A KILLER IN THE CORDGRASS

BRIAN THIEM

Severn River Publishing
www.SevernRiverBooks.com

ISBN: 978-1-64875-654-2 (Paperback)

ALSO BY BRIAN THIEM

Mudflats Murder Club Mysteries

The Mudflats Murder Club

A Killer in the Cordgrass

A Death in the Deluge

To find out more, visit

severnriverbooks.com

For my Southern brothers and sisters in blue. There definitely is professional law enforcement on this side of the Mason-Dixon Line

TIDAL MUDFLATS

Mudflats are found in tidal areas along the South Carolina coast, commonly in estuaries and along tidal rivers. They are formed by the rise and fall of the tide, which submerges and exposes the mudflats twice daily. They are a vital part of the Lowcountry ecology and form a habitat for shorebirds, crabs, shellfish, and fish.

SPARTINA (SPARTINA ALTERNIFLORA)

Smooth cordgrass, commonly found in coastal salt marshes along the Atlantic coast of South Carolina. The growth of Spartina stabilizes the soil, prevents erosion, and protects the fragile shoreline from storm surges. It also provides food, habitat, and protection for many creatures that make the tidal rivers and marsh home, including various fish, crabs, shrimp, and numerous different bird species. The Spartina grass, along with the twice-daily tidal flow and salt water, is an essential component of the Lowcountry tidal marsh ecology. Spartina is critical to the very life of Lowcountry salt marshes.

Placards on the River Lodge dock at Sea Island Plantation, Spartina Island, South Carolina.

1

WEDNESDAY

Sean Tanner picked up the soggy tennis ball and shook off the sand. Annie, his yellow Lab sat in front of him, her entire body quivering in anticipation. Sean tossed the ball about a hundred feet into the surf. Annie sprinted across the fluffy sand and into the shallow water until it got too deep for her feet to touch. She then dog-paddled out into the Atlantic Ocean, crashed through the small breakers, and made it to the calmer water. Annie looked right and left then headed with laser-like focus toward the small yellow ball bobbing in the water.

The sun crept over the horizon, appearing as a thin red line above the water. It was two days after Labor Day and the Spartina Island beach was deserted this early, most of the summer tourists back at their jobs up north and their kids back in school. Annie grabbed the ball in her mouth, paddled in a small circle, and headed back to land. Her nose barely cleared the water, and her otter-like tail trailed like a rudder. She bobbed with the ocean's swells until her feet touched the sand, then she splashed through the surf and onto the beach where Sean waited.

Annie dropped the ball at his feet and shook, spraying a gallon of water onto Sean. Although his Northern friends figured summer was over after Labor Day, summer weather lasted well into October in the South Carolina

Lowcountry, so Sean didn't mind Annie's shower. They had arrived at the beach at first light, a half hour before sunrise, and Sean had walked nearly a mile with Annie walking, running, and swimming three times his distance.

The red line on the horizon broadened, until the sun popped above the horizon as if it were rising out of the ocean. Sean pulled his sunglasses from the pocket of his shorts and was sliding them on when his phone rang. He looked at the screen: Sergeant Charlotte Nash.

"Morning, Charlie," Sean said.

"How are you feeling?"

Charlie had called him last week and suggested they get together. A date maybe. He wasn't sure. They had met a month ago when one of Sean's neighbors was murdered, and they worked together on that case and a forty-year-old cold case. He felt something for Charlie and sensed she felt something for him too. But after having been married to the same woman for thirty years, he wasn't sure precisely what he felt and whether Charlie actually felt something for him or was just being a friend. So when Charlie had called and asked him out—if that was what she was really doing—he'd panicked. He told her he had caught the flu, instead of leveling with her that he was in a deep depression over the one-year anniversary of his wife's death.

"Great, I'm back to normal," he said, referring to his faked illness, not the sadness over losing his wife.

"I'm out on a homicide, a body dump on the beach, and was wondering if you'd like to take a look, make sure we're not missing something."

When Sean's neighbor was murdered last month, Lieutenant Billy Green, Charlie's boss, asked Sean to examine the crime scene, utilizing his decades of experience as a homicide detective to help the less experienced detectives of the Campbell County Sheriff's Office. Although Charlie was royally pissed that a retired California detective was being allowed to enter *her* crime scene, they eventually became great work partners and even friends.

"I'm out on the beach with Annie and not dressed appropriately."

"Come as you are. It's just me and some deputies here. I'm texting you the address. That's where our cars are parked, so you'll need to walk from there down the public access walkway toward the beach."

Sean copied the address and pasted it into Google Maps. It was a half mile down the beach. "My car's a mile back the other way, but I can walk down the beach and be there in ten minutes."

2

Charlie stood alongside Deputy Don Hicks in the loose sand ten feet from the body. Hicks was one of the department's crime scene technicians. He was a few years from retirement, but he loved his job and would do whatever was asked of him to avoid being sent back to patrol, where he'd have to write traffic tickets, handle family fights, and chase down bad guys. The wind blew his comb-over, making it look like he wore a flag on top of his head. "Not sure what else I can do here," Hicks said.

The woman was lying in a slight depression in the coastal sand dune that separated the beach from the hotels and condos. Her body was surrounded by American beachgrass and sea oats, the native grasses that kept the sand from eroding. The sand was so soft that Charlie's feet sank down several inches with each step. The beach access pathway that connected the beach to the public road was twenty feet away, and a dozen people—the citizens who found the body, firefighters, paramedics, and deputies—had already trampled the route from the path to where the body lay.

"After the coroner picks up the body, you can do a better search under and around her," Charlie said. "Maybe get your metal detector and go over the entire area."

"Yes, ma'am," Hicks said. "I got lots of photos but haven't found anything that might look like evidence."

A uniformed deputy was telling a few people who wanted to walk down the access path they'd have to find another way to the beach. Another deputy had stuck some poles in the sand and strung crime scene tape on the beach side of the pathway to keep curious people away.

The victim was a small woman with long black hair. Although law enforcement officers were not permitted to search the body of a deceased victim until the coroner's deputies arrived, the paramedics had removed a phone from the back pocket of her shorts. In a sleeve attached to the back of the phone was an Illinois driver's license that identified her as Courtney Evanson, thirty-five years old, five feet tall, and weighing one hundred pounds. Next to the license was another picture ID card, known as a CAM card, issued by the Sea Island Plantation Community Management Association.

Charlie's phone buzzed and showed Detective Sherman Todd on the screen. "Hey, Sherm." She had sent him and Detective Jay Garcia to canvass the two-story condo building just south of their scene.

"Hey, Sarge," Sherm said. "I finally got a call back from Sea Island Plantation security. They have no record of Courtney Evanson in their vehicle registration system, and their resident directory shows no one with a last name of Evanson."

"Of course not. Sea Island is an active adult community, so people have to be at least fifty-five to own a house there."

"I thought there were exceptions, and some could be as young as fifty to buy there," Sherm said. "Our friend Sean Tanner isn't yet fifty-five is he?"

"Not quite," she said. Sean was fifty-four, ten years older than she was.

"Security said if Courtney was just visiting, she would only have a guest card, but since she has a regular picture CAM card, they assume she's a relative of a resident and staying there for longer than thirty days."

"They must know what resident is sponsoring her," Charlie said.

"Security said the community association office would have that information, but they don't open until nine o'clock."

Charlie looked at her watch—7:15. "Thanks, Sherm, I guess we'll have to wait until then to get some background on her. Let me know if you find someone on your canvass that knows anything."

Charlie's attention was drawn to the deputy blocking the beach side of the path forty yards away. "Stop right there, sir," the deputy said loudly.

Charlie saw Sean Tanner standing calmly on the other side of the crime scene tape. He was a big man, around six-four, with an athletic build. He wore a blue T-shirt, foam green shorts, and a khaki-colored baseball cap. Annie, the best trained dog she'd ever met outside of police canines, sat next to him. Charlie began walking toward them and said, "It's okay, deputy, this is Sean Tanner, a member of the cold case team. I asked him to come."

"I'm sorry, Sergeant Tanner," the deputy said. "I didn't recognize you, but after everything you did on those homicides last month, we all know who you are."

Sean smiled. "I'm retired now, so just call me Sean."

"Thanks for coming," Charlie said.

"Anytime." Sean gave Annie commands of down and stay, and she dropped to the sand by the deputy, but kept her eyes on Sean.

Charlie led him up the pathway, out of earshot of the deputy. "How's your mother doing?" Sean asked.

"She's still wearing the soft cast but started physical therapy this week." The weekend after they had arrested Beth Laughlin for three murders, Charlie invited Sean to join her and her brothers for a day trip to Charleston on her boat. She had figured a group excursion like that was casual enough that it wouldn't appear like she was asking Sean on a date, something her mother's Southern upbringing would cringe over. But on Friday, her mother fell off a stool while rearranging the top shelves of her pantry and broke her wrist. For the next two weeks, Charlie spent all of her off-duty hours taking care of her mother.

"I'll bet she was grateful to have you around."

"If you knew my mother well, you'd know saying thank you is not in her vocabulary. I'm sorry it ruined our outing."

"I'm sorry I then got sick."

"Thank God we have another murder to bring us together," Charlie said.

3

Charlie had said it with a straight face, knowing Sean would appreciate the kind of gallows humor common among big city cops at murder scenes. After working with him on the homicides last month, she was beginning to understand why he was the way he was.

Sean laughed. She liked how he seemed lighter at this scene than the one where they met last month. She did feel a bit guilty that someone had to get murdered for her to see him and wondered if it was her destiny that someone had to die for her to be brought together with a decent man.

"So, what have you got?" Sean asked, now all business.

She spent the next few minutes briefing Sean on what she knew so far. "Deputies should be finished with their written statements from the couple that found the body, and I was just getting ready to talk with them."

Charlie and Sean walked to the street where a uniformed deputy was talking to an older couple dressed in cargo shorts, T-shirts, and sandals worn over white socks. Charlie scanned the statements of Nigel and Clara Horton, introduced herself and said, "Your statements say you left your condo around quarter to six for a walk on the beach. That's pretty early to take a walk when it's still dark out."

"Our bodies are still operating on London time," Nigel said. "Just flew across the pond two days ago, so we were wide awake at five o'clock."

"Had our coffee and thought an early walk before the sun rose might be nice," Clara said.

"How'd you come across the victim?" Charlie asked.

"We walked down this beach cut-through," Nigel said. "I had a pocket torch—a flashlight to you Americans—and was shining it around, hoping to see a big sea turtle in her nest."

Charlie wanted to tell him that most of the loggerhead turtles had nested many months ago and most of their hatchlings had already scrambled across the beach to the ocean. She also wanted to tell them that baby turtles move toward light, often at night when the moon reflects off the ocean. That was one reason the island had a light ordinance, and locals knew shining flashlights on turtle nests could be deadly for hatchlings trying to get into the ocean. Back when Charlie worked for the regional planning commission, she spent three seasons volunteering with the Spartina Island Sea Turtle Patrol. She helped rope off sea turtle nests, cleared paths of obstructions so the hatchings could make it to the ocean, and educated beach residents and tourists. She had drifted away when one of the volunteers and environmental activists, Cory Bowers, began a fringe group that tried to close any beaches where sea turtles nested.

"And we saw something just off the path," Clara said. "Thought at first it was a big loggerhead, so we didn't approach at first."

"I could see it was a person," Nigel said. "Figured someone had a few too many pints and was sleeping it off."

"I used to be a nurse in Bexley," Clara said. "I thought the young lady might be in distress. I shook her, and when she didn't move, we rolled her over to get her face out of the sand so she could breathe."

"That's when we saw she had passed," Nigel said.

"Then you called nine-one-one?" Charlie said.

"I told the operator the woman was deceased, but I guess they didn't believe me," Nigel said. "Next thing we know, two fire trucks and an ambulance arrive with lights and siren."

"Did you see anyone around the body or during your walk?" Charlie asked.

"Not a soul," Clara said. "The body was cool, and rigor had begun to set in, so she'd been gone a while."

Charlie thanked them and walked back toward the body with Sean. "It would be nice to get a lead on who Courtney is and not have to wait for the Sea Island Plantation office to open at nine."

"Sometimes young adults, for one reason or another, move in temporarily with their older parents in our community," Sean said. "I see them at the fitness center and the club, but I don't recognize her from her ID photo. Maybe some of the others on the cold case team might recognize her."

"Feel free to ask them."

Sean took a photo of the CAM card and sent it out as a group text with a short message then looked down at the victim. "Unusual place to dump a body," he said.

"I agree. If they transported her in a car, they'd have to carry or drag her a hundred feet from the street."

"Same if they came from the beach," Sean said. "Could've encountered her on the path, killed her there, and just dragged her off into the sand dune."

"There's no indication someone dragged her from the beach."

"High tide was three hours ago," Sean said. "That would've wiped out all footprints to the high tide mark, and with the loose sand the rest of the way, there'd be no clear footprints or drag marks."

"And a bunch of people have been back and forth before we got here."

Several sea gulls screamed overhead as they swooped over the water.

"But she's not a big woman," Sean said. "When I was on the SWAT team in my younger days, we trained in the fireman's carry so we could rescue a wounded officer. Her driver's license says she only weighed a hundred pounds. I've carried men twice that weight."

"I could probably carry a woman her size myself, but wouldn't most killers dump a body at an easier location?"

"You're obviously checking for cameras."

"Yeah, I have Jay and Sherm out canvassing right now."

Sean crouched over the body. "Any indication of the cause of death?"

"The paramedics did a quick once over when checking for signs of life. They didn't see any GSWs or knife wounds. Didn't notice any blood except what we see on her face and neck."

"Yeah, looks like someone struck her several times in the face."

"All those scratches on her throat tells me someone with long nails choked her."

Sean shook his head. "The medical examiner will be able to give a better idea, but she probably caused those scratches on her neck herself. Someone was manually strangling her, and she scratched herself desperately trying to pull their hands away. I've seen it a few times before."

"Shit, I was hoping our suspect's fingernails would be full of our victim's DNA."

"Still could be if there was a prolonged struggle, which is common during manual strangulations," Sean said. "Your victim probably has some of the suspect's DNA under her nails, and your suspect might have scratches on his hands or arms."

"Her photo shows an attractive young woman," Charlie said. "If you ignore the battered face, her body looks clean and healthy. Not like she was living on the street and into drugs or booze."

"Guess we'll have to figure out who would want to kill a healthy, attractive young lady and dump her body on the beach," Sean said.

4

Sean was sitting on his backyard bench under a giant live oak that overlooked the salt marsh and Spartina River. Spanish moss hanging from the century-old tree swayed in the light breeze. When a deputy had told Charlie the coroner's van was pulling up to the crime scene and two reporters were waiting on the other side of the crime scene tape to talk with her, Sean made a quick exit. He didn't want Charlie to have to explain the presence of some retired homicide cop dressed in shorts and flip flops.

The tidal river was near low tide, and several egrets and a blue heron poked around for baby crabs or other food in the mudflats at water's edge. On the ground in front of the bench were two old memorial stones Sean had brought from their home in California when they moved here two years ago. Engraved on them were the names Amy and Amber, the two dogs that were such an important part of their family during their thirty years of marriage. After Amber, their previous yellow Lab, had passed over the rainbow bridge, they got Annie. Sean always thought it was one of the most unfair aspects of life that dogs didn't live as long as people. Lauren had said the universe designed it that way to teach us how to deal with loss. Sean wasn't sure he believed that, because when Lauren died, even after suffering the loss of two family dogs, he didn't have a clue how to deal with it.

A brand-new memorial stone lay alongside those of their dogs. Etched on it were Lauren's name and the dates of her life. His daughter, Rachel, had brought it over last week on the one-year anniversary of Lauren's death. They had sat together on the bench that day, one of Lauren's favorite spots, shared memories of the best wife and mother in the world, and laughed and cried until late at night.

His phone buzzed and the screen showed *Marvin Johnson*. "Hey, Beagle," Sean said. Marvin was a retired senior prosecutor with the Philadelphia District Attorney's Office and a member of the cold case team. He bore a striking resemblance to Morgan Freeman, with a voice nearly as deep and rich. The other members called him the team's legal beagle, and the nickname Beagle stuck.

"From your early morning text, I see that Miss Charlotte Nash invited you to a sunrise date on the beach. I hope it was every bit as romantic as I imagine."

"You guys are a laugh a minute," Sean said. "Did you call just to bust my balls this morning?"

"Actually, I have some info for you. I took Diva to the dog park this morning and showed the photo of your victim around," Beagle said, referring to his Golden Doodle. "People said they'd seen her coming there late mornings with a tan Cockapoo that belongs to Don and Karen Littleton. They assume the Littletons are the girl's parents. Our resident directory shows the Littletons live at 142 Leisure Lane."

"Thanks a million. I'll pass it on to Charlie."

"By the way, we're still working on a decent nickname for you. FNG doesn't seem as appropriate after your performance on your first cold case."

"Can't help you much there. Fellow officers back at Oakland PD just called me Sean."

"Not sure we all believe that, but I guess fucking new guy will have to be it until we get the real scoop from some of your Oakland PD buddies."

Sean hung up, called Charlie, and passed on what Beagle had told him.

"Appreciate it," Charlie said. "The coroner's transport will be leaving in a few, but I need to leave Sherm and Jay here to finish the canvass. Would you mind assisting me with the next of kin notification?"

Until the murder had occurred across the street a month ago and his involvement with the cold case team, Sean's life after Lauren's death had been boring. It had seemed all he had to show for his days was a lousy golf game and the fish he caught and released back into the salt marsh. Then there was the murder and an unsolved cold case. He had felt alive again. "Be glad to. Just need to shower and change."

"Great. I'll meet you there in about half an hour."

5

Leisure Lane was located between the club house and the main gate, but the active adult community wasn't so large that nothing was much more than a five-minute drive from Sean's house. He parked his Toyota Highlander on the street and waited for Charlie.

He wore khaki chinos and a blue, button-front shirt with a straight hem, designed to be worn untucked. He had adopted that style shirt years ago for casual wear so that he could still conceal a handgun when off-duty. Under his shirt, a Glock Model 19, 9mm semiauto resided in an inside-the-waistband holster. Although he was not a cop anymore, he would've felt naked being unarmed when working a murder case.

Charlie pulled up a minute later in her unmarked Dodge Charger and stepped out of her car with a steno pad in hand. She wore a black pantsuit over a lavender shirt. The jacket was far from formfitting, but that was necessary to conceal her Sig Sauer handgun, handcuffs, and other tools a detective must carry. She was five-nine and looked skinny in her baggy suit, but Sean had seen her in a tennis outfit and a swimsuit, and Charlie had an athletic figure that curved in all the right places.

"I didn't call first to avoid spooking them," Charlie said, tucking a strand of her long blonde hair back into the tight bun on the back of her head. "I'll just knock at the door and play it by ear."

Sean nodded in agreement. He hated doing death notifications when he worked homicide in Oakland and often left them to the coroner's office. But in a situation like this, they needed to talk to the family to learn more about the victim's life and point their investigation in the right direction.

The house was one of the dozen or so models available to new home buyers on the west side of the development. Gray stucco, navy blue shutters, with a dark shingled roof and a two-car garage facing the street. Nicely landscaped yard, probably cared for by one of the many landscaping companies that serviced the area. An oversized, solid wood door faced them. Charlie rang the doorbell. A dog barked and a petite woman in her sixties wearing a yellow knit top and black leggings answered the door.

Charlie showed her badge and said, "I'm Sergeant Nash with the sheriff's office, and this is Mr. Tanner, a member of the sheriff's cold case team. Are you Karen Littleton?"

A gray-haired man in a maroon T-shirt and shorts stood behind his wife and said, "Yes, and I'm Don Littleton. Can we help you?"

"Are you related to Courtney Evanson?"

"She's our daughter," Karen said. "What's this about?" Their expressions conveyed a sense of dread.

"May we come in?" Charlie asked.

They stood aside as Sean followed Charlie inside.

"Did something happen to Courtney?" Don asked.

"Maybe we could sit down," Charlie said.

Don and Karen led them into a spacious great room with ten-foot ceilings, and they slowly sat together on a cream colored sofa. A light brown Cockapoo jumped onto the sofa and lay next to Karen. Charlie sat on the edge of a striped Queen Anne chair arranged perpendicular to the sofa. Sean stood behind her.

Sean knew there was no easy way to handle a death notification. Sometimes, he would try to get all of his questions out of the way before he broke the news, fearing the parents would become too hysterical or even combative once they learned of their child's death. He knew that was selfish, handling the needs of his investigation before the needs of the victim's parents, but he had figured he was a homicide detective, not a social worker.

Charlie cleared her throat. "Early this morning, Courtney's body was found in the beach sand dunes, not far from the Westin."

Karen and Don looked at each other, and Don grabbed his wife's hand. "Is she dead?" he asked.

Charlie nodded. "I'm so very sorry for your loss."

Their eyes welled up and tears rolled down their cheeks. Karen buried her face in Don's chest and sobbed. Sean spotted a box of tissues on the kitchen island and brought it to them. After a minute or two, Karen's breathing slowed, and she slowly pushed away from her husband. Don dabbed his eyes and blew his nose. "How? Why?"

"We don't know a lot at this time," Charlie said. "The cause of death will be determined later, but she suffered some facial trauma."

"You mean like someone beat her?" Karen said.

"That's a possibility. Was she living here with you?"

"She moved in three months ago," Don said. "She had lived in Chicago. That's where we're from too. Karen and I retired and moved down here five years ago. Then Courtney got divorced and had no place to stay. She needed to start over."

"Was her divorce contentious?" Charlie asked.

"At first it was a fairytale romance," Karen said. "Dave was her high school sweetheart. They married after college and Dave became successful in the corporate insurance field, while Courtney worked as a social worker for different non-profits. At some point, Dave developed a gambling problem, lost his job, the house, and everything."

"But contentious, no," Don said. "There was nothing left to fight over. Creditors took everything. Courtney packed a few boxes of stuff, shipped it down, and flew here with two suitcases. The bank even took her car."

"I'm sorry to hear that," Charlie said. "How had Courtney been since she'd been down here?"

"About as well as you can expect from a thirty-five-year-old woman who's forced to move back in with parents who live in a retirement community," Don said.

"She's actually coping quite well," Karen said. "I guess, I should say, she *had* been coping well. *Had been*, as in she's not here any longer." Karen paused to wipe her eyes. "As a social worker, she had previously worked

with the elderly, and she said that the people who live in Sea Island Plantation are not elderly at all. She worked out at the fitness center, took Teddy to the dog park, and joined us for cards and stuff with neighbors."

"She spent a month just resting and recovering from all the stress of her divorce then went out and found two jobs," Don said. "Not in her field, but she said she needed time to get her head straight before she could even consider social work, which can be draining for the most emotionally strong people."

"Where did she work?" Charlie asked.

"She worked a few days a week at the Spartina Island Boutique and weekends as a bartender at the Atlantic Dunes Resort," Karen said.

"When did you last see her?"

"She was pulling extra shifts over Labor Day weekend at the Atlantic Dunes, so she worked Monday and Tuesday night," Karen said. "I think she left around three-thirty yesterday."

"What kind of car does she have?"

"She's still saving up to buy a new one," Don said. "We have two cars, so we let her use our older Subaru Outback." He scrolled through his phone and provided the license number.

"I have to ask some standard questions, so please don't be offended, but was Courtney using drugs?"

"Definitely not," Karen said. "After what she saw with her social work clients, she was totally against drug use."

"What about drinking?"

"She might have one or two, but that was it," Karen said.

"She did work as a bartender," Charlie said.

"The Atlantic Dunes is a boutique hotel that caters to people with more money than we have," Don said. "They prohibit employees, even the bartenders, from drinking on the job, and that's not the kind of place Courtney could afford to drink at."

"Has she mentioned any problems with anyone, or can you think of anyone who might want to hurt her?"

"Courtney is—was—the nicest, sweetest girl in the world. And I'm not just saying that because I'm her mother. She was just trying to put her life back together."

Don nodded but added nothing. Charlie looked at Sean and raised her eyebrows.

"Did Courtney have a new boyfriend?" Sean asked.

"She said she wasn't even interested in dating," Karen said.

Don pursed his lips but said nothing.

"Mr. Evanson?" Sean said.

"Sometimes I can't sleep—old age, you know—so I get up, and I've seen her come in at two in the morning or later. Very quietly and she'd head straight to her room. She was a grown woman, so I didn't pry, but to be quite honest, she might've been seeing someone after work."

"Do you know the names of any friends she might've met down here?" Sean asked.

They both shook their heads.

"The only thing we found on her was her phone with her driver's license and her CAM card," Sean said. "Did she carry a purse and have other cards?"

"That's all she carried when she was around Sea Island Plantation," Karen said. "Her license so she could drive, and her CAM card would get her into the gym, the dog park, and allow her to even charge at the clubhouse. But she carried a small clutch purse or larger handbag when she went out. In there she had a wallet with a new credit card—she was trying to reestablish credit—medical insurance card, and other stuff."

"Do you mind if we take a look in her room and the bathroom she uses?" Sean asked.

6

Charlie walked out with Sean after thanking the Littletons and leaving her card. Since Don and Karen had stood in the hallway as she and Sean searched the rooms, they knew they'd have to wait until they left to discuss their observations. Charlie unlocked her car and stood in the open door. "Find anything interesting?" she asked.

"Her closet had some nice clothes. Much of it looked like things a professional woman would wear in wintry weather. Probably brought it from Chicago. Also some casual clothes, similar to what my daughter wears when she's not at work."

"How old's your daughter?"

"Twenty-nine. I just found out she's pregnant with her first child." Sean smiled, obviously happy at the prospect of being a grandfather. She smiled back at him, trying to hide the realization that she was interested in a man who was almost a grandfather. Maybe the ten-year difference between them was a big deal, she thought.

"I also found several folders with papers," Sean said. "I took photos of a bank statement—Wells Fargo checking with a balance just over three grand. Also a credit card statement. Only a balance of a few hundred dollars, which was paid automatically through the checking account."

"She's trying to reestablish credit and apparently not blowing her money," Charlie said. "Bathroom had lots of empty high-end cosmetic bottles and lotions. The full ones were all typical drug store brands. Tells me she was used to spending money on herself, but now is making do with less. I found three prescriptions in the bathroom: an antidepressant, something for sleep, and birth control pills."

"So maybe there is a boyfriend," Sean said.

"Or maybe she didn't want to go off them after her divorce and wanted to be prepared should she run across a nice man."

"Unmarried women not in a relationship do that?" Sean asked.

"Many of us do."

She watched for his reaction, knowing he'd figure she was possibly alluding to herself. He blushed and looked away. She wanted to laugh, but didn't want to embarrass him more than she already had.

Sean quickly changed the subject. "The Atlantic Dunes Resort is not too far from where she was found."

"We can go there first, as long as you're still available."

Charlie grabbed an umbrella, a bag filled with fast food wrappers, and a gym bag from the passenger seat of her unmarked car and tossed them in the back. Sean hesitated. Charlie glanced at the floor where more stuff had collected: the boots she wore on the beach, the athletic shoes she used for CrossFit, and a box of nitrile gloves. "Just kick that stuff out of the way or toss it in the back."

Sean climbed in, gingerly pushed the items around with his feet, and shut the door. A half block down the street, Charlie slowed behind a white SUV meandering down the middle of the road at not much more than jogging speed. It stopped at a stop sign, and even though no cars were coming, sat there for at least five seconds before slowly turning right.

"The speed limit's twenty-five," Charlie said. "In the rest of the world, drivers would get a horn blast if they were going twenty-four."

"You get used to it," Sean said. "There's a guy in one of my golf groups who's ninety-two. His wife won't let him drive outside the gate, but he drives around inside just like that. I doubt his old car has gone faster than twenty miles an hour in years."

"They tout this place as an *active* adult community," Charlie said.

"Many of us are quite active."

Charlie caught his use of *many of us* as a play on her use of it when mentioning that many of us single women often take the pill. He had heard her loud and clear, she realized. She gave him a wink.

Ten minutes later Charlie pulled up to the front entrance of the Atlantic Dunes Resort. She knew the boutique hotel had only thirty rooms, all with ocean views. The cheapest rooms went for eight hundred a night during tourist season. A valet wearing black, knee-length shorts and a spotless white polo shirt jogged to her door. She swept her jacket back to show her badge and said, "Leave it there. We won't be long."

The valet backed away, and Charlie and Sean stepped into the lobby and across the ivory and robin-egg blue marble floor to the reception desk. A thirtyish redhead smiled and made eye contact as they approached. "Welcome to the Atlantic Dunes Resort. How may I help you?" She wore a perfectly pressed white shirt and black skirt. Her nametag read: *Hannah, Columbus, Ohio.*

Charlie showed her badge and said, "We're with the sheriff's office and need to see the manager."

Hannah picked up a phone and spoke softly into it. A moment later a fifty-something man appeared through a door marked *Staff* to the left of the reception area. He was buttoning the jacket of his black suit. He looked around the lobby before fixing his eyes on Charlie and Sean, apparently making sure none of his guests might notice the presence of police in his establishment.

The man looked at Sean. Typical, Charlie thought, for people to assume the man was in charge, even though she was wearing a suit and Sean was dressed casually. "Would you like to follow me to my office?"

He didn't wait for a response before holding the door open to quickly escort them out of sight of several guests sitting in the lobby. He went down a short hallway and into a small windowless office. "I'm Daniel Peterson, the hotel and resort manager."

"Detective Sergeant Nash with the Campbell County Sheriff's Office, and this is Mr. Tanner, with our cold case team."

Peterson settled behind a light-colored wood desk and motioned toward two guest chairs. Charlie sat down and said, "Is Courtney Evanson one of your employees?"

"She's one of our part-time bartenders. She's not in trouble with the law, is she?"

"We found her body a few hundred yards down the beach this morning," Charlie said without a hint of emotion.

"Her body? Is she dead?"

Charlie nodded.

"Oh, my! What happened?"

Peterson seemed appropriately surprised, Charlie thought. "We're just beginning to gather information, but we're investigating it as a homicide. How long has she been working here?"

"About two months. She was recommended by one of our servers in the restaurant."

"Her name?"

"Susan Gomez. She left a few weeks ago. I understand she's now a manager at the Spartina Island Boutique, over in the South Harbor Village."

"When did Courtney last work?"

Peterson clicked his mouse a few times and scanned his computer screen. "She checked out at ten-o-five last night. Our employees sign in and out on a phone app. Her normal schedule is four to midnight, Friday, Saturday, and Sunday, but we were at capacity over the weekend and Courtney volunteered to work extra shifts to cover for the normal Monday and Tuesday bartender."

"Her shift went until midnight, but she left at ten?" Charlie said.

"Our bar is small and intimate. It mostly serves our guests and a few local regulars who stop in occasionally for a cocktail. If there are no customers present, the bartender will close at ten."

"She was wearing shorts and a flowing top when we found her," Charlie said. "I take it that's not what she wears at work."

"All of our staff wear uniforms commensurate with their positions. Bartenders wear black slacks, with a skirt as an option for women, black vests, and white shirts. We provide all uniforms and handle laundering. Staff are not permitted to wear their uniforms off site, so they change into clean uniforms here before work each day. It's our way of ensuring our exacting standards."

"So that's what she could've worn to and from work yesterday?"

Peterson nodded.

"What else can you tell us about her? Any close friends among coworkers? Any problems with other staff or customers?"

"She was very personable and professional. She was a favorite of customers and received many positive compliments, but quite honestly, the bar is just a small part of my responsibilities. The restaurant manager oversees the bar and could tell you more. He comes in around noon."

Charlie glanced at Sean. "Do your employees have lockers where they change?" Sean asked.

"Yes, we provide male and female locker rooms, an employee break room, and even a dining area where they can eat while they're here."

"We'd like to look in Courtney's locker," Sean said.

"Employees use their own locks, so we—"

"I'm sure your maintenance people have bolt cutters," Sean said.

Peterson hesitated for a moment, then picked up his phone. "I'll have someone from buildings and grounds meet us in the ladies locker room."

7

Twenty minutes later, Charlie parked her car and walked with Sean past dozens of boats and mini yachts bobbing in the water next to The Village at South Harbor. Charlie was disappointed their search of Courtney's locker hadn't revealed anything useful. There were a pair of black pants and a black skirt in size four, two white shirts, and a vest so small that Charlie would've outgrown it by the time she started high school. On the floor of the locker were two pairs of black leather shoes, flats that looked comfortable enough to stand in for eight hours, and pumps with three-inch heels that Charlie couldn't imagine wearing for more than ten minutes while working behind a bar.

They stepped into Spartina Island Boutique and a dark-haired woman in her early thirties looked up from the counter where she was folding clothes and said, "Hello, Ms. Nash, have you come in to see our latest arrivals?"

Without even looking at him, Charlie could feel Sean rolling his eyes and thinking, *Well, of course, the clerks at one of the top high-end boutiques on the island would know Charlotte Nash by sight.*

"Suzie, this is Sean Tanner, a friend from work, so you can knock off the VIP customer service crap."

"How ya been, Charlie?" Suzie said, then quickly turned her attention to Sean, brushed her hair back from one ear and smiled. "So, Sean, are you a detective also?"

"Suzie!" Charlie said.

"I apologize, Sean, but it's not often that a tall, handsome man walks into a woman's boutique."

"Suzie!" Charlie said again.

Suzie laughed. "Since I doubt you brought Sean here to show him the really cute soft coral half-zip dresses that just arrived, and which, by the way, would look adorable on you, I'm guessing this is cop business."

"We were just down at Atlantic Dunes on a case, and I learned that you no longer work there. Congratulations on your promotion to manager here."

"Actually, Donna still calls herself the manager, but as the owner, she's got other things to do besides hang out at the store. I'm the assistant manager, but I handle the day-to-day operation."

"That's fantastic. It must be easier for you and Miguel not having to work nights."

Suzie turned to Sean. "I'm so sorry. As Charlie is pointing out, I am engaged and therefore should not be flirting with other men."

Sean winked at her. "Quite alright. I'm flattered, even though you appear to be about my daughter's age."

Suzie raised her eyebrows and nodded to Charlie. Although Charlie only knew her from the boutique and the CrossFit gym, Suzie was another person who seemed to think Sean was right for her.

"Sorry to interrupt your flirting," Charlie said, "but did you know Courtney Evanson?"

"Sure, she's a darling. Came in here and applied to a help wanted notice in July. She presented herself well, so we hired her to work part time three days a week."

"And at the Atlantic Dunes?"

"I was working the weekend dinner shift and heard they were looking for a bartender to work weekends, so I recommended her. Same thing—she learned the job quickly and the customers loved her. I left there a few weeks ago when Donna offered me the full-time position here. Why are you asking?"

"I'm sorry, but we found her body dumped on the beach this morning," Charlie said. "Looks like she was murdered."

The joyful expression that was always etched on Suzie's face dissolved instantaneously into tears. Charlie put her arms around her and held her until Suzie's breathing steadied. She wiped her eyes with a tissue, smudging her makeup.

"When did you last see her?" Charlie asked.

"She worked Saturday and Sunday at the boutique. From opening at ten until around three when she left for the Atlantic Dunes."

"Did she seem okay?"

"Sure, a bit tired, working two jobs, but you know how that is."

"Did she talk about any problems she had with anyone?"

Suzie dabbed her eyes with a tissue. "She was the sweetest, nicest girl in the world."

"Was she in a relationship? Seeing anyone?"

"Not really, but..."

"But..." Charlie parroted.

"When I was still waitressing at the Atlantic Dunes, I'd have to come up to the bar to get drinks for my customers. While Courtney was making them, we'd chat for a minute or two. One night, I went to the bar to get after-dinner drinks for one of my late dining tables. Eric, the chauffeur, was there having a drink—probably a soda—but they were both leaning over the bar and talking really close."

"Close like a conspiratorial kind of conversation or close like in intimate?"

"Intimate. I warned her about having a boyfriend hang out at the bar when she was working, and she said she'd tell him. She didn't want to mess up her job."

"Did you talk with her again about Eric?"

"At the store, I asked if she was seeing him. She said it was nothing, just two people occasionally fulfilling each other's needs."

"And you took that to mean?" Charlie asked.

"You know—friends with benefits. Just physical. Courtney had just gone through a nasty divorce and was working hard to start a new life. She said the last thing she wanted was a relationship."

"What's Eric's last name?"

"I don't know. I just saw him occasionally dropping off or picking up guests at the hotel. He drives a big black SUV and always wore a black suit, white shirt, and black tie."

"Does he drive for a rideshare company or something?"

"He was like a regular chauffeur, not just a rideshare driver."

"Can you describe him?"

"White guy, real dark brown hair. Late thirties or early forties. Tall, but not as tall as Sean, maybe six-two or so. Not skinny, not fat. I never felt comfortable around him."

"In what way?"

"He acted too slick, kinda sleazy, you know. He was just a chauffeur, but he acted like he was way more cool than the rest of us. Hell, we were all in the service industry. We served clientele that were quite a bit more well-to-do than us, but he acted like he thought he should've been one of them."

"Thanks, Suzie," Charlie said. "I'll watch the store for a minute if you wanna go in the back and fix your makeup."

Suzie gave her a quick hug and disappeared into the back of the store.

"Kinda sleazy," Charlie said to Sean. "I think we need to find Eric and bring him in for a little talk."

8

Sean arrived at the sheriff's office's briefing room ten minutes early for the cold case team meeting. This was where patrol deputies began their shifts, where a sergeant stood in front of the room, called roll, and where each deputy responded with, "Here, sergeant." It was a large, bright space with four rows of tables and modern video screens on the front wall. Wanted posters and crime alerts covered two bulletin boards, and a coffee machine and cubbyholes holding various report forms lined the back wall.

Frank Martin and John O'Shea were already there. Frank was eighty. He had retired from NYPD, then worked as an investigator with the Manhattan D.A. Office, and following that, he worked as a criminal profiler for the state police. John was known as Irish. He was a retired detective from Boston PD in his early seventies. Frank and Irish were the two original members of the cold case team.

"Saw the text this morning," Frank said. "You get your vic IDed?"

"Yeah," Sean said. "Beagle showed her photo around the dog park. Girl's name is Courtney Evanson and lived with her parents on Leisure Lane."

"They got any leads on the perp?" Irish asked.

"Too early," Sean said, "But she's got a boyfriend who people say is a real creep."

"I heard she was strangled," Frank said. "That's the kind of shit a creepy boyfriend would do."

Jason "Stretch" Andrews came in and fist bumped Sean. Stretch was in his early sixties and retired from the major crimes unit of the Vermont State Police. He was six-foot-two, but he usually told people he used to be six-four before he had half the vertebrae in his back fused. Even at six-four, he only weighed 160, so his fellow state troopers began calling him Stretch when he was a rookie.

Denise Sheppard stood in the doorway and announced, "All local cops should now rise, the nation's premier law enforcement agency has arrived." Known as Feebee, she retired from the FBI. She was in her mid-sixties, heavy set, and had short brown hair.

Bernard "Doc" Henderson walked quietly into the room and sat down with a soft, "Good afternoon, everyone." Doc was sixty-six and spent a career as a forensic pathologist in Columbus, Ohio.

Sean told the late arrivals about the body dumped on the beach and did his best to answer their questions. "Where's our legal beagle?" Doc asked.

"Beagle had to take his wife to a doctor's appointment," Frank said.

"Who's presenting the case today?" Irish asked.

"Don't know," Frank said. "Captain Cannon just said to be here at two sharp."

"If Cannon will be here, we should put on our buttons," Irish said.

Sean pulled his Mudflats Murder Club button from his pocket and pinned it on his shirt, as did everyone else. The metal button was the size of political buttons Sean saw around the Bay Area with a candidate's picture and *Vote for Me.* This one had a cartoonish drawing of a dead body lying in the pluff mud alongside what looked like the Spartina River and the words, *Mudflats Murder Club.*

Sean learned that Captain Cannon hated the button, saying it was immature and disrespectful to the values of professional law enforcement officers. Sean couldn't argue with that assessment. Although the team designed them as a joke, and they were only to be worn when they were out among themselves socializing, they made a point to wear them when Captain Cannon was around just to piss him off.

Suddenly, Stretch yelled, "A-Ten-Chun," and jumped out of his chair.

Sheriff Bob Donohue stepped into the room and said, "Sit down, y'all, and don't ever do that again. I'd hate to see one of you older fellas pull out your backs jumping around like that." Sheriff Donohue was in his mid-fifties with iron gray hair he wore in a crew cut. He retired from the state police a few years ago and ran for sheriff of Campbell County. He won against Captain Cannon, who thought he'd certainly be elected to replace his father, who had been sheriff for the previous twenty-five years.

"I know I already thanked y'all several times for your hard work and success in those murders last month, but I want to thank you again. I talked with my command staff, and we decided to do some things to make you more a part of our family. I know you're all retired, and I would never demand anything of you. I already appreciate you volunteering on the cold case team."

He scanned the room, focusing on the team's buttons. Sean removed his and stuck it in his pocket. The others did the same. Sheriff Donohue continued. "We're going to issue you employee ID cards containing an embedded chip that will allow you to enter the building without a deputy buzzing you in. Wear your ID on a lanyard around your neck and you no longer need an escort in the building. It will give you access to the general areas of the building, but should you think about going into my office and putting your feet on my desk, it won't open my door."

"How about Captain Cannon's office?" Irish said. "Always wanted to put my feet on his desk."

The sheriff rolled his eyes and grinned. "Fraid not, Irish, but it will get you into the investigations area, where you can utilize the vacant squad room. Your cards say, *Cold Case Team member, non-sworn*, on them. You are all professionals, so you know that if you use that card to impersonate a sworn deputy, it will get you—and me—in a heap of trouble. But you may use it to identify yourself as a cold case team member when appropriate.

"Gladys will pass them out later. Your next cold case was suggested by one of your own. It is the case of a man who went missing from our county ten years ago. He was a pillar of the community. The circumstances of his disappearance have been the talk around dinner and cocktail tables for years and the subject of scores of media reports, most of them nothing but speculation and recirculation of rumors. Since Sean Tanner was the one who suggested this case be reopened, and because of the way he demonstrated his ability a few weeks back, I decided to assign him as the cold case team's lead on the missing person investigation of Henry Nash. I'll now leave you with the detective who led the missing person investigation ten years ago, at that time Detective Sergeant Cannon."

9

Captain Clinton Cannon III moved to the podium as the sheriff left the room. He was in his mid-forties, about six feet tall and weighing around two hundred pounds, little of it muscle. He wore a blue pinstriped suit, a pink shirt, and a yellow paisley tie. Sean couldn't decide if he looked like a car salesman or an evangelical preacher.

"Not one itty bitty lead has surfaced since Mr. Nash disappeared," Cannon said. "But our sheriff wants y'all to look into this further. I was the assigned detective, and I did more than any normal man would expect for a missing person case. But I can't see no harm having you look at it again. Because of the sensitive nature of this matter—Henry Nash was Sergeant Charlie Nash's daddy—confidentiality and case integrity must be forefront in your minds. I know Sergeant Nash all too well, and I'll say this in a complimentary way, but the girl can be as stubborn as a mule and as persistent as a hound dog on a scent. She'll try to involve herself in your investigation. Don't allow that. Y'all know detectives cannot investigate matters involving their own family members."

Sean glanced at the other team members. They all nodded to placate Cannon.

"The sheriff and I talked at length about this. He, having been with the state police, said that in many progressive police agencies, civilian investigators handle missing person cases, to include interviewing witnesses and the sort. So, y'all have free rein, up to the point you find this is something more than a missing person. Which I can't imagine you finding. But, if by some chance, you discover Mr. Nash was the victim of foul play, then this becomes a criminal matter, and it'll have to be turned over to our detectives. Am I clear on this?"

Sean resisted rolling his eyes, but instead nodded.

Cannon looked at the report on his podium. "Ten years ago, Mrs. Abigail Nash called sheriff's dispatch just before midnight on May 20 to report her husband, Henry Nash, missing. Although we don't normally take a report on a missing adult unless they'd been gone twenty-four hours, the watch commander made an exception based on who Mr. Nash was. A deputy met with Mrs. Nash at her house, who said her husband received a phone call that evening around nine o'clock and left to meet with someone. Deputies checked the local hospitals and jails with negative results and put out a missing person alert. The next morning, deputies found his car in the parking area on the mainland side of the bridge to Spartina Island. They called me and I went to the scene."

Cannon glanced at his papers then looked up and said, "I looked at his vehicle, a new Mercedes G-series SUV. It was unlocked, and Mr. Nash's cell phone and wallet were in the glove box. It had rained the night before and we found no signs of foul play. I drove to the Nash's house and spoke to Abigail. She let me access Henry's cell phone. The last call was from Boyd Moretti, another land developer and Henry's partner in the Sea Island Plantation development.

"I met with Mr. Moretti, and he said it was not unusual for him and Henry to meet after dinner, smoke a cigar, and discuss their business ventures. Mr. Moretti lived on the island, so the parking area where they met was halfway between their homes. That night, they parted after about thirty minutes, and Henry said he was going to take a walk on the bridge and finish his cigar. Abigail had told me that it was not unusual for Henry to walk along the pedestrian and bicycle path on the bridge, often stopping at the halfway mark to admire the view of the island to the east and the mainland to the west."

Cannon slid the report back into a folder. "Over the next month or so, me and my detectives spoke to many of Henry's friends and business associates, but no one could offer any leads as to the victim's whereabouts or a clear motive for his disappearance. We had the sheriff's boat and the Coast Guard spend days checking the waters around the bridge, even following the tide's currents, but his body never appeared.

"There's been lots of speculation over the years. Some that he jumped because he recently found he had cancer. Some that he accidentally fell off the bridge. And all kind of conspiracy theories about him being killed. By mobsters out of Chicago. By Islamic terrorists. By hired killers paid by politicians in the state legislature. We found no evidence to substantiate any of that nonsense. Three years ago, we received a court finding that since he'd been missing for seven years, he was declared dead in absentia. Although it was still a missing person investigation to us, we retitled the case as an accidental death and filed it pending additional leads."

"There were a lot of newspaper articles written about this," Frank said. "They said Sea Island Plantation was in financial difficulty because of the downturn in the housing market back then."

"We done looked into all that," Cannon said. "But it didn't lead to any motive for someone to do harm to Mr. Nash."

"What kind of cancer did he have?" Doc asked.

"I believe it was prostate," Cannon said.

"Even ten years ago, prostate cancer was highly treatable, and certainly no reason for a man to take his own life," Doc said.

"That's what I been told too," Cannon said. "And Abigail said he was his normal, happy self."

"Are there any crime scene photos?" Irish asked.

"No. Y'all gotta remember, at the time this was just a missing person case. We all thought Henry would turn up in a day or two with a real good explanation of where he'd been."

"Then days and days passed," Feebee said, "and this became more than just a routine missing person case. But by then, it was too late to search the scene for evidence and process his car, I assume."

Cannon nodded. He stepped from the podium and handed two three-ring binders to Sean. "You've got two copies of all our official reports. I'll be your point of contact for this investigation. Any questions or needs beyond your capabilities, make them through Mr. Tanner to me. Like I said before, I think we did all the right stuff on this investigation back then, but there was nothing there. I doubt you'll find anything, but good luck anyway."

Cannon left the room.

"Did anyone else get the feeling he wasn't telling us everything?" Stretch asked.

"The question is why," Irish said.

"Covering his ass so it won't look like he dropped the ball," Feebee said.

"I was sensing a feeling of shame or guilt coming from him," Doc said.

"Or because there was evidence of foul play, and he's protecting someone," Frank said. "Political corruption and land development have a long history as bedfellows in the South."

Sean remembered Charlie telling him about finding a file in the captain's office filled with his notes on the investigation and labeled *Confidential.* He'd have to spend some time with the reports Cannon had provided to them, but he doubted Cannon gave them everything. He handed one of the binders to Feebee. "Can you start up one of those shared documents like you did last time?"

"Will do. And once I read this copy, I'll start passing it around."

"It's tradition that we meet tomorrow at Bubbas to plan our strategy," Stretch said.

"Sounds good," Sean said. "I think we've got our work cut out for us on this one."

10

Charlie sat in a chair across from Lieutenant Billy Green's desk. Billy was a big man, six-foot-three and 270 pounds, but to her, he was just a big teddy bear. He had been her field training officer when she went to patrol right out of the academy and had remained a mentor to her throughout her career. He was instrumental in bringing her to work for him in the Criminal Investigation Division to supervise one of the two general investigations squads under his command, making her the first woman in the sheriff's office to lead a CID squad.

"Was Chicago PD able to shed any light on your victim?" Billy asked.

"Never been arrested, although she made two reports of domestic violence against the ex-husband when he smacked her around. She refused to press charges each time."

"What's the status of the ex?"

"Chicago officers found him staying at a buddy's house, being that he lost his job and his house. But he hadn't left Chicago, so it wasn't him that killed her down here."

"Did they find out anything else about her?"

"One of their detectives talked to Courtney's former employer and some neighbors. Everyone said she was the nicest, sweetest person they knew. No drugs or other high-risk behavior, other than being married to an asshole."

"I wonder what kinds of people she ran into working as a bartender," Billy said.

"I spoke to the restaurant manager at length. Said Courtney was a fantastic bartender, her appearance and work ethic were impeccable, and she was friendly yet professional. Some locals came to the bar just because of her, the manager said. She was one of those bartenders who could act like she was listening to someone while still mixing drinks and serving people at the other end of the bar."

"Yeah, the Atlantic Dunes has lofty standards and caters to well-to-do guests. What about that chauffeur boyfriend?"

"Eric," she said. "The manager said he'd been stopping in the bar for weeks. Bartenders would give him a glass of water or a soda, he'd talk a bit, and then be on his way. The manager didn't notice anything going on between Courtney and him, although he said it was possible."

Billy jotted some notes on a pad sitting on his desk. "No ID on him yet?"

"It'll come. Jay and Sherm are still out in the area talking to people. They think some of the desk clerks must have Eric's contact info and informally reach out to him when a guest is looking for a car a step up from a taxi or rideshare."

"Who've you got attending the autopsy tomorrow?"

It was important to have a detective present at MUSC, the Medical University of South Carolina in Charleston, where autopsies were performed, to make sure the medical examiner received relevant details about the investigation and to bring back details of their findings before the written report came to them a week or more later. But it took a detective away from her team for most of the day, with a round trip to Charleston and the procedure. "I need Sherm and Jay here, so I'm planning on sending Darryl. Even though he's not cleared yet for full duty until the academy schedules him for refresher use of force training, he can certainly drive an unmarked car to Charleston unarmed and attend an autopsy."

Detective Darryl Pickett was the fourth member of her squad. He was fifty-three years old and the cousin of Captain Cannon. His family connection got him hired thirty years ago, when connections were more important than qualifications. During their murder investigations last month, Darryl had shot and killed a man who was brandishing what turned out to be a pellet gun. Since it looked like a real handgun, the shooting was ruled justifiable, but the sheriff decided it would be wise to send him for refresher training before he could carry a gun and perform full duties.

"Why don't you ask Doc Henderson from the cold case team if he'd like to go with Darryl?" Billy said. "Wouldn't hurt to have a set of professional eyes there."

"We can do that?"

"I don't know why not," Billy said. "The sheriff went on and on during our last command staff meeting about how great the cold case team is. He approved issuing them department ID cards with unescorted access to our building. And you had no problem calling Sean a few minutes after you arrived at your scene this morning."

Charlie was about to say that Sean was different, but for once, her mouth didn't automatically engage before her brain considered the outcome. "I'll reach out to him. I'm sure he'd be helpful. Darryl probably only writes down ten percent of what the medical examiner says, so this way we might get a fuller picture. How's the media circus?"

"Not too bad. A local woman found dead on the beach is not as earth shattering as a wealthy retiree killed in her house like we had a month ago. The sheriff will head a press conference in a little bit, but he's not concerned about media or political pressure so far. By the way, how's your mother doing?"

"Much better. She does physical therapy every other day and can drive short distances. The important thing is she can now get dressed on her own and do her own hair. For two weeks it felt like I was taking care of a child again."

"You seem so confident and self-assured with this murder," Billy said.

Charlie laughed. "As opposed to a neurotic worrier on the last one?"

Billy chuckled. "Well..."

"I think that after what we were up against last month and how well it turned out, I feel confident my team can handle just about anything."

"Having Sean Tanner helping out can't hurt."

She smiled. "I went from despising him to really respecting his talents. Plus he's unflappable. I'll bet he wouldn't even break a sweat if he were called out on a string of mob hit jobs."

"I doubt we'll ever see that on Spartina Island, but I'm glad you're working so well with Sean. He's a heck of a detective and an all-around good man."

"He doesn't seem to be busy with anything else, so I'll use him on this investigation too, if that's okay."

Billy looked at his desk for a moment then said, "Sure, just make sure he's got the time."

She nodded warily, getting the feeling Billy knew something he wasn't telling her.

11

Sean parked his Highlander on the street in the historic district of Dufftown, opened a wrought iron gate, and walked up a paver walkway to the largest antebellum house in the district. He climbed the steps to the wide front porch, containing a porch swing and several white rocking chairs, which he figured were required porch furnishings of southern mansions.

He touched the doorbell and an older Black woman wearing an apron over dark blue pants and a white shirt opened the door. "Good afternoon, sir. How may I help you?"

"My name is Sean Tanner. I'm here to see Mrs. Abigail Nash."

She gave him a once over, then said, "I don't believe Mrs. Nash is expecting anyone this afternoon, but I'll check and see if she's available." She closed the door, leaving him standing there.

A moment later, the woman opened the door and said, "Right this way, Mr. Tanner. Mrs. Nash will see you in the ladies parlor."

Sean fought to keep a straight face when she said the ladies parlor. When he had met Charlie here last month, Charlie said that was the family room, as opposed to the living room, although her mother insisted they be called parlors, as if she were living in Scarlett O'Hara's era. He stepped into the entry hall, where two curved stairways of dark, hand-carved wood ascended to a second-floor landing. Double doors to his left led to a large room with fourteen-foot ceilings.

The last time he was here, Mrs. Nash tried to escort him into the room to the right of the entry hall, the formal parlor as she called it. That room was filled with dark furniture and thick oriental rugs over a hardwood floor. This room was lighter and brighter. The furniture was upholstered in light blue and rose colors.

Mrs. Nash rose from a love seat set in a conversation group with other furniture in front of the windows overlooking the front porch and yard. She wore a teal dress that reminded Sean of the clothing he saw at the Spartina Island Boutique. He had noted some price tags while he was there, and realized he was out of his element when casual dresses worn around the house cost two hundred dollars. She held out her right hand, and Sean shook it gently. Her left arm was in a sling. "This is a surprise, Mr. Tanner."

"Please call me Sean."

"Very well. As I suspect we will be seeing more of you, you might as well call me Abigail. I was about to have some tea. Will you join me?"

The last thing he wanted to drink on a hot afternoon was hot tea, but he resigned himself to going along with this southern aristocrat custom. "Sure."

"Tea for two, please Rose," Abigail said, and Rose disappeared through a door at the back of the room.

She motioned to an upholstered chair. Sean sat down, finding it surprisingly comfortable. "As you probably know, Charlotte is still at work, so what brings you out this way?"

"I'm a volunteer on the sheriff's cold case team, and we've been assigned the missing person case of your late husband."

"I see." She placed a bookmark in a hardback novel that was sitting open beside her. "To be honest, Clinton Cannon called and said some of your people would probably be by to speak with me. I was not expecting you so soon."

"I didn't know he would call. I only thought it right to let you know we'd be looking into this again."

"Does Charlotte know?"

"I haven't told her. You're the first family member I've spoken to. Since she is family, it would be inappropriate for her to be involved in the investigation."

"I see."

Rose carried a sterling silver tray into the parlor and set it on the cocktail table in front of Abigail. "Is there anything else I can get you, Mrs. Nash?"

"No, thank you. Please close the doors on your way out."

Rose pulled the double doors that went to the entry hall closed, then left through the back door, shutting it behind her.

"Will you allow me to fix your tea, Sean?"

He nodded. Abigail lifted the lid of the teapot and looked inside. She then poured tea into two blue and white china cups, lifted sugar cubes from a bowl with tiny tongs and dropped one in each cup, then added a splash of cream from a tiny, matching pitcher. She placed a small spoon on a saucer next to one cup of tea and handed it to Sean. She stirred her tea and took a sip.

In those rare times Sean drank tea, he drank it straight. Or black. He didn't know the right terminology. He'd added sugar before, but never cream. He suspected Abigail fixed his tea to ensure he didn't do something as uncouth as drinking it straight. He told Abigail the details Cannon had told the team and what he'd read in the report. "What prompted Henry to go out at nine o'clock at night to meet with Mr. Moretti?"

"Over dinner that evening, Henry told me about his day, as he often did. He was rather upset. He said he drove through Sea Island Plantation and saw Gary Bowers, the man he uses for surveying, in the undeveloped area, surveying the area and staking out new lots."

"I take it that was without Henry's permission or knowledge."

"Mr. Bowers was not Henry's employee. He ran his own company, so he worked for other developers, although Henry kept him quite busy. Mr. Bowers was working off a new site plan that showed approximately eight hundred home lots, while Henry's plan called for two hundred."

"Did Gary say who gave him the new site plot?"

"Mr. Moretti, who also hired him to begin surveying it to see if his plan was feasible."

"I take it Henry and Moretti were partners in the Sea Island development."

"Yes, I later saw their partnership contract, and although it was rather involved, it basically made them fifty-fifty partners. However, Henry said that they had a verbal agreement that Henry's vision and original plan of three hundred home sites total for Sea Island Plantation was their development plan. You live in one of the one hundred homes in the river part of the plantation. The three-hundred home plan was what was presented to the county and what was approved."

"Was Moretti's new plan approved by the county?"

"At that time, no; however, I later learned that Mr. Moretti's attorney had begun the process with the county and the regional planning commission."

"So it sounds as if Moretti was taking some steps to show the feasibility of his new plan with four times as many houses, and he wanted to meet with Henry to propose this change."

"I believe that is correct."

"Was it just Henry and Moretti meeting for cigars?"

"Actually, Moretti brought his attorney."

"Wow, two against one." Sean took a sip of his tea and set the cup back on the saucer that he'd left on the cocktail table. He noted that Abigail balanced her saucer on her knees and wondered if that was the proper etiquette for everyone or just Southern ladies. "Who was his attorney?"

"Roger Medcalf."

"That name sounds familiar." Sean knew exactly who he was, but was playing dumb to see how forthcoming Abigail would be.

"Roger is Charlotte's former husband and the father of her son, Spencer."

"It seems I need to interview Mr. Moretti and Roger, since they were the last two people to have seen Henry."

"It seems appropriate."

"Since this was just a missing person case at that time, it is not surprising that the sheriff's office didn't process the scene or Henry's vehicle."

"Captain—at that time—Sergeant Cannon told me where it was found, and I had my sons pick it up and bring it back to the house."

"I'll speak to them also. Captain Cannon said Henry's wallet and phone were in the glove box. What happened to them?"

"He brought them to me. We accessed his phone log on his phone, and that's what led Captain Cannon to Mr. Moretti."

"I thought you said you knew he was meeting with Moretti."

"No, Henry had discussed his *issue* with Moretti, but when Henry left he didn't say specifically who he was meeting with, only he was going out for a cigar."

"Do you still have those items?"

Abigail rose and walked to an antique mahogany writing table on the other side of the room. She pulled a manilla envelope from a drawer and handed it to Sean. He examined the phone and wondered if it could be charged and brought back to life after ten years. The wallet was a thick leather bifold, darkened to a deep brown from age and use. There was a dark, crusty substance on both sides, as if someone held it with dirty hands.

"Any idea what this stain is?"

"No, and it's surprising. Henry was meticulous about his things. I'd even seen him using saddle soap on this wallet to clean it. Although I could never figure out how something a man carries in his pocket could get so dirty."

Sean understood. Sweat stains, mud that soaked through his jeans when he sat on the ground trying to fix the irrigation system when he lived in California, slush and grease on his hands when installing chains on his car during a trip to the Sierras in the winter. "Do you mind if I borrow them and have the crime lab look at them?"

"That's fine, no one, other than Henry, the detectives, and me should have had any reason to handle his wallet."

"When I have an investigation with no real leads, I often start with what we call investigating the victim. In a few days, I'd like to sit down with you and talk at length about Henry, so I can get to know him better."

Abigail walked to a bookcase that sat next to the writing desk. It was a traditional lawyers bookcase with glass doors that opened upward. She pulled out two thick albums. "I put these scrapbooks together over the years to memorialize Henry's accomplishments. He was the most humble man. He seldom talked about himself, but there were numerous articles written about him and many local awards given to him. Can I trust you to return them when you're finished?"

"Absolutely. Besides family, who might be his best friend or friends?"

"There are people at the Cusseta Country Club, where he became a member when he moved here more than forty years ago. My parents were members, so I've been going there before I can even remember. Then there are his many work acquaintances, some people he fishes with, former hunting partners."

"Could you make a list of those names with their contact information?"

She nodded.

"Since it's doubtful we'll be able to resurrect his phone, can you recall any other people Henry spoke to by cell phone the day or so before he disappeared?

"I remember Ray Mitro's name from earlier that day on his call register. He runs the CrossFit gym in Dufftown. Henry knew him before he moved here. He was sort of a father figure to Ray, although Ray has to be close to sixty by now."

"I'll stop by and talk to him."

"He's very private about his life. But he and Charlotte are friends. If she introduces you, I'm sure he would be more open."

"Okay. I'm sure I'll need to talk with you again in a few days. Do you have any questions for me?

"Only one. When do you intend to ask Charlotte out on a date?"

Sean stood and looked at her silently for a few seconds. "Thank you for the tea. I'll be in touch."

He opened the door from the parlor and stepped into the entry hall. Rose was there and walked him to the front door. "I don't know if you overheard, but I'm investigating Mr. Nash's disappearance, and I'd like to talk to you a bit."

"Mr. Tanner, as you can see, I'm working for the Nash house at this time, and I sure would not talk about the Nash family when I'm supposed to be working."

"When you get off? At your home, or we can meet for coffee or something."

She nodded.

He wrote his phone number on a page of his pocket notebook, tore it out and handed it to Rose.

"You call me, and we'll arrange a time," Rose said.

"But I don't know your number or even your last name."

"Mr. Tanner, if you can't find my last name and phone number, how do you think you can possibly find out what happened to Mr. Nash?"

12

Charlie was sitting at her desk eating a dinner consisting of a package of peanut butter crackers and a diet Coke, when a text flashed on her phone.

Spencer: *Just saw on a news feed you have another murder.*

Spencer had left for college a few weeks ago, but he called or texted every day, even if he had nothing to say other than he was doing fine and missed her. Like many divorced women, Charlie often said her son was the only good thing to come out of the marriage to her cheating, egotistical, slime-bag lawyer, ex-husband.

Charlie: *A young woman strangled and dumped on the beach.*

Spencer: *I know you'll solve it cause you're the best detective in the world.*

Charlie: *Thx. How's school going?*

Spencer: *Had Algebra exam today. Got 95.*

Charlie: *Awesome!*

Spencer: *Gotta go. Just wanted to let you know I miss you.*

Charlie: *Bye. Love you.*

Charlie blinked away a tear that was beginning to form and saw Darryl turn toward her and cover the mouthpiece of his desk phone. "I've got the security folks from Courtney's credit card company on the phone. They've listed her card as lost or stolen and said the card had two purchases today."

Her two other detectives, Jay Garcia and Todd Sherman, both looked up from their desks as Darryl returned to his phone call. A few minutes later, he hung up and said, "One purchase for fifty-two dollars at two-ten this afternoon at the Enmarket on Island Road and Town Beach Drive, and another for two-hundred-thirty at the Walmart at three-eighteen."

"Jay and Todd, you guys take the Enmarket," Charlie said. "I'll take Walmart."

Thirty minutes later, Charlie was sitting in the Walmart manager's office talking to corporate security on her phone. She was speaking to the third representative and hoping this one could do something. She learned that Walmart had security cameras covering the cash registers and most of the store, but no one at the store knew how to access the footage, so she ended up on the phone with someone at corporate level, where the security footage from every store was archived.

"Okay, Sergeant Nash, I have everything I need from you. We'll contact the credit card company for verification the card was stolen and related to a homicide. Their transaction reference number and the time of the transaction should help us identify the cash register that was used. With that, I'll request a review of the relevant video. Once they send it to me, I'll verify your identity and send it via email to your department email address."

"How long will that take," Charlie asked.

"I hope within a few hours."

"You do remember I told you this could identify a murder suspect, right?"

"Yes, ma'am. We get thousands of these requests from law enforcement agencies around the country every day."

"Thank you," she said, although she wanted to add *for nothing*, and walked out the door and across the hot asphalt parking lot to her car. The sun had just set, but the temperature hadn't dropped yet, and with the humidity, it felt close to a hundred. She had just started her car and was waiting for the AC to cool the interior when her phone rang over the car's speakers. She pressed the green phone icon on her dash.

"Sarge, we got a hit down here," Jay said.

"Good, because I got the corporate runaround from Walmart."

"Their cameras show a man bought fifty-two dollars' worth of cigarettes and beer from the convenience store. They gave us a copy of the security camera video and I sent a copy to three patrol deputies who work that area. One recognized the guy as Keshawn White."

"Is he in the system?"

"Sure is. Twenty-two, five-ten, one-fifty. Arrests for breaking into motor vehicles, shoplifting, drug possession, and other minor stuff."

"Last known address?"

"I'll text it to you."

Five minutes later, Charlie parked next to Sherm's unmarked Ford Explorer in front of a small apartment building. Like much of Spartina Island, this working-class neighborhood of apartments, small houses, and trailers existed in a pocket surrounded by gated communities with million-dollar homes and shopping plazas with fancy stores and restaurants. The building was two stories, with the apartments' front doors facing the parking lot and only windows on the back.

"Jay, can you take the back, and Sherm and I will knock at the front? If Keshawn is here, we'll arrest him for the credit card fraud and bring him to the office. Keep in mind, he might be our killer, but he's only wanted for the property crime at this time."

They both nodded their understanding. She gave Jay a minute to get around the back then knocked at the door. A heavy-set Black woman wearing jeans several sizes too small and a V-neck T-shirt answered the door. Charlie swept her coat aside to show her badge and said, "Ma'am, we're with the sheriff's office. We need to speak to Keshawn."

"What that boy done now?"

"We believe he was using a stolen credit card," Charlie said. "Is he home?"

"It's one thing after another with Keshawn. He my youngest son and the most trouble. But he don't live here, and I ain't seen him in months."

"If you'll let us take a quick look inside, then we can tell the rest of the deputies they don't need to come back here looking for him."

She stepped aside, and Charlie and Sherm walked through the living room and kitchen area. It was a small apartment but neat and clean. A reality show was on the television, and the place smelled like fried food. They walked into the single bedroom, checked the closet, and took a peek inside the bathroom.

"Any idea where we might find him?" Charlie asked.

"That boy stays here and there. No place permanent."

"Does he work?"

Keshawn's mother laughed. "He might work as a mover for a week, then he get fired for smoking weed at work. He then works with a landscaping crew until he just don't show up one day. Then he gets a job doing construction, but he fucks that up too."

"What's his phone number?"

She took out her phone and scrolled to a page of recently called numbers, tapped on Keshawn's name, and showed the phone to Charlie. She took a photo of the screen.

"But that was a month or more ago. He might've lost that phone or sold it and have a new one by now."

"Did he say anything the last time he called?"

"Yeah, he say he wanted me to give him money. That's about all he ever say to me. Look around. Do it look like I have money to be giving away?"

The three of them returned to their cars. "I'll put out a BOLO on him," Charlie said. "How about you guys knock on some doors here and see if anyone knows anything about Keshawn's whereabouts. I think his mother was honest about him not living here, but it never hurts to verify."

13

Sean got two more bottles of Blue Moon from the refrigerator and handed one to Stretch on the back porch. "How's your shoulder doing?" Stretch asked.

Sean's left shoulder was aching badly when he woke up Tuesday. It was the shoulder he fractured almost twenty years ago when some protesters dropped a chunk of concrete on him from a freeway overpass. He had several surgeries over the years and was always worried that he'd need another one or a total shoulder replacement because of the damage. He didn't know if he aggravated it in a yoga class, hitting golf balls on the range, or just the way he slept, but he'd been taking the maximum dosage of ibuprofen for the past two days to alleviate the pain. "Still hurts. Probably a good thing we have a case to work, because I sure can't swing a golf club or paddle my kayak."

"It sucks to get old," Stretch said.

They both sipped on their beers, puffed on their cigars, and stared into the darkness of the backyard and the river beyond it. The night was warm, but with the ceiling fans creating a breeze, it was comfortable sitting outside. Sean had already told Stretch about his encounter with Abigail and Rose, all except Abigail's question about when he was going to ask Charlie out on a date.

After he had gotten home from the little celebratory dinner at the Sandy Feet Bar and Grill with Billy and Charlie last month, he had decided he was ready. Probably Charlie playing footsies with him under the table indicated she wouldn't turn him down. The last girl he had asked out on a date was Lauren, when he was an Army MP at Ft. Steward, and she was a student at Georgia Southern. He had had no need to ever ask another woman out after that. Now he was totally out of practice dealing with rejection and didn't want to risk it.

Charlie had made it easy when she had asked him to join her family on the boat trip the following weekend. A date but not a date. Then that fell through because of Abigail's fall, and once Charlie was available, the memories of Lauren punched him right in the heart on the one-year anniversary of her death. Sean felt almost ready to try again, but he knew better than to ask when Charlie was in the midst of a murder investigation.

"I don't know how we're supposed to investigate Henry Nash's disappearance without talking to Charlie," Stretch said. "We need to talk to that Ray Mitro guy, and even Abigail said we need Charlie's introduction."

"I'd also like to talk to Rose," Sean said. "If anyone knows what goes on in a household, it would be the maid, but I don't even know her last name."

"And you probably don't want Abigail to know you're talking to the hired help."

"I have Charlie's brothers, James and Thomas, on my list. I'm sure they'll give me her last name and phone number."

"How do you want to handle Moretti and Roger Medcalf?" Stretch said. "If someone whacked Henry and shoved him over the bridge railing, those two are at the top of my list."

"Just treat them as witnesses. No pressure. No confrontation. See what they say, write it down, then see if other people say something that indicates they're lying."

Stretch took a swig from his beer. "I don't like Cannon's order that you have to keep him informed and go through him for everything."

"Yeah, I don't trust him. He's part of the old political machine in this county. I can imagine he and his father, the sheriff before Donohue, were all engaged in at least low-level corruption."

"What if that Moretti guy was greasing certain wheels to get those eight hundred houses approved and Henry was resisting? A lot of people might have some financial interest in seeing Moretti's plan happen. That could leave a lot of people who'd want to remove any impediments."

"Definitely a motive for murder."

Annie, who had been lying at Sean's feet, sat up and stared toward the side of the house. A red fox trotted from between Sean's house and his neighbor's, heading toward the river. Annie shot through the dog door built into the screened porch, barking. The red fox continued toward the river at an easy lope. By the time Annie got to the line where her invisible fence was buried, the fox was beyond it, and Annie stopped. The fox's head turned toward Annie as he trotted down the bank to the river. Sean thought he noticed the fox grinning.

"Annie's a good watch dog," Stretch said. "But those foxes are cunning and smart."

"Yeah, he passes through here a few times a week and has Annie's boundaries all mapped out."

Stretch puffed on his cigar. "I'm betting this is all about greed. Was the money involved in the Sea Island Plantation deal enough to kill for?"

"Anything's enough to kill for. In Oakland, I saw dudes kill over a ten-dollar bag of dope."

"Yeah, but rich people have a higher price tag for murder, I think."

Sean's phone vibrated. He looked at the screen and said, "Hey, Charlie."

"Don't hey me. When were you going to tell me that you and your Mudflats Murder Club assholes are investigating my father's disappearance?"

"The sheriff and Cannon just assigned us—"

"I know when you got the case, but you found time to sneak over to my house when I wasn't there and grill my mother."

"Come on, Charlie, I didn't grill—"

"I thought we were at least friends, Sean. You could've at least given me the courtesy of a quick text. I shouldn't have to find out about it from my mother."

"You're right, it's just that Cannon was adamant about—"

"I know—about keeping me out of it. Why do you think that is? Beyond the official reason that family can't investigate family. You, the brilliant California homicide detective, should be able to figure that out."

Sean was preparing to ask her what she meant when he noticed she'd hung up. He set his phone on the table and picked up his cigar.

"Should I pretend she wasn't yelling into her phone, and I couldn't hear everything she said?" Stretch said.

Sean took a long pull of his beer. He just shook his head.

"Look, buddy, everyone on the team can see you two have a thing going," Stretch said. "Okay, maybe not going yet, but you're both dancing around something beyond work partners."

"Oh, come on. Look at her. She's way out of my league. I'm flattered that you guys think she'd want anything to do with this old, worn-out murder cop, but if I had any feelings for her, it would be nothing more than a fantasy."

"Charlie is a very pretty woman," Stretch said. "I take that back. She's downright gorgeous. She's also smart and rich—yeah, we know she's just a cop, but her family has serious money. But give yourself some credit. You're not at all my type, but I can imagine some women might find you rather handsome. You're financially stable, so you wouldn't be sponging off of her. You're not a drunk or a drug addict. You're not crazy—at least not more than most cops. And most people who know you actually consider you a nice guy."

"Thanks for the compliments, I think."

"It seems she can be a pretty strong woman. That might scare the shit out of many men. I don't see you being scared of much of anything. You might even respect women like that. Granted, she can be a bit of a ball buster, as demonstrated by that last phone conversation."

"I wonder if she's more effort than it's worth."

"What the hell are you saying?" Stretch pointed at him with his cigar. "What it could be worth? How about what we all look for in life—having one person to love you no matter what. Lauren was one of a kind. And I know she would approve of you finding someone to share your life with. Hell, I can see it now, you and Charlie together for the next twenty years or so and jumping out of bed when the phone rings at night to send you both off on a fresh murder."

Sean laughed. "Is that your idea of living happily ever after?"

"Not for me, but what more could an old homicide dick like you want out of life?"

14

THURSDAY

Sean sat in an uncomfortable chair outside Captain Cannon's office at 8:05 a.m. reading the local newspaper. The headline read, *A Killer in the Cordgrass*. He just shook his head. It reminded him of those mornings seeing a silly headline of the newspaper article on one of his murders in Oakland. The police beat reporter often apologized and reminded Sean that the editors wrote the headlines. Something to catch the attention of the readers to entice them to read the article. His least favorite had been, *Detectives Baffled Over Mass Shooting*. For months, fellow officers called him the baffled homicide detective. When he arrested the killer, the teasing finally stopped. Sean figured some people might buy the local newspaper to see if there were killers lurking in the saltmarsh cordgrass on Spartina Island, even though the victim had been killed elsewhere and dumped in the sand dunes by the beach.

Captain Cannon walked past his admin's desk and said, "Morning, Ms. Gladys," then looked at Sean. "You waiting to see me?"

Sean nodded and stood.

"Come on in, but let me get a cup of coffee. You had yours?"

"Been up since six so I had my coffee long ago."

"You're retired now, son, you can sleep in a bit."

Sean wanted to go face-to-face with Cannon and tell him that he was ten years older than him, and he was certainly not Cannon's son. But he bit his tongue and sat in one of the guest chairs across from Cannon's desk, while Gladys brought the captain a cup of coffee.

Cannon took several sips. "What can I do for you?"

"Your report mentioned you had interviewed a number of people and took notes of the interviews. We'd like to see the notes, so we know who was interviewed back then and what they said."

Cannon stared at him for a moment then said, "No one in the world can read my scratch, so them notes wouldn't do you much good. I'll have to go through them and write up interview summaries. Could take a while."

Sean thought it best not to ask him for a time frame, although he was sure he'd never see a single interview summary from Cannon. He removed the manila envelope from his briefcase, tugged on one nitrile glove and slid out Henry's wallet. "Per your report, you found Henry's wallet and phone in his glove box and returned them to Abigail. I suspect the stains on the wallet are blood."

Cannon stuck out his hand.

Sean handed him a pair of gloves. "You should put these on if you want to handle it."

Cannon shrugged. "Just hold it up so I can see." After looking at it for a few seconds, Cannon said, "I'm not as certain as you, but could be blood. I don't recall noticing that when I found the wallet."

"Abigail was adamant that Henry cleaned his wallet whenever it got dirty or stained. Used saddle soap. I know it's a long shot, but if Henry didn't personally put his wallet and cell phone in his glove box, and I don't know why he would, then whoever was out there that night might've been bleeding and left their DNA on his wallet."

"That's a lot of ifs. Did you consider that Henry might've taken his own life, and he left his wallet and phone behind to make it easier for his family to handle his affairs?"

"I considered that among other scenarios, but at this stage of an investigation, I normally just collect facts. I found jumping to conclusions this early in an investigation can cause one to travel down the wrong path."

"A smart approach." Cannon took a few more sips of his coffee. "I take it you want this examined for the presence of blood, and if it's found to be blood, you want it typed."

"I'd have the lab examine it for DNA, focusing on the stain, but taking samples from the rest of the wallet and his phone as well. We could get elimination samples from Abigail as well as from you and any other detectives back then who might've handled these items."

"How would that play out, assuming it is blood, and we got a DNA profile? These items haven't been safeguarded against contamination for ten years and there's no chain of custody."

"It's certainly not ideal, but Abigail said she went through the wallet to make sure she stopped all credit cards, then put it back in the envelope, which she placed in her desk drawer, where it remained until she gave it to me yesterday. I'm not thinking forward to evidence being admitted at a trial, although I've seen evidence admitted in the California courts under worse circumstances. I'm only gathering facts, and if that is someone's blood on his wallet, wouldn't you like to know whose?"

Sean drove back to Sea Island Plantation and picked up Stretch at his house. Once Sean had convinced Cannon to test the wallet, Cannon called the evidence room supervisor to his office and instructed her to send it to the SLED crime lab overnight and provide him with the tracking number. Cannon assured Sean he would call SLED tomorrow and ask them to expedite the processing.

Sean was driving his Corvette today because it always picked up his spirit. In their years of marriage, Lauren had driven the newer family car, always a minivan or SUV, vehicles with plenty of room for the kids and their friends, while he drove an old compact pickup. It was good enough to drive back and forth to Oakland when he didn't have a take-home unmarked sedan, and it was useful for weekend trips to Home Depot and the dump. Sean had given up his dream of owning a sports car when he and Lauren got married and started a family. He never felt deprived in the least.

Shortly after he and Lauren had moved to Spartina Island, she'd surprised him by trading in his old pickup for a low-mileage, ten-year-old Corvette convertible. She said he deserved to live his dream. The truth was, being married to her and working together to raise a great daughter and son, with her unwavering support during those years he spent in Homicide, was a life beyond his wildest dreams. If Sean had planned the perfect life back when he was in the Army, he would've sold himself short, because the life he had was better than he ever envisioned. Until Lauren died.

Stretch hopped in the passenger seat, and they drove out the back gate, across Island Road, and into a commercial development called Spartina Village. The village was a cluster of one and two-story office buildings, restaurants, and small stores, with brick walkways, tall shade trees, and a central fountain to psychologically convince patrons that it was not as hot as it felt. He parked in front of a one-story building with a brick façade. Signs advertised a law office, a real estate office, and Spartina Island Development.

They stepped into a bright lobby with bleached wood floors and a wall with a painted mural of a map of Spartina Island and the surrounding area. An attractive Hispanic woman sat behind a reception counter and smiled when they entered. "Good morning, how may I help you?"

"I'm Sean Tanner and this is Jason Andrews," Sean said. "We have an appointment with Thomas and James Nash."

"They're expecting you. You can go on back. Right through this door," she motioned to her right. "Their offices are all the way to the back."

Sean was not accustomed to being allowed to just wander through an office without an escort. The brothers were either very trusting or the concept of Southern hospitality was alive and well in the Nash's business. They passed by several offices on their left, all with open doors and people working at desks, and an open area with workstations on the right. At the end of the hall was an open door to a corner office. From the office, a deep voice with a slight Southern accent said, "Come on in, gentlemen."

15

A tall man in his early forties met them as they entered the office. He had short blond hair and wore khaki chinos and a light blue polo shirt. "I'm Tom Nash. You must be Mr. Tanner." They shook hands.

"Please call me Sean. This is my partner, Jason Andrews."

"And this is my *little* brother, James."

James was also blond, with a well-trimmed beard and as tall as Sean. So much for him being the *little* brother, Sean thought. Last night, Sean had begun paging through the scrapbooks that Abigail gave him and noted that Henry had Norwegian roots. He could see that heritage—all tall and blond—in Charlie and her brothers. James wore jeans, a tan long-sleeved shirt, and boots, looking like he just stepped off the cover of an outdoor magazine.

James shook their hands. "Charlie has told us a lot about you. I'm glad we finally get to meet."

"Can I offer you a bottle of water?" Tom said. "By eight o'clock we're usually coffeed out for the day and try to focus on staying hydrated in our beautiful warm weather."

"Water's great," Stretch said. James brought them bottles of water from a small refrigerator, and they all sat at a round table surrounded by six chairs in the front of the room. Sean took a moment to look around the room. A large, light oak desk, flanked by windows overlooking a courtyard, sat in the back of the room. A standing worktable covered with rolled plans was on the other side of the room. Paintings and framed photographs of Lowcountry scenes—wading birds, marsh views, shrimp boats, and sandy beaches—adorned the walls.

"You have a great office," Sean said to Tom.

"This is James's office," Tom said. "It was empty for years after our father disappeared. Then once he was pronounced legally deceased three years ago, we flipped a coin to see who got the big room, and James won."

"We were supposed to rotate every two years," James said, "But Tom claimed he was fine in his office, and I should stay here."

"Not many older brothers would do that," Sean said.

A sly smile crossed Tom's face. "I actually did it because James works lots harder than me, and with him in the big office, people assume he's in charge and bother him with the problems."

"Not true," James said. "Tom handles the headaches of managing all the properties, and I get to drive around and stomp through the woods of our new developments."

"So, you don't just build these developments and sell them off?" Sean asked.

"Some we do," James said. "For instance, we dissolved the partnership of Sea Island Plantation, where you live, once the last house was sold. We turned it over to a homeowner's association, and they hired their own management company. This commercial area, Spartina Island Village, was the first major commercial development our dad built. We still own it and lease the space to tenants. Tom manages that. We have thirty different commercial and residential developments that Tom manages."

"I didn't realize your company was this big," Sean said.

"James is in various stages of development of fourteen different projects on the island and Dufftown vicinity." Tom handed him a glossy brochure. This is our annual report, which gives a fair overview of Spartina Island Development. We also own a number of other tracts of land that we, or our children, may develop in the future."

Although Sean was fascinated with the company and could talk with these two young men all day about it, he said, "What do you remember about the day your father went missing?"

"I saw him in the office that day," Tom said. "It was a typical day. He had put me in charge of property management several years earlier, so I didn't have many dealings with his developments, which was his focus."

"I'd been home from my military service for about two years..." James said.

"You were in the military?" Stretch said. Sean was surprised too. He figured the children of wealthy parents would send their kids off to private colleges then give them cushy positions with generous salaries in the family business.

James smiled. "My father believed in public service, as did his father. Dad worked for the State Department for four years after college, and only after that did he start working with his father in commercial real estate in New York."

"Sean and I both went in the Army after high school," Stretch said. "For us, it was a job and a steppingstone to our careers in law enforcement."

"Thank you both for your service," James said. "I was commissioned as an Army officer after college. Did four years active duty as an engineer officer, to include a deployment in Afghanistan. And my big brother here spent three years in the Peace Corps after college."

"I guess Charlie's work with the sheriff's office counts as public service," Sean said.

"That girl has been all about public service," Tom said. "After college, she went to work for the regional planning commission. She intended to work there for four years then come to work for the company as a landscape architect. But she stayed there until she went into law enforcement."

"Sorry we got off track," James said. "While Tom did the property management side of the company, I worked with my dad on new developments. He gave me projects to manage by myself, and although he was always there to help, our day-to-day responsibilities were separate."

"What about Sea Island Plantation?" Sean asked.

"That and Ocean Forest Plantation were his babies," James said. "I never got involved in them."

"Did you speak with him that day?"

"Sure, but nothing out of the ordinary. None of us knew anything was amiss until Mother called us around midnight, said he was missing, and asked if we'd heard from him."

"We all offered to come over to the house," Tom said. "But Mother insisted we stay home. The next morning, she told us they found his Mercedes G-Wagon. James and I went right there, and the detectives told us we could drive it back to the house."

"Charlie had told me that your father was adamant about his plan for only two hundred homes on the west side of Sea Island Plantation," Sean said. "What changed?"

"If you recall, the country back then was in an economic downturn," James said. "Dad wanted to wait it out, but Boyd Moretti, who was a fifty-fifty financial partner, wanted to build houses at a greater density and sell them."

"I understand your mother was the one who decided to go along with that," Sean said.

"She wasn't alone," Tom said. "Dad had written a will that included provisions if he became medically or otherwise incapacitated. Although we didn't know if being missing qualified, as a family we thought it would be his wishes. In it was how the company would be operated. All four of us, Mother, me, James, and Charlie, each had twenty-five percent ownership and control. Actually it was written that Mother had a tick over that and the three of us a tick under."

"To avoid a fifty-fifty tie vote?" Sean said.

"Exactly," James said. "Our first major decision was how to handle Moretti's proposal."

"I voted to approve it along with Mother," Tom said. "Charlie and James were opposed. In recent years, I've come to regret my decision."

"If you don't mind me asking, why did you support Moretti's proposal?" Sean asked.

"Purely for financial reasons," Tom said. "I was a business major in college, and I always believed in a conservative business plan."

"While Charlie and I were the dreamers," James said. "We often made decisions based on our emotions, Mother would say."

"How were the company's finances back then?" Sean asked. "Was sticking with your father's original concept too risky?"

"The four of us spent days with our accountant going over everything," Tom said. "I can't tell you precisely the finances of the company at that time, but we weren't ready to file bankruptcy or anything. We could've weathered either plan. I'm sure our accountant could give you a clear picture of ten years ago if necessary."

"Would it be okay if members of our cold case team spoke to him?"

The brothers looked at each other. James nodded. "Let me ask Mother if it's okay with her," Tom said.

"Last question," Sean said. "What do you think happened to your father?"

"I think Moretti killed him," James said without hesitation.

"I agree," Tom said.

16

Charlie huddled with her two detectives in the lobby of the Atlantic Dunes Resort. Javier "Jay" Garcia was the youngest detective in her squad. After four years in the Marine Corps and two years of college, he'd joined the sheriff's office seven years ago and was promoted to detective after five years in uniform. Sherman Todd was a soft-spoken, methodical investigator who had spent ten years in uniform before making detective five years ago.

The three of them had been at the resort for three hours, Jay and Sherm interviewing employees, while Charlie interviewed those guests who were present Tuesday night and reviewed the hotel's security camera footage.

"I spoke to two guests who had a drink at the bar Tuesday night," Charlie said. "Neither saw anyone showing unusual attention to Courtney. They agreed she was a friendly and charming bartender and had no issues with anyone. The hotel only has a few security cameras in the exterior and two in the lobby, one at the front door and one at the reception desk. The manager said there's also one in the elevator, but it's only activated if someone presses the alarm."

"Rich folks like their privacy," Sherm said.

"I think that's their philosophy," Charlie said. "Plus, they don't cater to the kind of clientele that typically cause security problems. A number of cars came and went during the time Courtney was working, but the camera angle and its low resolution made reading license numbers impossible."

"Any big black SUVs with an Eric-looking dude?" Jay asked.

"As a matter of fact, a black Cadillac Escalade drove up to the front at nine-fifteen and disappeared out of sight, possibly to park beyond the valet station. A man who could've been Eric walked in the front door and then back out fifteen minutes later."

"Ah-ha, a man visiting his sweetie at work," Sherm said.

"That's my assumption," Charlie said. "The two guests in the bar who I spoke to didn't mention him, so either they were there at different times, or it was a non-event to them."

"We probably need to return here in the evening," Jay said. "The day shift people we spoke with know nothing about Eric and hardly knew Courtney, other than all agreeing she was attractive, professional, and friendly."

Charlie looked at her notes. "A camera at the service entrance around back showed Courtney walking out that door at ten-o-five, the same time the manager said she checked out. She was wearing the same clothes she was found in. Two minutes later, headlights of a car in the parking lot came on and headed toward the exit. Hard to tell with the video quality in the dimly lit parking lot, but the car's appearance was consistent with the Subaru her parents said she drove."

"Looks like we have two potential suspects," Sherm said. "Keshawn White, who was in possession of her credit card, and Eric, because we all know boyfriends are the top suspects when a woman is strangled to death."

"We have the BOLO out on White, and I've reached out to a few of my C.I.s," Jay said, referring to confidential informants.

"We'll finish up here, grab some lunch, and meet you back at the office in a few hours," Sherm said. "If you want, Jay and I can come back later and talk to the evening workers. I'm sure a desk clerk or bartender has Eric's number in their phones so they can refer him to a guest looking for a driver."

"Thanks, see you later," Charlie said as she headed toward the door, not looking forward to returning to her office, where a pile of reports, phone messages, and a captain demanding answers would be waiting.

17

Sean pulled into a dirt parking lot at the end of Kelly's Landing Road. A rusty shrimp boat was tied to a dock that jutted out into a broad tidal river. A hand-painted sign announcing *Bubba's Shrimp Shack* hung over the front door of a weathered board building. Sean and Stretch pushed through the door and were greeted by a sixty-something man with a shaved head and a weathered face. "Hey, Bubba," he said to both Sean and Stretch.

"Hey to you, Bubba," Sean replied. The owner's real name was William, and he'd spent his life captaining a shrimp boat. After seeing the movie, *Forrest Gump*, he decided to open the shrimp shack restaurant and name it after Forrest's friend in the movie who had wanted to buy a shrimp boat after he returned from Vietnam.

"A couple of other Mudflats Murder Club bubbas are already here," William said.

Sean and Stretch walked through the small dining area, where all tables were already filled, and into the kitchen, where a cook was lowering a basket filled with assorted food into a vat of cooking oil. They went out the back door of the kitchen to a small deck, separated by a plywood wall from the larger deck occupied by regular customers.

Beagle and Feebee were seated on plastic chairs around small tables that had been pushed together. Feebee was drinking from a bottle of beer and Beagle had a glass of iced tea. A plump woman wearing a Bubba's Shrimp Shack T-shirt and apron stepped from the kitchen. Sean knew her name was Gwen, but she went by Bubbette. She said, "Hey, boys. Let me guess, a beer for Stretch and an unsweet tea for the FNG."

Sean didn't know how long he'd be considered the fucking new guy, but he learned last month that Bubbette's husband was with the sheriff's office, so she was not one to mess with. They both nodded as Frank and Irish came onto the deck. Frank was still walking with a cane, which Sean thought he'd be able to dispense with by now, since he had surgery two months ago after tearing ligaments playing pickleball.

While Irish and Frank were taking seats around the table, Bubbette returned with three beers and Sean's iced tea. "The police special today is the shrimp basket or the fresh fish of the day, which is flounder."

"Wasn't the shrimp basket the police special last month?" Feebee said.

"You, girly, are gonna be the smart ass today, huh?" Bubbette said.

"Yup," Irish said. "Feebee is the designated smart ass, and she wants to know what's in the shrimp basket."

"You Northerners is sure dumb," Bubbette said. "Everyone down here knows that shrimp is what's in the shrimp basket."

"Do you think you could put some fries and hush puppies in the basket with mine?" Beagle said.

"You think that cause you're a Black man, you get some special treatment," Bubbette said.

Beagle looked at the back of his hand. "I'm Black? Well lookie at that."

"Don't matter if you White or Black, fries and hushpuppies come with the shrimp." Bubbette looked at Sean. "Don't you try to tell me you want flounder, and you want us to grill it."

"No ma'am, I learned my lesson last time. I've been eating just oatmeal the past few days to save up my cholesterol quota, so I'm gonna go with the shrimp basket."

"For the FNG, you do learn fast," Bubbette said. "Six shrimp baskets, right?"

Everyone nodded and Bubbette disappeared into the kitchen. Feebee opened her laptop and said, "I set up a new shared document and summarized what Cannon told us in the briefing and what the reports said, which ain't a helluva lot. Sean submitted a summary of his interview with Henry Nash's wife Abigail last night."

"Sean and I interviewed Tom and James Nash, Charlie's brothers, just before we got here. I'll write up a summary of that interview."

Sean told them about his meeting with Cannon, who reluctantly agreed to send the wallet to SLED's crime lab.

"By the way, where's Doc?" Irish asked.

"He called me last night," Beagle said. "Lieutenant Green and Sergeant Nash asked him to go with Deputy Pickett to M.U.S.C for the autopsy on the woman murdered by the killer in the cordgrass."

"Deputy Darryl Dumbnuts," Irish said.

"That's bullshit," Frank said. "The sheriff's office can't start tasking our cold case team members without checking with me first."

"It's a new era," Feebee said. "I love that they're recognizing the expertise we bring to the table and utilizing our skills. They called Sean yesterday morning and asked him to come to the crime scene. How come *that* didn't piss you off?"

"They might as well just deputize us and issue us uniforms," Frank said.

"That ain't gonna happen," Stretch said. "I sure as shit don't want to wear a uniform again, and if we're deputized as reserves or something, then we have to play by their rules."

"Guys," Sean said. "Do we really need to refer to a killer lurking in the cordgrass?"

Beagle grinned. "The newspapers called it that, and you know the newspapers are never wrong."

Bubbette brought their food, and no one spoke for ten minutes. Despite the dietary risk, Sean relished the fried shrimp and hushpuppies. He figured his body could handle an occasional splurge like this.

Once most of them had finished eating, Frank said, "Sean, you're the lead on this, so what are we gonna do?"

"I think we need to learn a lot more about Henry Nash. His past is rather sketchy, and sometimes people get killed because of their secrets."

"You said Abigail gave you two scrapbooks," Feebee said. "If you give them to me, I'll start with them and do a deep dive into Henry and his family's background."

"Doc is a member of the Cusseta Country Club," Beagle said. "He and I can spend some time there and talk to people. You said Abigail's family were members going back at least sixty years, and Henry joined when he moved down here. People must know them well."

"Why you and Doc?" Stretch asked. "Because we low-class cops couldn't mix with the highfalutin country club set?"

"You said it, Stretch," Beagle said. "We attorneys and physicians fit in with society better than you guys."

Sean leaned forward in his chair and pulled his damp shirt away from his back. It was hot and muggy, and the industrial fan in the corner of the deck was the only thing that made it bearable. Two brown pelicans sat on rotting pilings in the river from a pier that had broken apart long ago.

"Irish and I can wander around old town Dufftown and talk to folks," Frank said. "They've lived there forever. People have to know things about them, maybe some problems with neighbors."

"That might require a lot of wandering for two old farts," Stretch said. "Maybe you should borrow two of them scooters from the Walmart."

"Next on my list is Ray Mitro," Sean said. "But I need Charlie to introduce us."

"Do you think that's a good idea?" Frank said. "If the captain finds out we're bringing Charlie into our investigation, he'll shit a brick. Besides..."

"Besides?" Sean said.

Feebee cleared her throat. "We know that you and Charlie have become...ah...well, friends. It might create an objectivity issue."

"Charlie cussed me out on the phone last night because I spoke to her mother without talking to her first. Now you guys think I'm not objective because I want to talk to her. And I personally don't care what the captain thinks. Cannon would be thrilled if we spin our wheels and get nowhere, so he can feel vindicated for never finding out what happened to Henry Nash."

"Sean's right," Irish said. "We all know Charlie and like her." He winked at Sean. "Some more than others, but it's impossible to thoroughly investigate her father's disappearance without dealing with her. Plus, Dufftown and Spartina Island are small towns. Even if we don't tell her shit, what we're doing will get back to her."

"I respect all of your opinions," Sean said. "You're all my partners, so if you think I'm not being objective or my judgment is clouded, don't be afraid to call me on it."

He looked around the table, and no one said a word.

18

Charlie was eating a salad at her desk when Darryl and Doc strolled into the office. "Broken hyoid bone in her neck," Darryl said, "Along with subdural hemorrhage in the neck that the pathologist said indicates manual strangulation. Scratches on the neck and more subdural hemorrhage on the left cheek bone and the nose. Suspect probably punched her good a couple of times."

"She had one broken fingernail and possible skin and dried blood under her nails," Doc said. "Of course they did scrapings and clippings to send to the lab."

"When Sean was at the scene, he noticed the scratches on her neck," Charlie said. "He thought that could've been done by the victim during a struggle to remove her assailant's hands as she was being strangled."

"From my observation at the autopsy and what I've seen myself during countless postmortem examinations, I think that's a reasonable assumption," Doc said.

Darryl handed Charlie a plastic zip lock baggie. "This was in the front pocket of her shorts. The assistants found it when they were removing her clothes and prepping her for the autopsy."

Charlie grabbed a pair of nitrile gloves from her desk drawer.

"I don't think those are necessary," Doc said. "I had the medical examiner's assistant do a wipe with a saline wetted gauze pad. We have it as evidence and can send it in to check for DNA if necessary."

"Very smart, Doc," Charlie said. She removed the necklace from the baggie and examined it. "I'm no jeweler, but this appears to be a nice ruby pendant. Probably a few carats. Not something you buy at *Costume Jewelry R Us*."

"I thought the same thing," Doc said. "So, why was it in her pocket and not around her neck?"

"Maybe she was expecting trouble," Charlie said. "Didn't want someone to steal it."

Darryl and Doc both nodded.

"I have the vic's clothing," Darryl said. "I'll have a crime scene tech go over it for blood or other potential evidence, and if there's anything at all, I'll have the evidence room send it to the lab."

"Of course the medical examiner is deferring the cause of death until they get the tox back, but everything points at strangulation as the cause of death and the manner being homicide," Doc said.

Charlie put the necklace with the ruby pendant back in the baggie and handed it to Darryl. "Make sure you book this into the evidence room right away. Anything else? Any thoughts?"

"The boyfriend, Eric, probably got pissed about something she said and choked her," Darryl said.

"Maybe," Charlie said. "Or she left work to go home and ran into someone else."

"Maybe that Keshawn White dude," Darryl said. "But a dirtbag like him wouldn't worry about dumping a body. He'd just leave her where he killed her."

"I know I'm not a detective like you guys," Doc said. "But moving the body indicates a somewhat clear mind. A suspect must have a reason for doing so. Quite often to protect the location of the murder from the police. If a man killed a woman in his home, for example, he'd not want the body there."

"Exactly," Charlie said. "But why the beach?

"Proximity to the location of the murder?" Doc said. "It would be smarter to drive across the bridge and beyond Dufftown. Plenty of places out there you could dump a body where it would never be found."

"But that takes time and increases the risk of gettin' caught," Darryl said. "Nothing worse than a sheriff's deputy stoppin' you for speeding when you got a dead body in the back seat."

"Was he not concerned with disposing of the body so that no one would ever find it?" Charlie said. "Just enough to get it away from where the killing occurred?"

"It must've been a decent place to dump her," Doc said. "It was dark and deserted enough that no one saw the suspect drag the victim in there. If that British couple hadn't been out on their morning walk looking for nesting sea turtles, she might not have been found until later in the day when people started frequenting the beach."

"Folks dispose of bodies or any sort of evidence in a place they're familiar with," Darryl said.

Another good point, Charlie thought. She thanked Doc for his help and took a few photos of the pendant before Darryl turned it and other evidence into the evidence room. She texted the photos to Suzie at the Spartina Island Boutique then called her.

"Hey, Suzie," Charlie said. "I know you have a keen eye for jewelry. Does this look familiar to you?"

"Sure, that was Courtney's."

"Did she say where she got it?" Charlie knew that Suzie would have gushed over it and asked Courtney a hundred and one questions about it.

"I noticed her wearing it a week or two ago. She'd only say Eric gave it to her. She was proud of it, but somewhat secretive at the same time."

"What do you mean?"

"She didn't want her parents to know she was seeing a guy. They thought she should stay away from all men and heal from her divorce for a while. She wore it at work, but always took it off before she drove home so they wouldn't see it and start asking questions."

19

Sean parked his Corvette and walked in the front door of the sheriff's office. He waived at the civilian behind the reception desk and used his new ID card to click open the door from the lobby. After the Mudflats Murder Club had finished lunch, he dropped Stretch at his house then met Feebee at his house to give her the two scrapbooks. He knew he'd have to face Charlie sooner or later, and if he wanted to interview Ray Mitro, it would have to be sooner.

He walked down a short hallway and into the CID office. Gladys looked up from her computer screen and said, "Good afternoon, Mr. Tanner."

"You can call me Sean."

"No, sir." Gladys shook her head. "I don't know how it was at your police department, but down here, law enforcement is a paramilitary organization. We address those of higher rank by their title and last name."

"I'm surprised that a civilian volunteer is considered a higher rank than the woman who runs the criminal investigation division."

"You are a sweet talker, Mr. Tanner, but the sheriff already told us the cold case team members are to be treated as equal to our detective sergeants." She pulled a lanyard from her desk and handed it to him. "When you're in the building, you must clip your ID card to this and wear it around your neck. Everyone without a badge must have their ID card visible at all times or else be escorted. You'll find lanyards hanging on a hook by the outside doors, so you can leave this one there and grab a new one when you come in."

"Thank you. Is Sergeant Nash available?"

"Last I saw, she was in her office. You can just go on back. You don't need my permission."

Sean walked past the A squad office on his right and the conference room and break room on his left and into the B squad office. The room had five modern workstations and a worktable in the center. Back at Oakland PD, all twelve homicide investigators had been crammed into an area not much larger than this. Darryl sat at a workstation just inside the door, and Charlie was seated behind a large U-shaped desk in the back corner. They both looked up when he entered. Sean looked at Charlie and smiled. "Have you got a few minutes?"

She didn't return his smile. She actually looked annoyed by his presence. "Not here." She got up and led him down the hall to a row of interview rooms. She stood by an open door and held her hand out. He stepped inside. She followed and shut the door.

"There's no privacy in this place," she said as she sat on one of the plastic chairs.

Sean pulled out another chair and sat down. "I'm sorry I upset you by talking to your mother before warning you, but I need your help."

She raised her eyebrows. "Oh."

This was not going well, Sean thought. "Your mother said a man named Ray Mitro was on your father's cell phone call registry the day he disappeared. She said he was a long-time friend of your father, but he would not give me the time of day unless you introduced us."

"So now that you need my help, you're willing to share a piece of your investigation?"

"Come on, Charlie, I'm doing the best I can here. But I value our friendship more than the missing person case of your father. If I can't have both, I'll tell Captain Cannon to find someone else to investigate your father's disappearance."

She sat there and just stared at him. Despite the seriously pissed off look on her face, Sean couldn't help but notice how beautiful she was. Her hair was done up in a tight bun and she wore minimal makeup. He knew female officers back at Oakland PD who did the same out of a concern men wouldn't take an attractive woman seriously. Her shirt and pants were loose fitting, but he could tell there was a slender, toned figure underneath.

"I've been wanting someone to reopen this case for ten years. And quite honestly, there's not another detective in the entire state of South Carolina who I'd rather see handle it. What disappointed me was that you didn't trust me. You could've asked me to keep a secret and then told me you were going to start off your investigation by talking to my mother. Besides, don't you think people talk to me? My mother told me everything she told you. My brothers told me what you talked about. They told me you're going to talk to our accountant. So I already know. You can trust that anything you tell me about your investigation, I will not repeat to anyone. And I mean anyone."

Sean looked at the floor for a few seconds. "You're right, and I'm sorry. I do trust you completely. I think I was afraid that if Cannon found out I was talking to you, he'd pull me from the case. I know how important this is to you, and I didn't want to do anything to jeopardize it. I guess I was even willing to risk our friendship to find out what happened to your father, so you can have closure."

"Wait here." She left the room and closed the door. Sean turned the doorknob. Locked. Although he had locked thousands of suspects in interview rooms like this, he'd never been locked in one himself.

A moment later she returned carrying her shoulder bag. Sean was standing by the door with his hand on the doorknob. She laughed. "Sorry about closing the door. Force of habit, but your new ID card actually opens the interview room doors. Just touch it to the proximity reader."

"I thought for a second you were so pissed that you were going to let me stew in here for an hour or so."

She touched his arm and smiled. "Naw, I'm over it already." She pulled out a large manila envelope and handed it to him.

Sean slid the twenty or so photocopied pages from the envelope.

"Remember when we were coming back from Marta Point last month and I told you I went into Cannon's file cabinet and found he had a confidential file on my father's disappearance?"

Sean nodded.

"And that I made a copy?"

Sean nodded.

"This is it. If it's discovered that I broke into his confidential file cabinet, I'd probably be fired. I'm giving you this, but you can't tell anyone what's in it or where you got it. I'm trusting you with my career. These are his handwritten notes of who he talked to and what they said."

"I asked Cannon directly if he had any papers or notes beyond what he turned over to us in the murder books, which consisted of only the official reports. He admitted he had notes, but no one could read them, so he had to write it up."

"Well, if and when he does write up his notes, you'll be able to see if he's still withholding anything."

"I'll lock these up in my house," Sean said. "If there's anything important in here to the investigation, I know I'll have to find another way to discover it."

"I know you'll protect me. I trust you."

"And I trust you."

"Good, shall we take a drive so I can introduce you to my dear friend, Ray Mitro?"

"That would be great."

"One more thing while we're in here." She gave him a hug and a kiss on the cheek. "Now I'm ready."

20

Sean sat in the passenger seat of Charlie's unmarked Dodge Charger and tried to relax despite her driving, where she either had the gas pedal mashed to the floor or was jamming on the brakes. On the way, she brought him up to date on the murder of Courtney Evanson. They pulled up to a light industrial building next to a furniture upholstery shop and went inside through an open overhead door. Sean had spent countless grueling hours in a CrossFit gym when he was on Oakland's SWAT team, and this one was little different. Cement floor, no mirrors on the wall, and no pretty girls wearing makeup and designer fitness outfits. Instead there was a lot of sweat, clanging weights, and plenty of grunting. A dozen men and two women were following the workout circuit of the day, consisting of dead-lifts, tire throws, pullups, and other exercises.

A man wearing a tight T-shirt and sweatpants made a beeline to Charlie and gave her a big hug. His face marked him as being around sixty, but he had the physique of a man twenty years younger. Charlie said, "Sean, this is Ray Mitro. Ray—Sean Tanner."

They shook hands. "I've heard a lot about you," Ray said. "Nice to finally meet you."

Even though Charlie had left her suit jacket in the car, Sean could see the sweat already dampening her skin in the hot building.

"Let's move over here by the fan." Ray escorted them toward a huge floor fan.

"I did CrossFit in the Bay Area," Sean said. "No air conditioning there either, but it never got this hot."

"You know the principles then," Ray said. "No frills, and warm muscles work better. You look like you're still in decent shape. Come on down for a workout and see if you want to get back into the greatest fitness program in the world."

"I'll think about it."

"Charlie's a regular here, as are a bunch of the others in the sheriff's office." Ray looked at Charlie. "I saw in the paper we had another murder, which means I won't see you for a while."

"I wanted you to meet Sean," Charlie said, getting right to the point. "The sheriff assigned him as the lead investigator for the disappearance of my father."

"Incredible, it's about time someone reopens that investigation," Ray said. "From what I hear about you, you're the right man for the job."

"We'll see about that. I understand you and Henry spoke the day he disappeared."

"I called him, and we met for lunch. We met almost fifty years ago, and after I settled here, we tried to get together occasionally."

"That's long before he moved here," Sean said. "Did you meet in New York?"

Ray glanced at Charlie. She nodded to him.

"Actually in Slovakia. Henry worked for the State Department and helped move me and my mother to the U.S. when I was fourteen."

"If I recall my history right, Slovakia was a Soviet satellite back then," Sean said.

"It ended its communist rule in 1989 and got its independence from Czechoslovakia four years later."

"Charlie said she's been coming to your gym for ten years now. Is that when you moved here?"

"It sounds like you're investigating me rather than Henry's disappearance."

"Sorry. It's just that I try to learn enough about possible witnesses to see how they fit with the victim."

Ray nodded. "I worked in the gas and oil business as an energy consultant. About ten years ago I semi-retired and settled down here. Henry found me a nice piece of property along the river, where my wife and I built our house. He also found me this site for the CrossFit gym that I run with a partner. Truthfully, it's more of a hobby than a business."

"During your lunch with Henry," Sean said, changing the subject abruptly on purpose, "Did he mention any problems with anyone, or any issues that could've caused him to disappear?"

"Henry loved Spartina Island and Dufftown and his family. He would've never left on his own. He mentioned some animosity toward a business partner in the Sea Island development, but I didn't get the impression it was anything that was insurmountable to Henry."

"Did he say what he was going to do about that problem?"

"Work it out," Ray said. "Henry had a way with people. He said there was no problem two people couldn't resolve if they were willing to talk about it."

"What do you think happened to him?"

"There's nothing in the world that would've caused Henry to leave his family. That means he's dead. He's not the sort of man to take his own life. What remains is he died accidentally, and his body disappeared. That's unlikely because Henry is not the kind of careless person who would just accidentally fall off a bridge as some people theorized. The only thing remaining is someone murdered him."

21

Charlie started the car and lowered the windows to vent the stifling air. She could tell Sean didn't trust Ray, but Ray had always been there for her after her father disappeared. He was the one who toughened her for the police academy. He was her sounding board when she needed to vent about her failed marriage, challenges working in the male-dominated sheriff's office, missing her father, or her overly present and domineering mother. He was there when she was sworn in as a new deputy and there again during the ceremony when she was promoted to sergeant, as proud of her as her father would've been had he been around.

Years ago, she had spent days reading about the history of Slovakia and Eastern Europe during the cold war, the period when her father was stationed in Germany and Austria with the State Department. She had many questions about how and why her father brought fourteen-year-old Ray Mitro and his mother out of a communist country through a militarized border to the west. Over the years, she had broached that subject with Ray, but he always evaded her questions entirely or changed the subject.

"Are you sure your father worked for the State Department?" Sean said.

"That's what he said. You think he was lying?"

"I think people working for certain government agencies are required to conceal where they work."

"You think he worked for the CIA or something?"

Sean shrugged. "I'm not sure getting foreign nationals out of communist countries is something the State Department does."

"What's it matter?"

"I guess it doesn't," Sean said. "That was almost fifty years ago. I can't see something that long ago being related to his disappearance, or as Ray has concluded, his murder. I just get suspicious when someone connected to one of my investigations is evasive. If something surfaces from the distant past, I might have to talk to Ray again."

"He gave you his phone number. I know he seemed guarded about his past, but that's his nature. Once he gets to know you, he'll be more open."

Her phone rang. "Hey, Jay."

"A C.I. of mine just called and said Keshawn White is hanging outside the smoke shop at Seagull Plaza. Sherm and I are just walking out of the office to head that way."

"I'm two minutes closer. I'm on my way."

"I'm not calling dispatch," Jay said. "If uniforms show up, he'll spook and run."

Charlie pulled the shifter into drive and punched the gas. She flipped on her lights and siren, made a right onto Spartina Island Road, and raced over the bridge. She slowed at a red light at the first intersection on the island, waited for the traffic to stop, then sped through. A minute later she turned off her siren, and a few blocks from the small strip mall, she switched off her flashing lights.

The smoke shop was on the south side of the plaza. They sold tobacco and vaping products, and it was a hangout for young people. She drifted slowly through the parking lot, seeing several people outside the front door. One fit the description of White.

"Young Black man in below-the-knee blue shorts, baggy, dark gray T-shirt, and red ball cap on backwards," she said.

"I see him," Sean replied.

"I'll park here, and we can both approach on foot from opposite directions. If he sees he's boxed in, he's less likely to rabbit."

Charlie parked her car in the back of the lot. She walked around to the left, and Sean went to the right. White and three other young men stood to the left of the door under an awning. They were talking to one another in an animated manner, while constantly looking around. From their wariness, she figured they all had plenty of run-ins with the law. She saw Sean coming in from the other direction. When she was about fifteen feet away, she swept back her coat to show her badge and her gun.

"Keshawn White," she said. "Sheriff's office. I'd like to talk to you."

Charlie didn't stop the other men in the group from slowly drifting away. As she had anticipated, White turned away from her and saw Sean. She used that as an opportunity to close the distance between them. Even though Sean was dressed casually and not showing a badge, his appearance and demeanor oozed cop. White looked back at her and sighed so loudly she could hear it. She figured he had resigned himself to the fact that there was no escape.

Then he ran toward her. She braced herself. He zigged to the left to try to slip past her, but she lunged at him and grabbed him around the waist. White twisted away. Charlie tried to grab him again, but he shoved her hard toward the building. She slammed into the plate glass window and collapsed to the ground.

Before White could take off, Charlie half-crawled, half-dove at him, grabbing his foot. He tried to shake her off, but she wasn't going to let go. White shifted his weight onto the foot she was holding and pulled back his other foot. She turned her head and braced herself for what she knew was going to be a brutal kick to her face.

Out of the corner of her eye she saw Sean, his head down and legs pumping, flying toward her. He was moving faster than she imagined a man his size and age could move. Sean hit White like a defensive end would hit a running back behind the line of scrimmage. White crashed to the concrete sidewalk. He then somehow struggled to his feet and looked around as if he was getting ready to run.

Sean grabbed a handful of White's T-shirt with one hand and White's shorts with the other. Sean lifted him off his feet and body slammed him to the ground.

Jay and Sherm screeched to a halt in front of the store and jumped out of their SUV. While they were handcuffing White, Sean helped Charlie to her feet. She wobbled and almost fell, but Sean put his arm around her waist to hold her up.

"Are you okay? Do you need to sit down?"

She felt embarrassed that she got her ass handed to her by a crook not much bigger than her. "I'll be okay. Just got my bell rung."

"Did you hit your head?"

"No, I don't think so. I just slammed into the metal frame of the window with my hip. It hurts but nothing's broken."

Sean relaxed his hold around her waist, and she slowly put weight on her throbbing leg. "Next time we do this, after you badge a bad guy and he looks my way, I'll just say I'm a civilian," Sean said. "That way maybe he'll run at me."

"Damn, Sean, the problem is you'll always look like a cop, and when crooks see big ole you and me, they'll always try to run through the skinny, blonde girl."

"It doesn't matter how we took him down," Sean said. "What matters is we're partners, and *we* got him."

22

Charlie stripped off her dirty suit in the locker room at the station and stuffed it in a bag to take to the cleaners. She stood in front of the mirror and looked at the purple and yellow bruise already developing on her hip. It would be all black and blue by tomorrow. Not a big deal, but she wouldn't be modeling a swimsuit for a while.

She washed her face and hands in the sink, let her hair down, and ran a brush through it. She kicked herself for not waiting for Sherm and Jay to arrive before she tried to contact White. Although Sean was more than capable, she had no business putting a civilian in a position where he had to help arrest a suspect. She was tempted to apologize to him for even asking him to assist with the arrest, but he would've laughed. He'd remind her again that *Once a Cop, Always a Cop*.

For a moment at the scene, she'd been worried about the way Sean body slammed White. He could've been seriously injured, and she'd have a lot of explaining why she put a civilian in the position to use that kind of force. Sherm offered to take White to the hospital to get checked out, but White refused. He actually apologized for fighting with them and for hurting her.

She put her hair back up, dressed in a clean shirt and the gray suit she kept in her locker for reasons just like this, and made her way to her office. "How're you feeling, Sarge?" Sherm asked.

"A little sore, but I'm fine."

"Well, you clean up well," Jay said. "You scared us for a moment there when Sean was helping you up and you were a bit wobbly."

"I should've waited for you guys," she said. "If he saw four of us, he would've just given up."

Jay nodded but said nothing, for which she was glad. It was hard for her to admit she'd screwed up and didn't need anyone else adding to it.

"We have him in interview one," Jay said. "He's scared and knows he's in a world of shit."

"Let's go talk to him."

White was sitting in a chair that he had moved into the far corner of the room. Charlie had him stand while they rearranged the chairs around the table then told him to sit at the end of the table. She and Jay sat on either side of him. She opened her leather folio and pulled out a rights waiver form.

"I probably don't need to tell you you're under arrest," she said. "We had one matter we wanted to talk with you about, but you're now also looking at assault on a police officer. What happens today is up to you, but before we talk, I'm required to read you your rights."

She went through the Miranda warning, and White waived his rights and agreed to talk with them. She slid a photocopy of the store video frame showing him in front of the cash register at the Enmarket in front of him. He looked at it and sighed.

"The credit card you used didn't belong to you."

"Yeah."

She placed a photo of Courtney's body in the morgue in front of him. He looked at it for a few counts then looked back at her. She was hoping for some telltale expression that would indicate guilt or remorse, but she saw nothing.

"It was her credit card," Charlie said.

"Is she dead?"

"You tell me," Charlie said. "What happened?"

"I never seen that girl in my life. I found the credit card. I didn't like take it or steal it from her or anyone."

"So you're just walking down the street, and a credit card dropped from the sky in front of you?"

"Not exactly."

"Then what?"

White said he was wandering around late Tuesday night or early Wednesday morning. He had no place to sleep, so he was just roaming the streets. He went through the parking lot of the Sunrise Apartments, a complex with three buildings a few blocks from Spartina Island Road. He was trying car doors until he found one that was unlocked.

"What kind of car was this?" Charlie asked.

"A small SUV. It was dark out, so I don't know what color."

"You're a guy," Charlie said. "Guys know cars, so what kind of SUV?"

"A Subaru. Not the Forester, the other one."

White continued with his story and said there was a purse on the passenger seat. He looked through it and found a wallet. He took the credit card and some cash, around thirty dollars. He used the cash to buy some drugs from a guy he knew, who also let him sleep in his place. The next morning he used the credit card at two places, but when he tried it at a third place, the clerk said the card had been reported stolen and kept it.

"Wait here," Charlie said.

Outside the room, she said, "What do you think?"

"Quite honestly, I don't see him as a killer," Jay said. "A thief, a drug addict, a general asshole, but not a killer."

"I tend to agree. Let's send Sherm out there to see if he can find the Subaru. That might verify his story. Meanwhile, we'll go back at him and see what else he has to say."

23

Sean drove down Jefferson Road past the Gullah Cultural Center on his way to the Freedman District. When Sean had vacationed here with his family years ago, they stopped at the cultural center with the kids to introduce them to the local history. As a teacher and a mother, Lauren believed their role as parents included educating their children about the world and other cultures. The original Gullah people had settled here after being freed during the Civil War. Over the years, many of them had sold the land they'd been given, but there were still about a hundred homes in the protected district. The weather and time had eroded all of the original homes, but newer ones took their place. Some of the current residents were descendants of the original Gullahs, while newer residents, mostly wealthier Black people, built more modern houses in recent years.

Sean had been to this neighborhood many times because his friend Lieutenant Billy Green lived here in a large, modern house that he had built on the same land where he grew up in a three-room shack. When Sean moved his arm to activate the turn signal, he knew he should be home icing his shoulder. He chided himself for reacting without thinking when he saw Keshawn White rush Charlie. It was instinctive for him to run toward trouble. When Charlie went down and White was preparing to kick her in the face, Sean lowered his shoulder and hit him like he was a tackling dummy back in his football days. Sean had ignored the screaming pain in his shoulder, and when White somehow got to his feet, he grabbed the guy, picked him up, and dropped him to take the fight out of him.

Sean had worked with female officers and detectives his entire career. Most could do the job as well as men. Some were good cops, some not so good, the same as male officers. But when it came down to knock-down-drag-out fights, few women could match the bigger male officers. Sometimes sheer size and brute strength ruled in a street fight. He was protective of all officers he worked with, but something within him—maybe his old-fashioned values—made him even more protective of female officers. So when he saw that asshole getting ready to kick Charlie in the face, he didn't think, he just acted.

He stopped in front of a white, vinyl-sided house with a huge live oak tree in the front yard. Red and pink annuals bloomed in the front yard. He walked down the driveway that ended at a two-car garage and along a walkway to the front door. Rosalyn Jackson opened the door before he could knock. "Please come in, Mr. Tanner."

He stepped into an immaculate living room with beige carpeting and a matching sofa and love seat that took up half the room. Family portraits adorned the walls. "You can call me Sean."

"Well, when I'm working for the Nash family, I call all of her guests by their title and last name. Just the way it is. I'm not working for them at this moment, but it seems you are performing duties for the sheriff's department. I always taught my boys to address law enforcement officers by their title and last name, therefore I think that so long as one of us is working at our jobs, I should call you Mr. Tanner."

Sean chuckled. "May I then call you Mrs. Jackson?"

"Only the young'uns in the Sunday school I teach call me Mrs. Jackson. I'd prefer you call me Rose. Sure is hot out there today. Can I get you an iced tea?"

"That would be wonderful."

Rose went into the kitchen and returned with two large glasses of iced tea. Sean took a sip. "Sweet tea."

"Mr. Tanner, when you drove into this part of Spartina Island, away from all the new developments, you traveled back into the South. Here, when you ask for tea, you get sweet tea. Shall we sit?"

Sean sat on one side of the sofa and Rose sat on a love seat where she could face him. "I don't know exactly where to start," Sean said. "As you probably know, the cold case team I'm a member of is investigating the disappearance of Henry Nash. I imagine that working for the household as long as you have, you might know something that can help. I can understand how you might be reluctant to say anything negative about the family for fear of reprisal, but I can promise you that what you say to me will remain confidential."

"Uh-huh."

Sean studied Rose's face, hoping for some sort of connection, a bit of commonality, but didn't see any at all. He continued. "I grew up in a working-class neighborhood, where some of my friend's mothers worked for wealthy families on the other side of the city. They'd leave early every day and come home after dark bone tired. Then they'd have to take care of their own children and homes. I've met Mrs. Nash. I can't imagine it's been easy."

Rose pursed her lips and smiled. "I know what you're trying to do, Mr. Tanner, but you don't understand diddly. I was twenty years old, a mother with two babies and working as a maid at one of the now shuttered resort hotels on the island. Mr. Nash and his pretty fiancé, the soon-to-be Mrs. Nash, offered me a job. You see, my mother was the maid for Mrs. Nash's parents, and she recommended me. They offered me twice the pay I was making. At first I commuted to Dufftown with two other ladies who worked for other families around there. Had to leave extra early and got home extra late. Mr. Nash saw that and bought me my own car, 'cause my husband needed our only car for his work."

"I'm sorry," Sean said. "I just assumed—"

"That I was an abused servant, spending my days on my hands and knees scrubbing floors and toilets?"

"Well..."

"Mr. Nash treated me like family. And Mrs. Nash, well, she could be a bit...well she did grow up in a privileged Southern family. Did you know that when I was pregnant with my third son, Mr. Nash still paid my salary when I was off for six months? Did you know that he paid for all three of my boys to go to college? Made them a deal when they were young—graduate high school, do a stint in the military, and he'd pay whatever the G.I. Bill didn't cover for their college education."

"I had no idea."

"Mrs. Nash and I are the same age. It wasn't easy for her early on. Married to a Northerner who her family and others didn't trust. Got pregnant with Miss Charlotte early on, before they even had a proper house to live in."

"I thought Mr. Nash bought their house when he moved down here."

"Dufftown and the Island is not what it is today. What is now their family house at that time was basically a boarding house. It was part of the old Dufftown Hotel, which is now long gone. They used it for long-term guests, which Mr. Nash was for a while. The house was once the home of the richest man in the county. During the Civil War, Union Army officers lived upstairs and had their headquarters downstairs. Then it was a Union Army hospital. After the war it changed hands a dozen times until the hotel bought it."

Rose took a sip of her iced tea. "Mrs. Nash bought it from the hotel with the money her daddy gave her as a wedding present, and Mr. Nash went about remodeling it and bringing it back to the grand house it once was, but with all modern features."

"So where'd they live during all that construction?"

"At first with Mrs. Nash's parents, but as you could imagine, that didn't work out. They rented a little house, but Mrs. Nash had a difficult pregnancy. There were no hospitals around back then, so Mrs. Nash went to her family's cabin up in the mountains in North Carolina. It wasn't far from a good hospital in Asheville and close enough to a great hospital in Charlotte. I stayed up there with her during the week, and I came home on weekends, and Mr. Nash stayed down here and worked during the week and came up there on weekends."

"That's where Charlie was born?"

She nodded. "Miss Charlotte was a few months old when the house renovation was all done, and they all came back and moved in."

"You must've overheard a lot during your years working there," Sean said. "Many people suspect foul play was involved in Mr. Nash's disappearance. Can you think of anyone who'd want to hurt him?"

"Back in the early days, back when Miss Charlotte and her brothers were toddlers, I spent more time working at the house. I helped raise them, or as Mrs. Nash often said, I raised them, and she helped. That was complimentary, but not true. Mrs. Nash was a good mother. I was too busy with the children and the house to worry much about Mr. Nash or his concerns. He often left early for work. Sometimes came home for lunch and I'd make him a sandwich or some soup. I'd be gone most of the time before he got home. But he was a good man. The very best husband and father."

"What about in recent years, like just before he disappeared?"

"The house was quieter those days. Miss Charlotte, Mr. Thomas, and Mr. James were all grown and out of the house. They didn't need me as much, so I probably only worked thirty hours a week. But Mr. Nash still paid me the same. Sometimes he'd be working at his desk in the library when I was cleaning. He always stopped to talk with me. Ask about my family. If I needed anything. But to answer your question, I never saw or heard of any problem anyone had with Mr. Nash."

"What did you hear after he disappeared?"

"The children were at the house a lot. Sheriff detectives there a lot too. Lots of worrying and crying. I tried to let them grieve and just do my job taking care of them and the house. A while later, Miss Charlotte moved back in with her son, Master Spencer. She said it was because after her divorce, she needed help with Spencer, especially being that she was going to be a sheriff's deputy and all. But I think it was also to be there for Mrs. Nash. Miss Charlotte can put on a tough veneer, but I've known her all her life, and she's actually the most caring and loving young lady in the world."

"The family dynamics must've changed a lot after Mr. Nash was gone and Charlie moved back in."

Rose smiled. "Actually, the house had been too quiet before with just Mr. and Mrs. Nash. I was used to it being full of laughter with all the children. Master Spencer was...what...maybe in the third grade when they moved back in. My favorite part of the day was when he got home from school, often bringing a friend or two over to play, and they'd sit in the kitchen with milk and cookies. Truth is, I was sad to see him graduate and go off to college. The house is too quiet again."

"What do you think happened to Mr. Nash?

"I heard all the gossip back then. We housekeepers...oh, yeah, some time ago, Mr. Nash said calling me a maid was outdated, that housekeeper was more respectful. Anyway, other housekeepers were talking that Mr. Nash had run off with a younger woman, or he took his life because of an illness, or he leaned over the railing on the bridge to look at something and fell. None of that made sense. Although I don't know why someone would want to hurt him, that's the only thing that could've happened to keep him away from his family and the life he loved down here."

24

Sean stopped at his house to feed Annie and let her out. He wondered if he was focusing too much on Henry's past. In all the murders he had investigated, the motive was nearly always over something that happened recently. His first partner had told him that solving a murder was easy, just find the last person the victim saw and convince him to tell you why he killed the victim. Except for a business dispute with Boyd Moretti, Sean had not heard of anyone who didn't love Henry Nash.

He took a quick shower, changed into shorts and a clean shirt, then said to Annie, "You ready to go see Rachel?"

She wagged her tail and jumped into the back of the Highlander. Once he crossed the bridge to the mainland, more questions swirled around in his head. He called Rachel.

"Hey, Dad."

"How's my favorite daughter?"

"Your only daughter?"

"That too. I'll be a few minutes late if that's okay. I need to stop and talk to someone."

Sean took a left, drove through historic Old Town Dufftown, and stopped under a giant live oak. He rolled down the windows for Annie and walked up to the front door and rang the bell.

After a long minute, Abigail opened the door. "Well, this is a surprise. I was in the back watching a show and wasn't expecting anyone."

"Sorry for the intrusion, but I was on my way to dinner with my daughter, when a bunch of questions began rattling around in my head."

"We can't have you being distracted with questions when you're with your daughter. Why don't you come in?"

She led him under the entry hall's majestic staircase to a room on the right. A grand piano stood in the front corner of the room, and a sofa and several upholstered chairs faced a large flatscreen TV in the back. She switched the television off. "This was originally the music room, but it is now mostly the TV room. Will this be just a few questions, or should I bring out some sherry?"

"I'll be quick. I'm learning Henry had an interesting life before he came to Dufftown. What do you know about his time with the State Department?"

"He never really spoke much about it. His father believed in public service, so Henry joined the State Department after college. After his training, he was posted in Germany and later in Austria."

"I guess Henry passed that tradition of public service to your children," Sean said.

"Yes, we were immensely proud of them. I still am."

"Did he ever tell you what he did over there?"

"Not really. He was a junior staff member in the diplomatic corps, so it was a lot of scut work, as he called it. When the kids were young, we took a vacation to Europe, and Henry showed us where he worked in the embassies in Berlin and Vienna."

"I saw on a map that Vienna is only around fifty miles from the border with Slovakia. Is that how he met Ray Mitro's family?"

"I don't know exactly, but we did take a day trip to Bratislava, the capital of Slovakia, and Henry was pleased by how much the border and the entire country of Slovakia had changed."

Sean couldn't tell if she really didn't know much about Henry's time with the State Department or if she was withholding what she knew. "I read some of the articles in your scrap books, but I still don't understand how the son of a successful New York real estate developer ended up down here."

"Henry and his father took a trip to Spartina Island, where another New Yorker owned a private hunting preserve. They saw the potential for development. A year later, Henry visited again and began buying land. He was staying at the Cusseta River Lodge, which was owned by my father. Henry's plan was to stay here a while, make some contacts to begin zoning and permitting, then return to New York while the paperwork made its way through the local bureaucracy."

"Let me guess," Sean said. "He met you."

She smiled warmly. "I was home for the summer from college and sunning at the pool at the Cusseta Country Club. This very charming, handsome, older man came up and introduced himself. He was thirty and I was only twenty, but I accepted his invitation to dinner, and the rest is history."

"So, he never returned to New York?"

"He was back and forth for a while, but he eventually moved here and only visited there for business and family matters."

"Is his father still alive?"

"He died twenty years ago. That left Henry and his younger brother, Richard, as the heirs to their father's real estate empire in New York City. You'll learn more about the financial fiasco when you meet with our accountant, but in a nutshell, Henry sold his interest in his father's business to his brother. Richard destroyed the business and declared bankruptcy shortly before Henry disappeared."

"That must've made Henry pretty angry."

"More like extremely disappointed. His brother owed Henry a great deal of money that was forgiven by the bankruptcy court."

"Sounds like they didn't end up with a cordial relationship."

"In the year prior to his disappearance, Henry made several trips to New York to meet with his brother, attorneys, and others. Richard wanted Henry to loan him money or delay the payments he was supposed to be making on his buyout of Henry's share."

"When Henry disappeared, did you suspect his brother might've had something to do with it?"

Abigail crossed her arms and looked at the wall beyond him. "I never told my children, but I hired a P.I. to investigate Richard's travel and whereabouts during that period."

"And?"

"He never left New York."

"He could've hired someone."

"I considered that, but the P.I. found no evidence to support it."

"But you never ruled it out," Sean said.

She shook her head.

25

Charlie stood with Jay and Sherm in the parking lot of the Sunrise Apartments. The complex consisted of moderately priced units that catered to young adults with decent jobs. Some retired people also lived here, but they were mostly those who didn't have enough savings to buy a house or condo in one of the developments that catered to retirees. The sun was hidden behind large trees on the west side of the complex.

When back in the interview room, Charlie and Jay had been pressing Deshawn White to admit to at least knowing Courtney or having encountered her the night she was killed, but he continued to deny it. She was beginning to believe him when Sherm sent her a text saying he had found the car. She walked around the Subaru and compared the license plate to her notes, confirming it was the vehicle registered to Donald Littleton.

"Have you talked to anyone here yet?" Charlie asked.

"I wanted to stay with the car," Sherm said. "But I spoke to a few residents in passing, and none of them knew anything about the car or who drives it."

"We'll have it towed back to the station where we can have SLED's crime scene team go over it," Charlie said. "I wonder if our mystery boyfriend, Eric, lives here."

"The manager's office is closed for the day," Sherm said. "But I have an emergency number if you think we should call them."

Charlie thought about it. It was 6:30 already. If they were to learn Eric lived here, would they just knock at the door and ask him to come down and talk to them? If he refused, they didn't have enough to arrest him and would need an arrest warrant to drag him out of his apartment. Then a search warrant to search it. By the time they got the warrants, assuming a judge would sign them, it would be ten o'clock. Although she'd done it many times before, it was not ideal to begin a crucial interview with a possible suspect when she and her detectives were already tired from a long day. Besides, she wanted something that pointed to Eric as the killer before she confronted him with Courtney's murder. Something besides him being her boyfriend and their experience of boyfriends sometimes killing their girlfriends.

Charlie tugged on a pair of gloves and opened the passenger door. A black leather handbag lay on the floor, its contents spread over the seat. Lip gloss, lip balm, two tampons, a key fob for the Subaru, a pack of tissues, a cellphone charger, two hair ties, a brush, a metal box of mints, and assorted business cards, but none in the name of Eric or for a limousine service. She opened the wallet, which contained no credit cards or cash. She was confident this was the work of Keshawn White. Maybe he was telling the truth.

She looked in the back seat and found an umbrella, a sweater, and a pair of pink running shoes. She popped the hatch. Nothing there. She opened the driver's door and saw beach sand on the floor. She wondered if Courtney regularly walked on the beach and tracked the sand into her car. Charlie knew her own personal car often had a sandy floor, but then again, she only vacuumed it when it got really bad.

She noticed the driver's seat was farther back than if five-foot-tall Courtney had last been driving. She wondered if White sat in the seat when he was searching the car for other things to steal and moved the seat back. She'd have to ask him. She searched through the console and door pocket but found nothing interesting.

She stepped out of the car and looked inside it again, trying to determine if this could be where Courtney was strangled. She saw no indications of a struggle, but then again, what would a struggle look like inside a car?

Nothing appeared broken, and other than the contents of her purse being strewn about, nothing else seemed out of place.

"What do you guys think?" Charlie asked.

"White could've gotten into the car and moved the seat back," Jay said, "but I don't think some thief, worrying about being seen, would sit in a car and get all comfortable. He'd stay outside so he could make a quick getaway if someone saw him."

"That's a bunch of sand on the floor," Sherm said. "Every place is sandy down here, even this parking lot, but for that much, either the woman never vacuumed her car, or someone stepped right off the beach into her car."

"Did she take a walk on the beach after she got off work?" Charlie said, thinking aloud.

"We saw her leave the hotel on the security camera, and a minute later her car drove off," Jay said. "Her workplace is right on the beach, so if she wanted to walk on the beach, why get in her car and drive somewhere else?"

"Good point," Charlie said. "Unless she was meeting someone."

"Like Eric," Jay said. "She got off work and hooked up with Eric. Then they drove to the beach for a romantic walk. The beach access walkway where we found her body is probably the closest beach access to where we're at."

"Okay," Charlie said. "Good theory. If we go with that, then Eric kills her on the beach, gets in the car with sandy feet, moves the seat back, and drives the car back to his apartment."

"Everything fits," Sherm said. "But wouldn't a guy think that driving the car of the woman you just killed and leaving it in your parking lot might bring the cops to your doorstep?"

"How many of the suspects you arrested were smart?" Jay said.

"You've got a point." Sherm said.

Charlie looked at her watch. "Sherm, you've got the parking lot. Walk around and record license numbers. Be on the lookout for an Escalade, but stay close to the Subaru so no one contaminates it and so you can see when the tow truck arrives. Jay and I will knock on a few doors, see if anyone knows anything about the Subaru or our mysterious Eric."

26

Annie leaped out of the back the moment Sean popped the hatch and raced to the front door. She barked twice and Rachel opened the door and stepped into the frenzied, tail-wagging, yellow Lab. After spinning around several times, Annie plopped onto her back, her tail still wagging so hard she kept tilting from one side to the other.

"Someone's happy to see me," Rachel rubbed Annie's belly then stood and jumped into Sean's arms.

"That's two of us happy to see you," Sean said.

She grabbed Sean's arm to lead him into the house, but Sean uttered a tiny grunt when he felt a hot pain in his left shoulder. "What's the matter?" she asked.

"I tweaked my shoulder the other day."

"The one you hurt back in Oakland during that protest?"

Sean nodded and followed Rachel into the house. She wore a pair of shorts and a tank top, her long brown hair in a ponytail. Sean was amazed how much she looked like Lauren when she was Rachel's age.

"Are you staring at my stomach?" Rachel laughed.

"Busted."

"I'm only ten weeks along, and I can't even see a bump yet." Rachel laughed. "I'll let you know when there's something to see. Now, let's get some ice on your shoulder, and I want to hear exactly how you *tweaked* it."

Sean sat on the sofa in the great room with an ice pack on his shoulder and told her about yoga, golfing, and sleeping wrong. When she gave him the same skeptical look that she had given him when he tried to convince her there was still a Santa Claus for one year longer than he should've, he confessed to helping with the arrest of Keshawn White.

"Don't you think you should let the younger cops handle stuff like this?"

Sean pretended he didn't hear the reference to him not being a young cop anymore. He finished the story with White being a second away from kicking Charlie in the face.

"Okay, I'll give you a pass since you were saving a pretty lady from severe injury. When are you going to ask her out?"

Rachel was the third person in two days telling him he should ask Charlie out. He knew they meant well, but it was still annoying that so many people wanted to get involved in his love life. "I almost did," Sean said, "then she invited me to the family thing on her boat. But then her mother broke her wrist. Once she was available after that, I really thought of it, but then...you know."

Rachel leaned against him on the sofa and rested her head on his right shoulder. "Yeah, I know. The one-year anniversary of Mom's death was hard. But you—all of us—got through it. We all know that Mom wanted us to go on with our lives, and I know Mom would approve of you and Charlie."

"I'll do it once this murder investigation she's involved in settles down. You remember back when I was working a case, I didn't even have time for you and your brother."

"That's not true, Dad. You'd go days without hardly sleeping just so you could be up and spend time with us. You never, ever, neglected us. But I understand. It would make sense for Charlie to get back to a normal routine so she can completely focus on you sweeping her off her feet with your charm and wit."

"When did you get so smart?"

She smiled. "I think I inherited it from you and Mom. Are you hungry?

I have chicken parmesan in the oven and apple turnovers and ice cream for dessert."

"Isn't that doting husband of yours joining us?"

"Austin's softball league has a game tonight, but he might be home in time for dessert."

As they were eating their dessert, Sean asked, "Have you talked with your brother lately?"

"We text, but we seldom talk."

"He sent me some texts, but whenever I call, he never answers," Sean said. "He said something about taking time off work and his boss being an asshole."

"Did you know Carson was taking Adderall? That a doctor diagnosed him with ADHD?"

"When he was young, one of his teachers thought he might have ADHD and could benefit from medication like Ritalin. Your mother took him to a doctor, and we decided to focus on behavioral change. We thought he outgrew it."

"As part of my teacher continuing education, I did a seminar on ADHD medications last year. Many therapists think that Adderall is overprescribed because it's a simple fix. Did you know that when I was going to college, almost half my classmates had a script for Adderall?"

"I don't know much about it. The drugs of choice on the streets of Oakland were heroin and crack. That's the extent of my drug knowledge."

"I'm not saying it doesn't have its uses, but some young adults abuse it. It's a stimulant, comprised of a mix of different amphetamines. It helps people focus, and that's why kids took it in college. Carson said all the programmers or coders at his work take it."

"He's probably exaggerating when he says all, but if it's prescribed by a doctor, that should make it okay, shouldn't it?"

Rachel picked up their empty plates and carried them to the sink. "I don't think he'd want me to tell you, but Carson and some other guys in his division were suspended. They were all buying extra Adderall from someone at work."

Sean was speechless. He'd taught his children the dangers of drugs, which he'd seen firsthand as a cop. Buying a prescription drug from someone was little different than buying an illegal drug in the eyes of the law. And just because one drug was safe when taken as prescribed, it didn't mean it wasn't dangerous when abused. He remembered the feelings of withdrawal he experienced when he stopped taking the pain meds he'd been prescribed after he was shot and had undergone multiple surgeries.

"I remember interviewing one young man we arrested for murder in Oakland. He was a heroin addict who stabbed another addict. Years before that, he was a successful insurance broker. Then he was in a car accident and doctors prescribed oxycodone after several surgeries. When the doctor wouldn't renew his prescriptions, he bought more on the street. Then he found out heroin was cheaper and went downhill from there."

"Stories like that are common," Rachel said. "Nowadays, young people are turning to fentanyl, which is even cheaper and more readily available, and overdoses are so prevalent that all the teachers in my district, even us in elementary school, keep Narcan in our desks. But we're not talking opioids and fentanyl with Carson."

"I should talk to him."

"Don't tell him I told you," Rachel said. "See if he'll bring it up himself."

"What will happen with his work?"

"He said it will be okay. The company needs them, so he thinks that after their internal investigation, they'll make them do a drug program and pee in a bottle for a while but let them come back to work."

Carson, now twenty-seven, was a grown man and didn't need his father to scold him about his mistakes in life. Although Sean wanted to help, he knew unsolicited advice was seldom helpful. He also knew that if Lauren were still alive, she'd know exactly what to do.

27

FRIDAY

Charlie got to the office at 7:30 a.m. and began calling Sunrise Apartments every ten minutes. Finally, the manager answered at 8:35. He said they had a tenant named Eric Robinson who drives a black Escalade. The manager said Eric had lived there for six months, paid his rent on time, and was never a problem. Because they only had enough covered parking for half the tenants, Eric was on a waiting list, but Eric and several other tenants with fancy cars rented unused garages from people in the condo complex next door.

Charlie ran a record check on Robinson. DMV showed the address of the Sunrise Apartments and a two-year old Escalade registered to him. His driver's license showed he was forty, six-feet tall, and 185 pounds, certainly big enough to carry or drag a hundred-pound woman to the beach. She found a domestic violence report from a year ago, where a neighbor reported an argument between him and his girlfriend at the time. Deputies interviewed the girlfriend who said nothing physical happened.

She sent Jay and Sherm to knock on doors at the neighboring condo complex to try locating the Escalade and walked into Billy's office. Billy looked up from his computer monitor and gestured toward a guest chair in front of his desk. She told him about identifying Courtney's boyfriend and said, "I'd like to pick him up and search his apartment and car."

"Your victim's car was in his parking lot," Billy said. "You have people saying he's her boyfriend. Your training and experience tells you that husbands or boyfriends are often responsible for women's murders. You have plenty for a judge to authorize the search, but you need more for an arrest warrant."

"How about if I also ask the judge to authorize a search of Robinson's body by a medical professional, looking for scratches or other injuries consistent with the murder?"

"Good idea. That would give you the right to detain him, transport him from his apartment, and if you find anything during the searches, arrest him on probable cause and bring him to the office for an interview."

"Even if we find nothing on him, his apartment, or his car to tie him to the murder, we'd still need to interview him," Charlie said. "Any normal citizen would expect to be questioned if his girlfriend was murdered."

"Absolutely, and going in with the search warrant will give you the upper hand should he be a dick and tell you to pound salt."

"I'm thinking about asking Sean to help with the search of the apartment. He has a way of seeing things we don't."

"I'm sure he'd be glad to help," Billy said. "The captain wants us to get a statement from him concerning his use of force during the arrest of Keshawn White."

Charlie leaned forward in her chair. "That's bullshit. He saved my butt from a real hurt out there, and this is the thanks he gets. It's going to feel like some sort of I.A. investigation to him. If a deputy did that, they'd just write up a supplemental report to justify their actions."

"But Sean's not a deputy. I'll talk to him and take his statement myself. Coming from Oakland where every use of force is scrutinized, I'm sure he'll understand."

"Then I'll leave it to you and say nothing, beyond thanking him profusely several more times for ensuring I don't need facial reconstruction surgery."

"I'm sure you've heard by now that the cold case team is reopening the case of your father's disappearance."

"It would've been nice to have heard it from someone other than my mother after Sean went to the house to question her."

"Don't blame Sean. That was the captain's orders. They were told they had to keep you out of the loop to avoid any appearance of improper involvement by you as the family member."

"I understand I can't head the investigation, but come on, boss. This is a small town and people talk, so I'm going to be aware of just about every move they make. Plus, the team will need me to make some introductions so people will talk to them. I already took Sean to the gym to meet Ray Mitro."

"We don't need to mention that to Captain Cannon. Just keep in mind that if it's shown your father was the victim of foul play and the cold case team does some magic and proves who was responsible, we can't have you testifying in court that you were involved in the investigation."

"Understood." Charlie got up and headed to the door.

"And Charlie," Billy said, "I know that with the nature of your relationship with Sean, it will be awkward keeping secrets from each other."

"The nature of our relationship?"

"Well, you know..."

Charlie studied his face, looking for him to say more. Like what he thought was going on between them.

Billy returned her look, as if he were waiting for an admission from her. Finally he said, "Ah, never mind."

"Don't worry. I can handle secrets." But she didn't have to like it, Charlie thought as she left his office.

28

Sean, Beagle, and Feebee sat at an oak table in a small conference room at the office of William Nichols, C.P.A. Will was a short, round man in his mid-fifties with a receding hairline and a ready smile. "My father was Henry's accountant when Henry first started doing business down here forty-six years ago. I began working with my father after I graduated college and took over the major accounts after he retired twenty years ago."

Sean had briefed Beagle and Feebee on everything Charlie's mother and brothers told him, and since they had a better grasp of financial dealings from their experience in investigating organized crime, he let them do most of the talking.

"Do you know where Henry's money came from and how he got started?" Beagle said.

"Henry and his father were visiting and saw potential for development. They met with my father and a realtor. Henry had two million dollars in cash from his father and a line of credit from New York banks for another twenty million."

"That's a lot of credit for development in what this area must've been back then," Feebee said.

"They would've been high-risk loans, but I'm sure the banks had done a lot of business with Henry's father and knew he was good for them," Will said. "Henry began buying tracts of land on the island and a few off-island locations around Dufftown. He worked with a lawyer for development permits, zoning changes, and political support for new infrastructure."

"If I recall my Spartina Island history correctly," Sean said. "The first bridge to Spartina Island hadn't even been built yet."

"That's right," Will said. "Henry was one of the major forces to make that happen. He got to know people in the state capital in Columbia and convinced them of the need for a way to connect the island to the mainland besides the state ferry system. The swing bridge opened a few years later, and immediately the value of all the land Henry had bought on the island increased tremendously."

"Getting the bridge would've required a lot of political support," Feebee said. "Did some of Henry's money go to campaign contributions and the like?"

Will shrugged. "I only know what my father told me, but when a developer is starting from nothing, it takes years before the first structure is built. Probably ten years or more before a positive cash flow is achieved."

"I understand his wife, Abigail, came from means," Beagle said. "I'm guessing she contributed to his company's operating capital."

"Actually, not at all. Henry's father didn't trust that pretty little Southern girl. Thought she was after Henry for his family money. And Abigail's family didn't trust Henry. Figured he was a Yankee carpetbagger. They both insisted on a prenuptial that would protect their families' estates. Spartina Island Development was solely owned by Henry, and Abigail's money remained hers."

"What do you know about the financials behind the Sea Island Plantation?" Beagle asked.

"Henry had bought part of that tract years earlier. About twenty years ago, he bought the rest and partnered with Boyd Moretti to develop it. Henry plotted it out and built the roads and infrastructure in the part between the river and the wetlands. He built and sold some houses and sold the other lots to people who would build their own houses. He was set to sell lots on the other side, but the market took a downturn, and no one was interested in building million-dollar houses down here."

Sean had heard all of this before, and although he wanted to interject to move things along, he let Beagle and Feebee handle the interview their way.

"We've reviewed some of the annual reports," Feebee said. "But to cut to the chase, how much was Henry Nash's business and the Nash family worth at the time of his disappearance?"

Will thought for a moment. "Abigail's parents were gone, and her share of the family estate was around five million. She owned the family home, equity in Cusseta Country Club and a few other properties, but sold the rest and invested in securities. Spartina Island Development and Henry Nash—it's hard to separate the two—was worth between thirty and fifty million, depending on how you appraise their land and other holdings."

Will paused for a moment. "That does not include the fifteen-million-dollar trust fund he created for his children."

Sean couldn't help raising his eyebrows. He remembered thinking he was rich when his deferred compensation account at work, to which he had contributed most of his career, had reached six figures. "Henry Nash did not seem like the kind of man who would raise his children as trust fund babies."

Will grinned. "He viewed that as a sort of insurance policy to make sure his children would be taken care of no matter what. Henry insisted they work; however, it didn't have to be in his company. The boys did a stint in public service then went to work for the family business. They received nice, but not outrageous salaries—around two hundred thou a year at the time of Henry's disappearance. Charlie decided to remain in public service, where her salary is a fraction of what her brothers receive, so the trust makes up the difference, so none of his children who dedicated their lives to public service suffer financially."

"When I graduated from law school and applied to the FBI, I accepted the fact I'd never make what some of my classmates would in corporate law," Feebee said. "But I would've loved to have someone supplement my salary to match what they were pulling down."

"Same here," Beagle said. "We prosecutors made more than cops did, but not what lawyers in private practice made."

Sean knew he and Lauren would never get rich working as a cop and a teacher, but the rewards of their professions could not be measured by dollar signs, and neither regretted their career paths.

"Charlie could care less about the money," Will said. "She stopped in to see me a few weeks ago and drove up in her old Prius. Her payments from the trust go right into an investment fund. She's not touched a dime of it and lives off her sheriff's salary."

That's got to be a pretty nice nest egg by now, Sean thought.

"Let's get back to Sea Island Plantation at the time when Henry disappeared," Feebee said. "It seems like Henry was financially able to sit on the property until the market changed."

"Yes, but at a cost," Will said. "A development of that scope might cost a hundred thou a month in interest and tax payments just sitting idle. You also have to factor in salaries of any workers who are doing nothing productive. The biggest non-tangible cost, though, is the delayed payoff."

"Can you explain that?" Beagle said.

"Let's say you have an investment that will pay out fifty grand," Will said. "You've been planning to spend that on a new car. Then you are told the payout will be delayed for five years. Or maybe you plan to retire at age sixty based on your investment return, but the market crashes and you have to work another five years. Therefore, you're without your dream car for five years or are forced to work five years longer."

"Was that Moretti's situation?" Feebee asked.

"I'm not his accountant," Will said. "However, he was more interested in short term returns on his investment in developments, while Henry looked at ten, twenty years or more into the future. If the Nash family had not gone along with Moretti's proposal for Sea Island Plantation, it would've been five or more years longer before a return was realized."

"Could Moretti's business have survived those five years?" Sean asked.

"Like I said, I'm not his accountant. He lives more lavishly than the Nash family does. His developments are mostly quick builds. He'll buy land, build twenty houses, and cash out within a few years. Or he'll buy land and sell it a year later if he can get more for it. His holdings in the county are not the size of Nash's Spartina Island Development, but his family has been builders and developers in the area for generations."

"How's Spartina Island Development doing today?" Beagle asked.

"More than solvent." Will handed a flash drive to Beagle. "Abigail authorized me to give you everything. You'll find that the company's assets minus liabilities show an equity well into nine figures and steadily increasing by ten to twenty percent a year."

It took a moment for Sean to realize nine figures meant at least a hundred million dollars, and that "well into" meant it could be a lot more.

29

A stand of loblolly pines stood on the south end of the parking lot of the Sunrise Apartments and provided a narrow slash of shade, where Sean found Charlie, Sherm, Jay, and a heavy-set uniformed deputy waiting. It was a few minutes before noon and the heat index was already near a hundred, which was hardly tempered by the warm breeze off the ocean.

"We located Robinson's Cadi in a garage next door," Charlie said. "We have a deputy standing by with it until we clear the apartment. Although we don't have an arrest warrant for Robinson, we have a warrant to search his person, so if he rabbits, we have every right to stop him. Jay, you take the back. His apartment has a sliding door that opens into the courtyard where the pool is. The rest of us will go to the front and knock. Keep in mind that although this is just a search warrant, he could be our murder suspect."

Sean followed the file of deputies to unit 156. Charlie pressed the doorbell and knocked at the door. After a moment, she did it again and said, "Mr. Robinson, this is the sheriff's office." She waited another moment, then rang the doorbell, knocked loudly, and yelled, "Sheriff's office. Search warrant. Open the door."

The breeze died down and Sean caught the whiff of an odor he had smelled all too often. "Does anyone else smell what I do?"

Charlie put her nose near the edge of the door and said, "I think I know why he's not answering the door."

She pulled a key from her pocket, twisted it in the lock, and pushed open the door. The uniformed officer stepped aside, and Sean followed Charlie and Sherm inside. The stench was overpowering. He often compared it to the smell when someone throws the packaging from chicken into the trash and it sits there for a week, only ten times stronger.

The kitchen was to the right. On the far side of the kitchen counter, a round dining table was surrounded by six chairs. Tied to one of the chairs was a body with a plastic bag over its head. Sherm opened a folding knife, cut the bag, and peeled it off the victim's head.

Back in Oakland, Sean and his fellow homicide investigators would never have tampered with a body with no signs of life. They'd wait for the coroner. They wouldn't risk possibly smudging the one fingerprint on the plastic bag that would identify their killer. But he couldn't blame Sherm. It was a natural reaction to rip a plastic bag from a man's head, even if there was only a one in a million chance he was still alive.

"Looks like we found Courtney Evanson's killer," Sherm said.

"If Eric didn't kill her, we now have two murders with no suspects," Charlie said.

"Stay with the body," she said to Sherm. "Sean and I will do a quick walkthrough." She backtracked to the front door and peeked into a utility room, where Sean had noticed a washer and dryer when he entered. She walked through the living room, past a sofa, loveseat, and coffee table to a patio door. Sean followed. She slid the glass door open and told Jay he could come inside.

Sean followed Charlie to the bathroom, where she pulled back the shower curtain to make sure it was empty. Sean doubted a killer would still be in the apartment, but good cops always checked. They went into the bedroom, checked the closet, and peeked under the bed. Charlie opened the bedroom window and returned to the main room. She turned the thermostat down to sixty to force the system to pump more cold, fresh air into the room.

"Should I call for paramedics to officially pronounce him dead?" Jay asked.

"I'll go out on a limb," Charlie said, "Based on the smell and the bag tightly taped over his head, I think we can conclude he's dead and just call for the coroner."

She took a few photos of the body with her phone. Although the face was bruised, swollen, and covered in dried blood, Sean was sure it matched the photo he had seen of Eric Robinson.

Sherm handed Sean a pair of booties and gloves, which he put on. Charlie photographed a set of keys that sat on the kitchen counter and handed them to Sherm. "Do a cursory search of the Cadi, then call for a tow. I'll call for a SLED crime scene unit to process the apartment and then do the car back at the station. Have the deputy wait for the tow, and then you and Jay can start a door-to-door canvass of the building."

As Charlie stepped outside where the air was fresher to make her notifications, Sean scanned the apartment. Not a luxury unit, but more upscale than average. Granite countertops, stainless steel appliances, nice tile in the kitchen and entry, quality laminate wood floors in the living room, and a pleasant view of a lush courtyard and pool through the patio door. The kind of place that would cater to those young working professionals who had not yet made the transition to home ownership.

Robinson's body was tied to the chair with a nylon rope that had been wrapped around the body and the back of the chair twice and tied with a square knot. The end of the rope was wrapped around his right wrist and tied to the arm of the dining chair with another square knot. The teal and gray braided rope ended in a loop, like the ropes he'd seen attached to the cleats of boats.

The other hand and both ankles were duct taped to the chair. Dried blood that had run from Robinson's head soaked his white T-shirt, creating a deep brown crust that extended to his beltline. His face had been battered. One eye socket and cheek bone appeared shattered, the nose broken and off center on his face. His left pants leg was torn and soaked with blood, and his right hand was mangled and bloody.

Charlie returned to his side. "I called for the coroner's office and SLED's crime scene unit and notified Billy."

Sean pointed out his observations to Charlie.

"How long you think he's been dead?" she asked.

"At least a day, probably longer."

"As long ago as Courtney?"

"That's a reasonable guess," Sean said. "I had a similar scene in Oakland. A Vietnamese restaurant owner tied up and beaten like this in his house. The home safe was open and empty. His children said he kept the restaurant receipts in his home safe and only went to the bank once a week."

"Years ago, we had one like this, but that victim was a drug dealer," Charlie said. "The grate for the air return was removed from the wall, so we assumed they beat him until he revealed that was where he kept his stash. The question is, what did Eric have that his killer wanted?"

While Sean and Charlie waited for the coroner's office and SLED, they began searching the apartment. Sean went through the bathroom then joined Charlie in the bedroom. "Only thing I found of interest was a prescription container with eight oxycodone acetaminophen pills remaining. Made out to Robinson last year."

"I guess we can rule out Robinson being a drug addict," Charlie said. "Those pills wouldn't have lasted a day in the home of an addict."

They searched the dresser drawers and closet, methodically examining each item of clothing for blood stains or rips that might indicate a struggle or involvement with Courtney's murder. When they finished with the clothes and shoes, Sean stretched to pull a box off the top shelf. He groaned when he grabbed the box, and its weight triggered pain in his left shoulder.

"What's wrong?" Charlie asked.

"No big deal. I tweaked my shoulder the other day."

"You mean yesterday when you saved me from getting my face kicked in?"

"It was sore before that, but yeah, that did aggravate it," Sean said. "It's an old on-duty injury that still acts up sometimes." He told her the story about responding to a major protest when he was in uniform and someone dropping a block of concrete on him that narrowly missed his head but broke several bones in his shoulder.

"You were shot once, tore up your knee making an arrest, and had concrete dropped on you." She took his right hand and held it with both of hers.

"You forgot all the blood, sweat, and tears I left on the streets of Oakland."

She kept hold of his hand and looked up into his eyes.

30

Sean made eye contact with her. Her lips parted, and he was sure she was going to kiss him. On the lips. A real kiss. He knew it was inevitable. He just never expected their first real kiss would be at a murder scene with the stench of a decaying body filling the air.

Charlie blinked and shook her head as if she were coming out of a trance. She stepped back. “I’m glad most of you made it out of Oakland in one piece. Let me get that box.”

The moment evaporated and Charlie was back to business like she had flipped a switch. They finished the bedroom without finding anything important and returned to the main room. The air conditioning and open windows had lessened the smell to the level that he no longer felt like gagging every time he took a breath. She started searching the buffet sideboard that sat against the wall in the dining area, while he went into the kitchen.

“Check this out,” Charlie said. Sean sidled up next to her as she paged through a ledger book filled with dates, dollar amounts, addresses, and “c” or “cc” codes.

“Could be his driving log,” Sean said. “C standing for cash, and cc for credit card.”

Charlie pulled a wood cigar box from a drawer, set it on the sideboard, and opened it, revealing a stack of cash, mostly twenties, several inches thick. "I'll have to count it to see how much is in there, but it looks like more than normal tips for a chauffeur."

"The stack looks at least two inches thick," Sean said. "Figure two hundred bills in an inch, so that would be around eight grand if it were all twenties."

"Whenever I see that much cash, I always think drugs," Charlie went back to her search of the sideboard drawers, while Sean returned to the kitchen. Thinking Robinson might be a drug dealer, he methodically searched containers in the refrigerator and freezer, opened boxes of cereal, and cannisters of sugar and flour. He noticed a smear of dried blood on a roll of paper towels in a holder on the counter.

He called Charlie over and she took a few photos. "Good possibility the killer grabbed a few paper towels to clean the blood off his hands or clothing," Sean said. He checked the trash can but found no bloody paper towels. Every kitchen had a junk drawer, and Robinson's was no exception. Behind several screwdrivers, rubber bands, AA batteries, pens, and other oddities was a roll of duct tape. He called Charlie over again.

She photographed it and picked it up with a gloved hand. "Looks the same as what was used on his body, but isn't all duct tape the same?"

"Not at all," Sean said. "If we went to Home Depot, we'd probably find ten different kinds." He glanced at the body for a moment, then opened the doors under the sink. "This box of garbage bags look like what's on his head."

Charlie squatted down, took a photo of the garbage bags, then picked up the box and set it on the counter next to the roll of duct tape.

"The lab can eventually compare the tape and garbage bags to what's on his body," Sean said. "If we're lucky, the killer didn't wear gloves, because it's about impossible to strip tape off a roll without leaving prints. I think we can say with near certainty the killer got his killing supplies from right here."

"Which indicates this was not premeditated."

"Or the torture part wasn't planned."

"So, what happened?" Charlie said. "The killers planned to just ask

Robinson nicely to give up whatever they were looking for, and when that didn't work, they tied him up and beat him until he gave it up?"

"Maybe. We don't know enough to know."

"That must be Oakland homicide wisdom," Charlie said. "We don't know enough to know. And if the killer pulled out the box to get a garbage bag and got the duct tape from a drawer, why would he put things away?"

"Murder is usually an irrational act, so you can't expect killers to do things that make sense."

"More Oakland homicide wisdom. Did Robinson kill Courtney then someone else killed him, or did the same killer murder them both?"

Sean smiled.

"I know," Charlie said. "We don't know enough to know. How many men do you think it would take to overpower Robinson and tie him up like that?"

"At least two to really overpower him, hold him down, and tie him up," Sean said. "There's no signs of a struggle. If several killers fought with him and forced him in the chair, we'd see indications in the house. There's nothing broken, no scuff marks on the floor, no blood anywhere except where the body is. Let's assume the killers came in with a gun or other weapon and ordered him to sit in the chair. Most people do exactly what they're told to do when a gun is pointed at their head."

"If we go with that theory, it's even possible someone the size of Courtney killed Robinson."

"That's a possibility."

Charlie sighed. "Which means we're no closer to figuring this out than we were before we stepped foot in Robinson's apartment."

31

"Another beer?" Billy asked.

Sean nodded. They were sitting on the back porch of Billy's house. The sun had just set, and mosquitoes were out in force, but an oscillating fan on top of a small refrigerator mostly kept them away. Billy grabbed two bottles of Budweiser from the refrigerator behind him and handed one to Sean.

Billy lived on two acres in the Freedman District on Spartina Island, land given to the freed slaves when the Union Army took control of coastal South Carolina in the latter days of the Civil War. Billy grew up on this land in a three-room shack, where his father operated a small farm and a shrimp boat. When Billy came back from his Air Force enlistment and joined the sheriff's office, his father was tired of farming and let Billy build his own house where okra, corn, and sweet potatoes once grew.

"How come every time I'm here, you're drinking Bud, but when we're out somewhere, you drink Yuengling, Blue Moon, or some craft beer?" Sean asked.

"I want people to think I'm cultured." Billy gave him a toothy smile. "At home, I'm just a Bud kinda guy. Besides, I like their Clydesdales."

"You know you're full of shit, don't you?"

"Yeah, I don't much care what people think about me. I like a little variety sometimes, but at home I'm a creature of habit. I like coming home to my loving wife, eating a comfortable dinner, and maybe watching a little TV while drinking a few beers. That's my idea of nirvana."

Sean remembered those days with Lauren. The simple times of having dinner at home and sitting on the sofa together were also his favorite. "Your wife is a great cook. You're a lucky man."

Billy patted his stomach. "And that's why I've got probably sixty pounds on your skinny ass. How are you coming on the Nash investigation?"

"It's a longshot, but I think there's blood on Henry's wallet. I saw Cannon, and he sent it to SLED."

"I heard the captain said he'd call to expedite the DNA work. Personally, I wouldn't count on that happening."

Sean had been hopeful, but it didn't surprise him that Billy suspected Cannon would do nothing. "Is there anything I can do?"

"Back when I was a detective, I knew that to get anything done you had to have a relationship with people. I took a day off and drove to the crime lab in Columbia with a big box of pastries. I made lots of friends, so when I needed something special—and I was careful not to abuse it—I had friends I could call. Sometimes they asked me for favors, like a place to stay on the beach when they came here on vacation. I'll make some calls on Monday."

"Thanks. As you know, when you've got nothing going with an investigation—no suspects or motive—you start by investigating your victim. I'm looking into the Nash family. The people who know the most, Abigail and her longtime housekeeper, are rather evasive. They're protecting some secrets that could be the reason behind Henry's murder."

"I like hearing you say it's a murder," Billy said. "Although everyone knows that's what it is, we still officially call it a missing person, as if Henry Nash is wandering around in the world lost and unable to find his way home. Abigail's image is everything to her. If she was given the choice of finding out who killed Henry or protecting the family's reputation, she'd let the killer go free."

"I spoke to Rose, and she's very protective of the family."

"Rose is part of their family. Of course she'd be protective. She helped raise Charlie and the boys, and if you want to get on her wrong side, say something negative about them. I've known Rose ever since I was a little boy. Living here in the Gullah community, she was one of my many aunties.

When I misbehaved in the neighborhood, she spanked me the same as my momma did. My mother and Rose do lots of church activities together. I'll have her talk to Rose and get the real skinny about anything going on in the family before Henry's disappearance."

"Especially involving Henry's dealings with Boyd Moretti."

"For a long time, people figured he had the most to gain by Henry's disappearance," Billy said. "Because his family's been around these parts for generations, most people either love him or hate him. The rest of us just keep our distance from him."

"So far, I haven't found anyone else with more to gain from Henry's disappearance, but that's a long way from saying he killed him. Charlie doesn't think much of him."

"How are you two doing?"

Sean took a pull from his beer and looked at the edge of the yard where a group of four deer were grazing, one of them a small fawn that still had its spots. "She's a damn good detective, and I'm happy to work with her any time."

Billy took a hearty swig of his beer. "You know that's not what I'm asking."

"It's complicated. We work well together. I like her. As a detective and as a person."

"You know she likes you too, right?"

"Has she said something?"

"When she was planning the search warrant on Eric Robinson's house, she asked me if it was okay to include you."

"So she values my investigative expertise."

"When I told her the captain directed we take a statement from you on the arrest of Keshawn White, she immediately came to your defense."

"The same as you and I would with a fellow officer."

"Come on, buddy, you can bullshit your friends, and I'll bullshit mine, but let's not bullshit each other. I can see it, and if you can't you're blind."

"Billy, just look at me. Charlie is a very attractive woman, she's smart, she's successful, and, I recently learned, she's rich. I'm an old has-been who's trying to still play cop because I have nothing else in my life. I have this broken-down body that's developing more aches and pains every day. I live in a decent place, where they might call the facilities at Sea Island Plantation a country club, but compared to Cusseta, where she's a member, it's more like a YMCA with a gym and swimming pool."

Billy drained his beer and pulled another from his fridge. "Although you've got some gray around the edges, many women would still consider you a handsome man. You live in a damn nice house in a wonderful, gated community, where most retirees in the country would love to be. You might not be rich, but I know what your pension pays you every month, which by the way is a lot more than I make working full time. Most of all, Sean, you're a nice guy. Women like Charlie don't need a man for his money or his social connections. What they want is a nice guy."

"I never knew matchmaker was part of a lieutenant's job description."

"I love Charlie, not only as my best sergeant, but also as my friend. She deserves happiness."

"This is all moot. I think she's still royally pissed at me for keeping our investigation on her father from her."

"Charlie gets pissed at me at least once a week. That's who she is. Ever want to know what Charlie is feeling? Just look at her. She shows her emotions on her face, and quite often, even if you don't ask, she'll tell you straight up exactly what she's feeling. She likes being in control, so you running the investigation without her input is gonna rile her up. I do lots of boss stuff that she lets me know she doesn't like. She ain't the kind of girl to pretend everything is peachy when it ain't. I can guarantee she's thrilled the case has been reopened, and she knows there's not a better detective anywhere to handle it than you."

32

SATURDAY

Charlie parked her car a few minutes before 10:00 a.m., grabbed her umbrella, and walked into the Village at South Harbor. A steady rain had been falling all morning, and although the air temperature was lower than normal, the humidity made it feel just as hot. The sand-colored buildings contained shops and restaurants on the bottom level and condos on the two top floors, all of which had a view of the harbor filled with recreational boats, ranging from twenty-five-foot pleasure and fishing boats to eighty-foot yachts.

After her divorce, she had thought she might like to live here, a lovely place on the water where she could jump into her boat anytime. But she quickly realized South Harbor was not her. The restaurants were so fancy that a scone and coffee for breakfast would set you back fifteen dollars, and if you tried to drink a beer out of a bottle at the waterfront café, they'd probably call security on you. Most people who lived in the condos also owned a place in New York or Boston. The women put on makeup and styled their hair just to go out on their boats, which were skippered by men wearing linen shorts and silk shirts that cost several hundred dollars each.

She pushed open the door of Village Jewelers at ten o'clock sharp. Eva looked up from the counter and said, "Charlie, it's been a long time."

Eva was in her mid-fifties with a platinum bob that never had a hair out of place. She and her husband lived in a big house two rows from the beach in Ocean Forest Plantation. She worked part-time at the jewelry store to keep busy on the three days a week her husband played golf and for the employee discount on jewelry. Her jewelry purchases far surpassed the pay she made working.

"I don't get around the club much these days," Charlie said. "How's Brent and the kids?"

"The kids are great. Both came down for Labor Day weekend. And Brent is—well, you know, he's just busy being Brent."

Charlie parroted Eva's smile. Brent was a four-handicap golfer at the Cusseta Country Club and let everyone know he used to be a scratch golfer until a torn rotator cuff took twenty yards off his drive. Eva reached into a display case and pulled out a gold ladies Rolex with tiny diamonds on the face. "This would look exquisite on you. Understated, but makes a statement in the right circles."

Charlie laughed. "I have so much stuff in my jewelry box at home I never wear most of the time as it is. See this." Charlie held out her wrist, showing a stainless-steel watch with a white face. "Citizen eco-drive. It cost two-hundred dollars, keeps perfect time, and never needs winding. I also have one in gold color and a dive watch."

Eva smiled. "I wish I could be like you."

Charlie wondered if the Evas of the world truly wished they weren't so caught up in having to wear the right clothes and jewelry, drive the right car, and belong to the right club, or did they just say that to excuse their vanity?

"I'm actually working and was wondering if you can look at something and tell me what you think?" Charlie shook the ruby pendant that was found in Courtney's clothes from the plastic bag onto the counter.

Eva looked it over and hefted it. "Is this connected to one of your investigations?"

"It was found on the body of a murder victim. I thought knowing more about it might tell me why someone would want to kill her."

Eva looked at it through a jeweler's loupe for several moments. "I'm not a certified gemologist, so if you need an accurate appraisal, you'll have to leave it until Monday when the owner comes in."

"I just need an idea whether it's something you can buy at the mall for fifty dollars or if it would be worth the price of one of those Rolexes."

"Although some jewelers will use unofficial quality names like good, better, and best, officially natural gemstones are graded from B to AAA. B grade gems are common. Grade A rubies are the top twenty percent of rubies and are used for fine jewelry. This is an A or possibly an AA. It's around three carats, which is a substantial size ruby. With the white gold chain and the setting, it's worth around fifteen thousand if it's grade A, and forty thousand if it's AA. Now if it were AAA, heirloom quality, it would be worth nearly a hundred thousand."

"But definitely not a piece of cut glass?"

"No, and it's a natural ruby. There are nice ones that are lab-grown, but discriminating women like you and I would never wear them."

Charlie wanted to snicker. A discriminating woman? Sure, one who wears solar-powered watches and stud earrings. The only other jewelry she normally wore was a sapphire ring on her right hand, a gift from her father when she turned sixteen.

"I also found an engraving on the back of the setting," Eva said. "It's really tiny."

"Something that says to so-and-so from so-and-so?"

"Appears to be a number, 11-6-71. Maybe a date to memorialize a special occasion. The setting and clasp on the chain are typical of how necklaces were constructed fifty years ago. Sometimes old jewelry like this ends up in estate sales and can pass through several owners in fifty years."

"Thanks. You've been an immense help."

"We should get together for coffee and catch up," Eva said. "Even better, maybe dinner. Are you seeing anyone?"

"Not really."

"Brent plays golf with a nice man about your age. Was a big wig in pharmaceuticals and took an early retirement. Recently divorced and just moved here from Atlanta. If you're interested..."

"I'll call you once this investigation settles down," Charlie said, although she doubted she really would. She wished she had a few girlfriends she could do things with, hang out, and just talk, but it seemed women like Eva were so different from her that they had nothing in common. She had girlfriends back in high school and college and even during the early days of her marriage. They could talk for hours about everything, from the stresses of school or work to their boyfriends or husbands. Then when she had Spencer, she had a lot in common with the other mothers.

Everything changed when she joined the sheriff's office. Her old friends drifted away, or maybe she pushed them away. She had changed, she knew. After dealing with life and death matters, it was hard to show much empathy for one of her privileged girlfriends who was fretting over the right window treatment for her bedroom or was jealous because her friend just got a new Mercedes while she drove a year-old BMW. Still, she missed her old college girlfriends. Women she could tell that she didn't know what the hell overcame her, but she almost kissed a man at a murder scene just feet away from a dead body. Women who would listen and tell her she was okay even when she didn't know what the hell was happening to her.

As Charlie walked to her car in the rain, she forced her brain to switch back to her investigation and wondered where a divorced bartender got a piece of jewelry worth more than she made in several months.

33

Sean drove across River Drive and down Riverside Lane. The ten largest houses in Sea Island Plantation were on this street. All backed up to the river and marsh. All on lots of an acre or more. Although Sean had a nice house on the marsh, these homes and their grounds were more like estates. Sean parked his SUV alongside two other cars in the circular driveway of the Mediterranean-style house, opened the hatch, and said, "Okay," to Annie.

She raced to the front door and barked once. As Sean jogged up the steps, he heard Diva, the Johnson's golden doodle, barking inside. Beagle opened the door and Annie rushed inside. After the two dogs sniffed each other for a minute, Diva took off running deeper into the house, with Annie in pursuit.

"Thanks for letting me bring Annie along," Sean said.

"If Diva saw you here without Annie, she'd never forgive me. Come on in. Everyone's in the kitchen."

They walked past the formal dining room and an office with dark wood built-ins to the back of the house. Massive glass doors opened from the great room to a covered porch and swimming pool. Beyond that was the Spartina River. Here, it was wider and deeper than it was farther upstream behind Sean's house. Frank and Feebee sat at a round table in the breakfast nook behind plates piled high with food. They both looked up, waved, and went back to eating.

The kitchen island was filled with platters of pancakes, scrambled eggs, cheese omelets, bacon, croissants, and rolls. It was ten o'clock, and since Sean had already eaten his customary bowl of cereal four hours earlier, he figured this would be his lunch. He took some scrambled eggs, a few slices of bacon, and a roll. "Did you make all of this?"

"Hell no," Beagle said. "You know me better than that. My wife made everything then left just before you guys arrived. Said she had an exercise class, but I know she wanted to be far away when my uncivilized cop friends showed up."

"Who you calling uncivilized?" Frank said. "Look here, I have your fancy cloth napkin on my lap and not tucked into my shirt."

Feebee opened her mouth wide. "See here, I have no food in my mouth while I'm talking."

"I can't see why your wife didn't want to be here," Sean said.

Diva pushed between Frank and Feebee's legs to get under the table, where she gobbled a piece of bacon Feebee was holding under the table. Annie stood nearby, watching. Sean snapped his fingers, pointed to the living room, and said, "Go lay down."

Annie trotted off and lay on the oriental rug. "Gotta get you to train Diva," Beagle said. "I give her a command and the wife countermands it."

"Diva knows who's really in charge in this house," Feebee said.

"No denying that," Beagle said. He filled his plate and sat down. "We hear the killer in the cordgrass is dead. You solved another one for the sheriff's office, huh?"

"Beagle, you're not going to let go of that killer-in-the-cordgrass crap, are you?" Sean said.

"You do know that I do it just to get a rise out of you, right?"

Sean told them about the murder of Eric Robinson and his assessment that instead of one murder being solved, they most likely had two unsolved murders with no real leads. "Did you guys learn anything more from the flash drive the accountant gave you?"

"Beagle and I spent most of yesterday looking at the reports," Feebee said. "Pretty much like the CPA told us yesterday. The Nash's company is more than solvent. With conservative estimates of the value of their land and the completed developments, the company is worth about a hundred and twenty million today. At least forty million when Henry disappeared ten years ago."

"Damn," Frank said. "I remember my father talking about millionaires when I was a kid as if they were some sort of gods."

"A million dollars is not what it used to be," Feebee said. "I met with a financial advisor when I was nearing retirement. He said that with what I was getting from my FBI retirement and social security, it would take an annuity of almost two million dollars to match it."

"My pension is more than I ever thought possible back when I started as a beat cop," Sean said. "And living here is a lot cheaper than in the Bay Area, but still, these people have some serious money."

Feebee got another plate off the counter, plopped three pancakes on it, and smothered them with maple syrup. "The main takeaway is that the Nash family had no money problems ten years ago and certainly doesn't today. The question is whether someone else had money issues that would motivate them to make Henry disappear."

"If I were still with the D.A.'s office, I think I could get a subpoena for Moretti's finances," Beagle said. "That would give us a better idea if he had a financial motive to make Henry disappear."

"We both thought there were some significant accounting gaps in the business between Henry and his brother," Feebee said. "We saw money coming in monthly to pay off Henry for the sale of his share of his father's business. Then significant legal expenses to an attorney in New York, which we assume was related to the bankruptcy."

"The next logical step would be to interview Henry's brother," Beagle said. "He might have another perspective about what occurred. It seems too much of a coincidence that all this was happening around the time Henry disappeared."

"Yeah, that makes total sense," Frank said. "We citizen volunteers just go tell Captain Cannon we need to travel to New York to interview a witness. Oh, wait, he's not even a witness to anything. And we can't even prove the elements of any crime."

"Why do we need permission?" Beagle said.

"You're starting to sound like the FNG," Frank said, looking at Sean.

Sean spread some peach preserves onto a roll from a jar with a label saying it came from a local farm. "As much as I'd like to have a talk with Henry's brother, I can't see paying my own money for that trip, and I can tell you that back at Oakland PD, where we had a much bigger budget than they do down here, they'd never approve a trip like this."

"I've got like a gazillion miles, and since my wife hates flying, I'd never use them all," Beagle said. "We could fly up there, interview him, and return that night. Wouldn't cost much, besides subway tickets, or however people get around up there."

"We'd have to do background on Richard Nash," Feebee said. "Interviews like this work best when we just pop in on him and catch him by surprise."

"Four would be a crowd," Beagle said. "Should only be two of us. Frank knows New York City, and it's Sean's case."

"There's a million reasons I left that city," Frank said. "Besides, I'm too old for this shit. A one-day trip means getting up at oh-dark-thirty and getting back home well after my bedtime."

"I went to New York once as part of a homicide investigation," Sean said. "I never had a clue where I was or where I was going, but an NYPD detective picked me and my partner up at the airport and drove us around for the two days we were there."

"I still got friends on the job," Frank said. "We always did that for out-of-town detectives. It would've been embarrassing if one of them got lost or mugged in our city."

"It should be Beagle and Sean," Feebee said. "Beagle understands all the financial stuff better than I do and he can dazzle people with all his legal mumbo jumbo."

Frank hobbled to the kitchen island and poured himself another cup of coffee. "I'm still not agreeing we should do this, but let me put out some feelers on this Richard Nash character. If he still has an office, the building security officer is probably retired NYPD, and Mr. Nash certainly lives in a fancy apartment with a doorman, who has to stay on the good side of the department. Captain Cannon might be more amenable to this trip if he doesn't have to find money in his budget for it."

"I'm more a believer in seeking forgiveness rather than asking permission," Sean said. "If we decide to do it, I say we just go and let the captain read about it later in our reports."

Beagle and Feebee nodded, and Frank just shook his head. "If you guys worked for me back in my NYPD days, I would've been drinking on the job and had an ulcer."

34

Her computer read 12:07 p.m. when Charlie finished typing up her report on the murder from yesterday. She printed it, stuffed it into a folder, and headed to the breakroom to read it over while she ate the bag lunch she'd brought from home. It was Saturday, so she expected to be alone, but Frank Martin, the oldest member of the cold case team, was sitting at a table, a cup of coffee, a murder book, and a laptop in front of him.

"Hello, Frank, what brings you here on a Saturday?"

"Afternoon, Sergeant Nash—"

"Charlie."

"Afternoon, Charlie. We just had a meeting about the case we're working—"

"The missing person case of my father?"

"Yeah. As much as I love my wife, sometimes it's best that we spend some time apart, so I came down here to review the investigation. We have passes—"

She smiled. "I know you were given access badges, and you've been assigned the empty squad room to use whenever you want."

"Well, the coffee maker's in here and I figured I'd spill half of it hobbling back there."

She looked at the black cane leaning against the table. "Didn't you have surgery following a pickleball accident?"

"Surprised you knew."

"I like to keep up on my friends' medical challenges."

"That's a subtle way of saying we old farts have loads of medical issues and it's polite to listen to us talk about them. I had surgery and been doing physical therapy, but now the docs say there's issues with my knee and I may need another surgery to take out some worn parts and put in new ones. I heard about your second murder yesterday. How ya coming with it?"

"Like most investigations early on, I have more questions than answers. Like why'd someone torture Eric Robinson, and why did Courtney Evanson have a valuable necklace in her pocket that might've been given to her by Eric, who by the way, was renting an apartment and making payments on the car he used for his business."

"The simplest answers are sometimes the right one. The necklace wasn't Eric's to give. Someone beat him until he admitted he gave it to Courtney, then they killed her, but didn't think to search her pockets."

"Could be." Charlie slid a tuna salad sandwich from a paper bag, unwrapped it and took a bite. Frank was eighty, only five years older than her father would've been if he were still alive, but he seemed so much older. He was grumpy in an endearing way. She wondered what her father would've been like today if he were still alive.

"When me and the wife got married, we never had much money. Me working as a patrolman in New York, and her as a clerk in a department store. She never asked for jewelry like that. She understood our money was better spent on the important things, saving to buy a house, car payment, little bit of money in the bank. Been married more than fifty years now, and now we have some money. Wonder if she always felt like she'd been cheated in life because she never had jewelry like this."

"I have lots of jewelry at home I never wear, but I know many women feel very special when the man they love gives them jewelry as a present." Charlie pulled out the pendant that was still in her pocket from her morning trip to the jewelry store and held it up. "This is not my style, but I can see why some women would adore it."

Frank stared at the pendant necklace for so long Charlie began to wonder if he was having a senior moment. “It can’t be,” he said.

“Can’t be what? I didn’t mean to make you feel uncomfortable for not giving your wife something like this.”

“No, it’s not that. This looks like the necklace a girl was wearing when she was murdered years ago. The cold case team looked into it about four years ago. Came up with no clues. There’s photos of it in the case file. Her name was Sarah something-or-other. She was killed and robbed in the woods behind the Island Rec Center.”

“Sarah Fitzpatrick?” Charlie said.

“Yeah, that was it.”

“Sarah and I went to school together. She was a senior when I was a junior. Her murder shocked the entire county. She was dating Anthony Capozzi, one of the stars on the football team. He got her pregnant, and the next thing you know they were engaged. Both their families were Catholic, and that was the right thing to do back then. A week later she ended up dead.”

“I recall the boy’s mother gave Sarah a ruby pendant necklace to welcome her to the family,” Frank said. “The mother had been given it by her husband when they got engaged years earlier. Sarah always wore it, and when her body was found, it wasn’t on her. That’s why the sheriff’s office thought it was a robbery.”

“Do you remember if it was engraved with a date?”

“I recall something like that in the report,” Frank said.

Charlie left the break room and returned with a three-ring binder and an accordion folder filled with papers.

Frank paged through the binder, the same murder book the cold case team had been given four years ago. He flipped to a page with a color photo of a ruby pendant necklace.

Charlie studied the photo and the pendant. “Exactly the same. Is there an insurance appraisal document or anything like that in there?” Charlie asked.

Frank paged through the book. “This is a copy of the purchase receipt. A 3.2 carat ruby pendant on a white gold rope chain. Bought by Marco Capozzi along with a diamond engagement ring from a jewelry store in

Savannah. He had both engraved with 11-6-71, the day he was engaged to his wife, Ann."

"You wouldn't be able to read it without a magnifying glass, but that's the date on this pendant," Charlie said. "Sarah was a cheerleader at our high school. She was pretty and bubbly. She came from a working-class family, and Anthony's father owned one of the largest construction companies in the county, so most of the kids at school figured she and Anthony would never have a future together. I recall Anthony was planning to go to college, get an engineering degree, and return to work at his father's company, eventually running it."

"Sounds like he was on the road to success until he knocked up his girlfriend," Frank said.

"There was talk that Anthony's father wanted Anthony to marry someone of his *social level*, as if that should've mattered, but Anthony's mother thought the idea of family money equaling status was nonsense. She loved Sarah and immediately treated her like a daughter. Because all of us kids liked Sarah, we loved Mrs. Capozzi for accepting her."

Frank scanned a page in the murder book. "I remember that detectives had interviewed Anthony and scores of students at school. Anthony was with six friends and two parents on a fishing trip in the sound from the time school let out until eight o'clock that night, which was when Sarah's body was found. The detectives concluded Anthony and Sarah were in love, he'd never hurt her, and no one at school had a bad thing to say about Sarah."

"I remember kids saying Anthony wasn't upset that Sarah's pregnancy changed his life plans. He never really thought he was college material, and he would've been happier working at his father's company and learning the business from the bottom up."

"Reading between the lines of the original detectives' reports, it seemed the only person unhappy about Sarah's pregnancy, was Marco, Anthony's father. Marco was a big wig around town, and that might've been the reason the detectives didn't pursue him as a possible suspect."

Charlie thought back to her high school days. Her father and Marco were friends back then, did business together, and were both members of the Cusseta Country Club. If Marco was a big wig around town, as Frank said, then her own dad must've been considered a super big wig to most people, because Marco often worked for her dad, doing the construction for his projects. Although she knew they were comfortable growing up, she never thought they were wealthy or that she was higher on some sort of social pecking order than the other kids.

She didn't see much of Anthony after high school. She had gone off to college, and soon after, she married Roger. She heard that Anthony eventually married Kristin, another girl a year ahead of her in school. Kristin's family were members of Cusseta, but instead of lounging around the pool or playing tennis like many of the country club kids, she was into horses. She had two horses of her own and competed in both dressage and jumping. While Sarah was slim and blonde, Kristin was big and brunette. Not fat, but tall, stocky, and muscular for a girl. While Sarah was outgoing and always surrounded by friends, Kristin was a loner. Charlie was surprised when she heard Anthony and Kristin got married. Kristin seemed totally different from Sarah back in high school. Before Sarah died, Anthony was a happy kid, sometimes the class clown in school. When she saw him years later, he seemed sad, like the fun and jovial part of his personality had been buried with Sarah.

"Who was your lead investigator when you guys looked into this murder?"

"Bert, a retired Cleveland detective," Frank said. "He died two years ago, but Irish John was his partner and did most of the heavy lifting because Bert wasn't very computer savvy."

"How'd you like to reopen this case again? You and Irish reexamine everything that was done back twenty-seven years ago through the prism of what we just learned about the pendant?"

35

Sean sat in his recliner watching a college football game on TV with an ice pack on his left shoulder. He'd rather be doing something other than sitting on his butt on a rainy Saturday afternoon. He had gone to urgent care yesterday afternoon on the way home from Sunrise Apartments. They took x-rays and twisted his shoulder in every conceivable direction and concluded he should continue with ice and resting it then see a physical therapist Monday morning.

His phone buzzed with a call from Carson.

"Hey, Dad, sorry I haven't been taking your calls. How's everything?"

"Nothing new or exciting here. How are you doing?"

"Oh, fine. Rachel tells me you're working another cold case. One of a man who went missing ten years ago but was probably murdered."

Sean told him a little about the Henry Nash investigation, but didn't mention his involvement in the fresh murders of Courtney Evanson or Eric Robinson. "How's work going?"

"What did Rachel tell you?"

"Not much," Sean lied. "Only that you had some stuff going on there and I should reach out and talk to you."

The phone was silent for a few beats, then Carson said, "It's not a big deal. Just normal company bullshit, so I'm taking a little time off."

"You've been with Intuit a while, so vacation is always nice."

"I left Intuit a month ago."

"Really?"

"That's normal in the tech world. A headhunter got me a contract position with WWW-AI, a relatively new company that's using artificial intelligence for all kinds of neat stuff. It's in the same area as the Intuit and Google campus. My pay is almost double what Intuit was paying."

"A contract position?"

"Working for tech companies is not like when you worked for Oakland. They don't actually hire us. We're hired by a staffing agency as part of a contract with the company for a particular project."

"So, it's not a permanent job?"

"No, but contracts are usually extended. One guy I work with has been there for two years, ever since the company went public."

"One of the wonderful things about my career with Oakland was the security."

"We don't have that kind of long-term security, but WWW-AI is hesitant to just terminate contract workers, because then the project we're working on comes to a screeching halt until they bring new people in and bring them up to speed."

"So, you're not worried?"

"Everything's fine, Dad. Hey, a friend just came over and I gotta go. We'll talk again soon."

"Love you, Son."

"Love you too, Dad."

In all his years working in Oakland, Sean seldom talked about his job at home. He sometimes told some funny stories or discussed the people he worked with, but he never mentioned the horrors of what he saw and did or the personal toll it took on him. Sean realized during this conversation with Carson that his son had learned more from him than he ever imagined. He didn't know if Carson thought he had to protect him from his troubles at work or if he was afraid his father would try to tell him what he did wrong and how to fix it. Although Sean wished Carson would open up and talk about what was going on and how he was feeling, he realized his son had grown up to become a lot like him.

His phone vibrated with a group text from Frank: *We've been assigned another cold case. Occurred 27 years ago and is connected to the recent murder of Courtney Evanson. If you're available, come to the sheriff's office. I'm here waiting.*

If Sean had been doing something other than watching a football game he cared nothing about, he'd be ticked about being called in on a weekend, especially since it wasn't at overtime pay like when he was with OPD. But a cold case warming up with a link to an active case would be a lot more interesting than the nothing he had planned for the rest of the day.

A half hour later, Sean was sitting in the empty squad room that had been assigned to the cold case team. Like Charlie's squad room, it had five workstations and a table in the center of the room. Two guest chairs sat in front of the sergeant's U-shaped workstation in the back of the room. Frank, Irish, Stretch, and Doc had pulled chairs around the table. After Frank said Feebee and Beagle couldn't make it, Frank reviewed what he and Charlie had discussed to bring everyone up to speed.

"Since Irish was the co-lead on our reexamination of this murder four years ago, I only think it fitting he take the lead this time around," Frank said.

"Bert and I visited the scene four years ago," Irish said. "It was in a wooded area between the high school and the rec center, both of which were only a few years old when the murder had occurred. From the crime scene photos, the body was about ten feet off a path that ran from the high school to the rec center."

"An established path or one that people or animals created?" Stretch asked.

"When we saw it, it was well worn, but it obviously began as a shortcut between the school and rec center," Irish said.

"It was *the* shortcut," Charlie said from the doorway. "Sorry for barging in, but I want to first thank everyone for showing up. It's great having investigators around who are familiar with this case. When I went to school there, kids that weren't involved in organized sports or other activities often went to the rec center after classes were over. I walked that path hundreds of times. The woods were thick and there were little trails off the main path where couples sometimes went to make out or whatever."

Sean noticed Charlie raised her eyebrows when she said "whatever," and he wondered if she had ever snuck off into the woods behind the school to do *whatever*. She was dressed casually today, in a pair of dark denim stretch jeans, black athletic shoes, and a V-neck pullover tucked into the jeans. If it weren't for the wide belt that held a holstered Sig Sauer 9mm, extra magazine, badge, and handcuffs, she wouldn't even look like a cop. Because Sean thought they'd just be in the office among other cold case team members, he was wearing shorts and a T-shirt and was only armed with his tiny Ruger LCP in a pocket holster. He wished he had changed into something more professional looking.

"When we worked this four years ago," Irish said, "Bert and I conducted phone interviews with a few people in the presence of a sheriff's detective. We talked to Ann Capozzi, the mother of Anthony, and Sue Fitzpatrick, Sarah's mom. Neither had heard anything new that could help us. Neither Anthony nor his father, Marco, returned our calls, so we never spoke to them."

"If you still have their phone numbers in your file," Charlie said to Irish, "how about calling them up. Tell them there's been a new development in the case, and you and I would like to come to their house and talk to them."

"You mean I'd go with you and do a face-to-face interview?" Irish asked.

"Oh, yeah, this ain't the old passive cold case team that can't leave the office," Charlie said with a smile. "You guys are the famous Mudflats Murder Club. I'll be down the hall in my office. If you get through to either of them, we'll leave right away."

As soon as Charlie walked away, Irish John raised his right hand for a high-five. Sean, Stretch, and Doc all smacked palms with him. Frank just sat there and shook his head.

Stretch leaned across the table toward Irish. "She's an attractive woman, Irish, but don't you get any ideas when you're alone in her cruiser with her."

Doc laughed and Frank rolled his eyes. "Don't worry," Irish said. "My three kids are all older than her, and besides, I'm so old that my idea of a fun time with a woman is watching Jeopardy after dinner and falling asleep together in our matching recliners."

36

Charlie and Irish sat at opposite ends of a long white sofa in the Capozzi's living room. Ann sat on a matching sofa across a glass coffee table from them.

"When Mr. O'Shea called and said you were reopening the investigation into Sarah's death, I think my heart skipped a beat," Ann said. "And Charlotte, dear, you look wonderful. I always knew you'd grow up to be a stunning woman."

Charlie blushed. Ann had to be seventy-five, Charlie figured, but her eyes and smile made her look years younger. "I'm sorry to hear about Marco. How long's it been?"

"He passed two years ago. Had heart issues for several years. Mr. O'Shea, I remember talking to you four years ago. I had no idea you were a senior. You sounded so young on the phone."

Charlie tried not to smile too much at Ann's flirting with Irish. He obviously recognized it and said, "Well thank you. I'll be sure to let my wife know that despite all my wrinkles, I still have a youthful voice."

Ann laughed. "So what's the development that brings you out here today?"

"We're not at liberty to say much, but we're investigating two recent homicides that might overlap with Sarah's murder," Charlie said. "Can you tell us about that ruby pendant necklace that Sarah was given?"

"It was a special gift to me from Marco to celebrate our engagement. I cherished it, but as time went on, I didn't wear it much anymore. When Anthony told Marco and I that Sarah was pregnant and they would marry, I knew I should pass the necklace to her. It was made for a young woman, something I no longer was by then."

"When did you last see it?"

"The evening after Anthony told us he intended to marry Sarah, we invited her to dinner at the house. After dessert I presented her with the pendant and wished she and Anthony as many wonderful years together as Marco and I had."

"That's the last you saw it?" Charlie asked.

"A few days later, Sarah's parents had us over to their house for dinner. Sarah and Anthony were there, and I'm certain Sarah was wearing it. Anthony told me later that she never took it off."

"Did it ever resurface after Sarah's death? Did anyone mention seeing it again?"

"If Marco, Anthony, or I heard anything about it after that, we would've immediately called the sheriff. That would've meant whoever had it was the person who killed Sarah, right?"

"Quite possibly," Charlie said. "That must've been quite a family challenge back then to find out your son got a girl pregnant."

"Marco and I were shocked. We thought we raised Anthony better. Marco was also angry and yelled at Anthony about how he ruined his life. He said terrible things about Sarah. That she seduced him to trap him. We prayed on it and came to the realization that this was God's will, and He would take care of everything."

"I'm Catholic as well," Irish said. "I'm afraid my reaction might've been the same as your husband's if one of my boys got a girl pregnant in high school."

"Sarah was such a sweet girl. She and Anthony had been together since freshman year. They were so cute together. She was a shining light and brought Anthony out of his shell. I know it sounds trite, but Anthony said she was his soulmate, and seeing them together, I agreed. Once Marco calmed down, he went into problem-solving mode, like how he operated at work. They would both finish high school, and we'd help them with a place to live. Anthony would work with Marco and earn a paycheck to properly support his young family. I knew he'd mature quickly and become responsible, and Marco and I would be there for them."

"How did Anthony take her death?" Charlie asked.

"He was devastated. Like his heart had been broken. He went off to college that fall but did so poorly, he dropped out. He came home, worked for his father, and tried college again the next year. He did better and graduated in four years, but he was never the same."

"In what way?"

"More solemn and serious, and, well, just not as light."

"Then he married Kristin?"

Ann nodded. "Anthony and Kristin were childhood friends. They grew apart in high school. Anthony was into sports and socialized with the cheerleaders. Kristin was into riding. But they reconnected after Anthony returned from college."

"They're still together?"

She nodded. "Marco felt she'd be a good wife for Anthony, but I got the sense that Anthony had settled, that he accepted he'd never find anyone like Sarah. Kristin could never have children, and that was a struggle in their marriage, but they stuck it out."

"What's Kristin like?" Irish asked.

"She's quieter. Not really into social things at the club. Not as outgoing, but she's a good person and a good wife."

"But she's not Sarah," Charlie said, taking a gamble that Ann wouldn't get angry at her comment.

Ann smiled weakly. "No, she isn't Sarah."

37

Sean took the murder book to the copy machine, put the pages into the feeder, and pressed the button for three copies. As he was pulling out the collated copies, Detective Jay Garcia walked in through the station's back hallway. "Sergeant Nash said a missing item from an old robbery homicide is the necklace found on the Evanson victim. She asked me to work with you guys until she gets back."

Sean ran another copy and briefed Jay on what they knew so far.

"What can I do to help, beyond being another set of eyes on the old reports?" Jay asked.

"None of us can work your computer system, so maybe you could start running out the people from the original report," Sean said. "Maybe we'll get lucky and one of the kids from back then has been identified as a serial killer."

"I doubt we'll be that lucky, but it wouldn't hurt to have current contact info on everyone if we want to reinterview them. By the way, where is Sergeant Nash?"

"She's out with Irish John interviewing Ann Capozzi."

"John, the thin old guy?"

Sean smiled. "The thin old guy is Frank. Irish John is the short, fat old guy."

Jay laughed. "Okay, I'll stop using *old* when trying to describe members of the cold case team."

Sean held up his ID card that was hanging around his neck. "And I'll get the other guys to start wearing their ID cards so you can see their names."

Jay took his copy of the report to his office, and Sean went down the hall to their squad room. He passed out a copy to Frank, Doc, and Stretch then sat down in one of the comfortable desk chairs at an empty workstation and began reading.

His first impression was how thoroughly the sheriff's office had investigated the murder. A murdered high school cheerleader would get the attention of the public, media, and every law enforcement officer in the area. There were statements from dozens of fellow students, teachers, and parents. The area around the body was searched methodically, and the autopsy was thoroughly documented. The entire school knew Sarah was pregnant. Obviously, it was hard to keep a secret in a small town. Some of the girls and boys felt sorry for her, and some of the parents expressed surprise Sarah was pregnant because she seemed like such a "good girl."

Sean had heard about friends of Rachel and Carson becoming pregnant in high school. There, abortions were commonly seen as the solution to an unplanned teenage pregnancy, but he suspected California was different from South Carolina, especially twenty-seven years ago. Still, Sean could imagine an unwedded pregnancy would create a scandal, especially in small-town South Carolina. Although none of the students from whom statements were taken had anything negative to say about Sarah, he wondered if there were whispers of gossip that the detectives never heard.

The autopsy noted the cause of death as asphyxia caused by manual strangulation. The medical examiner noted two impression contusions on the front of the victim's throat, which he suspected were from the thumbs of the assailant. Dirt and vegetable matter consistent with the location where the body had been discovered was found in the victim's hair, indicating she was probably strangled on the ground. The body was sixty-one inches in height and 103 pounds, so Sarah was a small girl. Although Sean suspected that being a cheerleader she was very fit, it wouldn't be difficult for an adult or even an average-sized boy in high school to overpower her.

Her boyfriend, Anthony Capozzi, was a six-foot-two, two-hundred-pound lineman, playing both offense and defense on the football team, which was common with smaller schools. He had an ironclad alibi. The detectives who interviewed him noted his overwhelming grief, and they were convinced he was not the one that harmed her. If he hadn't had an alibi, Sean wouldn't have given much credence to his expression of guilt, because he had interviewed people who went from sobbing over how sad they were that someone was dead to confessing to killing them a few hours later.

Charlie returned to the office just as Sean had finished reading the reports. She filled them in on their interview with Ann Capozzi.

"Where's Irish?" Stretch asked. "He didn't get lost again, did he?"

Just then, Irish walked into the office. "I had to pee. This fieldwork is not easy for us old guys with one-hour bladders."

"He didn't embarrass you out there, did he?" asked Frank.

"He was the utmost professional," Charlie said. "He even flirted with the senior citizen widow to get her to open up."

Doc slapped Irish on the back and Stretch gave him a thumbs up.

"Let's brainstorm this," Charlie said to the group. "What are your thoughts?"

"Courtney was just in grade school when this murder occurred," Frank said. "And not even living in this state, so there's no obvious connection."

"Supposedly, Eric Robinson gave the pendant to Courtney," Charlie said. "But Robinson would've been around twelve or thirteen at the time of Sarah's murder, and he was living in Atlanta until moving here just a few years ago."

"We should maybe be thinking about why someone would want to kill Sarah," Doc said, "Other than the obvious motive of robbery."

"Good thought," Sean said. "Of course, the prime motive points at Anthony, because becoming a father at his age could change his life significantly, but he's got a tight alibi."

"But his father, Marco, was initially pretty pissed about having his boy's future trashed," Frank said. "Even blamed Sarah."

"The autopsy didn't provide an accurate time of death, so all we know is Sarah was last seen when school let out at three and she was found at eight," Stretch said.

"The first responding deputies and detectives all thought she'd been dead for at least a few hours," Doc said. "We don't know what observations caused them to conclude that, but most seasoned cops can tell if a body is a fresh kill versus been there a while."

"That still gives us a window from three to eight," Frank said. "Maybe three to six. Marco was at his office until five, where other people saw him, then straight home, where his wife was the only one present."

"You think Marco just happened onto the path between the school and the rec center when Sarah was walking along it?" Irish asked.

"No other students saw Sarah after class were out," Doc said. "Even though she was just two months along, the school wouldn't allow her to participate in any sports or physical activities without a doctor's permission. Other students said that she, Anthony, and other kids often went to the rec center when they didn't have sports practice or anything else after school."

"Anthony and a bunch of his friends were going fishing," Sean said. "Can we assume it's likely that Sarah went to the rec center on her own right after classes let out?"

"That would make sense," Charlie said. "Since she wasn't seen hanging around school and no one saw her arrive at the rec center, I think it's reasonable to assume she was killed shortly after school let out. What about Sarah's parents? Her body wasn't found until eight. If I had a pregnant daughter who wasn't home by eight, I'd be out looking."

"Unless they—" Stretch said.

"No," Doc said. "According to two statements I read, Sarah's mother actually made some calls to other parents to see if they knew where Sarah was. One parent told her about the fishing trip Anthony was on, and although that parent thought it was just for boys, she thought they might've taken Sarah along due to her circumstances."

"What about some kid who was a religious fanatic who hated Sarah because she sinned by having premarital sex?" Stretch said.

"When I did criminal profiling for the state of New York, I handled serial murders by killers who were motivated by religious extremism beliefs," Frank said. "Not that they don't exist, but in all my experience and training, I never knew of one that was a teenager."

"With teenagers, it could be just plain jealousy," Sean said. "A boy is jealous of Anthony for having a pretty girlfriend. Maybe a boy was hoping Anthony would leave for college and Sarah would then be available for him, but she got pregnant and messed up his fantasy."

"Or a girl was jealous because Sarah was getting all the attention because she's pregnant," Charlie said.

"I never even considered it could be a girl," Irish said. "I guess that's my gender bias, ignoring the fact that women are just as capable of murder as men."

"It's not being misogynistic," Charlie said. "Ninety percent of all murders are committed by males, so it's a reasonable assumption to make."

Jay burst into the office holding a sheaf of paper in his hand. "When I was running out all the names in the old murder report, I found Anthony Capozzi made a burglary report two weeks ago. Someone broke into his house when he was out of town and stole around two hundred grand worth of jewelry."

"By any chance was the ruby pendant among the loss?" Charlie asked.

"Afraid not," Jay said. "But only a fool would report it as stolen if it was last seen on his dead girlfriend twenty-seven years ago."

38

Charlie convinced the cold case team to go home. She needed to review the Sarah Fitzpatrick investigation and the burglary report on her own and come up with a plan of action. Sean was the last to leave, and she caught him at the back door. "I'm tempted to pick up Anthony, put him in an interview room, and keep him there until he tells me everything."

"But you know that would be premature," Sean said.

"I know he could be the killer, and I need a whole lot more answers before I question him, but still..."

"I agree it would be too much of a coincidence for the jewelry getting ripped off from Anthony's house and the ruby pendant turning up on Courtney's body for there not to be a connection. But until we figure out how the pendant got to Anthony and then to Courtney, I wouldn't interview Anthony."

"It had to be Marco," Charlie said. "Somehow he or his wife got the necklace back after Sarah was killed and gave it to Anthony for sentimental reasons."

"Eric then stole it from Anthony, and when Anthony found out, he tortured him until he admitted giving it to Courtney?"

"So you're thinking Anthony killed Courtney too?"

Sean shrugged.

"Maybe Eric has some other connection to Anthony," Charlie said. "I'll bet Anthony has been to the Atlantic Dunes restaurant or bar. Could've seen Courtney there wearing the pendant. Maybe he ran into Eric. Per the burglary report, the jewelry was in a wall safe that they supposedly forgot to lock when they went out of town. Pretty suspicious to me."

"Anthony didn't have a home security system?"

"Not according to the report," she said. "He lives in Ocean Forest Plantation. Because it's gated with their own private security, a lot of the residents feel safe there."

"There must be a reason why two women who wore that pendant necklace both ended up dead."

"After I digest all of this, Jay and I will go to the hotel bar where Courtney worked to ask more questions. Thanks for your help, but there's not much more you can do here." It would've felt like the most natural act in the world to lean in and kiss Sean goodbye, but she had to resist that impulse. She looked around to make sure Jay was still in their office, then reached out and squeezed Sean's hand before turning and walking into her office.

She spent an hour scanning the old murder case and the burglary report then drove to the Atlantic Dunes Resort with Jay. Although she was fairly certain their Eric Robinson, murder victim, was the Eric people at the hotel had been talking about to them earlier, now that they had his picture, she could get a positive ID. The manager didn't recognize Eric Robinson when she showed him his photo, but he was willing to give them a printout of credit card receipts from the bar on the days Courtney had worked.

They spoke to the desk clerk, who recognized the photo of Eric, saying she knew him as a limo driver who picked up or dropped off guests at the hotel. She also acknowledged Eric was Courtney's "friend." Charlie and Jay sat in the lobby and looked over the printout the manager had given them.

"Here we go," Charlie said. "Four weeks ago on a Saturday night, a charge by Anthony Capozzi for twenty dollars plus a ten-dollar tip. Another one Sunday night three weeks ago, fifteen dollars and a five-dollar tip."

Jay retrieved his tablet from their car and brought up a recent DMV photo of Anthony. They went into the bar, which was empty. A thirty-something man dressed in a black vest over a white shirt and black slacks appeared through a doorway between shelves of liquor. "We didn't think you were open," Charlie said.

The man smiled. "I'm a server in the restaurant, but I take care of the bar until the evening bartender comes in."

Charlie showed him the DMV photo on Jay's tablet. "Do you recognize him?"

"Sure, he's a local, Mr. Capozzi. Comes in with his wife for dinner occasionally. Been coming here for years. Sometimes comes in alone and eats in the bar."

She showed him the photo of Eric Robinson.

"Seen him a few times. He's a chauffeur."

"Ever seen the two of them together?" Charlie asked, pointing at the photos of Robinson and Capozzi.

"Never noticed."

"How about either of them together with Courtney?"

He shrugged. "When Courtney was here, I had no reason to come to the bar except to pick up drink orders for people dining. Just in and out. Never paid attention to people she might've been talking with."

At seven-thirty that evening, Charlie parked her car once again near the restaurant door of the Atlantic Dunes Resort. The sun had set, and rain had turned to a light drizzle, the kind of warm evening made for lovers to stroll under the same umbrella. After their earlier visit to the hotel, she had sent Jay home to spend the rest of the weekend with his family then worked on her report at the office for an hour.

There were no urgent leads that couldn't wait until Monday, but Charlie had nothing to go home to. With her son off at college and her mother out with her group of *lady friends*, as she called them, she didn't want to spend a Saturday night alone in the big, quiet house. She left the office and drove to the fitness facility at the Cusseta Country Club. Being late afternoon, it was empty. She was sure all the regulars were home getting gussied up for romantic evenings with their significant others. She spent forty-five minutes on an elliptical machine, keeping her heartrate at 140, the upper level of her target pulse. She then hit seven different machines, doing three sets on each one, to work her arms, shoulders, and back.

After she had showered and changed in the locker room, she was tempted to step into the dining room at the club for dinner. Except her jeans were against the dress code, although they were dark and fit her figure very well, and she was sure that with a smile, she could convince the maître d' to let her sit at the bar. The main reason, though, was that she could only imagine what others would think if they saw her eating alone on a Saturday night. She felt pathetic enough without showcasing she was alone on a Saturday night in front of the Dufftown and Spartina Island elite. Instead, she had climbed into her car and driven to the Island.

She walked past the hostess stand at the Atlantic Dunes Resort Restaurant to the small bar. Four of the tables were filled. She climbed onto a stool at the end of the bar where she could view the entire room. A pretty, thirtyish woman with strawberry blonde hair placed a napkin in front of her. She wore a black skirt, white shirt, and a black vest with a nametag that read "Maddie."

"Do you know what you'd like to drink?"

"How about a club soda with a twist for now," Charlie said. "Do you have a bar menu?"

Maddie filled a tall glass with ice and soda and pressed a wedge of lemon into the rim. She placed the drink on the cocktail napkin and handed Charlie a laminated menu. "You can order from the regular restaurant menu also if you'd like."

Charlie scanned past the fifteen- and twenty-dollar martinis and wine by the glass starting at twelve dollars to a dozen food items. She looked twice at the filet mignon bistro burger, but instead asked for the bar steak salad. Maddie tapped on an electronic screen next to a cash register, looked around the bar to see if anyone needed another drink, then returned to Charlie. "Are you visiting the island?"

"Actually I live in Dufftown." Charlie took a sip of her soda. "Have you worked here long?"

"A few years. I'm normally a waitress, but I just finished a crash course in bartending to fill in until they find a new weekend bartender."

"To replace Courtney?" Charlie said.

"You heard about that?"

Charlie pulled a business card from her jacket pocket and handed it to Maddie.

Maddie's eyes opened wide. "So you're working now?"

Charlie nodded. "But I'm hungry too."

"It's the saddest thing. Courtney was really sweet."

"Did you know her well?"

"Just from working here, but we talked. She told me about her divorce and how it forced her to move in with her parents."

"Did you know Eric?"

Maddie smirked. "Yeah, Eric hit on me a few months back. I thought Courtney could've done better than him."

Charlie showed her a photo.

"That's Mr. Capozzi," Maddie said. "Anthony. I've served him and his wife, Kristin, in the restaurant several times. He's a semi-regular. He also stops in at the bar for a drink several times a week."

"Did he know Courtney and Eric?'

"I'm sure Courtney served him at the bar."

"Anything unusual about him or his wife? Problems with anyone? Drunk or obnoxious?"

She shook her head. "This is not the sort of place where people cause problems. His wife gets tipsy and a bit loud sometimes, but never a problem."

"So, they're heavy drinkers?'

"Not Anthony. He's a cocktail-before-and-a-glass-of-wine-with-dinner kind of man. His wife drinks the rest of the bottle and has a double cognac for dessert."

"Ever seen him and Eric together?"

A kitchen worker appeared with Charlie's salad as Maddie made her rounds to the bar tables. As she ate, Charlie watched Maddie bringing fresh drinks to people in the bar and clearing a table that had been vacated.

Maddie brought Charlie a fresh soda. "I've entered "DD" for your sodas. There's no charge for nonalcoholic drinks for a group's designated driver, and since you need to drive yourself, that seems to apply."

"It's not necessary, but thanks."

"I've been asking around. See the silver-haired man at the end of the bar?" Maddie said, referring to a distinguished-looking older man wearing a Tommy Bahamas silk shirt and white pants. "He and Anthony sometimes chatted together at the bar. Should I ask him to come over?"

Charlie said okay, and Maddie walked down the bar and whispered something to the man. He walked toward Charlie, nodded at the empty stool beside her and said, "May I?"

"Please."

He set his drink, a Manhattan or something similar, on a cocktail napkin that Maddie tossed in front of him.

"Maddie tells me you're a detective investigating Courtney's murder. I also read Eric was murdered."

"That's right, I'm Sergeant Nash, and you are?"

"Colton Davis. Maddie said you're interested in interactions between Anthony and Eric. Are you thinking Anthony killed them?"

"I'm thinking nothing yet. I'm just running down leads as they appear. What can you tell me?"

"A few weeks ago, or maybe a month, I was talking with Anthony over a drink. He was saying he and his wife had to fly to Michigan for some family thing, and he hated leaving his car at the airport. I suggested he talk to Courtney because her boyfriend, Eric, is a chauffeur and does runs to the airport and back."

"Do you know if he did?"

"When I saw him a few days later, he said he'd been in contact with Eric. Although it was more expensive to have a car service like that than taking your own car, it was worth it to avoid the hassle of driving and parking."

Charlie recorded Colton's name and contact info into her pocket notebook, handed Maddie two twenties, and thanked her for her help. She scanned the bar on her way out, noting the only person there alone was Colton, and he was old enough to be her father. Definitely not the place for her to meet men on a Saturday night, had she been so inclined.

39

SUNDAY

After coffee and breakfast, Sean had Annie jump into the back of his SUV and he drove to Ocean Forest Plantation, a two-thousand-acre private development on the southern tip of the Island. He pulled up to the security gate and showed his new sheriff's ID card. He wasn't sure it would work. After all, it said *Cold Case Team Member* rather than deputy, sergeant, or another rank, he was obviously not driving a department vehicle, and his golf shirt and shorts were clearly not work attire. If challenged, he was prepared to say he was visiting a cold case team member who lived here to discuss a case.

The security officer didn't even flinch. "Have a nice day," he said, and the barrier arm raised to allow Sean to drive through. The resort had miles of roads that wound through a maritime forest of pine trees, oaks, maples, and sweetgums. Miles of sandy beach lined the southern edge of the development, where a four-star hotel and golf country club were also located. Throughout the development were numerous homes, ranging from simple wood-sided houses and condominiums built thirty years ago to waterfront mansions worth more than ten million dollars.

Sean parked at the Ocean Forest Preserve, undeveloped land in the center of the development, popped the hatch, and snapped the leash on Annie. His sunglasses immediately fogged over, and he used his T-shirt to wipe them. He'd checked a weather app when he got up at six this morning, and it was seventy-eight with the dew point the same. Sometimes a storm would bring cooler and crisper air, but yesterday's rain only brought more humidity. They walked along trails that weaved through the forest and around several freshwater ponds teeming with egrets, storks, and cormorants. He spotted the head and long neck of an anhinga moving through the water. Known as snake birds, they had dense bones that allowed them to stay submerged under the water to stalk fish. Tourists often mistook them for snakes when only their head and neck could be seen in the water.

They walked along a bicycle and walking path that ran alongside the road leading to the beach. They stopped when they encountered other walkers with dogs so the dogs could sniff each other. Sean always offered Annie's new furry friends a small treat from a baggie he carried in his pocket. Sean had wonderful memories of walking these same trails and paths with Lauren, but this was the first time he'd been out here with Annie since her death. It was about time he began making new memories, he thought.

He stuck an earbud in his left ear and called Charlie.

"Morning, Sean. It's Sunday, so don't tell me you're working on your cold case?"

"Sundays are just another day when you work Homicide. Don't tell me you're taking the day off?"

"You old Homicide detectives are such bad asses, always busting the chops of us small-town cops." She told him about what she'd learned about Anthony Capozzi yesterday at the Atlantic Dunes. "I'm home today but doing some work at my desk. I sent in a request to compare Eric Robinson's prints to the lifts from the burglary of Capozzi's house."

"I remember sitting home many weekends when I knew there were things to do on one of my cases, but nothing urgent enough to justify working on a Sunday."

"That's where I'm at, plenty to do, but nothing that can't wait until Monday. What are you up to?"

"Taking Annie for a long walk at Ocean Forest Plantation. I think we've gone five miles so far, but..." Sean paused, not sure if he was willing to admit his life was so empty that he had no other plans until dinner with his daughter. "I can't golf or kayak because of my shoulder, so I was wondering if you could maybe reach out to your father's old surveyor, Gary Bowers, and see if he's willing to meet with me today. He was one of the last people to talk to your father."

"Gary's not the most welcoming man. I doubt he'd open up to someone he didn't know, that is if he'd even agree to meet with you."

Sean heard the tinkle of a bell behind him. He looked over his shoulder to see two bicyclists approaching. He stepped off the path and held Annie's leash tight as they passed. "I understand. I guess I'll have to try another approach."

"Let me call you back," Charlie said and hung up before he could respond.

Sean had barely gone another block when Charlie called back. "I couldn't say I was bringing an investigator to interview him, so I told him I was coming by to show a friend my father's old hunting camp."

"I don't know."

"What? You're afraid I'm going to insert myself in your investigation? Afraid Captain Cannon might find out you're not keeping me in the dark?"

Those were exactly his thoughts. "No, actually, that's fine. I'll leave my thumbscrews and bright lights at home."

"It's on a dirt road that might be muddy after the rain, so if you meet me at my house, we can take our SUV."

"It'll be an hour," Sean said. "I need to drop off Annie and change into something more appropriate for an interview."

"Sean, we're going to a hunting camp out in the woods. Come as you are and bring Annie along. She'll love it out there."

Charlie was sitting on a rocking chair on her front porch when Sean pulled up. She was dressed in brown shorts, a light green button-front shirt, and canvas sneakers. "Come on in and bring Annie. My mother's at church, so we won't hear her complain about dragging dog hair into the house."

Sean and Annie came up the steps. Charlie gave him a head-to-toe once-over and said, "You look perfect for where we're going."

"I wasn't expecting to be seeing you and going out on an interview. I haven't even showered and shaved this morning."

"Oh, my, you mean you didn't shower before you took Annie out on a five-mile hike in summer-time heat and humidity? Shame on you."

Charlie looked like a model in an upscale resort wear catalog. "But you look so..." Sean couldn't finish his sentence because he was afraid he'd get so gushy about how beautiful she was, even when dressed casually, that he'd make her uncomfortable. Granted, California was different than South Carolina, but fellow officers back there had gotten sexual harassment complaints for complimenting women on their appearance.

She smiled. "Come on in. We'll grab some waters and head out."

Annie rushed through the door and into the living room, her nose twitching as she ran around the furniture.

"You have a cat?" Sean said.

"Yeah, Lexi. She's a Tonkinese."

"I'm not really a cat person."

"She's a cross between a Siamese and Burmese. She's used to dogs."

"Annie's never been around cats."

"Don't worry. Lexi's upstairs napping, which is what cats do most of the day. When we have more time, we'll introduce them. I know they'll be fine together."

Annie came out of the living room and looked up the stairs. "No!" Sean said, and Annie trotted to his side with her head down, obviously disappointed she couldn't search the entire house to find the source of the cat scent. They walked through the house to the kitchen, where Charlie grabbed several bottles of water, then out the back door to a long, single-story building that matched the style and colors of the main house.

Sean and Annie followed her into the six-bay garage. Inside were Charlie's unmarked Dodge Charger, her old blue Prius, an Audi sedan, and a metallic blue G-Class SUV, which looked like a jeep on steroids. Charlie swung the heavy back door open, and Annie jumped inside without hesitation. When Charlie closed the door, Sean noticed the chrome *G63* and *AMG* badges on the back. He climbed into the SUV and settled into the soft leather passenger seat, as Charlie started the engine and pulled out of the garage.

"Was this the car your father drove the night he disappeared?" Sean asked.

She drove down the alleyway to the main street. "He bought it a month before he disappeared. Traded in an older one that he had for ten years."

"I wish they would've processed it for prints and trace evidence back then."

"Agreed," she said. "But it was only a missing persons case at the time. Besides, I doubt there was anything of value to find inside and it had rained, so any prints or DNA on the exterior would've been washed away."

"I believe someone put his wallet and phone in the glove box."

She nodded. "At the time, the sheriff's detectives assumed my dad put them there himself, but that made no sense."

They turned left and roared westbound on Spartina Island Road. "This thing is amazing," Sean said. "I expected it to ride like a jeep or pickup truck."

"Rides like a luxury car, yet can take on the roughest terrain. It'll do zero to sixty in under five seconds, which is faster than a lot of sports cars."

"Quite different than your Prius."

"Yeah, my old environmentalist pals from college would unfriend me if they saw me driving this. My mother keeps it for nostalgic reasons, but my brothers sometimes use it, and I drive it when I go out into the woods."

"So where are we going?"

"My father bought a three-hundred-acre hunting tract out in the far western part of the county when he first came here. It had a little cabin on a lake that was filled with bass, trout, and catfish. The surrounding land had deer and turkeys, which my dad liked to hunt. About twenty years ago, he was finding signs of poachers and other trespassers, so he asked Gary Bowers if he'd like to be the caretaker. Gary had just gone through a divorce and was living in a tiny apartment. My father built a little house on the property, and Gary lives there for free in exchange for watching over the land."

"Sounds like Gary was more than just the man your father hired to do his surveying."

"He was. Gary and Dad were good friends."

40

After more than thirty minutes of driving on increasingly narrow roads, Charlie turned onto a dirt road blocked by a metal barrier. Annie stood up in the back, awake from her nap now that they had stopped. Several *No Trespassing* and *Private Property* signs hung from the barrier and along a fence that extended from both sides of the road. She gave Sean the combination to the lock, and he got out, opened the padlock, and swung the gate open before she drove through. He relocked the gate and climbed back into the Mercedes. Tall Loblolly and Longleaf pine trees lined both sides of the road.

In a hundred yards they came to a clearing with a red brick, ranch-style house. They parked next to a Chevy pickup, and an older man with white hair and a beard stepped out of the house. He wore jeans, brown leather boots, and a short-sleeved shirt the color of the dirt road. They got out of the Mercedes, and Sean stood by his door as Charlie and the man hugged. He was slightly shorter than Charlie, so Sean pegged him at five-eight. He had a weathered face, which would make sense for someone who had spent a career working outdoors.

After they finished their *good-to-see-yous* and *how-have-you-beens*, Charlie said, "Gary, this is my friend, Sean Tanner."

Gary extended a calloused hand. He had a strong handshake. Gary was slim, with a wiry build and ropy muscles in his arms. "You must be a very special person, Sean, because Charlie is very particular about who she considers a friend."

"You have a nice place here," Sean said, looking across a green lawn filled with magnolia, maple, oak, and different fruit trees.

"Sean is a retired detective from California," Charlie said. "The sheriff assigned him to reinvestigate the disappearance of my father."

"Such a sad situation," Gary said. "Henry was a good friend, and I still have trouble accepting it was an accident or suicide."

"I don't believe it was," Sean said.

Charlie's eyes shot daggers at him.

"Sean and other members of the cold case team are looking into all possibilities," Charlie said.

Gary glanced at his watch. "I've got something in the oven. Why don't you two run up to your camp, and I'll see you there in a little bit."

When they were back in the SUV, Charlie said, "I thought you said you were leaving your thumbscrews at home."

"I needed to see his reaction."

Charlie skirted around the house, past a red barn, and along a muddy dirt road that continued into the forest. "And what did you see?"

"I'm not sure. Maybe surprise."

"Although my dad's friends didn't want to admit it, suicide or accident were the most reasonable explanations for his disappearance."

"I'll try to keep it lighter when we talk again."

The road got bumpier as they splashed through mud puddles that hid the ruts in the road, but the G-Wagon maintained its smooth ride, even when crossing areas where the road was washed out. A small lake, about ten acres in size, soon appeared in front of them. On a small rise above the lake sat a weathered wood cabin with a brick chimney extending above the metal roof. Charlie parked and opened the back door. Annie leaped out and looked at Sean. He waived his arms, said, "Okay," and Annie dashed up a small hill.

"I know where she's going," Charlie said. "A herd of deer like to bed down up there."

They walked up a path that ended under a giant live oak. Annie sniffed the ground next to a rustic bench made from logs. Charlie sat on the bench and held her hand out to Sean. He took her hand and sat beside her.

"This was one of my dad's favorite spots," Charlie said. "There's always a breeze up here, and just looking out over the lake makes you feel cooler."

Charlie gestured toward three small white crosses to their right. "That's where we buried Sammy and Lucy, our Boykin Spaniels," Charlie said. "My dad got them for hunting, but they were mostly family pets."

Sean thought of the placards for the two dogs that were no longer a part of his family. He noted the Spaniels' names in black paint on the crosses. "The third cross?"

"That's where Cory buried his rescue. Cory is Gary's son. He found this mutt when he was out tromping around the marsh, which he often did. Cory brought him home and was nursing him back to health, when he ran off and was hit by a car."

"What a sad story."

"Yeah, it happened shortly after Dad disappeared. Cory hadn't even named his dog, but Gary let him bury him up here with Sammy and Lucy."

They walked down the hill to the cabin. Annie ran ahead taking in the smells along the ground on the way. The main room had an old cast-iron woodburning stove in one corner and a bunkbed built into the wall next to it. A tweed upholstered sofa that looked like one his parents retired to the basement thirty years ago was against the far wall. Two upholstered chairs and a coffee table completed an intimate seating area. At the back of the cabin was a compact kitchen and a round dining table with four chairs.

"When my dad bought this place, this was the extent of the cabin. It had only been used by men for hunting or fishing trips. It had no electricity, and the only running water came from a hand pump. An outhouse was out back." She stepped through a doorway. "He added on this bedroom and a real bathroom, brought in electricity, and drilled a deeper well."

Sean noticed there was no television anywhere in the cabin. "This feels really peaceful."

"We'd come out here when I was a kid. My mother didn't like roughing it, but she'd put up with it for a few days once or twice a year."

"Sounds like great memories."

"In the early days of my marriage, before Roger began cheating on me and when he was better at hiding his true asshole nature, we would come out here for romantic weekends together." She walked back into the main room, opened a door between the kitchen sink and the dining table, and stepped onto a screened porch that overlooked the lake.

"If this were my cabin, this is where I'd spend most of my time," Sean said.

"As kids, we usually slept out here in sleeping bags. It was like camping outside, but without the mosquitos."

Gary appeared around the back and opened a screen door to the porch. "I figured you'd be out here." He handed Charlie something in a paper bag.

"You're still making your sourdough bread?" Charlie said.

"Sure am. I had two loaves ready to go in the oven when you called."

"From as far back as grade school, I remember when Dad brought home a loaf of your bread. We'd devour half the loaf before dinner."

"Make sure you share it with your mother," Gary said.

Trying to take things a little slower for Charlie's benefit, Sean said, "You from here originally, or are you a northern transplant like most folks down here?"

"I was actually born in the Lowcountry," Gary said. "My father, like all of his family, was a logger in the mountains of Northern Georgia. When the timber industry started up down here, he and my mom moved here for work. I was born a year later. Followed in my father's footsteps for a while, but then found surveying was lots easier work."

"Bet you've seen lots of changes in the area," Sean said.

"Sure have." Gary glanced at Charlie before looking back at Sean. "So you think it might've been more than an accident or suicide?"

Sean was prepared to continue the small talk longer, but since Gary initiated the conversation shift, he said, "People I talk to say Henry Nash would never commit suicide. He loved his life and his family too much. People also say he wasn't so careless that he'd somehow fall off the bridge."

Gary nodded slowly, as if he were contemplating that fact. "You know I saw him that day."

"That's what I understand. Can you tell me what happened?"

"The week before, Boyd Moretti hired me to start a preliminary survey of the west side of Sea Island Plantation. He had a hand-drawn plan that added more streets and home sites and wanted to know if it was feasible. I was out surveying it when Henry drove by and wanted to know what I was doing."

"Had you already surveyed this land for Henry?" Sean asked.

"Sure had. I prepared a final site plan, all certified to send to the county for approval."

The aroma of the fresh bread was intoxicating. Sean peeked into the bag. "I guess Henry was surprised to see you there."

"More like fuming mad. I thought Boyd and Henry were together with this new idea. I should've guessed something was up when Boyd was the one who came to me with the new plan, because he never got involved in the details. But I'd done work for him before on other projects. He signed my standard agreement and paid my retainer."

"What did Henry say?"

"I don't remember his words, but there was plenty of cursing. Not at me, but about Boyd, for going behind his back. I told Henry I didn't want to get between him and Boyd, and I would just stop work until they settled whatever they needed to settle."

"When did you next see Henry?"

"That was the last time I saw him. He went missing that night."

"Did you call Moretti and tell him about Henry seeing what you were doing?"

"I figured Henry would do that. Henry gave me more business than any of the developers. For a bunch of years, I was pretty much working for him full-time with all the projects he was doing. And we were friends. We went hunting and fishing together and had lots of man-to-man talks. He kept me from going postal when the missus decided she wanted a divorce."

"Did you know they were meeting that night?"

"No, but Henry wasn't one to let a dispute fester for long."

"Did you speak to anyone else about what happened between them?"

Gary thought for a moment. "The next day a sheriff's deputy came by, told me Henry was missing, and asked what happened. Told him the same I just told you. I went to the house and saw Abigail that evening."

"What do you think happened to Henry?"

Gary was quiet for a minute. "People were saying that he jumped or fell off the bridge, but just like you said, Henry wouldn't do that. And he wouldn't just run off and leave his family. I never wanted to think about it, and never said this to anyone, but most likely someone killed him. Might've been an accident or maybe someone lost control of themselves."

"What do you mean?"

"You know, like two men been drinking in a bar and get to arguing and then fighting. One has a heart attack and dies. Something like that."

"Like maybe him and Boyd?"

"I won't be pointing no fingers at anyone."

"You eventually went back and finished surveying the land according to Moretti's plan," Sean said.

"Couple months later, Boyd said Abigail agreed to his plan. I spoke to her, and she said it was okay, so I redid the plot plan just as Boyd wanted."

"How did you feel about that?"

"I liked my job. Only retired because I just got too old for field work. But I love the land, and I don't like seeing it disappear. Henry, Charlie, and I all agree that development is inevitable, but anything we can do that results in more trees and grass and fewer buildings and asphalt is good."

41

On the drive back, Charlie thought about what Gary said. Her dad had seldom gotten angry, so it surprised her to hear he was so mad he was swearing. She wondered if he carried that anger with him to his meeting with Boyd later that night. Did they fight, as Gary suggested? Did her dad die at the scene and then Moretti disposed of his body? These were possibilities she had not previously considered.

She was glad she finally spoke to Gary about his conversation with her dad on the day he disappeared, but she had an ulterior motive for bringing Sean to meet Gary. She was pleased that he loved the rustic camp on the lake. She wondered if he would think she was too forward if she were to invite him out there for a picnic or early dinner once she had wrapped up these murders.

"Do you know his son Cory?" Sean asked.

Charlie turned on the radio. The voice of Billy Joel singing "Just the Way You Are" filled the cabin. He noticed the presets on the display were almost exactly the same as the Sirius stations Lauren had programmed in his Corvette for him. Yacht Rock Radio, advertised as, "smooth-sailing soft rock from the late-70s and early 80s," was one of Lauren's favorites. "Never pictured you as the rock and roll type," Sean said.

"Why, because my generation grew up with grunge, punk, and hip-hop?

I listened to that with my friends when I was young, but the music from the sixties and seventies puts a smile on my face. What about you?"

"I grew up with this music, then disco killed it. I hated hearing the boom of rap music in my early days as a cop, and quite honestly, I seldom listened to music after that. It seemed like a distraction from whatever I was doing."

"A nice distraction at times," she said. "Here we are talking about my father's disappearance or murder, but with the right song playing, it's less painful."

Sean couldn't disagree.

"Cory is eight or nine years younger than me, so I didn't really know him growing up," Charlie said. "My brother James knew him from school and said he was wicked smart, but always a troublemaker as a kid."

"A guy who rescues stray dogs can't be all bad."

"Cory had a lot of great qualities, but he got involved with the radical ecological movement and was arrested several times. The sheriff's office caught him and some other idiot friends of his sabotaging the construction equipment at one of my father's developments about fifteen years ago."

"I worked a bombing murder linked to *Earth First* back in Oakland. They were into spiking trees, blowing up bulldozers, and firebombing college buildings."

"Cory was headed in that direction. He was the ringleader of a little group that caused thousands of dollars of damage and delayed work for weeks."

"Was he prosecuted?"

"My dad talked to the circuit solicitor and asked him to give Cory a break. Cory had been doing this stuff for a while and was looking at five to ten. Instead he got six months in jail and probation."

"Did he change?"

"He continued his protesting and letter-writing campaign against development, but stayed away from the violence and vandalism. He was a teenager when his parents split, and Gary blamed himself for Cory's acting out. But he's doing better now. When he wasn't working with his father, he worked as a dockhand and first mate on fishing and dolphin-tour boats. A few years ago, he got his captain's license and actually skippers a boat for a dolphin tour company now."

Billy Joel's voice trailed off and Sade began singing about a guy being a smooth operator. He remembered listening to this song with Lauren, and she accused him of being a smooth operator. They had both laughed because they both knew that was the furthest from the truth. "Seems like your father's compassion paid off with Cory."

"I know it hurt Gary a great deal to learn his son had done that to my father. Six months behind bars was the wakeup call Cory needed."

Her phone vibrated. She looked at the message and said, "I get a text when someone leaves a voicemail on my work phone." She listened for a moment, then said, "That was Sarah Fitzpatrick's mother. Said she's willing to meet with me anytime. I could call in Jay or Sherm to assist, or if you're not doing anything..."

An hour later, Charlie pulled up to one of the smaller two-bedroom stucco homes in Sea Island Plantation in her unmarked Charger. Sean was waiting outside his Highlander, dressed in khaki pants and a dark blue shirt. She had changed into the dress jeans she had worn yesterday and a yellow cotton blazer, something more appropriate for an interview than her shorts and sneakers. Continuous loud pops from the pickleball courts across the street filled the air, and Charlie wondered what it was like living next to that constant noise. Sue Fitzpatrick opened the door as they approached. She was a small woman around seventy, with short gray hair and round, wire-framed glasses.

"I can't believe you're reopening your investigation."

"Some new information has come up," Charlie said. "This is Sean Tanner, with the department's cold case team."

"Come in. I see you're going to be writing," Sue said, looking at Charlie's steno pad. "Let's sit at the dining room table." She led them into a house that was so neat it looked hardly lived in.

Charlie started by getting background information. Sue's husband had passed away five years ago from a heart attack, and she and another friend who was recently widowed sold their family homes and bought this house together. Something easier to take care of and in a community with countless activities to keep them busy. "My husband and I spoke to detectives daily back then for months. They told us they interviewed dozens of students and other people, yet never got anywhere. I can't believe it's been twenty-seven years since Sarah died."

"When did you last speak to Sarah that day?" Charlie asked.

"When she left for school. Everyone didn't have cell phones back then. Although she wasn't allowed to participate with the cheer team because she was pregnant, she said she was going to watch their practice after school. The team was preparing for some sort of exhibition. Sarah's friends later told me that she left cheer practice around four-thirty and was going to the rec center to watch some other girls play basketball."

"Is that the last anyone saw her?"

Sue nodded.

Charlie doubted Sue knew anything about the murder that wasn't in the reports, so there was no need to rehash it. What she wanted from Sue was her impressions of others, so she planned to toss out open-ended questions or comments to get Sue to talk. "It must've been hard for a teenage girl to suddenly learn she's pregnant."

"When she first found out, we were all disappointed—Sarah, me, and her father. But we soon accepted it and decided to make the best of it. Sarah was an incredible young lady, and we knew she'd be a good mother. And I'd be there to help."

"How about Anthony?"

"My husband and I both approved of him dating Sarah. He was a likable kid. My husband blamed him at first. You know, it's always the boy's fault, but Anthony accepted responsibility and seemed to grow up overnight. Anthony's father was initially an A-hole and made disparaging comments about Sarah. But Anthony's mother was a gem. She put her husband in his place, and all four of us parents promised we would work together and be the most supportive parents in the world."

"Must've been quite traumatic when you learned she'd been murdered."

"It was like our world ended. We were all in shock. I didn't sleep right for months. Anthony's parents were the same. Ann, that's Anthony's mom, and I saw each other every day for probably a year. It was like we had both lost a daughter."

"How did Anthony take it?"

"The poor boy. He was distraught. He'd stop by after school and just sit in the kitchen while I made dinner. Said he felt Sarah's presence in our house. He eventually moved on, went to college, and married Kristin, another girl they all went to school with."

"What was Kristin like?"

"She was nice, but very unlike Sarah. She was very proper and reserved. Other girls said she was stuck up. She was into horses and riding at her country club, stuff that was foreign to Sarah and the rest of us middle-class folk."

"Sarah was wearing a ruby pendant necklace, but it wasn't with her when she was found," Charlie said.

"Sarah cherished that necklace. It had belonged to Ann, given to her by her husband when they were engaged. It meant the world to Sarah when Ann presented it to her. It told her she was accepted by their family."

"Have you heard if the necklace has been seen again?"

Sue had a puzzled look on her face. "No. Has it turned up somewhere?"

Charlie didn't intend to answer. "Do you still keep in touch with Anthony or his parents?"

"Anthony and his mother take me to dinner every year on Sarah's birthday. Anthony and both of his parents came to my husband's funeral, and when I had to clean out our old house to downsize, Anthony came to help and brought some of the young men from his construction company to help me move."

"How is Anthony doing today?"

"He's a grown man now and very successful, but he's different. He never laughs and goofs around like he did when Sarah was here. Maybe he's just gotten older, but Sarah brought out the best in him, and when she was gone, that part of him never returned."

42

Charlie stood by her car and looked over at Sean. "What do you think?"

"She still misses her daughter. What parents wouldn't? The cynical detective part of me thinks Anthony staying connected with Sarah's mother could be out of guilt."

"Of course Sue thought the world of Sarah, but everyone interviewed back then loved Sarah. When I spoke to Anthony's mother with Irish John, she also said that Sarah was the best thing that ever happened to her son."

"And Anthony has a solid alibi, right?"

"Airtight, but I'm gonna have Jay and Sherm try to contact all those people who said they were with him to see if their stories have changed over time. For now, I'm confident Anthony couldn't have killed her."

"Anthony's father is at the top of my list, motive-wise. He was probably thinking this little tart seduced his angelic son to trap him into marriage so she could access the family riches."

"I don't doubt that didn't go through his mind at first," Charlie said. "Even his wife alluded to that. He was upset that it curtailed Anthony's plans for college and taking over the family business. But he eventually came around."

"Excuse the cynical detective again, but we don't know if the father really came around, or if he was just acting like he had to placate his wife."

"Since Marco died two years ago, we can't ask him."

"If we assume Marco did kill Sarah and take the pendant, at some point he must've returned it to Anthony."

"To follow your logic, then Eric and Courtney stole it when they burglarized his house, Anthony found out, and he killed them both."

"You know I don't like to make assumptions without evidence, but it would be too much of a coincidence for Anthony's house to be burglarized and Courtney just happens to be wearing the pendant."

"When Irish John and I spoke to Ann Capozzi, I specifically asked if she'd seen the pendant since Sarah's murder. She said she hadn't, and if she had, she'd immediately call us, because that meant whoever had it killed Sarah."

"Maybe talk to her again," Sean said. "Mention the burglary of Anthony's house and ask if it's possible the pendant somehow got back to him."

"We've been holding off talking to Anthony, partly because of your suggestion that if he is Eric and Courtney's killer, we'd tip him off. If we mention the burglary to his mother, it will surely get back to him, along with our suspicions."

"If he is the killer, he tortured Eric and didn't get the pendant, then killed Courtney and didn't find the pendant, so he might assume it's lost for good."

"If you feel like spending more quality time together this fine Sunday afternoon, we could go and visit Ann."

"If it means I don't have to stand in this blazing sun and sweat my butt off discussing theories, I'm all in."

Sean followed her in his car to Ann Capozzi's house at the Cusseta Country Club which happened to be near the stables. Charlie had taken riding lessons when she was young, but it was one of those skills that her mother thought kids in her social class had to acquire, like tennis, ballet, and piano. She never had a passion for it, and there were so many other activities she enjoyed more.

Although not one of the newer mini-mansions on the golf course or along the river, the Capozzi's house was a large Lowcountry-style house with an inviting front porch and a detached four-car garage that resembled a classic carriage house. Ann led them to the same formal living room where Charlie and Irish John sat yesterday. Ann looked at Sean and said, "I met your associate, John O'Shea, yesterday. I understand most of you live in Sea Island Plantation, but you don't look as old as most of the residents there."

Charlie sometimes began an interview with a comment or question to make the person uncomfortable and to let them know she was in charge. She found it interesting that Ann had done that to Irish yesterday and was trying to do the same to Sean.

"Thank you, Ms. Capozzi." Sean didn't take the bait and justify his decision to live there or explain the advantages of living in an active adult community.

"We just left Sue Fitzpatrick's house," Charlie said quickly to get the interview on track. "She tells me you two have remained in touch all these years."

"Sue is a very nice lady. We grieved together over Sarah's death for a long time, and now we have another commonality, both of our husbands gone."

"She downsized to a nice house in Sea Island Plantation," Charlie said. "You have a beautiful home here, but it must be a lot of work taking care of it alone."

"It's home. I'm sure your mother feels the same way after she lost your father. Besides, it helps having a son who runs a construction company. It's like having an army of home handymen on call whenever something needs fixing."

Charlie opened her notebook, scanned a page, and said, "The reports from back then show Marco was at work until five o'clock the day Sarah was killed. Did he have another activity before he came home?"

She shook her head. "He came straight home. I'm positive. We were both home when Sue called to ask if we had seen Sarah. And we were home when everyone began calling each other to say Sarah's body was found."

Charlie didn't put much faith in spousal alibis. Wives lied for their husbands all the time. She knew that if Marco had actually gotten home much later—late enough to have had time to kill Sarah—Ann wasn't about to change her story now. "I just learned Anthony was recently the victim of a home burglary."

"He and Kristin were away on a trip and discovered it when they returned. They lost nearly all of their jewelry, not that Kristin wore any of it anymore."

"Any sentimental family heirlooms?"

Ann looked at her with a puzzled expression on her face.

"I was just thinking," Charlie said. "When Anthony announced his engagement to Sarah, you gave Sarah that ruby pendant."

"Sarah was different. I knew she would appreciate it. The pendant was so her, bright and vibrant. Kristin came from means, so she already had quite a collection of jewelry by the time she married Anthony."

"I remember Marco around the club when I was young," Charlie said. "He always wore big gold chains and bracelets. Was any of that stuff stolen during that burglary?"

Ann laughed. "Marco always said wearing bling was part of being Italian. I think he watched too many old gangster movies and thought that was how all Italian men were supposed to be. That was also the style back then. In the last twenty years or so, Marco seldom wore any jewelry besides a nice watch and his wedding ring."

"Did he pass on any of the stuff he no longer wore to Anthony?"

"Marco sometimes splurged. Years ago, I learned that he got a huge state contract to widen Spartina Island Road when he came home wearing a Breitling watch and towing a horse trailer with a new horse for Kristin. That was Marco. Marco was also the man who walked around the house turning off lights and telling us we were wasting money on electricity."

Charlie sat quietly. Waiting.

"Marco loved me and Anthony deeply, but he wasn't a demonstrative person. When he was dying—he had congestive heart failure and kidney and lung issues—he gave me a wrapped cigar box and asked me to give it to Anthony after he was gone. He was here, under home hospice care. A few days later, with me and Anthony at his side, he passed. Later that evening, I gave the box to Anthony, and he took it in another room and opened it."

Ann removed a tissue from a drawer of an end table and dabbed her eyes. "Anthony was reading a letter his father had written and was crying. I hadn't seen him cry since Sarah died."

"Did he tell you what the letter said?" Charlie asked.

"I never asked. Figured if he wanted to tell me he would."

"Was there anything else in the box?"

"I never saw what was in there, but the next day, I saw Anthony wearing that Breitling watch. He's worn it every day since his father died."

Fifteen minutes later, Charlie and Sean sat in the parking lot next to the stables in their respective cars, nose to tail, their driver's doors inches apart. "Do you believe she didn't know what was in the box or what the letter said?" Sean asked.

"I don't know. But I suspect that letter was Marco's deathbed apology for killing Sarah. And I'll bet the pendant was in the box."

"If so, Anthony must've hidden it where Kristin wouldn't find it," Sean said. "He could never tell her about it."

"Then it was stolen by Eric and given to Courtney. Anthony had to get it back, not only for sentimental reasons—he was still in love with Sarah—but if it resurfaced, the world would know Marco killed Sarah, which would tarnish his family's reputation forever."

"That's a good theory, but how do we prove it?" Sean said.

"I'd like to interview him. Sarah's still an emotional issue with him. I could use that to break him."

"If he denies it, you have no evidence to confront him with."

"I could do a low-key interview. Just sit down and talk, see where it goes."

"If he gets all nervous, he could destroy evidence," Sean said. "He's sure to have kept the letter. Maybe he's got other evidence linking him to the two recent murders."

"I'll sleep on it," Charlie said.

Sean looked at his watch. "I've gotta go. I'm making dinner for my daughter and her husband tonight."

"You cook?"

"Nothing fancy, but I make do. Why don't you join us? I know you and Rachel would get along great."

Charlie wondered if Sean's invitation was just the sort of casual invite one would make to a co-worker, or if it meant something more. And if, in his mind, it meant something more, meeting his daughter was a huge leap, one she wasn't sure she was ready to take. "Wish I could, but I promised my mother I'd join her for dinner tonight," Charlie lied.

43

Sean stood at the kitchen sink rinsing dishes and loading the dishwasher. "You sure I can't help?" Rachel sat on a stool on the other side of the counter, while Austin was in the living room watching football, with Annie sitting on the floor beside him and resting her head on his knee.

"I'm sure. Besides, you should be taking it easy."

"Oh, Dad, I'm just pregnant, not disabled. Have you talked to Carson yet?"

"We finally spoke on the phone, but he didn't really say much."

"The important thing is that he's talking to you," Rachel said. "Did he mention anything about drugs?"

"Not at all. He said he was taking some time off, but he didn't come out and say he'd been suspended."

"He's afraid he'll be terminated. He's already reaching out to other people he knows to see if other tech companies are hiring."

"I wish there was something I could do," Sean said.

"You're already doing it. Just being here and loving him no matter what. That's what Mom would do," Rachel said. "The story you told me about Sarah is really sad. Do you really think her boyfriend's father killed her because she was pregnant?"

"That's only a theory, and remember, you can't talk about this to anyone, right?"

"I know." She ran her finger over her lips. "It could compromise the integrity of the investigation."

"I like how you've got the cop lingo down pat. Granted this was twenty-seven years ago, but it's still hard to fathom how people could be so closed-minded."

"You're thinking like a Californian, Dad. Although teenage pregnancies aren't the social stigma they once were, that was a different time and in a Southern small town. It's dangerous to judge people from a different era or a different culture through our own societal values in present day."

"Geez, Rachel, how did you get so smart?"

"You sent me to college. I also learned from you and Mom. Don't forget, Mom was born and raised in the South. She told me that she had a lot of adjusting to do when she moved to crazy California after college."

Sean looked past Rachel into the backyard. It was dusk, and birds were flocking to the feeders to fill up before heading off to wherever birds slept at night. First there were chickadees, nuthatches, and Carolina wrens. Then a pair of cardinals swept in, followed by a red-bellied woodpecker that flew to the suet feeder.

"Living in our gated communities on Spartina Island is sometimes like living in a bubble," Sean said. "We aren't much exposed to life outside."

"When I left the Bay Area for college in Georgia, it was like going back in time in many respects. But it was still college, where young people challenged the norms they grew up with. Then coming here to teach was another step back in time. I was talking to one of my old California friends recently, and she could not believe there are parts of the country where you can't buy liquor on Sundays."

Sean put the last glass in the dishwasher and closed the door. "Not that it was a big deal to me, but that was a surprise to me too when I moved here."

"What I really loved about Sarah's story was how both her parents and her boyfriend's parents, despite the community values, eventually came around to support Sarah and Anthony and pledged to help them out however they could."

Sean nodded. Except for the possible exception of Anthony's father, he thought.

After Rachel and Austin left, Sean kicked back in his recliner with a recent crime thriller Stretch had given him. It was good escapism, but unlike the real world of homicide investigations, the detective solved every murder by the end of the book and usually ended up in bed with a new woman. His phone buzzed. "Hey, Feebee."

"I've been doing a deep dive into Henry Nash and his family, and I discovered some startling facts."

"Yeah, like what?"

"I think I should show you."

Sean looked at his watch—8:50 p.m. "It's getting late, can it wait until tomorrow?"

"I don't think so."

Ten minutes later, Feebee was unloading an old-style leather briefcase with buckled straps onto his dining room table. She laid out pages of printouts that documented a timeline of Henry's life, from his birth certificate to school records to his college diploma, with all sorts of supporting papers and news clips in between. She then did the same from the time he first visited Spartina Island to the day he disappeared.

"Our official sheriff office's email address has worked wonders to get access to different people and databases," she said. "Almost as good as my old FBI email address and official status. I got into O.P.M., that's the federal Office of Personnel Management, and confirmed Henry was a foreign service officer for five years. It showed his overseas postings in Germany and Austria, but there was nothing more available where I was digging."

"Okay, that's pretty much what we know," Sean said.

"Right, but an hour ago, I got a call from an agent with the Bureau's counterintelligence division who wanted to know why I was investigating Henry Nash."

"Shit! They called you on a Sunday evening?"

"That's not unusual. Those guys work twenty-four-seven. I'm thinking my search just popped onto his radar."

"What did you tell him?"

"The truth. That I'm just a volunteer helping the sheriff's office on a missing person investigation."

"And?"

"The agent asked me three times who I was really working for and whether I remembered everything I was taught at Quantico about working for a foreign power or an organization that had ties to such."

"Did this FBI agent say what Henry did with State that was so sensitive that he had to question you?"

"He said nothing, but I didn't expect him to. He didn't call to provide information."

"How'd your conversation end?"

"I'm certain he believed me, but it was obvious I was digging into an area where they preferred I not dig."

"I don't understand any of this," Sean said. "You were the fed, so what do you make of it?"

"My best guess is that Henry actually worked for the CIA, and they wondered why someone was investigating one of their former officers. Or maybe, he was, in fact, assigned to the State Department, but was doing intelligence work in conjunction with the intelligence community. Back then, the lines between agencies like State and CIA were blurred."

"We should keep this between the two of us and not put it in our report. We'll keep this in the back of our minds as we continue our investigation, but if we learn Henry Nash was killed because he was a spook, I'm not sure how we will ever get to his killer."

"Agreed. There's something else."

"You're not going to tell me Abigail Nash is a Russian agent."

Feebee grinned. "No, she's exactly who we thought she was, but I found Charlie has two birth certificates."

"Huh?"

Feebee slid a photocopied birth certificate across the table. "This shows a Charlotte Kensington was born at Mission Hospital in Asheville on June second, forty-four years ago." She handed another one to him. "This shows

Charlotte Nash was born on July twenty-eighth in a private residence in Buncombe County. That's the county Asheville is in. The registration of birth was submitted to the county vital records by an RN named Dorothy Jones."

"Who is Charlotte Kensington?"

"Kensington is Abigail Nash's maiden name."

"Okay..."

"There's no record of Charlotte Kensington anywhere. No school records, no death records. Nothing. She never existed, except for her birth. The record of Charlotte Nash's birth is nine months following Henry and Abigail's wedding."

"Oh, my god! Are you saying?"

"It sure looks like it. Charlie was actually born in the hospital around seven months after her parents married. Then a nurse, who I learned was doing home visits at a mountain home belonging to Abigail's parents to look in on a newborn baby and mother, submitted a registration of birth form to the county to document a birth showing Charlotte was born nine months after her parent's marriage."

"Do all of Charlie's official records show that July date?"

Feebee nodded. "Driver's license, employment records, as well as a birth announcement in the Spartina Island weekly newspaper."

"I wonder if Charlie knows."

Feebee shrugged. "This is some more of my fantastic sleuthing work that I will not put into our report."

"Good idea."

44

MONDAY

Charlie was sitting outside the CrossFit gym when Ray Mitro arrived at ten to six to open. "Couldn't sleep, huh?" he said.

"I stayed up half the night trying to figure out these damn murders then woke before five and immediately my brain starts thinking about murders."

"I promise you a routine so grueling this morning that your brain will only think about finding a way for your body to survive. Why don't you stretch and jump rope to warm up while I write up the workout of the day."

The workout consisted of five different exercises, each done non-stop for a minute. A minute rest was allowed before starting the next round. The board said to do three rounds, but Charlie did five. At the end, she could hardly lift the medicine ball, much less throw it against the wall for the prescribed minute.

Ray tossed her a towel. "Did that clear your brain?"

"Of the murders, but not of my visit to my dad's camp and the conversation with Gary yesterday."

"How's he doing?"

"Taking good care of Dad's land and still baking bread."

"What's nagging at you?"

"Sean wanted to talk to him because he was one of the last people to see my father alive. I realized I never once in the ten years talked to him about that day my dad disappeared."

"Why do you think that is?"

She shrugged. "Maybe I didn't want to know what he might have to say."

"And what was that?"

"It wasn't so much what he said, but...I don't know, I got the feeling that he knows more than he told us."

"Did Sean get that same feeling?"

"We didn't really discuss it. Sean doesn't talk much about what his gut is saying. He wants hard evidence and facts."

"I can't say I know him as well as you, but Sean strikes me as a man with fine-tuned intuition. He might not say it, but I'll bet he has a strong feeling about what Gary said or didn't say."

"I gotta get home to shower and change for work."

"Come by anytime you need a brain cleansing."

Charlie was at her desk by 7:30 and typing up the summaries of her interviews with Sue Fitzpatrick and Ann Capozzi as Jay and Sherm drifted into the office well before their 8:00 a.m. starting time. Darryl was on the road to Charleston again with Doc Henderson for the autopsy of Eric Robinson. She assigned Jay and Sherm to confirm Anthony's alibi for the murder of Sarah, by recontacting everyone who had previously said he was with them on that after-school fishing trip.

After they left, she called a fingerprint technician at SLED crime lab who she'd gotten to know over the years and asked if they could put her request to compare Eric's prints to the latents found at Anthony's burglary at the top of their list. Charlie was just finishing up her interview summaries when she got a call back from SLED. "This is preliminary until it goes through my supervisor for certification, but I matched twelve points on two of the lifts taken off a desk drawer in Capozzi's home office to Eric Robinson."

She thanked her friend, grabbed her notebook, and headed down the hall to brief Billy on everything that had developed since she last saw him on Friday.

45

At ten o'clock, Sean left the physical therapy office. His shoulder was sore, but he was feeling good about his prognosis. The therapist had started by stretching and bending his left arm in every possible direction. She then used dry needling to stimulate the nerves and trigger points that were causing his pain and limited mobility. He would see her two more times this week, and if he didn't improve, she'd refer him to an orthopedic surgeon, who'd probably start with an MRI. He tried to push the possibility of another surgery from his mind.

Although he was supposed to go home, apply heat, and take it easy, instead he stopped at the Nash house. Rose answered the door and escorted him into the kitchen where Abigail was arranging flowers in several vases. "Since you surely know Charlotte is at work, I imagine you came here to see me."

"I think I told you that when we have an investigation with no obvious leads, we often begin by investigating our victim, hoping that will lead us to a reason someone would want to hurt them."

"You did, and you seemed to believe this was related to the disagreement between Henry and Boyd Moretti."

"Additional possibilities are surfacing. We uncovered something from

Henry's past that might have nothing to do with his disappearance, but secrets are always discerning to me during an investigation."

"Henry was a private person, so I'm not surprised you're finding things that are not exactly public knowledge."

Sean removed copies of the two birth certificates from his leather folio and set them on the counter. Abigail set her scissors down and looked at the papers. She sighed and said, "Would you like a cup of tea?

Neither said anything as Abigail boiled water and poured it into a white porcelain teapot with pink and red roses. She carried the teapot, cups, saucers, spoons, cream, and sugar to the breakfast table and sat down. Sean sat across from her. She sighed again.

"Does Charlie know?" Sean asked.

She shook her head. "I've always intended to tell her. Then more time went by, and I never did. When I learned I was pregnant, Henry promptly proposed. Just like that. He said he wanted to spend the rest of his life with me, however, he was hoping we would've had time to plan a proper wedding, one that would be talked about in Dufftown for years."

She poured tea into both of their cups. Sean pulled his in front of him before she could doctor it up with cream and sugar. "You cannot imagine the reaction when I told my mother. She said the most unkind things about me and, of course, Henry. She went on and on about the scandal it would cause if I walked down the aisle with a baby belly stretching my wedding gown, and what the town would think. So Henry and I agreed to a quick wedding. The story was that we were so much in love that we could not wait, and Henry, being a Northerner, was uncomfortable with an extravagant Southern wedding."

"I understand," Sean said.

"I doubt that you do. Dufftown society forty-some years ago is not something you can understand unless you were born and raised in it. We had a small wedding the following Saturday at our church. By small, I mean only a hundred guests. Then a reception at Cusseta Country Club. My mother decided I needed to leave town before I started to show. We used the excuse of renovating our new house and some medical complications that demanded I be near a large hospital."

"Which could've meant Savannah or Charleston," Sean said.

"Of course, but that was too close, so mother found a fine doctor in Asheville, which was close to our family cabin in the mountains. Rose accompanied me, and I had a nurse that came by a few times a week. When it was time, I had Charlotte in the hospital in Asheville. She was a healthy and beautiful seven-pound-two-ounce girl."

"You used your maiden name at the hospital."

"My mother's idea. Then seven weeks or so later, we had another birth certificate made up."

"Someone had to complete a registration of birth form and send it to the county to get a birth certificate."

"My mother convinced my nurse to do so. Our story, and the one we told of Charlotte's birth, was that I began having contractions at home and called my nurse. The baby was coming so fast, we didn't have time to drive to the hospital."

"So that's the story of how Charlie came into the world that she's been living with for her entire life."

"You must think I'm a monster."

"I've met many monsters in my years working homicide, and you don't come close."

"Do you intend to tell her?"

"That's not my place."

They talked for another hour about Abigail and Henry's life, filling in some of the pieces that were missing after Sean's conversations with Rose, the accountant, and Charlie's brothers. He learned that Henry's father and family had never approved of Henry making a life for himself down here. Henry was surprised that his father left him half of his estate when he died, but Henry didn't want to help manage the business in New York, so he sold his share to his brother for a hundred million dollars, a fraction of what it was worth, to be paid over thirty years.

Abigail said Henry was angry when his brother filed for bankruptcy to avoid continuing to make the payments to Henry. Although the monthly six-figure checks from Henry's brother were more than welcome, their lifestyle had not changed once they stopped. Henry's brother didn't expect Henry to join his brother's other creditors and seek partial relief in federal bankruptcy court. Henry's lawyers settled for a fraction of what his brother owed him, but after everything was settled, Henry owned his brother's five-million-dollar apartment, and his brother was broke. Henry told his brother he could continue to live there as long as he was alive, and Henry gave him a monthly allowance to live on.

"It sounds like Henry's brother had a motive to go after him," Sean said.

"I hardly know the man, but from what Henry had told me, his brother never accepted responsibility for his own business failures. He blamed Henry, saying that having to pay Henry off for his share of the business was what caused him to go under. Then he said Henry bled him completely dry after the other creditors took their share."

"At some point, we may go to New York and speak with his brother," Sean said. "What about any other people who might be upset with how Henry fought the bankruptcy?"

"Henry's brother was left with no assets besides a small bank account, so when he passes, there will be nothing to leave his son. I imagine growing up as a Nash, his son had expected something. So, if you're looking for people who might be angry enough at Henry to kill him, I think you need to put his brother, Richard, and his son, Patrick, on your list."

Sean got up from the table. "If you think of any other secrets that I should know, please give me a call."

"Thank you for not telling Charlie about her real birth."

Sean nodded and began walking to the door.

"And Sean..."

He turned.

"When do you intend to ask my daughter out on a date?"

46

Charlie and Sherm pulled into the circular driveway of Anthony Capozzi's house in Ocean Forest Plantation at ten-thirty. It was a gorgeous house in the third row from the beach. Beach area lots on Spartina Island were priced by their size and how far away they were from the beach. Obviously, houses right on the beach were the most expensive, starting at around ten million dollars. A house one row back, exactly like one on the beach would sell for two or three million less, and the same house in the third row was worth another two or three million less. Still, no houses in the beach area of Ocean Forest Plantation could be considered affordable housing.

She and Lieutenant Billy Green had talked for a half hour about the wisdom of interviewing Anthony at this stage of the investigation and weighed the pros and cons of doing so. She told Billy that Sean had recommended against it, but that was before they had proof Eric Robinson was the thief who burglarized the house, which led to the conclusion that he stole the ruby pendant along with other jewelry.

They both had thought an initial interview to talk about the burglary was warranted. Billy reminded her to keep it casual, with no accusations that might trigger the necessity of a Miranda warning and no confrontation that would cause Anthony to think they suspected he was the killer. Since

Charlie had grown up with both Anthony and his wife, Kristin, she thought she could keep the conversation friendly.

She rang the doorbell, and Anthony opened the heavy oak door. He was around six-two and weighed at least two-fifty, looking like a stereotypical former high school football player who had gone to seed. His black hair was slicked back, and he wore a pair of blue jeans, a long-sleeved white shirt, and fancy cowboy boots, attire that could take him from a construction job site to a meeting with investors, she thought.

"Charlie, it's been a long time." Anthony opened his arms. Charlie didn't hug people on duty. It gave the wrong impression, and it was a major officer safety taboo, but if she were to keep the interaction relaxed and casual, she had to make an exception. He was, after all, an old high school friend, right?

She gave Anthony a loose hug. "It's nice to see you. Sorry it's under these circumstances. This is my partner, Detective Todd."

Sherm and Anthony shook hands. "Come on in. Kristin's in the back, and she's looking forward to seeing you."

They walked across the marble tile foyer, past a wood-paneled office and dining room, through a huge living room with a two-story ceiling, and into a glass-walled Carolina room that overlooked a backyard that could be a stop on a house tour showcasing the finest gardens on Spartina Island.

Kristin got up from a lounge chair and gave Charlie a cold embrace. Charlie smelled the odor of alcohol on her and wondered if she'd been drinking already this morning or if it was residue from a night of heavy drinking. Kristin was probably six feet tall, a good three inches taller than Charlie and weighed at least one-eighty. She didn't strike Charlie as being fat, but rather big boned and solid. She wore a dark green polo shirt tucked into Wrangler jeans.

"I keep on reading about you in the paper," Kristin said. "I still can't believe you became a cop."

"The career is interesting, and I like to think that what I do is about something much bigger than myself," Charlie said.

"You always were about having purpose in life," Anthony said.

After a few minutes of small talk about their families and local gossip,

Charlie asked if she could see the site of the burglary. Anthony and Kristin led them into a large master suite, complete with a four-poster canopy bed and a separate sitting area with a bar and gas fireplace. Down the hall were two walk-in closets, and beyond that was a spa-like bathroom. A full-length mirror was mounted in the hallway across from Kristin's walk-in closet. Anthony grabbed one side of the mirror and pulled on it. It swung away from the wall like a door, revealing a safe with a digital keypad.

"When we got home, the safe was open and cleaned out," Anthony said. "We can only figure we didn't lock it when we left."

"If you don't mind telling me, what was your combination?"

"It was the date we installed the safe," Kristin said, slurring her words. "We've since changed it."

Charlie nodded. "Your garage door also has a keypad. What was that combination?"

"Our wedding date," Anthony said. "I know. Not smart."

"If you're here to tell us we were stupid," Kristin said, staring at Charlie. "I've heard it from too many people already."

Charlie ignored her comment, but caught Sherm's eyes, which showed his shock at Kristin's outburst. "Were other areas of the house searched?"

"All the dresser drawers and my desk in the home office," Anthony said. "They took some cash and other pieces of jewelry: cufflinks, rings, and a few other less valuable necklaces and earrings of Kristin's."

They walked back to the Carolina room. "I noticed you have a home security system," Charlie said. "Did you set it when you left?"

"We were rushing to get ready," Anthony said. "Our driver was early, and I didn't want to make him wait, so I guess I forgot to turn it on. We hardly ever use it, so it's not a force of habit."

"We just got a hit on fingerprints found on the desk in your office," Charlie said.

"No prints on the safe?" Anthony asked.

"According to the burglary report, the deputy took elimination prints from you both when he responded. The only prints on the safe and the mirror that covered it were yours. Do you know someone by the name of Eric Robinson?"

They both shook their heads. She showed them his photo and carefully observed their reactions. They looked at each other for a few seconds. Charlie figured they were silently checking with each other to see if they should admit it.

Finally, Kristin said, "He was our driver."

"Your driver?" Charlie said, pretending she was surprised at the revelation.

"Oh, yeah," Anthony said. "He was the man who drove us to the airport."

"Any idea how he got the code to your garage door?"

Anthony shrugged. "When he arrived, he helped us with our luggage. We came out the front door and I locked it."

"But I realized I forgot my sunglasses," Kristin said. "I'd left them in my car."

Anthony smacked his forehead. "And I opened the garage door, using the keypad, while he was standing right there putting our suitcases in the back of his SUV."

"That could explain it. Do either of you know Courtney Evanson?"

They both shook their heads. "She was a bartender at the Atlantic Dunes," Charlie said.

"That Courtney," Anthony said. "Sure we know her."

"How'd you end up hiring Eric as your driver?" Charlie asked.

"That's right," Anthony said. "It was Courtney who gave me his name."

Charlie had figured out within a minute of talking with them that both Anthony and Kristin were not about to offer anything or even admit they knew Courtney and Eric until she shoved it in their faces. She wasn't sure if Anthony was lying about Colton Davis actually being the person who told him about Eric, or if he actually got Eric's number from Courtney and it was easier to gloss over the details.

"You know they're both dead?" Charlie said.

Again, Kristin and Anthony looked at each other before Anthony said, "We heard about Courtney. I stopped at the bar for a drink a few nights after, and everyone was talking about it. But Eric too?"

"Did you see Eric after he took you to the airport?"

"He picked us up when we returned," Anthony said. "But not after that. How'd he die?"

"We're not releasing those details at this time. Have you heard anything about their murders?"

"Like my husband said, we last saw Eric when he brought us back from the airport. We didn't even know he died. And all we know about Courtney is what Anthony heard at the bar and we saw in the paper."

"Which was?" Charlie asked.

"That someone killed her and then dumped her body on the beach." Kristin stood up from the chair in which she'd been sitting. She swayed and staggered two steps until she got her balance. "I'm not sure I like your tone and what you're insinuating."

Charlie smiled as she looked at Kristin, noticing her pupils were dilated even in the bright light of the room. "Kristin, I'm not insinuating anything. I'm investigating two homicides, and one of those victims burglarized your home and stole two hundred thousand dollars' worth of jewelry from your house. I'd be negligent if I didn't come here and talk to you about it."

"Yeah, right," Kristin said. "You never did like me. You and all your little friends from school and the country club. You always thought you were better than me."

Anthony put his hand on Kristin's shoulder and helped her into her chair.

Charlie nodded to Sherm then said, "We best be leaving. Thank you for your time."

Anthony followed them to the front porch. He closed the door and said, "I apologize for Kristin. She took a spill from her horse two years ago and had two back surgeries. She's still in pain and has been taking strong pain meds, which sometimes affects her personality."

"I had no idea she might still be holding onto grudges from high school," Charlie said. "The truth is, we ran in different crowds, and other than us saying 'hi' and 'bye' to each other, I don't recall us ever really talking."

"I'm sure it was just her pain medication talking."

"Can she still ride? I know that was her passion."

"She has good days and bad days, but on the good days she still rides. Her days of jumping, which she really loved, are over."

"I hope she feels better, and you might want to talk to her about mixing alcohol with her pain meds," Charlie said.

"I'll mention it to her again."

47

Sean stopped at Gladys's desk in CID. "Is the captain available?"

"Honey, despite what he might think, I'm not his personal secretary, I'm the division admin. If his door's open and he's inside, anyone can go in."

Sean figured he was wasting his time after what Billy had told him, but he wanted to give Cannon the benefit of the doubt before he went around him. Sean knocked on the door jamb and stepped inside. Cannon looked away from his computer monitor. "I'm busy as a dairy farmer during morning milking," Cannon said. "But what can I do for you?"

"I was wondering if you made any progress on that request to expedite the processing of the wallet?"

"I spoke to the lab director personally. Asked him to prioritize the matter. He reminded me it was just a missing persons case, but he'd do what he could."

"That doesn't sound very promising," Sean said. "Is there something I can do?"

"I'm not sure how y'all interact with your criminalistics laboratories in California, but down here, all we can do is ask real polite." Cannon shuffled through a stack of papers on his desk, wrote something on one and handed it to Sean. "Here's a copy of the lab request with the director's phone number. Feel free to call him yourself. Doubt he'll even talk to you though. He don't make it a practice to talk to anyone below the rank of captain."

Sean went next door, dropped into the chair in front of Billy's desk, and told him what happened.

"Just like I expected," Billy said. He picked up his phone, dialed a number, and spoke to someone for five minutes. Sean couldn't hear much of the conversations beyond "darling," "honey," "how's your boy doin'," and the mentioning of Sean's name several times. When Billy hung up, he wrote a phone number on a slip of paper, handed it to Sean, and said, "This is Blanche's phone number. She's expecting your call, but don't use your cell. Go into your new office and use a desk phone. That way it'll show up as Campbell County Sheriff CID on her phone display."

"That's it?"

"Once things settle down here, I'll set up a tour of SLED's crime lab for you folks on the cold case team. You'll go to Columbia, listen to their dog and pony show, act all impressed with how Southern forensic science is cutting edge, and collect a bunch of business cards from your new friends. And you'll bring several boxes of pastries."

"I'm learning that to expect favors from people down here, the secret is bringing a box of pastries," Sean said.

Billy shrugged. "Don't know. I just like pastries and it's not polite to eat them in front of folks without offering them one."

Sean sat at one of the empty workstations in the cold case team office and called the number Billy gave him. "Mr. Tanner, it's a pleasure to meet you. Lieutenant Green told me about you and how you were instrumental in solving the three murders in Campbell County last month. I did the DNA work on them. I knew I had heard your name before, so I did a quick web search, and then it came to me. You were the lead investigator on the Coffee Girl Murders!"

"You heard of them?"

"Heard? I was at a seminar in Atlanta a few years back where a presenter talked about the DNA work on that case and how it led you and other investigators to Columbia—the country, not our city—additional victims, and then in a grand finale, to the identification and arrest of the suspect."

"I didn't solve that case alone. It took some amazing work from Oakland PD's crime lab and a lot of other investigators and professional staff from a dozen different agencies."

"It will be an honor to work with you on this case. I already looked it up on the computer, and the problem is, it's listed as a missing person investigation. Unless it is DNA from a body that has not been identified, this is the lowest priority. What I'll do is change the subject to murder. That's why you're looking into it, because you suspect the missing person was possibly murdered, right?"

"Well, yes."

"I'm sure I don't need to tell you, not with all your experience working homicides, but the way we process DNA evidence these days is in batches. I'll add this to a batch we'll handle this week or shortly thereafter. I should have a profile for you by the end of next week at the latest. Give me your official email address, and I'll let you know as soon as we have results."

Sean talked with her for a few more minutes, asking where she was from, where she went to school, and the like. He stuck his head into Billy's office and gave him a thumbs up. "I should find a bakery in Columbia that delivers."

48

Sean was on his way out of the building when Charlie stepped out of her office. "How's your shoulder doing?"

He told her about his physical therapy, then said, "I came in to see your captain about the lab request on your father's wallet."

She raised an eyebrow. "And how'd that go?"

"Much as I expected, but Billy came through, and I had a nice conversation with a SLED lab tech who will prioritize it."

"Captain Cannon rarely uses his rank for our benefit, but Billy has friends everywhere."

"Any progress on your murders?" Sean asked.

She filled him in on her interview with Anthony and Kristin Capozzi. "Although there's no evidence to prove he killed Courtney and Eric, there's something about the burglary that doesn't feel right."

"I can understand Eric seeing them operating the garage keypad. That could get him into the house easily, but how would he know the safe combination? I don't buy that Anthony left it open."

"And the fact that we found Eric's prints on a desk, but nothing on the safe, which is where our crime scene tech would've devoted most of his efforts."

"Are you thinking insurance fraud?" Sean said.

"Could be. We found no jewelry at Eric's apartment. I'm assuming he found something more than the ruby pendant, but not whatever was in the safe."

"But we found a bunch of cash. Where'd a thief go to fence stolen jewelry on Spartina Island?"

"I know who would know." Sean followed Charlie down the hall toward the interview rooms. She stopped at the last door on the left where a sign read *Special Investigations.* They stepped inside. A man dressed in jeans and a black T-shirt sat at a corner workstation. Sean guessed he was around forty, but with his long hair and beard, he could've been younger.

"Sean, this is Sergeant Garrett Shilling," Charlie said, "He handles gangs and narcotics."

Garrett stood and shook Sean's hand. "Nice to meet you, Sean. I've heard great things about you."

Charlie told him about her murders and the burglary.

"There's an up-and-coming dope dealer named Jared Dorovic who's rumored to take jewelry as payment for drugs from his dealers and then fences the jewelry with his supplier down in Florida. We've done some surveillance on him, but so far, we're just learning his pattern and associates."

"Has the name Eric Robinson come up?" Charlie asked.

"Not that I recall, but I'd have to check surveillance logs. You said he's a chauffeur. When Dorovic isn't driving his brand-new, mid-engine Corvette, he likes to be driven around like a movie star."

Charlie left the office and returned a moment later with the ledger they had found in Eric Robinson's apartment. She opened it on Garrett's desk. "There are a number of entries showing *J.D.* followed by cash amounts."

Garrett scrolled through different documents on his computer. "An informant said Dorovic has been seen as a passenger in a black Escalade. Do you think he could be your killer?"

"We don't know enough to say he isn't," Charlie said.

Garrett jotted down the dates of the murders, made a phone call, then said, "SLED Narcotics is working with DEA on Dorovic's supplier in Florida. They said Dorovic was in Jacksonville around the time of both of those murders. They have no problem with us taking him down as a link to your murders, as long as they get to talk to him when we're done with him."

"I went after drug gangs plenty of times to solve murders back in Oakland," Sean said. "You need to have a hammer over them to get them to talk."

"Dorovic is a level up from the street dealers," Garrett said. "One of his dealers, an old man named Donnie Bowers, is probably the weakest link. He sells out of bars and mostly to the older crowd—people in their sixties or older, including people here on vacation."

"How old's this old man Bowers?" Sean asked.

"Mid-fifties at least," Garrett said. "I can pull his file."

Although it should've been obvious to Garrett, Sean was in his mid-fifties. Garrett must consider him an old man too. "Can you get a buy into Donnie Bowers and see if he'll flip on Dorovic?"

"We know Donnie hangs at Clancy's Sports Bar," Garrett said. "We've been meaning to try to buy from him, but my oldest undercover is in his thirties. We need a cop with lots of gray hair that isn't known around here."

"Although Sean is almost old enough, he'll look like a cop until the day he dies," Charlie said. "But I think we know some other old guys who might be able to help."

Twenty minutes later, Sean, Charlie, and Garrett met Frank, Irish John, and Stretch at Manuel's Restaurant and Cantina on Spartina Island. It was two-for-one-lunch-special day at Manuel's, and Sean had joined Stretch there for lunch before. Sean ordered fish tacos, and Charlie and Garrett both ordered beef enchiladas at the counter, then joined the other three at their table.

Charlie made the introductions and told Frank, Irish, and Stretch what she needed.

"My only undercover work was pretending I was a hit man when we heard a woman was looking for someone to kill her husband," Stretch said.

"I was the supervisor and undercover handler on a number of undercover operations," Frank said. "But me, buying drugs? No way."

"I worked Vice in my mid-twenties at Boston PD after my first stint in uniform," Irish said. "For two years, I basically picked up prostitutes and bought drugs for a living. But that was forty years ago."

"How many years ago?" Stretch said.

"Okay, closer to fifty." Irish picked up his second burrito and took a bite. "You need someone to pretend to be an old guy down here on vacation and looking to score some recreational drugs. You wouldn't tell my wife, would you?"

"Yeah, his wife would kick his ass if he got himself shot in a drug deal gone bad," Frank said.

"Donnie Bowers is the least dangerous dealer we've ever seen," Garrett said. "That's one of the reasons we've never really targeted him. He's small-time, and only deals weed, coke, and some pills. We're all known in Clancy's, but we can wire you up and get some video inside. We'll be right outside in case something goes sideways, but I can't imagine it."

Frank took a drink of his beer. "If you're using one of my guys on the cold case team, I need to be there as his handler."

Garrett looked at Charlie with furrowed eyebrows. She nodded.

"Okay," Garrett said, "You can be with me and Charlie in the surveillance van, but don't worry, we won't let anything happen to Irish."

49

Charlie rode in the front passenger seat of the white van as Garrett pulled into the back of Clancy's parking lot. On Saturday nights, the lot was packed, but on this Monday afternoon, there were only a half dozen cars there.

Garrett pointed out a light blue Honda CRV. "That's Donnie's car, so he should be inside."

With the darkly tinted windows and the sunshade Garrett placed on the front windshield, no one could see inside the van, as he and Charlie climbed into the back where Frank and Irish were sitting. Garrett opened a laptop on a table mounted along the left side of the van. It showed two camera feeds. The one from the miniature camera on the front of Irish's shirt showed Frank and Charlie as they sat in the van The other camera showed the ceiling of the van.

"Take off the baseball cap and hold it visor down," Garrett said to Irish.

The other screen now displayed Garrett as he sat at the worktable.

"Okay, so I go in and hang the hat on the coat rack so the button on the top is pointing to the middle of the bar," Irish said.

"Right," Garrett said. "From that camera, we can see everything in the bar, and the one you're wearing will show us everything in front of you."

"Got it," Irish said. "Say something on your radio so I can make sure these damn earbuds work."

Garrett whispered a five count softly into his microphone, then said, "The earbuds look exactly like hearing aids, so no one will think twice if they notice them. We can hear everything you hear or say."

"I'd feel lots better if you'd let me carry my gun," Irish said.

"We've covered that, Irish," Charlie said. "Retired vacationers from Boston don't carry guns. Besides, you've got me, Garrett, and two of his detectives right outside."

"And, you old fart, you haven't qualified with your firearm in ten years," Frank said.

"Neither have you, you old coot," Irish said.

"That's why I don't carry anymore," Frank said. "And because the bulge of a gun spoils the lines of my physique."

"I think we're all set if you are," Garrett said to Irish.

Irish John slid open the van's side door, stepped out, and walked into the bar.

Charlie and Garrett watched the camera feed on the laptop, showing Irish stopping just inside the door. The hat video feed blurred for a few seconds while Irish took it off his head and hung it on the coat rack. It then showed the interior of the bar, a bald-headed fiftyish man behind the bar, two other older men sitting at the bar, and two others at tables. Irish climbed onto a barstool. The bartender approached. "What can I get you?"

"You got Samuel Adams?"

The bartender pulled a bottle from the cooler and poured it into a frosty mug.

"Sure is hot down here," Irish said.

"Where you from?"

"You can't tell?"

The bartender laughed. "Sounds like you have a New England accent, and you drink Sam Adams. I'll take a wild guess and say Boston."

"Bingo. You don't sound like a Southerner yourself."

"Detroit originally. Been here five years and won't ever go back." The bartender waved his hand around the room to the ten TVs all showing different games. "Anything you want to watch?"

"The Red Sox ain't playing till tonight, so nothing's worth watching now."

For the next twenty minutes, Irish and the bartender debated pitchers and batters playing for the Tigers and Red Sox, as the bartender bounced between bar patrons to refresh their drinks.

"Let's get on with it," Charlie said to Garrett.

"He's an expert at this. We'll just let him do his thing," Garrett said. "Irish glanced around the bar when he entered and noticed Donnie sitting in the corner nursing a drink and playing on his phone. He then ignored him, because in his role, he wouldn't know him or even be concerned with him. He knows he has to make friends with the bartender for an introduction."

"How long will that take?" Charlie asked.

"As long as it takes," Garrett said. "I once went to the same bar every night for two weeks before I thought the bartender was comfortable enough with me to introduce me to a guy who would eventually sell me a bunch of fully automatic rifles."

"We don't have two weeks."

"Irish John knows that," Garrett said. "I had to learn patience when I first began doing surveillance and undercover assignments."

As much as she didn't like it, she went back to watching the video and listening to the audio.

"Friends in Boston told me not to risk even bringing a joint when I flew down here," Irish said. "Is it true that weed is really still illegal in South Carolina?"

The bartender chuckled. "Technically it is, but it's such a low-grade crime, the cops could care less as long as you're not selling pounds of it or smoking in front of an elementary school."

"Do you know where I can get some down here? And maybe some other stuff too?"

The bartender poured Irish another beer without him even asking. "What other stuff?"

"I'd love to get some coke. My wife said she wanted to try ecstasy before she died, but I hear that can make a woman crazy."

The bartender laughed. "Don't take this personally, but you might be

too old to do molly. I'd hate for you or your wife to have a heart attack while screwing all night long."

"You're probably right. We've been smoking weed and doing coke since we were in our twenties, but to tell you the truth, I'm not sure I'm all that interested in having all-night sex with a horny seventy-year-old woman."

The bartender waved his hand toward the back of the bar, and a minute later, a skinny man wearing blue shorts and a cheap-looking Hawaiian shirt climbed onto the barstool beside Irish. "Donnie," he said as he stuck his hand out.

"Irish John."

"How can I help you?"

Irish glanced at the bartender, who was mixing a drink for a customer at the other end of the bar. "I guess you're the guy who can tell me where I can get some weed and coke."

"How much you looking for?"

Irish pulled out his wallet and removed five twenty-dollar bills, the bills Garrett photocopied before he passed them to him.

"That'll get you a quarter ounce of quality weed and a gram of blow."

"Sounds fair."

Donnie reached for the money, and Irish pulled the money back. "Nothing personal, Donnie, but we just met. Show me the product and I'll hand over the cash."

Donnie nodded. "Drink your beer. I'll be right back."

"I'll take a leak while you're gone," Irish said.

Charlie watched Donnie exit the bar through the front door. He opened his car's trunk, stuffed something in his pocket, and disappeared back into the bar, where he reappeared on the computer screen. Meanwhile, Garrett turned the laptop away from Charlie so she wouldn't have to watch Irish at the urinal.

Irish said, "This might take a minute."

Frank grabbed the mic from Garrett and said, "I told you to see a urologist, you old fart. They have medication for that."

"Shut up, Frank," Irish said. "And get the real detective on the radio."

"I'm here," Garrett said. "Donnie went to his car, got something out of the trunk, and returned to the bar. When you're done in there, he'll be waiting on the same barstool."

Irish zipped his pants and left the men's room.

Charlie smiled. "It's not that I've never seen a man peeing, but I appreciate not having that image imprinted in my mind."

Irish returned to his barstool, took a swig of his beer, and turned to Donnie. Donnie pulled two small packages from his pocket and held them under the bar. Irish took them, slid them in his pocket, and handed the hundred dollars to Donnie.

Donnie handed him a card with his name and number on it. "Call or text if you need more. I'll even deliver if it's for a C-note or more."

Irish shook his hand, stood, and drained his beer. He waved at the bartender, left a twenty dollar bill on the bar, and headed to the door, where he grabbed his hat from the coat rack and pushed open the door.

50

"What are you doing the rest of the day?" Sean asked Stretch after the others had left the Mexican restaurant.

Stretch looked into his empty beer mug. "Sad to say, but lunch with those two cranky old geezers was the highlight of my day."

"Wish I could play golf or kayak."

"There must be some people we can go talk to on your case."

Sean drained the rest of his iced tea. "I need to interview Boyd Moretti and Roger Medcalf, but since they're the prime suspects, I'd like to know more about what happened before I talk to them."

"They were the last two people to see Henry Nash alive. Wouldn't that be a reasonable starting point if this were an active homicide case?"

"Yeah, but—"

"You've investigated way more murders than me, so I hate telling you how to run your case, but this thing has gone nowhere in ten years. It's time to stir things up. Shake the trees and see what falls out."

"You're right," Sean said. "I think I've been tiptoeing around this case because of Charlie and her family."

"You don't want to offend them. I get it. But you had a reputation in Oakland for allowing nothing to interfere with you getting your killers. Are you really going to allow the possibility of hurting Charlie's feelings to stop you from finding out who killed her father?"

"I'm already digging up secrets that the family would just as well prefer remain buried."

"Somewhere in those secrets might be the lead that will solve your case," Stretch said.

"That's some pretty wise thoughts for a Vermont country boy."

"I think I'm just recycling detective wisdom you've share with me before."

"Since we both have nothing going on in our lives, let's see if we can find something worthwhile to do." Sean pulled out his phone and made a call.

Thirty minutes later, Sean and Stretch sat in a bright conference room in a new office park in Dufftown. On tables against one wall were models of various developments on Spartina Island and Dufftown. A short, thin man in his mid-sixties entered. He had jet black hair that Sean figured was surely dyed.

"Mr. Tanner and Andrews, I'm Boyd Moretti." He walked to the head of the black laminate table in the center of the room and sat. "My lawyer would say I'm a fool for meeting with you without him, but I have nothing to hide."

Sean and Stretch sat down. "You know why we're here?" Sean said.

"I know you both work the sheriff's cold case team and have been reinvestigating the disappearance of my friend and former partner, Henry Nash. My first question is what gives you authority to question me?"

"Authority to do what?" Sean asked. "To sit and talk with people?"

"Touchè!" Moretti smiled. "Since you're not armed with a search warrant or taking me into custody for questioning, I guess one needs no special authority to talk."

"You can always call Sheriff Donohue to verify we have been assigned to investigate this case," Sean said.

"Not necessary. I've known for days that you've been nosing around. I'm surprised it has taken this long to get to me."

"In a criminal investigation, it's often best to gather background before interviewing key people."

"Do you mean suspects? Or persons of interest?"

"Mr. Moretti, I have not assigned a label to you," Sean said. "What I do know is you're the last known person to have seen Henry Nash alive."

"Are you assuming he's dead?"

"I avoid assumptions without supporting evidence, so I'm assuming nothing. However, if I were to give it a probability weight, I think there's about a ninety-five percent probability Henry Nash is dead."

"Does that mean you think Henry was murdered?"

"It's hard to prove cause of death without a body, so right now, I'm just gathering facts."

Moretti grinned. "Okay, ask away."

"Why don't you start with you and Henry agreeing to meet that night."

Moretti said Henry had called him early that evening, very angry about him initiating the survey for a new plan without consulting him. They met at the parking lot on the west side of the bridge that evening, a place they'd met and smoked cigars before. For the next half hour or so, they discussed, debated, and argued over the best way forward with the development of Sea Island Plantation. After they got nowhere toward a solution, Moretti and Roger Medcalf left.

"You just left?" Sean said. "There must've been some final words."

Moretti rolled his eyes. "Roger, being a lawyer, couldn't help himself. He threatened an injunction, a lawsuit, and other legal actions. Henry said he'd be talking to his attorney in the morning to get a restraining order preventing me from stepping foot on the property. That sort of thing."

"Did anything physical occur?" Sean asked. "Shoving, chest bumps, slaps, or punches?"

"We're businessmen. We don't resort to violence."

"Raised voices?"

"I guess so. We were all angry...or I think passionate about our beliefs would be a better description."

"Why were you so passionate about your new plan?"

"For decades, my family was the largest developer in the county. Then Henry showed up with a huge bag of money and deep pockets of credit from New York. I couldn't compete with him in large-scale developments, which was where the big profits were. I had approached Henry about buying the land for Sea Island. I needed him, not only for his half of the capital, but to convince my bank of the safety of the loan. We agreed to build two hundred houses total, and we figured we'd make a sizable profit."

"Then the recession hit," Sean said.

"Yes, and that would've pushed back any return on my investment by years. I was already taking a huge financial risk with a project that large, and if I needed to pay the loan for additional years, I could've lost everything."

"So you were desperate."

"Although I don't like your choice of words, yes, I was motivated to come up with a solution. Increasing the number of houses, more modest homes that would sell more quickly, was what I came up with."

"Did you discuss other alternatives?"

"Henry proposed buying out most of my share for a discounted rate, but that amounted to highway robbery. I would've walked away with nothing after all my years of work."

Although Sean didn't understand the world of real estate development and investing, he was beginning to feel for Moretti's plight. "It sounds like you were at an impasse. What was your plan moving forward?"

"Roger and I were going to meet the following day and discuss alternatives that we could present to Henry. We thought that once we all cooled off, we could work out something without resorting to legal action."

Although Sean and his fellow cold case team investigators had discussed getting a court order to see Moretti's financials, since he had admitted his desperate need to restructure the plans for the development, Sean no longer thought that was necessary. "You've probably heard that Henry's wallet and phone were found in his car's glovebox. Did you see him with those items that night?"

"When we first arrived, Henry was irritated that I'd brought Roger with me. He pulled out his phone and threatened to call his own attorney to come down, so it was definitely not in his car at that time."

"Some people assumed Henry might've taken his own life. What are your thoughts on that?"

"I told the detectives the next day the same as I'm telling you now, Henry wasn't depressed or suicidal in any way. He had the upper hand in our dispute. Looking back on it, I think Henry was just taking a strong initial position on what would've been days of negotiations. The end result would've been something we could both live with."

Sean exchanged glances with Stretch, who shook his head. "I've got to ask directly," Sean said. "Did you harm Henry Nash or know of anyone else who did?"

Moretti shook his head. "That's not my thing. Even as a kid, I avoided schoolyard fights. Roger might be aggressive, but it was just with his mouth. Like all good lawyers, he loved to debate and argue, but I can't imagine he'd ever lay a hand on someone. I've seen him get into shouting matches with other lawyers during settlement conferences and in court, but when it was over, they'd go out to lunch and talk about sports and such."

51

On their drive to Ocean Forest Plantation, Sean said, "Did Moretti strike you as a murderer?"

"No, but I arrested plenty of men who didn't strike me as being murderers," Stretch said.

"Me too. I learned long ago that everyone is capable of murder."

"After his initial hard-ass attitude, he seemed forthcoming about his financial situation and desperation to change the development plan."

"That still doesn't rule out them getting into a yelling match that escalated into a physical altercation," Sean said.

"And Henry suffering a fatal injury, even if it wasn't intentional."

"They'd still have to dispose of the body."

"Dump it in the water and let the tides and sea life take care of it," Stretch said. "That still doesn't account for how Henry's wallet and phone ended up in his car."

"I've been thinking about that. Either the killer wanted it to look like a suicide, thinking the victim would leave those items behind for the benefit of his family, or the killer was close to the Nash family and left those items for them."

"If it's the latter, that adds weight to the possibility of it being an accidental homicide, something that was the unfortunate result of a shove or simple punch," Stretch said. "I guess we'll see how we feel once we talk to Attorney Medcalf."

Sean parked in the driveway of a huge Mediterranean-style house that overlooked the sixteenth fairway of the Ocean Forest Golf Links. Sean had read the background Feebee did on Roger, which showed when he and Charlie divorced ten years ago, Roger bought a 3500-square-foot house in Ocean Forest. Five years ago, he bought this much larger house for twice what he sold the old one for.

When Sean had called Medcalf upon leaving Moretti's office, he was surprised that Roger was willing to meet with them. He said he was working out of his home office, and they could come by. Roger answered the door dressed in a floral golf shirt and white shorts. He was just shy of six feet tall and looked to be a soft 190 pounds. Sean guessed the only exercise he got was walking from his golf cart to the putting green.

"Detectives," he said. "Come in. Let's go to the back." He led them to a great room that overlooked the pristine golf course. "I would offer you something to drink, but I can't imagine this taking long."

"In that case, let's get right to it," Sean said. "What brought you to the meeting with Boyd Moretti and Henry Nash the night he disappeared?"

"Boyd called me and said Henry wanted to meet at the bridge parking lot that night. Boyd and I had planned to get a preliminary survey for our new plan for Sea Island Plantation and then meet with Henry to convince him of its feasibility. Henry found out about it before we were ready and insisted we meet."

"We spoke to Mr. Moretti about your meeting with Henry, but we'd like your version of what occurred," Sean said.

"Ah, yes, the old detective trick of focusing on any differences in our stories to accuse one of us of lying. I won't go there. Whatever Boyd said is what happened."

"How do you know what Boyd said?"

"Mr. Tanner, I apologize for previously referring to you as detective, since you are a civilian, the same as me, but so long as you don't assume Boyd and I conferred to concoct a story between us, don't you think it reasonable that when Boyd's business partner goes missing, and we were the last ones to have seen him, that we would've talked about it at length over the years?"

Sean was accustomed to attorneys asking long, multi-part questions to confuse witnesses on the stand, so Roger's long response that he turned into a question was typical for Roger's profession. He was not about to allow Roger to turn the tables on him and become the questioner. "I understand the discussion that evening became rather heated."

"Whatever Boyd's response to your obvious question, which you presented as a statement, you can use as my response to the same."

"I get it." Sean looked around the house and at the view through the sliding glass doors that opened to a spacious patio. "You've come a long way from your government legal position with the coastal commission."

"Thank you. I have."

"How's it work in your type of law? Do you bill hourly or work on a percentage of the contract?"

"Not that it should be your concern as someone investigating a missing person, but in this type of law, we can get paid either way. When I left the coastal commission and first went into private practice, I billed by the hour. As I became better known and my own financial situation improved, I worked on commission. It can be riskier, but more lucrative in the long term."

"So in a sense, you owned a percentage of Boyd Moretti's half of Sea Island Plantation?"

"In a sense, that's correct."

"So you stood to benefit from the greater number of homes in Moretti's plan as compared to Henry's initial plan."

"Does that make me part of some sort of evil cabal conspiring to eat up all of nature and turn it into housing and retail development?"

"I understand you were instrumental in convincing Abigail Nash to go along with your plan once Henry was out of the picture."

"*Out of the picture*, wow, that is loaded language. If we were in court, the judge would sustain you and direct you to rephrase the question. I will, however, respond because I know you're trying to rile me up so I'll say something that you can use against me. I presented Abigail with the facts. She made twice the profit as she would've under Henry's plan."

"As did you and Moretti," Sean said. "But that wasn't Henry's or Charlie's vision for the development."

"I admit to being rather idealistic in law school, believing I should use my time and new skills for the public good. I then saw that no matter what I did, the elite would still become wealthier. Except in a pure, utopian, socialistic society, making money is not evil, so I figured I should be allowed to get paid properly for my work."

"In the criminal justice system, there were lawyers who started off as prosecutors then went into private practice as criminal defense lawyers to make money," Sean said. "We said they went over to the dark side."

"So to you, working for developers is that same dark side?'

Sean shrugged. "I guess there is socially responsible land development and then there's other development that is solely focused on making money for the developers to the detriment of what's best for society."

"Are you saying Henry Nash was socially responsible, but the different vision that Boyd and I proposed was not?"

"From what I hear, Henry would've never agreed to your plan for Sea Island Plantation."

"Let me guess, you heard that from my ex-wife."

Sean shrugged.

"Charlie lives in la-la land. She had a huge trust fund and a daddy that would always take care of her, so she never had to worry about making a living. Even now, she's just playing detective. She doesn't need to work there to put a roof over her head or pay our son's college expenses. I've read about you and your work with her on those crimes last month. She's got you hoodwinked. The beautiful blonde who's dedicating her life to law enforcement. Wait until you see the real Charlotte Nash, the ice queen, who pretends she's a commoner, but is nothing but a spoiled rich girl."

Sean felt his face getting flushed. "You best be careful how you talk about her."

Roger grinned. "So the rumors about you two are true. I can see how that tight little body of hers has got you mesmerized. But just wait, and you'll see how it will turn on you if you don't let her have her way all the time. That's what spoiled, rich, trust-fund babies demand."

Sean rose from his seat and was getting ready to tell Roger exactly what he thought of him, when Stretch put his hand on his arm.

"Thank you for your time," Stretch said. "We'll see our own way out."

Sean stood there for a solid minute and glared at Roger. He hoped Roger would make a move. Lay a hand on him. Something that would justify him beating him to a pulp. But Roger just sat there grinning.

"Come on, Sean," Stretch said. "It isn't worth it."

Sean nodded and followed Stretch out of the house.

52

Charlie let Garrett debrief Irish John and collect his remaining buy money, earbuds, and cameras while she went right to her office. Darryl was hanging up his blazer and getting ready to sit down at his desk. "You just got back?" Charlie said.

"Yeah, the pathologist assigned to our case had to testify in court, so they handed it off to another one who didn't get started until late," Darryl said.

"What did they find?"

"A bunch of busted bones," Darryl said. "Cause of death was asphyxiation."

"A fractured tibia," Doc said. "The medical examiner and I concurred that took a powerful blow with a hard impact instrument. Also at least seven fractured bones in his hand. Had he survived, his hand would never fully function. Fractures of the skull with indentations consistent with blows from a hard impact weapon. Brain hemorrhage, which might've killed him, but the plastic bag over his head caused his death first."

"What about Sean and my theory that this was torture?"

Doc took a deep breath then said, "That's beyond what a postmortem exam can ascertain, but the progression of subdural hemorrhage indicates the injuries likely began with the tibia, where it appears the assailant struck him in the shin numerous times, which would've caused significant pain. The blows became increasingly greater until the tibia fractured."

"Can you tell which one occurred first?"

"The injuries to the leg and hand especially showed significant hematoma, which is a bad bruise. It's caused when the capillaries rupture from a traumatic injury and pool under the skin. If I were to guess, and it would be mostly a guess based on the coloring of the different hematomas, I'd say the tibia injury occurred first, followed by the hand injury, and finally the blows to the head."

"Thanks, Doc," Charlie said. "We sure appreciate you helping out." Charlie returned to the special investigations office, where Garrett and two of his detectives were talking around a table filled with packages of narcotics, while watching a computer screen showing Donnie sitting in an interview room. "We arrested him without incident," Garrett said. "He gave consent, and we searched his car. My guys will inventory everything and weigh it, but it looks like several thousand dollars' worth of marijuana, cocaine, methamphetamine, and an assortment of pills we've yet to identify."

"What kind of time would he be looking at?"

"Sales alone of coke can be fifteen years. We don't need to tell him that judges never give that to a first-time offender."

"Shall we go talk to him?"

"You're not going to mention the murders are you?"

"I think it would be easier to get him to flip if he thinks this is just over drugs," Charlie said.

"I'll then introduce you as one of my narcotics detectives."

Charlie undid her bun and shook out her hair, then pulled her shirttail from her pants and unbuttoned two top buttons of her shirt.

"Not quite grungy enough, but you'll pass to Donnie," Garrett said.

They walked into the room and sat on opposite sides of Donnie.

"Donnie, I'm Garrett," Sergeant Garrett Shilling said. "This is..." he paused. "Carol. We work narcotics."

"This is entrapment. That old guy isn't a cop."

"He's what we call a citizen agent," Garrett said. "You know, like if we want to bust the Enmarket for selling beer to minors, we send in a sixteen-year-old police explorer. Well, in this case, we sent in an old guy who volunteered to help us out."

"That can't be legal."

"It is. I already spoke to the district solicitor, and he says it's not only legal, but we need to throw the book at drug dealers that prey on the elderly."

"I have a clean record."

"That can help. The judge might give you a few years less than fifteen. But, if you want to work with us..."

"I'm no snitch."

"Okay." Garrett got up from his chair, stepped to the door, then turned. "How old are you, Donnie?"

"Fifty-six."

"Let's see, fifty-six plus fifteen. The good news is that when you get out, you'll be eligible for social security."

"Wait. I can't go to prison?"

"You can avoid most or all of that time if you tell us what you know and work with us."

"That old guy, was he a snitch?"

"Oh, yeah, deputies busted him and his wife for smoking a doobie outside their hotel. He didn't want to sit in jail, so he worked for us. His arrest is gone. He gets to go home to his grandkids without a criminal record."

"What do you want?"

"Who's your supplier?"

"Oh, man, he's bad news. He'll kill me."

"Donnie, do you think you'll last fifteen years in a South Carolina prison? Work with us and we'll help you relocate when this is done if that's what you want."

"A guy called J.D."

Garrett showed him a photo of Dorovic, and Donnie nodded. "Walk me through the process of how you re-up from him."

They spent the next half hour talking with Donnie about everything he knew about Jared Dorovic and his drug network. Garrett put Donnie's phone on speaker and returned it to him. "Remember, you tell him that you'll have the money ready anytime tomorrow afternoon."

Donnie placed the call. "Donnie, my main man, how ya doin'?"

"Good J.D. Business is good. I'm running low."

"How much ya got to spend?"

"Like last time, five G."

"What do ya need?"

"Weed, blow, and oxy. The old guys are loving the oxy this month."

"Send me a text with how much you want to put on each. I can have it ready tomorrow morning."

Garrett grabbed Donnie's face and turned his head to make him look at him. He shook his head.

"I got a doctor's appointment in the morning. Can we make it the afternoon?"

"Send me the list. Be available at two o'clock. I'll text you the location tomorrow."

"Okay, and J.D., one of the dudes I take care of has come into some jewelry. He wants to trade that for product. Do you do that?"

"Donnie, these two-bit thieves are more trouble than they're worth. You don't know a diamond from cubic zirconia, so you're smart if you only take cash. If you come across a big score—and by that I mean at least fifty G worth of quality jewelry—then we can talk."

"Okay. I'll shoot you the text in a minute."

Garrett ended the call.

"I can go home now?" Donnie said. "Call you tomorrow when he texts?"

"Donnie, Donnie, Donnie," Garrett said. "Right now we text him your order, sort of like ordering food with DoorDash. Tonight you get your own private cell in county detention. No phones, no contact with other inmates. Tomorrow we bring you back here and wait for J.D.'s text and go from there."

"You ain't gonna get me killed, are you?"

"Not to worry, Donnie. My boss gets real pissed when someone working with me gets killed."

Charlie arrived home at 8:30 p.m. after spending several hours at her desk writing up everything she did throughout the day. She was startled when she came in through the kitchen door and saw her mother sitting at the breakfast table in the dark with a decanter of sherry in front of her.

"Mom, what are you doing here?"

"Charlotte, please sit down. I need to tell you something. You should get yourself a glass because you're going to need a drink after you hear what I have to say."

53

TUESDAY

Charlie awakened in Ray and Jacque's cozy guest room. Her head was pounding, and her mouth tasted like it was full of pluff mud. She stumbled into the en suite bathroom and found bottles of aspirin and ibuprofen. She popped two of each and stepped into the shower. After she toweled herself off, she ran a comb through her wet hair, wrapped herself in a thick robe she found hanging on the door, and made her way to the kitchen.

Ray was sitting at the table with a cup of coffee and iPad in front of him. "How are you feeling?

"Like a quartet of tiny percussion musicians are banging their cymbals inside my head."

After her mother had told her she had actually been born nearly two months earlier than she'd believed her whole life, she was unable to speak. Her entire life had been a lie. That endearing story of her origin—the baby that was so eager to enter the world that she couldn't wait to go to the hospital—was a lie. The people dearest to her—her parents, her mother's parents, even Rose—allowed her to live that lie. The truth was, she was nothing special. She'd been born in a hospital like everyone else. People had told her she was big for her age as an infant. She wasn't. She was actually two months older than the fictitious birth certificate that had become her official entry into the world. That fake date had been when she celebrated her birthday, signified when she could get her driver's license at sixteen, and would even mark when she'd officially qualify for social security benefits.

Charlie couldn't remember ever seeing her mother cry, but her eyes had glistened with tears last night at the kitchen table. She begged Charlie to forgive her. She made excuses and tried to justify what she had done. Charlie went into the library and locked the door. She didn't want to hear any more lies. That had been her father's room, and he had never locked the door. Even when he was working at the roll-top desk, she and her brothers were always welcome. She could almost accept her mother had lied to her, but her father too? That hurt even more.

She had gone to the liquor cabinet in the corner of the room. Their town of Dufftown was named after a burgh of the same name in Scotland, which produced more whiskey than any other town in Scotland. Her father collected Scotch whiskies from all of the distilleries in Scotland's Dufftown, the most famous being Glenfiddich. She hardly ever drank hard liquor, but if there was ever a time to partake, Charlie figured this was it. She selected a bottle of Glenfiddich Millennium Reserve and poured three fingers into a crystal glass. After a third, or maybe a fourth, she couldn't remember, she knew she couldn't stay in the house and called Ray.

Ray poured a cup of coffee and a glass of green stuff from a blender. "Drink this," he said.

"What is it?"

"You don't want to know, but it's good for you."

She drank the green stuff. It wasn't horrible. "I'm sorry about last night."

"Whatever happened must be awful."

She told him what her mother had shared with her last night.

"Wow," was all he said.

"My whole life is a lie. All the people I trusted betrayed me."

"This doesn't change who you are. I know your mother had her reasons. It doesn't justify it, but it might explain it. One thing I do know is your mother, in her own way, has always loved you with all her heart. And you know your father did as well."

"I know my father loved me, but he's gone. And I now feel so alone."

Ray pulled her to her feet and wrapped his arms around her. "I'm here. Jacque is here. You have two brothers and many friends and co-workers who love and respect you. You are definitely not alone."

After several minutes, Charlie slipped out of Ray's arms, sat down, finished the rest of the green drink, and took a few gulps of coffee. "Speaking of Jacque..."

"She went over to your house to pick up some fresh clothes for you. We figured you wouldn't want to show up at work wearing the same clothes as yesterday, especially when you look like you closed down the Sandy Feet Bar."

"I'm not very good at getting drunk."

Ray laughed. "I think that's a good thing. How did this come up after so many years?"

"The cold case team did background on my father to see if anyone in his past might've had a reason to hurt him. They found I had two birth certificates. The one that showed I was born in the hospital in Asheville never developed a life history, no school records, no social security card, no nothing. That baby Charlotte ceased to exist after she left the hospital. Sean Tanner asked my mother about it, and she told him everything."

"I think everyone has secrets they don't want the world to know. I'm sure that your mother never considered how hurtful this would be for you."

"Sean should've told me."

"In his role as the investigator into your father's disappearance or as your friend?"

"If he were a friend, that should trump everything. Withholding it from me is no different than lying. He betrayed me too."

"Don't friends sometimes withhold things that could be hurtful?"

"I'm not some delicate little Southern belle. I'm tough and can take anything. Except friends lying to me."

Just then, Jacque came in carrying a light gray suit on a hanger and a paper bag. "I think I got everything you need," she said. "There's a blow dryer in the guest bath and I can set you up with makeup or other things you need."

"Did you see my mother?"

"She let me in and helped pick out your clothes. After seeing her condition this morning, I did learn one thing."

"What's that?" Charlie asked.

"If I were ever planning to get stinking drunk, I'd sooner do it on twenty-year-old Scotch than Palo Cortado sherry."

54

The Dufftown Diner was the oldest, continuously operated restaurant in Dufftown and Spartina Island. It sat on the north side of Cusseta River Road, which was the original road to Spartina Island, before there was a bridge and the four-lane Spartina Island Road. The diner was housed in a rustic, wood-sided building surrounded by two-hundred-year-old live oaks.

Sean stepped through the doorway and slipped his sunglasses into his pocket. The large room was filled with mismatched tables and chairs, some tables that would accommodate only two people and two large ones for eight. A counter with ten stools ran along one side of the room, behind which was the kitchen, partially visible over a half wall.

A heavy-set man wearing dark blue slacks and a white, button-front shirt waved at him from a table in the far corner. Sean made his way through the breakfast crowd that filled every other table to the man sitting with his back to the wall. He stood and offered his hand. "Mr. Tanner, thank you for accepting my invitation."

Sean had just showered after returning from a long walk with Annie when he'd gotten the call from Clinton Cannon II. He'd never met the man, but he knew of him. The father of Captain Cannon, Cannon II had been the sheriff for twenty-five years, assuming the position from his father, who had been the sheriff for the previous twenty years. Sean shook his hand and sat across from him. "How could I refuse?"

A server wearing a brown apron set a huge plate of food in front of Cannon. "Do you need a menu?" she asked Sean.

"I'll just have coffee."

"You're missing out," Cannon said. "I've been eating breakfast here for more than fifty years. Always have the same thing."

Sean looked at his plate filled with three sunny-side-up eggs, a pool of grits dripping with butter, and a large biscuit covered with sausage gravy. "That's okay. Coffee is fine."

The server left and Cannon began dicing up his eggs and forking them into his mouth. "You've made quite a name for yourself in the short time you've been here, Mr. Tanner."

"Just trying to help out the sheriff's office where I can."

"My son says much the same. You were an immense help with that cold case last month. Made for some good press for the department. I must tell you, though, you're making some folks awful uneasy with some of your questions about Henry Nash's disappearance."

"Really? Who am I making uneasy?"

Cannon waved his hand as if he were shooing away a fly. "The interest in what happened to poor Henry had dwindled over the years to about nothing. Now, folks are starting to talk about it again, saying it might've been a murder. Makes folks worry they've been living with a killer in their midst the past ten years."

"You were the sheriff back then. Were you comfortable with the belief that he had committed suicide?"

Cannon shoveled some grits into his mouth, put his fork down, and wiped his mouth with a paper napkin. "You've been a death investigator for a long time. Not as long as I've been in law enforcement, but still a long time. You must agree you don't always reach a conclusion with every investigation. That some cases always have unanswered questions."

"Sure, after I had done everything humanly possible, the answers in some cases still eluded me."

"Exactly. That's where my son found himself with that case."

"Is it Captain Cannon who's feeling uneasy with my inquiries?"

"How'd you feel if some young detective started scrutinizing one of your old unsolved homicides back in Oakland?"

"If someone else could bring a killer to justice when I was unable to, I'd cheer him on. I'd like to know who else is feeling uncomfortable with my investigation. Seems to me, the person who feels most uncomfortable might be the person who killed Henry."

"None of us, not me, not my son, would get in the way of you finding a murderer. But you're digging into areas that have nothing to do with his disappearance."

"Since we didn't have a video camera shooting footage of what happened that night, I have to start by investigating my victim and those close to him. Isn't that what you would do with a murder with no eyewitnesses and no physical evidence?"

"I understand you're looking into Henry's and Boyd's financials."

"Greed is often a leading motive for murder," Sean said. "What are people afraid I'll find?"

"Mr. Tanner, things were different in Campbell County and at the state house up in Columbia in years past. Getting things done sometimes required more than just asking nice or presenting a valid proposal. Henry realized that when he showed up down here dressed in his New York City duds forty-five years ago, back when my daddy was sheriff. Henry visited Columbia, wined and dined the right folks, and wrote checks for the right campaigns. Boyd's daddy did the same. You don't think we got our first bridge to Spartina Island by just asking nice."

"And local zoning laws and building permits," Sean said. "Did that take wining and dining and such at the county level? Did contributions to your reelection campaigns every four years as sheriff affect how you allocated police services?"

Cannon waved at the server, who removed his plate and poured them both more coffee. "I don't know what you think you know, but I don't like what you're inferring."

Sean hadn't intended to reveal what Feebee and Beagle had discovered in their background on the Cannon family, but since he'd already gotten a rise from Cannon, he figured he'd poke the bear a little more. "We looked at the county budget for every year you were sheriff. Your salary was pretty modest, even by rural South Carolina standards, yet you live in a house that is worth close to two million dollars, and you've been a member of the Cusseta Country Club going back forty years. Not even talking about the buy-in, the monthly dues for that club membership would take a huge chunk of your monthly pension. Even in South Carolina, political contributions have been public record for a while now, and we couldn't help but notice one of the largest contributors to your reelection campaigns was Boyd Moretti."

"You never cease to surprise me, Mr. Tanner. Not only that you would investigate me, but that you have the balls to lay it out in front of me. We Southerners are more polite than that. We might think it and even hint around that we know something, but we'd never come right out and accuse a man of corruption. Here's the gospel truth, and I *am* a churchgoing, God-fearing man. Yes, when Henry went missing and my boy was the detective sergeant on the case, I told him not to drag Boyd to the station and grill him. Not because Boyd was one of my supporters, but because it was a damn missing person investigation. Unless you have some evidence of foul play, you don't drag people to the station just because they were the last one to see a person who went missing."

Cannon drained the rest of his coffee and continued. "After time went by and Henry never appeared and his body was never found, we considered the possibility of murder. But by whom? Boyd is a developer who might grease some palms, and Roger Medcalf might be a slimebag attorney. But murderers? That's not how they do business. And me, as a sheriff, would never take a payoff to let a murderer skate."

Sean didn't really expect Cannon to confess to taking graft or whitewashing the investigation to protect Moretti and Medcalf. But if Cannon's purpose for this little breakfast meeting was to get Sean to back off, he now knew he'd wasted his time.

Cannon stood and dropped a twenty dollar bill on the table. "Why don't you just sit here and enjoy your coffee. Someone else wants a moment of your time."

55

Sean moved to the chair Cannon had been sitting in. He felt more comfortable with his back to the wall, and where he could watch the door. A moment later, Captain Clinton Cannon III came in and sat down across from him. He was the only man in the diner wearing a suit and tie.

"Did you have a nice meeting with my daddy?" Cannon asked.

"He seems like a nice man."

"He said he tried to educate you about our culture down here."

"Have you ever read the homicide investigator's creed?"

"Never heard of it," Cannon said.

"I know it by heart," Sean said. "*No greater honor will ever be bestowed on you as a police officer, or a more profound duty imposed on you than when you are entrusted with the investigation of the death of a human being. It is your moral duty, and, as an officer entrusted with such a duty, it is incumbent upon you to follow the course of events and the facts as they develop to their ultimate conclusion. It is a heavy responsibility. As such, let no person deter you from the truth or your personal conviction to see that justice is done.*"

"Kinda like a dog with a bone. You just ain't gonna let go."

Sean nodded.

"Even if what you find hurts a lot of people who had nothing to do with Henry's disappearance?"

"Let's call it what it is. Henry didn't disappear. He was murdered and his body was disposed of."

"Let's say you're right. How do you prove it?"

"I keep digging. I keep asking questions. You could've helped at the beginning by turning over your file to me."

"I told you I'd write up them notes for you."

"That was five days ago. I had to find out on my own that it wasn't just Moretti who met Henry that night. Nowhere in the official reports you gave us did it even mention Roger Medcalf. I've taken over investigations from detectives before, and they hand over everything. If you make me a copy of your notes, I can come back and ask you about anything I can't read or understand."

"And you were supposed to keep me updated on your investigation," Cannon said.

"You mean like telling you I interviewed Roger, who you intentionally withheld from your report? Or tell you that I spoke to a nice woman at the SLED DNA lab who will expedite my request to have the blood on the wallet typed, after you said you would have that done yourself? Captain, I've worked for a bunch of command officers in Oakland who didn't exactly do much to help me, but I never experienced one who tried to prevent me from solving a case."

Cannon's face turned red. "Is that an indirect way of accusing me of—"

"You tell me, do you want us to find out who killed Henry Nash?"

"Of course, but..."

"But don't upset anyone in the process, right?"

"That's not what I was going to say." Cannon leaned forward in his chair. "Do you think Moretti or Medcalf killed him?"

"I don't know. They had several million motives measured in dollar signs."

"Who else had a motive?" Cannon said.

Sean paused for a moment as he thought about how much he should reveal to Cannon. "Henry had a brother in New York, who Henry went up against in a bankruptcy filing. Also several million motives. And Henry worked overseas for the State Department before he moved here and may have run afoul of some people."

"I never heard anything about either of those."

"Of course not. It was just a missing persons case back then, right?"

"I did the best I could at the time."

"I know," Sean said, although he wasn't sure he believed it.

"You know I could pull you off this case."

Sean locked eyes with Cannon. "Could you?" It was a risk to challenge the captain, but Sean wanted him to know he could go straight to the sheriff if Cannon followed through with his threat. He wondered if winning this little battle with Cannon might cause him to lose the war.

"I'll make a copy of everything in my file as soon as I get back to the office and leave it with Gladys. But if you don't tread a bit more lightly and stop accusing everyone in the county of killing Henry Nash, we will have another conversation."

56

Sean walked onto the back deck of Bubba's Shrimp Shack at noon. A fishing boat motored down the river under a cloudless blue sky. If it weren't for the thermometer reading ninety-three, the negligible breeze, and the heat index well over a hundred, it would've been a perfect place to eat lunch. Stretch, Feebee, Beagle, and Doc were there. He ordered a grilled fish sandwich and iced tea and pulled up a chair closest to the industrial-strength fan. "Where's Frank and Irish?"

"They worked with Sergeant Nash doing a drug buy yesterday connected to her homicides," Doc said. "They're helping again today."

Sean felt hurt that Charlie would ask them to help out on her active murder cases instead of him. Maybe she figured he was too occupied with his own case. Her current murders were also linked to the cold case of Sarah Fitzpatrick, which Irish and Frank had worked, so Sean supposed it made sense for them to work with her.

"I accompanied Detective Darryl Pickett to the autopsy of Eric Robinson for her yesterday," Doc said.

Everyone was working with Charlie, except for him, Sean thought. "I think I made an enemy of our good captain and his father." He told them about his meeting with the Cannons.

"Beagle and I spent both afternoons this past weekend at the Cusseta

Country Club," Doc said. "I'm a member and pretended I was showing Beagle around as a prospective new member."

"Hey, how come you didn't ask me to be your pretend prospective member?" Stretch said.

"Because you look and act like a north woods hick," Feebee said. "Beagle is a lot more cultured."

Doc ignored Feebee's jab at Stretch. "It gave us the opportunity to talk to a lot of people I don't normally speak with under the auspices of introducing Beagle. As we had discovered, Cannon II is a social member, but he doesn't golf or have anything to do with the stables. He's one of the dealmakers there, introducing people to each other and that kind of stuff. The Nash family has been members forever, but other than Abigail, the rest of the family, her two sons, their families and Charlie, don't spend much time there. Plenty of people knew Henry Nash. Everyone liked him, despite him being a Yankee. And yes, many people called him that. Many members were happy to tell us their opinion about what happened to him, but no one knew anything besides rumors."

"What about the Capozzis?" Sean asked, still interested in Charlie's investigations even though he'd apparently been put on the sidelines.

"Ann is there a lot," Beagle said. "Lunches and card games with other older women. A lot like Abigail Nash. Anthony golfs there once a week or so and then has drinks afterward, but it's Kristin who's there most days. She has two horses in the stable and often spends three or four hours a day there."

"We'll go back this afternoon," Doc said. "The story we'll use is that Beagle's granddaughter is into horses, so if he becomes a member, she would like to take riding lessons. That might allow us to get close to Kristin and learn more about Anthony."

"It feels like we're spending more time and effort on Charlie's homicide cases than our own investigation," Stretch said.

"You're starting to sound like Frank," Feebee said.

"Frank, the guy who's off working an active case with the sheriff's detectives rather than attending a Mudflats Murder Club meeting?" Stretch said.

"There's no reason we can't do both," Sean said. "I don't know about the rest of you, but it's not like I have anything more important to do. Just be sure to shoot Charlie an email if you uncover anything relevant to her cases. Anything new on your Henry Nash background and financial sleuthing, Feebee?"

"You already know what I discovered about Cannon II. It doesn't appear like Captain Cannon has any money coming in apart from his sheriff's salary. When he ran for sheriff he had a campaign account, but everything seemed up and up. When the campaign was over and he lost, the account had a few thousand left in it, but it hasn't been touched or added to. He's either clean or he doesn't flaunt his graft like his father does."

Sean was glad Feebee mentioned nothing about Charlie's double birthdates in front of the others. It didn't seem like that had anything to do with Henry's disappearance, so there was no reason to mention it in their reports or tell anyone else.

"I also did some background on Ray Mitro," Feebee said. "As you documented after your first interview with him, he moved to the U.S. when he was fourteen. Although he said he was from Slovakia, his visa shows he immigrated from Austria with his mother on a special business nonimmigration visa. They settled in Clairton, a former steel mill town near Pittsburgh, and two years later, his mother's status was changed to permanent immigrant E-3, which is for skilled workers. The employer that sponsored her was Henry Nash, Senior, the president of the New York City commercial real estate development empire and our Henry Nash's father."

"That's interesting," Sean said.

"Ray later attended Penn State and got a degree in chemical engineering. He became a U.S. citizen upon graduation, then worked for different oil companies as an energy consultant, including several contracts with the U.S. government. His mother passed away fifteen years ago. He sold his consulting business ten years ago for twenty mil and paid for his house and his gym with cash."

"I think we need to reinterview him," Sean said.

"Let me know," Feebee said. "I'd love to go with you."

57

Charlie heated up a microwave dinner in the breakroom for lunch and brought it back to her desk. Her hangover headache had dissipated, and she was starting to feel halfway normal. Irish and Frank had arrived at 9 a.m., and she paired them up with Sherm and Jay to reinterview everyone they could find from the Sarah Fitzpatrick case. It was always best to have two investigators conduct key interviews, so by using the cold case team members, Sherm and Jay could cover twice the territory.

She was convinced that Marco Capozzi had killed Sarah, and she was hoping someone her detectives spoke to could help her prove it. From there, it would be easier to make the leap that Marco passed on the ruby pendant to Anthony, and then Eric Robinson stole it, which set him and Courtney up to be murdered by Anthony. She realized this was nothing more than a theory at this time, but hoped that if Jay and Sherm turned up something and the drug operation this afternoon got people talking, she'd be on the way to solving these murders.

She was eating her last spinach artichoke ravioli when Garrett came through her office door. "I have Donnie in an interview room with one of my guys waiting for the text from Dorovic."

"Do you know yet where Dorovic stores his drugs?"

"We're pretty certain he doesn't keep them in his fancy apartment,"

Garrett said. "SLED narcs have had him under surveillance since last night. He bedded down around midnight, drove to his gym at eight this morning in his fancy Corvette, then ate breakfast at a place on the water. He picked up another dude, who we haven't yet identified, and just returned to his apartment."

"It's your operation, but what's your plan for arresting Dorovic?"

"In the drug world, you have to be flexible. We'll wire up Donnie and let him make the meet. I'll have my team shadow him. Meanwhile, the state narcs will follow Dorovic to wherever he keeps his stash and then to the meet. After Donnie gets his product and Dorovic goes on his way, we'll grab Donnie and do a field test to verify it's actually illegal narcotics. At that time, we can arrest Dorovic on probable cause as long as he's in a public place. All my guys and the state narcs will be in U.C. surveillance cars, so I don't want to burn them by making an arrest on the street."

"I can handle that," Charlie said. "I'll be in one car, and two of my detectives in another. I'll have dispatch assign two marked units to assist. Should we wait for Dorovic to light somewhere, like back at his apartment or his stash pad, or make a car stop on him?"

"If he returns to either of those places, we'll just sit on them until we get the search warrant. We can then arrest him when we make entry. We have the warrant affidavit all done except for some fill in the blanks, so we can probably have it signed within the hour."

"And once we bring Dorovic to the station?"

"You get first crack at him. Homicide trumps drugs. He'll be shocked that you want to talk about hot jewelry and is more likely to roll on that than his connection. Once you're done with him, me and the SLED guys will play let's make a deal to get him to give up his supplier."

"Sounds good," Charlie said. "I'll call my detectives back in and we'll be ready to roll when you give us the word."

58

"Did you get anything?" Charlie asked when Jay and Sherm returned to the office with Frank and Irish.

"I met with three of the people on our list, fellow students of Sarah back then," Sherm said. "Frank and I had them talk about the day Sarah was murdered. Their stories were the same. Nothing new that points to Marco Capozzi or anyone else."

"Irish and I talked to four people who were teachers at the school back then," Jay said. "Same story. Nothing useful."

Irish looked at his watch. "I hate to be a party pooper, but if there's nothing urgent, I should be getting back home. My wife's been home all day, and I hate leaving her alone for too long."

Charlie knew Irish's wife was in a wheelchair and they lived in a transitional living facility. Although Irish had said she had support there if she needed anything, Charlie understood him not wanting to be away too long. "That's no problem. I appreciate all you did today."

After Irish left, Charlie briefed Sherm and Jay on the operation, then said, "Frank, there's not much for you to do. You're free to hang out at the office until we get back, but I have no idea how long this will take."

"How about I come along?"

"I'm not sure that's a good idea."

"Sherm and Jay are in one car, and you're in the other. Who's your partner?"

Charlie looked over at Darryl, who was still restricted to the office. "I'm fine alone. Besides, at the most, we'll be making a low-key traffic stop and taking Dorovic into custody."

"Then you shouldn't mind a ride-along. Someone to monitor the narc radio and the phones while you're driving."

"He's got a point, sarge," Sherm said. "Frank was a good partner on the interviews."

"Drug operations are old hat to me," Frank said. "Heck, I was doing stuff like this when you were still in...hell, you weren't even in diapers yet, cause you hadn't yet been born."

Charlie couldn't help but smile. She couldn't imagine how Frank would be of any assistance during this operation, but at the same time, he and his other cold case team members had been helpful, and she didn't want to dampen their enthusiasm. "Okay, but you know the rules if by some chance something goes down."

"Yeah, Sherm told me. Stay in the car, don't touch anything, and don't get shot, because that would mean a whole shitload of paperwork."

They went out the back door to the lot where the department vehicles were parked. She grabbed her tactical vest from the trunk of her car and pulled it over her civilian clothes. Emblazoned on the front and back were the words *Sheriff* in yellow letters. If she or one of her two detectives had to stop the car, there would be no confusion as to their identity.

Sherm and Jay donned their vests and climbed into their unmarked SUV. She started the engine of her unmarked Charger, made sure her phone was paired with the vehicle's Bluetooth and turned on her car radio and the small portable radio that would allow her to communicate with the narcotics teams.

Garrett's voice came over the narc radio, "Game time everyone, our C.I. just got the text from our target. The location is the back parking lot of the Palmetto Dinner Club. The C.I. will drive there in his car," he said, referring to Donnie as a confidential informant. "I'll shadow him. Units two and three, find a place to set up where you have an eyeball on the parking lot."

A voice Charlie couldn't identify said, "Roger that, boss. The club doesn't start rocking until later, so that parking lot will be mostly empty. There's no cameras back there, so that's probably why Target picked it. We can set up across the street in the shopping center."

"This is SLED One," said another unfamiliar voice she assumed was the SLED team leader over the narc radio. "The Corvette just pulled into the driveway of a doublewide off West Road. He backed in and popped the hatch. Target and his friend—let's call him Target Two—are going into the trailer. I'll get you the address later."

Charlie called Sherm on his cell and told him to start heading in the direction of the supper club and to stage at a gas station about a half mile away. She then got on her car radio and asked the dispatcher to have the two patrol units she had requested meet her at the back of the gas station.

"This is SLED One," said a voice on the narc radio. "Targets One and Two are loading several duffle bags into the back of the Corvette. They're leaving northbound on West Street. My guess is this is delivery day, and our targets will be meeting more than just our C.I."

"Copy that," Garrett said. "It'll take them about ten minutes to reach the meet location. Our C.I. will be there in five."

"SLED One, I'm leaving one surveillance car sitting on the trailer until we get the warrant. Three of us will shadow the Corvette to the meet location."

The radio was quiet for a few minutes. "Your narcs run a damn professional operation for a bunch of Southern rednecks," Frank said.

"Are you surprised?"

"Nah, I bust your chops all the time about being country bumkins, but good cops are good cops no matter which side of the Mason Dixon line they live," Frank said. "Except for the funny accents."

"Garrett is one of the best, and those guys from SLED are the cream of the crop. They've all done this a thousand times."

She pulled into the back of the gas station and talked with the two uniformed deputies. Sherm and Jay joined her, and Frank hobbled over on his cane. She explained their mission, which was to conduct a traffic stop on the Corvette and take both occupants into custody if necessary.

Charlie turned up the volume on the narcotics portable radio and everyone listened to Garrett's play-by-play from Donnie's wire and his visual of the meeting. Dorovic and his friend pulled behind Donnie's car in his scarlet red Corvette. Donnie stepped from his car with a paper bag in his hand. The three men talked about the weather and the hottest clubs with the hottest chicks on the island for a few minutes, then Donnie gave the bag to Dorovic, who looked inside and fingered through the stack of money.

"I hear Target over the wire telling C.I. that it looks like it's all there," Garrett said. "Target is handing a small black duffle bag from his trunk to C.I. C.I. shook Target's hand and got back into his car. The Corvette is pulling away. SLED, have you got the eye?"

Charlie and her team jumped into their cars. Once the Corvette was a minute ahead, Charlie pulled out and began following, trying to stay several blocks behind the surveillance units. The marked units would follow several blocks behind her. They proceeded south on Spartina Island Road, with the SLED surveillance units keeping everyone updated on the Corvette's location, so they would not get too close. One of Garrett's detectives advised over the narc radio that the product Donnie had received tested positive.

Over the sheriff office's radio, the dispatcher advised of a man with a gun making threats inside the Soloman Funeral Home. The closest two deputies available were on the Dufftown side of the bridge, around five miles away. The funeral home was less than a mile from where Charlie was. The dispatcher updated the call, "Shots fired in the funeral home. Units respond Code Three. Are there any units closer?"

Charlie didn't hesitate. She grabbed the mic, "I'm releasing the two patrol units on my detail. Have them respond." Both marked units made a quick right turn and sped off toward the funeral home.

She touched her car's screen to call Sherm on his cell. "We're on our own," she said.

"An active shooting is more urgent," Sherm said. "We can handle this."

As long as everything goes according to plan, Charlie thought, which all too often it didn't.

59

"I'll keep this line open, so you can hear the narc net traffic from my handset," Charlie said to Sherm.

Charlie determined from the radio traffic that there were three SLED cars on the surveillance, one of them the team supervisor. Garrett was quiet, but Charlie knew he was floating in their wake in his nondescript gray Camry. A SLED unit advised the Corvette just pulled into a Starbucks drive-through, and a few minutes later, it headed back the way it came. Charlie saw the Corvette pass by going north on Spartina Island Road from the side street she had pulled into to wait. When it was out of sight, she pulled onto the road a block or two behind the surveillance cars.

"I thought he was headed to his apartment," Garrett said on the narc radio. "Now he's going back in the direction of his stash pad."

"Unless he's making another delivery and needed a cup of Joe for a long trip," one of the SLED narcs said.

"If so, we should make the stop," Garrett said.

Charlie keyed the mic on the narc radio. "I don't know if you heard, but there was a shooting at a funeral home, and I released my two marked units. I still have two unmarks with three of us in tactical vests, so we can make the stop."

"Roger that," Garrett said. "The undercovers can stop behind you, pull on their raid jackets, and be available to assist if things go to shit."

"He just passed the turn he would've taken if he was going to his stash pad," a SLED narc said.

"CID units, you're free to make the stop when you're ready," Garrett said.

"Copy," Charlie said as she accelerated down the road.

"I've got the point in a white Accord," said a SLED narc. "We're in the left lane. When I see the unmarked cars come up on me, I'll pull off."

"Copy," Charlie said into the radio. Then into the air where her cell was connected to Sherm's. "You're the two-man unit, so the stop's yours. I'm backup."

In a few seconds, she heard the roar of Sherm's Police Interceptor Utility as it sped past her. She pulled behind him.

Charlie glanced over at Frank. "You doing okay?"

Frank smiled broadly. "Haven't had this much fun since my wedding night."

She saw one of the SLED surveillance cars, a Honda Accord, a block ahead. It pulled into the right lane, and she hugged the rear of Sherm's SUV as it weaved through traffic and zipped around the Accord. The red Corvette was ten car lengths in front of them. Charlie had been listening to the sheriff's radio in the background. Deputies advised they had the suspect in custody at the funeral home and that no one had been shot.

Charlie said over the handsfree cell phone link to Sherm and Jay, "We've got about a mile until we reach the bridge off the island. Let's make the stop on this side."

"Roger that," Sherm said.

The red and blue flashing lights and white strobes on the Explorer lit up, and cars in front of them began pulling to the right lane. Sherm sped up until he was just behind the Corvette and blipped his siren. Charlie could see the eyes of the Corvette driver in his sideview mirror looking back at them. Then the Corvette rocketed forward.

Charlie turned on her emergency lights and followed Sherm's Explorer as it tried to catch the Corvette, which had accelerated from thirty-five to eighty in about two seconds.

Jay broadcast on the sheriff's radio net that they were in pursuit, the direction, and a description of the Corvette. The two patrol units that were no longer needed at the funeral home announced they were responding. Charlie knew they were several miles away, and with the speed the Corvette was going, they were not going to catch up in time.

The SLED team leader yelled into the narc radio, "All SLED units fall back. You're not operating emergency vehicles, so you're not to participate in a police pursuit. I don't want to see none of that *Miami Vice* bullshit."

Charlie saw the Corvette about a quarter mile ahead, brake lights flashing as it weaved through traffic. Her speedometer read eighty, and she knew the only thing keeping the Corvette from hitting twice that speed on the bridge were cars in front of it. She glanced at Frank.

"Keep your eyes on the road," Frank said. "I've been in more high-speed pursuits in my career than you'll ever be in, so don't worry about me."

She nodded as she swerved around a pickup pulling a boat trailer in the left lane. They reached the high point of the bridge and started down toward the mainland. The Corvette slowed to fifty as it came up on a pack of cars traveling abreast in both lanes. The Corvette weaved from the left to the right lanes, trying to squeeze through. Finally, a minivan pulled to the right, and the Corvette shot through the opening. Sherm's SUV followed, with Charlie on his tail.

Charlie had the accelerator pressed to the floorboard. Her speedometer needle tickled the one hundred mark, but the Corvette was still pulling away. Her Charger and Sherm's police-package Explorer had engines rated around three hundred horsepower. They were fast, but no match for even a base-model Corvette that had five hundred horsepower in a car hundreds of pounds lighter. But she'd been taught the police didn't have to *catch* cars they pursued. All they had to do was stay with them until they got bogged down in traffic or wrecked. Instructors at the academy stressed that with the training she had received, she'd be much better at high-speed pursuit driving than the people they chased. The drivers, not the cars, were what mattered.

They sped down the bridge into Dufftown. Ahead was a traffic signal at an intersection that was always backed up. The Corvette slowed. She saw the nose of Sherm's SUV dive as it braked as hard as it could. The light ahead turned green, but there were at least ten cars in front of them blocking both lanes. The Corvette swung into the right-turn lane and shot into a shopping plaza, with Sherm now on his tail, his emergency lights flashing and siren blaring.

The Corvette sped through the parking lot and banged over a speed bump. The nose of the Corvette, only a few inches above the ground, struck the speed bump. Pieces of red plastic flew in the air. At the next speed bump, the Corvette braked hard, and Sherm rammed into its rear with the metal push bar mounted on the front of his vehicle. The Corvette scraped its bottom, and more pieces of the car flew in the air. It then shot toward the exit. It made a quick right onto the main road into blaring horns and squealing tires.

Sherm raced toward the exit. A bicycle, with the rider wearing earphones, cut right in front of him. Sherm swerved to the left to avoid hitting him and smashed into a light pole. Charlie stopped alongside and rolled down her window.

"We're not hurt," Jay yelled. "Go get him."

Charlie pulled onto Spartina Island Road and mashed the accelerator. She grabbed her radio mic and advised dispatch she was alone in the pursuit, the vehicle was now a half mile ahead of her, and it was traveling westbound on Spartina Island Road. She weaved through traffic and saw the Corvette stopped behind cars backed up at the next light.

The Corvette tried to squeeze through on the left of the cars. Its left wheels tracked along a grass median that fell off quickly into a drainage ditch. Charlie slowed and pulled around the cars, following the Corvette.

"Ram him," Frank shouted. "Knock his ass off the road. That low-slung piece of shit will bottom out."

Charlie squeezed between the line of cars and the ditch. When she got twenty feet behind the Corvette, she floored the gas pedal and slammed into the back of the car, spinning it off the road and into the ditch.

Charlie yelled for Frank to stay in the car then leaped out with her gun in her hand. Dorovic was slowly rolling out of the driver's side. Out of the corner of her eye, she saw Frank getting out of their car. "Stay in the car, Frank," she yelled, then immediately directed her attention back to Dorovic

—her primary threat. *Damn it, Frank, if you get yourself killed, the sheriff will have my ass.*

"Hands up," she yelled at Dorovic.

Dorovic stood then stumbled and fell on the uneven ground. She was ten feet away when he finally got to his feet again and stared at Charlie's Sig Sauer pointed at him. She ordered him to turn around and put his hands behind his back. She was preparing to holster her gun and handcuff him when she saw Frank hobbling on his cane toward the passenger door of the Corvette.

The passenger opened the door, and the man got out. She had to cuff Dorovic and secure him before she could deal with the passenger. "Frank," she yelled. "Stay back. Let him go."

She stuck her handgun in her holster, grabbed one of Dorovic's hands, and ratcheted a cuff on it. The passenger stepped away from his door and faced Frank. She heard Frank saying something at him, but she couldn't make out his words over the traffic noise.

The man stepped toward Frank with his hands outstretched. Frank crouched and lunged forward, thrusting his cane into the man's solar plexus. The man doubled over. Frank spun his cane around like it was a martial arts staff. He hooked the curved end behind the man's knee, stepped back, and pulled. The man's legs flew toward the sky, and he landed on his back. Frank stood over him with his cane in a two-handed grasp, ready to hit him again if he got up. The man didn't move.

60

It was four o'clock by the time Charlie finally sat down behind her desk. She knew the results of the drug operation would take the rest of the day and maybe half of tomorrow to write up. One pursuit through the streets, two vehicle collisions, and one use of force. By the time she had cuffed Dorovic, Garrett had pulled up in his undercover car. He flipped Dorovic's passenger onto his belly and cuffed him, but the man was groaning and in obvious pain, so he called for an ambulance. By that time, several patrol units had arrived. Charlie's knees had felt wobbly as the adrenaline slowly oozed from her system. The smell of burned oil and rubber filled the air, and the tick-tick-tick sound of overheated engines cooling down was amplified due to her heightened senses resulting from the heart-pounding chase.

Marked units arrived. One took Dorovic to the station, another followed his passenger to the hospital, and the third did a traffic collision report and towed the Corvette after Garrett had thoroughly searched it.

Once that scene was clear, Charlie drove her car to Sherm's accident scene. A patrol deputy was handling the collision report. Since part of the SUV's fender was rubbing on the front wheel, they would need to have Sherm's vehicle towed back to the station. Although Charlie's car was drivable, she'd smashed the front bumper, and it would need to go to the body shop tomorrow as well.

Frank hobbled into the office carrying two cups of coffee. "You take yours black, right?"

"I don't normally drink coffee this late," Charlie said, "But what the hell."

Sherm and Jay were at their desks, Sherm typing up his report and Jay working on a search warrant affidavit for Anthony Capozzi's residence and vehicles, contingent upon the next phase of their operation. "You think I'll be okay with the accident review board?" Sherm asked.

"You'll be better off than me," Charlie said. "Yours was an accident to avoid killing a bicyclist. Mine was intentional."

"Ending a high-speed pursuit, which could've ended with Dorovic killing someone with his Corvette," Jay said.

Garrett stepped through the doorway. "I'll be there to give my two-cents worth to the board. Overall, it was some damn good police work. Don't worry about what the brass thinks. The only cops who never face a department review board are those who never do any work."

"I guess we'll be driving one of the pool cars with a hundred thousand miles on its odometer until ours get back from the shop," Sherm said.

Charlie nodded dejectedly.

"Then there's your Mudflats Murder Club ass kicker," Garrett said. "I never saw a man yield a cane like a PR-24 baton before."

"It's not just any cane," Frank said. "It's a TDI Self-Defense Cane. It's made from high-strength aluminum and designed as a self-defense tool for old, handicapped men like me."

"Did it come with instructions, or did all those fancy moves just come natural?" Garrett asked.

"There's a bunch of videos online. I looked at them, because an old geezer like me shuffling along on a cane is an easy target for muggers."

Charlie just grinned and shook her head.

Garrett told them the SLED narcs recovered at least a kilo of cocaine, several kilos of marijuana, and thousands of pills, as well as packaging materials and stacks of cash at the stash house. Garrett's detectives found a large box of cash, jewelry, and ledgers that documented Dorovic's drug trade in his luxury apartment.

"I already let Donnie go," Garrett said. "I'll review his case with the solicitor's office next week, but as far as I'm concerned, a plea deal with just probation would be a fair trade for what he gave us. Dorovic is sitting in Interview Two, whenever you're ready."

Charlie finished her coffee and followed Garrett down the hall.

Garrett opened the door and walked right up to Dorovic with his hand out. "We haven't formally met, but my name's Garrett Shilling. Since we're going to be friends, you can call me Garrett."

Dorovic shook his hand. "I'm Jared."

"And this is Sergeant Nash," Garrett continued. "You can tell by the way she dresses and how clean she is, she doesn't work narcotics."

Garrett and Charlie sat at the table. "Dorovic," Garrett said. "What kind of name is that?"

"My family originally came from Montenegro."

"That's that tiny little country by Bosnia, isn't it?"

Dorovic nodded.

"Now that we've got that out of the way, let's talk about your situation."

"Don't you need to read me my rights and get me a lawyer?"

Garrett grinned. "I only have to give you Miranda rights if I want to ask you questions about the crime we arrested you for, to use against you in a court of law. But I don't need you to admit to anything. You see, we have you on video selling drugs. You then fled from us in a car filled with drugs. We saw you leave that old trailer with several duffle bags filled with drugs. We went back to the trailer with a warrant and found a whole shitload of drugs and money. We then went to your apartment and found more money than me and Sergeant Nash make in a year. Sergeant Nash, can you tell him how much time he's looking at?"

"Based on the weight of the drugs we found, that makes you a major trafficker, which is punishable by twenty-five years."

"What happened to my cousin?"

"The guy in your car?" Garrett said. "Your fellow narcotics trafficker? He's under a deputy's guard in the hospital with a concussion and cracked ribs. But he'll live."

"The old man did that to him? That's police brutality."

"That old guy is a citizen volunteer," Garrett said. "He was attempting a citizen's arrest when your cousin appeared as a threat. Our volunteer felt his life was in danger and defended himself."

"That ain't right."

"Jared, that *old man* is eighty years old. He's like my grandfather. Ain't no one gonna blame him for what he did."

"If you don't need my confession, then why are we talking?"

"I told you at the beginning that I want to be your friend," Garrett said. "I want you to work with us, so you don't have to sit in prison for twenty-five years."

"I'm no snitch."

"Funny," Garrett said. "Everyone I talk to says that. Snitch is a nasty word. We never use it. We prefer the term source. You can be a source of information for us. If you tell us things we don't already know, I can help keep you from spending twenty-five years in prison."

"You want to know my supplier," Dorovic said.

"That might be nice to know later, but first Sergeant Nash needs to clear up some other things. You see, she's investigating a homicide, and it sort of looks like you might have something to do with it. If you think twenty-five years for narcotics is bad, you don't even want to hear how long you'd spend in prison for murder."

"That's bullshit," Dorovic shouted as he stood up and crossed his arms.

"Sit down, Jared," Garrett said calmly. "We're your friends, and people shouldn't yell at their friends."

After Dorovic sat back down, Charlie slid a photo of Eric Robinson in front of him. "He was your chauffeur. He also sold your drugs to clients of his. He's dead."

"I know he's dead, but I didn't do it."

"You were the last one to see him alive," Charlie lied. "People are saying he stiffed you, so you had to teach him a lesson."

"That's bullshit. He never stiffed me, and it's not like he was a real customer. I just helped him out with some recreational product so he could take care of his limo clients."

Charlie pulled a stack of jewelry insurance appraisals with photos from her folio and lay them in front of Dorovic. He looked through them. "So," he said.

"Have you seen that stuff before?"

"Maybe."

"Jared, you should show more respect to Sergeant Nash or else we'll start thinking we can't be friends," Garrett said.

"Eric, the guy in the photo, he gave me some of that stuff."

She showed him the photo of the ruby pendant.

"I never saw that piece."

That told Charlie Eric gave it directly to Courtney, as she had suspected. "And you gave him money or drugs in exchange for jewelry," Charlie said.

"Yeah."

"That's a couple hundred grand worth of jewelry," Charlie said. "I know a fence doesn't pay dollar for dollar, but Eric didn't have that much money on him or at his place."

"Eric only had a little bit. Someone else had most of the jewelry. A rich guy that lives in Ocean Forest."

Charlie showed him a photo of Anthony Capozzi.

"That's him."

"Help me figure this out," Charlie said. "You got some of the jewelry from Eric and some from Anthony, but I know it all originally belonged to Anthony."

"What's in it for me?"

Garrett began writing numbers on a legal pad, beginning with a one and ending with twenty-five. With his pen, he crossed out twenty-five and twenty-four. "So far, you've told us a tiny bit of stuff we didn't know, so we're down to twenty-three years in prison. You've got a long way to go."

61

"Rich guys are the biggest crooks," Dorovic said. "My man, Eric, came to me a few weeks back with some quality jewelry. Like I tell everyone, I'm no expert, so I take everything on consignment. When I visit my friend in Florida, I give him the stuff and he gives me a price. Most people I get stuff from just tell me to get what I can for it."

"That's the deal you had with Eric?" Charlie said.

"Yeah, he didn't exactly have the royal jewels. I got him a few grand. Then the next day, I get a text from Anthony."

"How do you know him?" Charlie asked. "Is he one of your dealers?"

"Hell no, he's got a straight job, owns a big company. About a year ago, I was kicking with some friends at a place on the water, having some cocktails. Anthony comes up to my friend. I don't get involved because they do their own business. Anthony goes back to his table with his wife, and my friend tells me he's been selling oxy to him. A bottle of fifty every week or so. Anthony tells him he wants to buy in quantity, like a regular thing, like once a month."

"And since you only deal to those who buy in quantity, you cut out your middleman and connected directly with Anthony," Garrett said. "What did he want?"

"Oxy fifteens. A hundred fifty of them. My guys sell them for fifteen or twenty a pop. I give it to them for ten a pop. I tell Anthony I'll give him three bottles of fifty for two grand. He was happy with that. Anthony would text me every three or four weeks, and we'd meet up for a drink at some nice place and do the exchange. He'd always buy the drinks."

"Anthony doesn't look like an addict," Charlie said.

"His wife is like one of them Beverly Hills housewife junkies. He said she had back surgery a while back and the docs gave her pills for the pain. After a while, he cut her off. Anthony first figured he was helping her out until she could taper off, but she was a bitch if he rationed her, so he just figured he'd get her whatever she wanted to keep her happy."

"Okay," said Charlie. "What about the jewelry?"

"He texted me a week or so ago and we met. He takes me to his car and shows me all kinds of jewelry. Says it's all real, but he doesn't need it anymore. Says someone broke into his house and stole a bunch of stuff when he was on vacation. He saw an opportunity to unload all this other stuff. I knew that meant he'd tell his insurance company it was stolen with the other stuff, so he'd collect from them and collect whatever I could get for it from my friend."

"This was all his wife's jewelry, right?"

"He said she never wore it, but she'd never let him sell it. He told her it was all stolen when the guy broke in."

"Did you happen to mention you knew Eric?"

Dorovic laughed. "I have like lawyer-client confidentiality. I put two and two together, especially when one day Eric was driving me and said he was able to case these big mansions when he drove for people. But I never said a word of it to Anthony."

"How much did you give Anthony for his jewelry?"

"Nothing yet. My friend delivered forty-K yesterday. Take out my fee and I owe Anthony thirty. I had it in my car, and I was gonna text Anthony and drop it off after...well, you folks interrupted my delivery schedule."

Charlie and Garrett left the room, conferred in the hall for a few minutes, then returned.

"We'd like you to call Anthony and tell him you have his thirty grand for the jewelry and you're ready to meet," Charlie said. "We'll wire you and you'll make the exchange." Charlie had wanted to have Dorovic ask

Anthony about the ruby pendant and try to get him to admit killing Eric, but Garrett convinced her that would be too big a stretch, and Anthony was sure to be suspicious.

Dorovic looked at Garrett's legal pad. "If I do this, how many more numbers will you cross off?"

Garrett crossed off five more numbers on his pad, leaving eighteen as the highest number on his list.

Dorovic nodded. "What can we do about all those other numbers?"

"Let's focus on this for now," Garrett said. "Tomorrow I'll introduce you to some state and federal people, and we'll start talking about your friend down in Jacksonville."

Charlie handed Dorovic his cell phone. "You know what to do."

62

Sean sat in his recliner, reading the latest Michael Connelly novel. Although he liked the earlier books featuring Harry Bosch, Sean understood that Harry was getting awfully old, so it made sense that Connelly had added Renee Ballard to do a lot of the heavy lifting. Although Sean was the youngest member of the Mudflats Murder Club, it made sense that the active detectives, Charlie and her team, would do the heavy lifting on Spartina Island murder investigations. But just because it made sense, it didn't mean he had to like it. He was young enough to still be relevant.

After lunch at Bubba's, Sean had come home and spent an hour going over the Henry Nash file he had put together, now fifty-some pages long. He hoped some hidden clues would materialize, but all he came up with were more tasks to add to his to-do list. Next up on his list was reinterviewing Ray Mitro, but Feebee said she was playing in a bocce tournament this afternoon with her husband, so that would have to wait until tomorrow. Bocce was something you could play with only one good shoulder, but Sean might as well check into a nursing home when that was the only activity he could participate in.

As Sean read the novel, occasional text alerts from Frank and Doc would ding on his phone. They were sending updates on the murder investigations of Eric, Courtney, and Sarah to the entire Mudflats Murder Club.

Sean read about the car chase, the arrest of Dorovic, and the searches of his apartment and stash pad. Sean wished he were there. Sean had called and texted Charlie several times, offering to help, but she never responded.

Since he couldn't golf or work out at the gym because of his shoulder, he had puttered around the house, doing laundry and vacuuming the carpets, all the time missing being part of a homicide investigation as it came together. As he was fixing himself dinner, a ferocious storm swept through, beginning with thunder and lightning, and followed by torrential rain. He called Rachel.

"You getting a thunderstorm there?"

"The rain just started tapering off, so the storm must be heading your way," Rachel said.

"It's here."

"Dad, ya doin' okay?"

"I'm great. Just thought I'd call and see how you were doing."

"I'm fine. Austin's fine." She paused for a few counts, then said, "Carson is leaving California."

"Why? Where's he going?"

"They're not giving him his job back, and the recruiter he used before said there was nothing available for him in the Bay Area. He asked if he could stay with me and Austin while he looks for work on the east coast."

"How are you and Austin with that?"

"It will take some adjusting. We already got rid of the furniture in what was the guest room, so we can turn it into a nursery. The other spare bedroom we've been using as an office. We have a blow-up air mattress we can put in there."

"You know that when your mother and I bought this house, she insisted there be two spare bedrooms, one for you and your husband, and one for Carson and his future wife."

"I remember. She wanted us all waking up there on Christmas morning, so her future grandchildren could open presents under your tree," Rachel said. "I actually went with Mom to the furniture store to pick out the bedroom sets. Is the furniture still in Carson's bedroom?"

"Just like your mom left it. Queen-size bed, dresser, two nightstands, probably even toothbrushes and toothpaste in the bathroom. He knows he's always welcome here."

"Maybe you could tell him. I'd never turn away my little brother, but with the baby coming and all..."

"I totally understand. I'll call him."

"Thanks, Dad. And Dad, be easy on him. He already feels bad about getting fired, so what he needs right now is support while he reassesses his life."

"I will." Sean was ready to say good-bye, but asked, "Do you listen to music much?"

"You've been in my house. I often have music playing when I'm alone. When you come over, I turn it down. Why?"

"I don't know. I was just wondering."

"Mom liked her music. It made her happy."

"I remember."

Sean called his son's phone, which went straight to voicemail. He told Carson he heard he was coming for a visit and that he was more than welcome to stay with him. Sean did his best to sound as excited as Lauren would've been over Carson coming home.

He went to the TV remote, turned Pandora Radio to the light rock station Lauren had liked, and ate his dinner at the kitchen counter. When a song by Neil Sedaka came on, an old memory popped into his head. He, Lauren, and the kids were at a craft fair one Saturday afternoon just before Halloween when it started raining. Their car was a half mile away and Carson, a first grader at the time, was on the verge of a meltdown. Lauren took Carson and Rachel by their hands and started singing "Laughter in the Rain." In no time, Carson was singing along as the three of them skipped through the rain puddles. Sean was surprised the memory brought a smile to his face, instead of sadness over the loss of Lauren. Maybe he was on the road to getting on with his new life.

63

Charlie twisted the air vent in Garrett's Camry away from her. The biker-looking cop beside her had the air conditioning cranked low enough to keep ice cream from melting. They were sitting in the parking lot of Ocean Forest Harbour. In front of them were shops and restaurants, and beyond that were boats ranging from thirty-foot speedboats to eighty-foot mini yachts bobbing in the water. Garrett steadied his iPad on the center console, which showed Dorovic walking to a high-top table by the window on the second floor of Harbour Restaurant. He fiddled with a portable receiver plugged into a USB outlet until the audio from Dorovic's wire was audible.

"Where'd you put the camera?" Charlie asked, referring to the video she was watching on the iPad.

"One of my guys is sitting a few tables away having a cocktail. He's got a novel on his table with a pin-hole camera in it," Garrett said. "The boss will probably flip when I expense a fifteen-dollar glass of wine for a surveillance operation."

Charlie had eaten at the Harbour Restaurant before, but when an appetizer and a glass of wine sets you back thirty bucks, it wasn't a place cops typically frequented. She returned her focus to the iPad.

Dorovic shook hands with Anthony Capozzi. "Ant, my main man, how ya doin'?"

"As well as possible under the circumstances," Anthony said.

A petite Asian waitress with waist-length black hair stopped at their table and took their order. When she left, Dorovic said, "What's up, man?"

"I wish I never would've done this jewelry thing with you."

"Sorry, man, but the stuff is gone, and you told me you already made the claim with your insurance company."

"At the time, I was boiling mad. My wife's pain med cost was pissing me off, and it seemed like a way to say, 'fuck you,' to her. Figured it was only fair I sell her jewelry to pay for her stuff."

"I don't get involved in marital issues with my clients," Dorovic said. "I'm not an addiction counselor either, but you got the money to get her into rehab or whatever."

"Yeah, I know. After this batch, I'm going to put my foot down."

The waitress set two glasses of beer on their table, smiled, and left.

"I have your money from the jewelry here. You still want the three bottles of oxy?"

Anthony nodded.

Dorovic handed Anthony a large manilla envelope. "I took two grand out for your product. Sorry I couldn't get more for your jewelry, but you reported it to your insurance company and the cops'll put the items in their big computer, so my friend has to break everything down and send it overseas. It would be too hot to try to offload here."

"This will be the last deal."

"People used to call folks like me pushers. I never push anything on my friends. If you don't want anything after this, I'm cool with it. We can still meet for a drink and talk."

"I can't keep on like this. Two detectives came to see me. They said they were looking into the burglary, but they were really investigating the murder of Eric Robinson."

"Eric was a good man," Dorovic said. "He used to drive for me."

"A good man? Bullshit. He ripped me off and set this whole thing in motion. Now the cops are all over me, and my junkie wife is not even concerned. She's so numb she doesn't care about anything but her stupid horses and her pills."

"I guess the cops assumed you'd be pissed at Eric for ripping you off," Dorovic said.

"I didn't even know for sure it was him until the cops came to my house. They can't really think someone like me could kill someone. I wouldn't even know how to kill a man."

Dorovic laughed. "All you gotta do is watch some of them crime shows on Netflix. Shoot them, stab them, bash their head in. Anyone can kill a man."

"You didn't..."

"No way. Eric was my bud, and murder ain't my thing."

"Sorry I even asked. Eric probably ripped off plenty of other people. You can't do that and not eventually piss off the wrong person."

"You know Eric brought me jewelry too."

"I figured as much. He took a bunch of stuff that wasn't in the safe."

"If I knew it was yours, I wouldn't have fenced it with my friend."

Anthony shrugged. "It's done with, so nothing I can do about it."

Dorovic drained his beer. "I gotta run. I can pick up the tab if you want."

"No, I got it."

"See you around." Dorovic got up and headed to the door.

"I wish Anthony would've said more about Eric," Charlie said to Garrett.

"Only in the movies do people go bragging about whacking someone. I will say, Dorovic is a smooth operator. I think he'll be able to help dismantle a major trafficking network for us."

"I've still got some work to do before I have a solid murder case on Anthony, but this was a huge step."

Dorovic walked across the parking lot and climbed into the back seat of the Camry. "How'd I do?"

"Real well," Garrett said. "If you weren't a criminal drug dealer, you'd make a great undercover narcotics officer."

A moment later, Anthony walked to his Range Rover and opened the door. Jay and Sherm approached him, flashed their badges, and handcuffed him.

"I'm gonna take a look in his car before we tow it," Charlie said. "You okay with our friend in the back?"

"Jared, you ain't gonna do something dumb like jump out of the car on the way back to my office, are you?" Garrett asked.

"Fuck no. I'm gonna work with you until we cross out all the numbers on that page."

Charlie walked across the parking lot to Sherm and Jay's car, where a uniformed deputy had just arrived and was putting Anthony into the back seat for transport to the station. "Let's do a quick search then have it towed back to the station to be fully processed," Charlie said.

While Jay and Sherm gloved up and searched the interior, she opened the rear hatch. She saw six reusable grocery bags, but other than that, the rear trunk was empty. She grabbed a strap and pulled up the trunk lining. Inside was a spare tire that looked brand new, a jack, and lug nut wrench. She looked at the lug nut wrench carefully, thinking that could've been used to beat Eric instead of a hammer as the medical examiner had suggested. Next to the jack was a plastic garbage bag that looked like the same type used to suffocate Eric.

She pulled the bag out. Inside was a claw hammer, a small handgun, and a wad of paper towels with dried blood.

64

Charlie and Jay entered the interview room where Kristin Capozzi had been sitting for the past hour. Kristin raised her head from the table and looked at them with a vacant stare. After they had finished searching Anthony's Range Rover and sent it off on the back of a tow truck, they drove to the Capozzis' house. They handed Kristin a copy of the search warrant, and while Sherm watched over Kristin in the living room, Charlie and Jay conducted a methodical search of the house and their other car, a burgundy Mercedes SL Roadster.

Their search had turned up several mostly empty bottles of Oxycodone with no prescription labels attached. They collected several rolls of duct tape and garbage bags, although Charlie was fairly certain the killer had acquired what he had used for the murder from inside Eric Robinson's apartment. Charlie was confident they had found the blunt instrument used to beat Eric in the Range Rover, but they still seized two hammers from a toolbox in the garage. Even though simple possession of narcotics was not a major crime, it allowed them to arrest Kristin and take her to the station for questioning.

"How are you doing, Kristin?" Charlie asked. Kristin's hands shook, and she was sweating, despite the air conditioning in the room. Charlie suspected it was from more than just fear.

"I need my meds."

"You don't have a prescription for the pills we found in your house," Charlie said. "We don't know exactly what they contain, so I can't let you have them."

"Look at them," Kristin said. "I have a prescription for oxycodone, and these have the same markings as those I was getting from the pharmacy."

Charlie had examined them. They had a large *M* on one side and *15* on the other, which was how oxycodone 15 milligram tablets were marked, so they could've been diverted from legitimate supply channels, or they could've been made in a clandestine lab and marked the same as real oxycodone. "Your prescription expired well over a year ago, and these were bought on the black market from a drug dealer."

"I'm sick."

"It's called withdrawal," Charlie said. "We're going to take you to the hospital. We'll talk to you tomorrow unless you feel well enough to talk now."

"Let's get it over with."

"We've arrested Anthony for insurance fraud and buying drugs. We know he fenced the contents of your safe to a drug dealer in exchange for thirty thousand dollars. That was after he made a two-hundred-thousand-dollar insurance claim."

"That asshole."

"So you didn't know about this?"

"Hell no. It's not like Anthony needed the money. He hates me. He can't stand being with me anymore. He goes out most nights just so he doesn't have to spend time with me."

"He does buy drugs for you," Charlie said.

"He wouldn't be able to live in the same house with me if he didn't. He's threatened to take my horses away. We signed a prenup when we married. Most of the money from my parents' trust is gone. I can't afford to live on my own."

Charlie nodded, trying to put on her compassionate and empathetic face as Kristin spewed her problems and frustrations. "We believe Anthony found out Eric Robinson broke into your house, and then he killed him along with Eric's girlfriend, Courtney Evanson."

Kristin's face showed no emotion for several moments. "I wouldn't put it past him. He's gotten increasingly angry the past year or so."

Charlie showed Kristin a photograph of the ruby pendant. "Have you seen this before?"

"That was the pendant worn by Anthony's old high school girlfriend, Sarah."

"But have you seen it since then?"

She shook her head.

Charlie told Kristin the day and approximate time when they determined Eric and Courtney had been murdered and asked her if she knew where Anthony was at that time.

"Like I said, he goes out most nights, while I stay home and watch TV or whatever. We don't even sleep in the same room anymore, so he could be gone all night, and I wouldn't know it. You said you believed Anthony killed them. How do you know?"

"We have quite a bit of evidence. We arrested Anthony after he picked up money and drugs from a dealer. We then searched his Range Rover, where we found a hammer that we believe he beat Eric with and a gun he used to threaten him. We'll send both to the lab, but I'm sure we'll find Eric's blood and Anthony's fingerprints."

Kristin stared blankly at Charlie and Jay. "How long will that take?"

"A week, maybe a bit longer," Charlie said. "But we have enough to hold him until then."

"What about me?"

"I'm going to have Detective Garcia take you to the hospital, where they can see you through a medical detox. I'll also call a friend who runs a treatment facility, so when the hospital releases you, you'll have a place to go."

"But after that? Anthony's going to prison, and what will I do?"

Charlie scrolled through her phone and jotted down a name and a phone number on a piece of paper. "This is the name of a great divorce attorney. Once you get situated in the treatment facility and meet with a counselor, you may want to give her a call."

Kristin nodded. "Thank you for not arresting me tonight, Charlie. I'm sure that when we were back in high school, neither of us imagined our lives would turn out this way."

Charlie smiled. She never imagined she'd be seeing Kristin under these circumstances, and although being a detective and investigating homicides was never her career goal back then, Charlie was mostly satisfied with how her life had turned out.

65

When Charlie returned to her office, she was surprised to see Frank and Doc sitting around Darryl's computer, watching the video of the interview room with Kristin.

"Darryl has been keeping us updated on the activities," Doc said. "He said your team had been working without a break, so Frank and I thought you might like some pizza."

Charlie glanced at her watch. No wonder her stomach was growling. When she got involved in an investigation, eating was the last thing on her mind. She grabbed a slice of sausage pizza from one of the two boxes.

"Darryl showed me the hammer you collected as evidence," Doc said. "If I were the medical examiner who did the autopsy, I'd say that hammer could've been the weapon used to cause the injuries we noted on Eric Robinson."

"There was obvious dried blood on it," Charlie said. "The crime lab should be able to match it to Eric."

"What's your take on Kristin?" Frank asked.

"A woman in an unhappy marriage who's another tragedy of opioid addiction."

"She's a fucking junkie," Frank said. "The junkies I knew back in my day shot heroin and lived in shit places. Because she's rich, she lives in a mansion and takes her drug with a glass of water, but they're no different."

"I feel sorry for her," Charlie said.

"I don't think anyone held her down and forced her to take drugs," Frank said. "She makes Anthony out to be the devil, but he still supplied her pills. Misguided compassion, but he thought he was helping."

"Was it out of love, or did he do it to keep her numb so he could do whatever he wanted?" Charlie said. "Still, everything she said makes sense and fits into what we already know."

"Junkies are master manipulators," Frank said. "I don't trust them."

She wasn't going to argue with Frank. He came from a different place than she did. He saw the street crime and the heroin addicts lying dead in New York's streets with syringes hanging out of their arms. But he'd never lived with a lying, deceitful husband like she had. She finished her slice of pizza, snagged a fresh legal pad from her desk, and said to Sherm, "You ready to take on Anthony?"

Anthony stood when she entered the interview room. "Charlie, I'm so glad it's you. You've got to believe me—"

"Anthony, despite knowing each other, I have to do my job here," Charlie said. "If you're uncomfortable with that, I'll find someone else to conduct this interview."

"No, I trust you."

They sat at the small table and Charlie read Anthony his rights.

"I'll make this easy on you," Anthony said. "Yes, I've been buying drugs for Kristin. I know it's wrong, but she was still in such pain and so miserable. Her doctor wouldn't authorize additional refills. I know I should've refused, but Charlie, she's my wife, and I love her."

Charlie knew that under the circumstances, if it were only about the drugs, a judge would let Anthony off with probation. They were not going to lock up a man who, in his own misguided way, thought he was helping his wife. "Tell me about the jewelry."

Anthony looked at her, pretending to be confused.

"You should know that we arrested your pal, Jared Dorovic. He told us everything and was wearing a wire when he met you at the bar."

Anthony covered his face with his hands and sighed loudly.

"Tell us about it, Anthony. Eric Robinson broke into your house and stole some jewelry. You decided to tell your insurance company the thief also took everything in the safe, which wasn't true. You then had Dorovic fence it for you."

He nodded.

"Why?"

"I tried to be a good husband, but enough was enough. Every time I turned around I was spending a thousand dollars to feed her addiction. She refused to get help. I figured if she was going to use drugs, they should be bought with her money."

Charlie put the photo of the ruby pendant in front of him. "Eric stole this also."

"What? Where'd you get that photo?"

"From Courtney's body," Charlie said. "After you killed her."

"That's crazy! I had nothing to do with Courtney's death."

"You found out Eric stole the pendant, and you tortured him until he revealed he gave it to Courtney. You then killed her, but you didn't know the pendant was buried deep in her pocket."

"That's ridiculous."

"Okay, maybe you saw Courtney wearing it at the bar and confronted her first," Charlie said. "After you killed her and didn't find it, you then went to Eric. I understand why you had to get it back. It was your memory of Sarah. Your father left it for you after he died. You couldn't have the pendant resurface. It would smear your family name if it came out that your father killed the girl you loved. The girl you still love to this day."

"I never saw the pendant after Sarah was killed. I don't know what kind of fantasy story you've concocted, but it's all wrong."

"Anthony, it's over. We found the hammer you used to beat Eric, your gun, and paper towels covered with blood in the trunk of your car. The lab will show your prints on the hammer and gun, and Eric's blood on the paper towels and hammer."

"My car?"

"Your Range Rover."

Anthony's eyes opened wide. Surprise? Or sudden realization Charlie knew everything? She waited.

"I want to talk to my lawyer."

66

After Sean finished eating dinner and cleaned up the kitchen, he went back to reading his novel, with Pandora playing softly in the background. Annie leaped from her dog bed, raced to the front door, and began barking. Sean looked at his watch: 9:04. The doorbell rang, and Sean opened the door to see Abigail Nash standing there. She was impeccably dressed as always, wearing light blue slacks and a peach-colored blouse. "I apologize for coming to your home unannounced and this late at night, but..."

"Would you like to come in?"

She nodded and followed him into the great room. "You have a beautiful house, Sean. Very modern, yet decorated very traditionally."

He was about to mention that he had nothing to do with the decorating, but instead just accepted the compliment. "Can I get you something to drink? I have tea, but only those normal Lipton tea bags."

"Do you have something stronger?"

"I have beer in the fridge, and I'm sure there's some bottles of wine and some whiskey in the kitchen cabinets."

"Whiskey would be nice," she said. "Neat."

Sean poured three fingers of Bushmills into two glasses and brought them to the living room, where Abigail had already perched on one side of the sofa. Annie rested her chin on her leg and looked up at Abigail's face.

"We used to have dogs," Abigail said. "They can be a great comfort during difficult times."

Sean handed one of the glasses to Abigail, who took a sip and set the glass on a coaster on the coffee table. "They do seem to have a sense when people need comforting," Sean said.

"I told Charlotte about her real birth last night," Abigail said.

"How'd she take it?"

"Not well. She left and spent the night at a friend's house."

Sean took a sip of his whiskey. "That must have been a lot to process. I'm sure that given time, she'll understand."

"I don't know. Our relationship has always been strained. My friends tell me that's normal for mother-daughter relationships, but I think with us it's more than that."

"My wife and our daughter were always close," Sean said. "So I can't offer any advice in this area, but I have a son who pushes me away more and more the older he gets."

"What do you do?"

"Continue to reach out, apologize when he's upset over something I did or said, even when I did nothing wrong, and let him know that I'm always here for him and will always love him."

"That's good advice, but I'm afraid Charlotte will never forgive me for what I had done. I must also apologize to you, because I had to mention you were the person who brought this up to me, and Charlotte was very angry you didn't tell her yourself."

That explained why she didn't reply to his calls and texts. "It wasn't my place to tell her."

"You have a strong moral code, Sean. There aren't many people like that. I can accept Charlotte's anger toward me, but she should understand why you left it for me to tell her."

Sean took another sip of his whiskey. "I learned a long time ago I can't make another person agree with me or even understand me. I care about Charlie and wish she weren't upset with me, but I'm powerless to change how she feels."

"That's very enlightened of you."

"Not bad for an old homicide cop, huh?"

She smiled. "From the first time we met, I knew you were more than just an *old homicide cop*. I surmised that you had become a master of human nature to do your job well. You are demonstrating that tonight as we talk. What do you think we should do?"

"I take it you've already apologized."

"Profusely."

"Show her you will continue to love her no matter what, and that you'll always be there for her. She has every right to be angry, so allow her to work through it at her pace. If Charlie is the woman I think she is, she'll eventually come around."

"And you?"

"I need to tell her I'm sorry. Understand why she's angry. See if she'll allow me to explain."

Abigail took a final sip of her whiskey and stood. "It would be a shame if this destroyed your friendship with Charlotte. She needs someone like you in her life."

Sean walked Abigail to the door. "And when you two settle this, you truly should ask her out on a date."

67

It was almost midnight when Charlie parked her replacement unmarked car behind her house. It was a five-year-old, white Chevy Malibu with 140,000 miles on the odometer. The driver's seat had lost whatever lumbar support it might've once had, but the air conditioning worked. It had a more powerful two-liter engine than the sluggish, smaller one that was in a rental she had once driven, but she definitely wouldn't be chasing Corvettes in it.

The house was dark except for the assortment of LED nightlights built into electrical outlets around the house. She made her way upstairs, closed her bedroom door, and packed a small suitcase and garment bag. She didn't know when she'd return, but she gathered enough clothes for four or five days. By then she should have a better idea of her future. After Spencer left for college last month, she knew she no longer needed to continue living with her mother. She had thought about buying a nice condo on the beach or a house on the river, where she could dock her boat. But her family home was comfortable and convenient, and she had considered how her mother would feel living all alone. Right now, she didn't care a bit about how her mother felt.

She heard a soft meow and cracked the door. Lexi stalked in. She picked up the Tonkinese cat and held her to her chest, feeling the vibration of her purrs. Although she had wanted to get another dog when their last Boykin Spaniel died, her mother was against it, so they got a cat. She wondered if her mother would fight her if she took Lexi with her when she moved out.

She drove to Ray's house and entered through the back door. Ray was sitting in the living room with the TV on. "You didn't have to wait up for me," she said.

"And miss the opportunity to debrief my favorite detective?"

"I really appreciate you letting me stay here until I sort things out."

"You're welcome to stay as long as you want, sweetheart. If you decide to make it longer, we can move you into the apartment over the carriage house, where you'll have more space and privacy."

"I've been thinking about buying my own place. If I do, I may take you up on that while I'm looking for the right house."

"Whatever you need. You must be bushed and ready for some sleep."

"I'm too wound up. I usually sit up for a while to unwind first before sleeping after days like this."

"Why don't you get yourself settled in your room and changed into something comfortable. There's a full moon tonight, and the dock is a beautiful place to have a beer and unwind."

Ten minutes later, Charlie and Ray sat in Adirondack chairs at the end of his dock. She could see all the way across the river in the moonlight. An offshore breeze made it feel almost chilly, even though the temperature was still in the high seventies. She wondered if there was any riverfront land available near Ray's house. She had the money to buy it and build a comfortable house, not something as big as Ray's five-thousand-square-foot house, but something that would more than meet her needs and Spencer's when he came home for the summers.

She told Ray about her investigation. She was elated the way it came together with the arrest of Anthony Capozzi. Although she'd never be able to prove beyond a reasonable doubt that Marco had killed Sarah, she was confident he was the killer. Once she finished her report, she could clear the case and provide a sense of closure to Sarah's mother.

"This last week must've been tough," Ray said. "Now you can relax a bit."

"We might have the killer in custody, but there's still a lot of work to do and a mountain of paperwork."

"Jacque had lunch with your mother today."

"Jacque is too sweet to be dining with that witch."

"It's rare for you to speak so negatively about someone."

"How about deceitful bitch?"

"Your mother feels awful about what she did. What she feels even worse about is that she might lose you over it."

"Of course," Charlie said. "It's always about her. How would you feel if this were you?"

"I'd be incredibly hurt just like you. But then I hope I'd forgive her. Have you ever done something that hurt a friend and asked for forgiveness?"

"This isn't about me."

"Yes it is, Charlie. I'm sure your father wasn't all in on this lie, but he loved your mother so much that he went along because she asked him to. You and I both know how insistent your grandmother could be about maintaining the family image. Don't you think she was maybe the force behind the way in which your mother had to handle this?"

"I'm sure, but it was up to my mother—"

"Who was a twenty-year-old girl who got pregnant by a man ten years older than her out of wedlock in a Southern aristocratic society."

Charlie drained half her beer and looked at the moonlight bouncing off the silvery ripples of the river. "I've been an adult for what, twenty-five years now. She's had plenty of time to tell me."

"Sometimes the longer a secret has been buried, the harder it is to dig it up and bring it to the surface. Have you spoken to Sean?"

"He called a few times today, but I've been busy."

"Does he know that you know?"

She shrugged.

"You know it was not his place to tell you, right?"

"A friend would've."

"A man of character would've gone to the person responsible for telling you and first given them the chance to make it right."

"You might be right about this, but I'm still stinging from the revelation that my origin is not what I had believed it to be. I got drunk over it last night, and today I blocked it out of my head so I could focus on taking down a killer. I'll sleep on it tonight." She looked at her watch. "For at least a few hours. Maybe I'll be a little less angry at the world tomorrow."

Ray clinked his beer bottle with hers and stood. He put his arm around her shoulder, and they walked back to the house.

68

WEDNESDAY

Sean drove from his physical therapy appointment to Feebee's house on the west side of Sea Island Plantation, arriving just before nine o'clock. "Doc and Beagle want to meet with us after we're done with this interview," Feebee said.

"Why don't they just type up whatever they've done in our case chronology?"

"It has to do with the active investigations that Charlie's team is handling."

"Those two and Frank and Irish spent most of yesterday working with her. Why didn't they just share whatever with her then?"

"What are you so grouchy about?" Feebee said. "Did someone piss in your Cheerios this morning?"

"I'm not grouchy."

"Ah, I think someone feels left out because the other guys got to spend quality time investigating murders with Charlie, and you weren't invited."

"I never assumed I had an exclusive murder-investigating relationship with Charlie."

Feebee laughed. "I think Detective Tanner is jealous."

Cops were famous for busting each other's chops, and Sean knew the only way to end Feebee's teasing was to ignore her and pretend it didn't bother him. He turned on the radio and drove the rest of the way in silence.

They walked into the CrossFit gym. A muscular man wearing a red T-shirt reading *Retired Marine* said Ray wasn't coming to the gym today. The man called Ray at home and said Ray would see him there.

Sean followed the directions on his GPS and turned off Cusseta River Road onto a dirt road. The road was lined with a few small brick houses and double-wide trailers. The road seemed to end where a pair of red brick pillars stood guard over an open, ornate wrought iron gate. Plaques on the brick advised this was a private residence and trespassers would be arrested. The dirt road turned to gravel as it continued through a thick forest for a hundred yards. The woods ended at a lush lawn that would be the envy of the most exclusive golf course. Beyond the lawn sat a sprawling Lowcountry-style house and two-story carriage house. Past the house lay the Cusseta River.

Sean stopped his Corvette in front of the house, and Ray Mitro met them on a wide front porch that ran the length of the house. He was barefoot and wore a faded T-shirt and cargo shorts, not how Sean expected a man who recently sold a twenty-million-dollar business would dress. "Nice to see you again, Sean," he said then turned toward Feebee. "You must be retired FBI Agent Denise Shepherd."

Feebee shook his hand. "I don't believe we've met."

"Our little newspaper had brief backgrounds on the cold case team members after you solved that forty-year-old murder last month," Ray said. "Come in and let's sit on the back porch. It's actually a bit cooler today than it has been."

They followed him through a casual, yet beautifully decorated house to a large, screened porch that overlooked the river. A stone path led to a dock that jutted into the water. A red racing-style boat was tied to one side of the dock and a pontoon boat to the other. The porch contained a massive outdoor kitchen, several lounge chairs, a dining table with ten chairs around it, and a conversation grouping with eight cushioned chairs.

Ray motioned them to the cushioned chairs surrounding a low bronze table that held two pitchers and glasses. "Cold water and iced tea, not the sweet tea the South is famous for, but just straight brewed tea. Help yourself."

Sean poured himself a glass of iced tea as did Ray. Feebee stuck with water. "Thanks for meeting with us," Sean said. "As I said when we spoke previously, all we're trying to do at this point is delve into Henry's past deep enough to see if there are people who would want to hurt him. You're his friend, and we did some background on you, which turned up some interesting things."

Feebee repeated everything about Ray that she had told Sean and the others at Bubba's yesterday.

Ray was quiet for a moment. "I'm a private man, and I didn't expect you to investigate me. I wasn't being secretive earlier, just private."

"I understand," Sean said. "We're not accusing you of lying. Can you fill in the pieces for us, so we better understand your relationship with Henry and Henry's early life."

"My family lived in Slovakia when it was a part of the Czechoslovak Socialist Republic. My father was an executive with a company that provided materials to the army. That's all I knew growing up. One morning before I left for school, several men wearing cheap suits came to our house and asked my father to come with them. My mother was frightened. She kept me and my brother, Andie, home from school.

"That evening, Henry Nash came to our house. That was the first time I met him. He was with three other Americans. My mother had already packed our bags, one suitcase each was all we were allowed, and we left with the men. Andie was sixteen and either very brave or very foolish, but he refused to come. We traveled by car and then on foot through the woods at night and ended up inside Austria. My mother and I remained there for several months. We then flew to the United States, where we lived with another family in Clairton. You know the rest."

"When did you next see Henry Nash?" Feebee asked.

"About a year later, he came to Clairton to see how we were doing. My mother was working nights as a custodian in an office building. Henry got his father to sponsor her as an employee of his New York company to change her immigration status. She could then get an accounting job, which was her occupation in Slovakia."

"What happened to your father and brother?" Feebee asked.

"Henry was now out of his government job and working in New York, so he would visit us every month or so. During one visit he told my mother that my father had died in a prison operated by the state security. My brother ended up in a labor camp, where he stayed until the end of the communist rule in the early 1990s."

"Your brother must've been very bitter," Sean said.

"I've seen him several times over the years, and yes, bitter is an understatement. He blamed the American government for getting our father killed."

"When Henry and the other Americans rescued you from your home, who did you think they were?" Sean asked.

"You mean like soldiers or something?"

Sean shrugged.

"Henry Nash said he worked for the State Department. I'm not so naïve as to believe State Department diplomats cross the iron curtain to rescue families of people who worked with the Americans. I never questioned Henry about what government agency he actually worked for, but the other men with him that night didn't look like members of the State Department's diplomatic corps."

"Did your mother blame Henry for causing your father's death?" Sean asked.

"My mother knew what my father was doing and respected him for it. She was enormously grateful Henry brought me and her out. Otherwise, we would've likely died in a labor camp."

"And your brother?" Sean asked.

"I lived and traveled throughout the world during my career. I had tracked down Andie the year after Slovakia became a sovereign nation from the Czech Republic. The country's economy was transitioning from socialism, which, quite honestly, had been still developing into socialism in the aftermath of World War II. Andie was working with a group selling farming implements. The black market was the primary commerce at the time, so Andie was associating with some rather unsavory individuals."

"Was he angry at Henry?"

"Andie was angry at everything, but his top concern was making money.

It took a while, but the government grew stronger, and capitalism took hold, so people like my brother converted into legitimate entrepreneurs. He still sells agricultural equipment today, but it's done out of an office instead of alleyways."

"I have to ask," Sean said. "Has Andie had any contact with Henry?"

"We're not close. Our lives turned out so different it's as if we didn't even come from the same parents. When I was living in Washington, he just showed up at my townhouse one day. Said he was there on business. Years later, when my wife and I were getting settled in the Spartina Island area, he showed up here. We spent time together, but we never talked about what happened in Slovakia when we were young. It was something we both wanted to forget."

"I'll have my contact check his passport and visa history," Feebee said. "But was he here during the time Henry disappeared?"

Ray nodded. "That time he came to Spartina Island was a few weeks before Henry disappeared."

"Did you ever consider..." Sean said.

"I only saw him for a few days. He left without saying goodbye. I figured he had just moved on. But he's still my brother, so no, I never even considered he might've had something to do with Henry's disappearance."

69

Once they were back in Sean's car, Feebee said, "Another suspect just materialized out of the blue."

"Yeah," Sean said. "Now we have Boyd Moretti, Roger Medcalf, Henry Nash's brother in New York, and Ray's brother in Slovakia, along with Captain Cannon's father, who might be just a shot caller. The more we get to know Henry Nash, the more people we find with motive to kill him."

"What do you always say about motive?"

"Motive is not a crime," Sean said.

"Are you still thinking about going to New York and interviewing the brother?"

"I'd like to, but I'm not sure we can justify it."

"I wonder if the sheriff's office will spring for travel to Slovakia. I hear it's really nice there."

"In your dreams. I got a text when we were talking to Ray from our new sheriff's office voicemail system."

"I'm glad you set that up," Feebee said. "Just call your voicemail and listen to it."

Feebee walked him through the process, and Sean heard a message from Blanche, the woman in SLED's DNA lab. He punched in the number.

"Thanks for calling back," Blanche said. "I have the DNA results back from the wallet you submitted. It's a mixture. We identified Henry Nash's DNA as part of the mixture, but there's another DNA profile present that is not in the system."

"That doesn't do us much good."

"We'll keep the profile on file and periodically resubmit it," Blanche said. "The person with this DNA could be arrested tomorrow and their DNA profile submitted to CODIS. But there's another route you may want to consider. Have you heard of investigative genetic genealogy?"

"Hi, Blanche, this is Denise Sheppard," Feebee said. "I'm in the car with Sean, and yes, I'm familiar with it. We used it on a case when I was with the FBI."

"Excellent," Blanche said. "We at SLED don't get involved with it for a myriad of legal and regulatory reasons, but if you can get the funding for Parabon, I can send them a DNA extract."

Sean thanked her and hung up. "Is this like using Ancestry.com to see if I have a long-lost rich uncle?"

"Sort of," Feebee said. "It starts with sending extracted DNA from SLED to a company called Parabon Nano Labs."

"Why can't they just use the DNA profile the SLED lab compiled?"

"Without getting too deep into the weeds, forensic DNA typing looks at around twenty STRs markers," Feebee said. "That stands for short tandem repeats, which I know means nothing to us cops. Parabon examines more than a half million SNPs, which are single nucleotide polymorphisms."

"Which means even less to me, so we can just call them SNPs, whatever the hell those are."

"Just think of it as two different ways to look at DNA. STRs can only show a direct match or a very close relative. Blanche told us CODIS doesn't show a match, so that's a dead end. SNPs can give us relative matches for many generations. The science behind this is that larger blocks of SNPs are shared between close relatives and smaller blocks between more distant relatives. Parabon enters the profile into one of the publicly available DNA databases."

"Like Ancestry.com?"

"Not exactly, since Ancestry is private and restricts law enforcement use, but it's loaded into another database with DNA profiles representing more than a million people."

"So, if the brother of whoever left the blood on the wallet is in that database, it will tell us," Sean said.

"That would be a lucky hit. It might only match someone who's a more distant relative, like a second or third cousin. From there, we have to talk to people and build family trees, which will hopefully lead to someone with a link to Spartina Island or Henry Nash."

"Sounds involved."

"It can be. The case I worked at the Bureau took us six months to lead us to the likely suspect. We surveilled him until he tossed a Starbucks cup in the trash, and we got DNA from it, which showed a match. For a cleaner chain of custody, we got a warrant for his DNA, which showed a forensic DNA match. We then arrested him, and when confronted, he confessed."

"Blanche mentioned funding. How much will this cost?"

"Around five grand for Parabon to do the work."

"Our Cold Case Team's budget is zero, so this is ruled out," Sean said.

"While you male members of the Mudflats Murder Club play golf and beat your chests and grunt at each other, I do lunch with the women who really run the sheriff's office. Gladys told me there are several grants and some other special accounts with citizen donations earmarked for different purposes. Captain Cannon dips into them as his personal slush fund, but Gladys has assured me that if we need money for special equipment or training, she can find it."

"And you think..."

"I'll talk with Gladys, the agent from the Bureau I worked with on the genetic genealogy case, Parabon lab, and Blanche, and see what I can orchestrate," Feebee said. "Now, let's go back to my house. There are some people waiting to talk to you."

Frank, Doc, and Beagle were sitting in Feebee's living room with Feebee's husband when Sean and Feebee arrived. Feebee's husband quickly excused himself, and Sean and Feebee sat down. Feebee told them about their interview with Ray Mitro and the conversation with the DNA technician.

"We need to put that on hold," Frank said. "It's waited ten years, so it can wait a little longer. We uncovered some new evidence on the murders of Courtney Evanson, Eric Robinson, and Sarah Fitzpatrick."

"Why don't you just visit Sergeant Nash and tell her," Sean said. "You guys are part of her CID squad now, aren't you?"

"Feebee said you were grouchy today," Frank said.

"I think he's jealous that he wasn't picked for the kickball team this time," Feebee said.

"Sean," Doc said softly, "We have some information that might be merely hearsay, some deductions that may be unsupported by facts, and some things people have told us under surreptitious means. When we put it together, we believe Sergeant Nash arrested the wrong person for the murders."

"Come on, Doc, speak plain English," Sean said. "What do you know?"

"We've told you that I've been frequenting the Cusseta Country Club with Beagle under the pretense that he's considering becoming a member."

"And they took me over there twice because I'm pretending my granddaughter and Beagle's might want to take riding lessons," Frank said.

"Okay," Sean said. "Go on."

For the next hour, they told him what they had discovered. The five of them discussed the best way to proceed to prove their theory and develop the necessary evidence for Charlie to act on it.

Finally Sean said, "Let's see if she'll even talk to me."

Sean called Charlie's cell phone.

"Hello," she said.

"Hey, Charlie, this is Sean."

"I can see that on the caller ID."

"I understand you're not really happy with me right now, but our cold case team has come up with some new evidence on the three murders you're working."

"You mean the three murders we've solved?"

"Well, yes, but there's some things you need to know that might change that."

"Like what?"

"It's complicated, and some of it we need to show you. I'd like to take you to lunch and talk about it."

"Sean, I know what you're trying to do, but I'm not ready to talk. I don't know if I ever will be."

"Let's meet for lunch and we'll only talk about murders. Nothing else."

"I'm up to my eyeballs in paperwork to get this case ready for the solicitor."

"You need to eat, and we think you should know this stuff before you present your case for charging."

"It's against my better judgement, but okay."

"Great. Meet me at the Cusseta Country Club at one o'clock."

"Sean, you need to be a member to get a table there."

"I have people in high places. We have reservations already."

"Very well. I'll be there, but just because I agreed to have lunch, doesn't mean I'm not still mad at you."

70

Sean waved to Charlie as she entered the Cusseta Country Club's dining room. As she approached, Doc, Beagle, and Frank got up from the table. "We're finished," Frank said to Charlie. "We'll see you when you're done eating."

Sean held a chair for Charlie. She furrowed her eyebrows to let him know she wasn't pleased, but she sat down anyway. A server set a large dinner salad in front of her.

Charlie turned to Sean and said, "How do you know this is what I wanted?"

"This nice woman said the last three times you had lunch here, you had the arugula and cucumber salad topped with pan-seared ribeye, so we thought it was a safe choice."

"If you'd like something else, Ms. Nash, I'll be glad to bring it," the server said.

"This is fine," Charlie said. "I just don't like being so predictable that Mr. Tanner thinks he can order for me."

The server smiled demurely. "Can I also bring you an iced tea, one quarter sweet tea, the remainder unsweet?"

"Yes, thank you. I'm surprised Mr. Tanner didn't have that waiting at the table when I arrived."

The server smiled again, and another server standing right behind her placed a glass of iced tea in front of Charlie.

"So you had my drink planned as well," Charlie said.

"Well, ma'am, we were anticipating it." The server left.

Charlie speared a cherry tomato and began eating her salad. "You're not eating?"

"The four of us already ate," Sean said. "Doc, Beagle, and Frank had a few last-minute things to check into before you arrive."

"Arrive where?"

"The stables."

"You do know that I know, don't you?" Charlie said.

"Your mother told me."

"I hear she came to your house last night."

"I thought you two weren't talking."

"I have sources," Charlie said as she stabbed a slice of meat and cucumber and popped them into her mouth. "Jacque, Ray's wife, had tea with her this morning."

A server topped off Charlie's iced tea glass.

"Bring me the check when you get a chance," Charlie said.

"Sorry, Ms. Nash, but this is already on Doctor Henderson's account."

When the server left, Charlie said, "You must be very proud of yourself."

"For what?"

"Getting me to lunch. Getting Doc to pay for it. Conspiring with my mother. You know, all of that."

"Charlie, I never wanted to hurt you."

"I thought we were only going to talk about my murder cases."

"Okay. Did you know that Kristin Capozzi showed up at the stable at eight-forty this morning, went into one of her stalls, retrieved a bottle of pills, and left?"

"The hospital told me they cleared Kristin for release, and at seven this morning, a woman from the treatment facility picked her up."

"Beagle spoke to the treatment facility, and Kristin walked out halfway through the intake process and called a rideshare to pick her up."

"She came to the stables to retrieve some pills she had apparently stashed here?" Charlie said.

Sean nodded. "Doc and Beagle talked to the stable manager. That's who called them when Kristin showed up. We have his contact information if you need a statement from him later. She left after about five minutes in the same rideshare. Stretch and Irish set up on her house. She came out at about ten o'clock and drove back to the horse barn in her husband's burgundy Mercedes."

"You mean *her* Mercedes," Charlie said. "Her husband drove a Range Rover."

"According to three women who have horses here, Kristin drove the Range Rover. The only time she drove the Mercedes SL was when her Range Rover was low on gas. She'd then leave it for her husband to fill and drive his car. Frank has the names and contact information of the women."

"Shit," Charlie said.

"Anthony had stopped at the gas station on his way to the meeting with Dorovic. If you're done eating, let's go to the barn. Doc has something to show us."

Charlie followed him in her car. They parked by a long, white building that opened on the far end to a pasture and several riding arenas. Feebee, Doc, Beagle, and Frank were waiting.

"Kristin is out riding one of her horses, the one she uses for dressage competition," Feebee said. "Her other horse is in its stall. While all you guys have been dining in the fancy country club, I've been hanging around here smelling horse manure." She led them through the center of the barn, where there were twenty stalls on both sides.

Doc stopped at a stall marked with a brass plaque containing Kristin's name and the name of her horse. "I never knew much about horses until Beagle and I began frequenting the equestrian center. This horse of Kristin's is considered a warmblood. He's sort of halfway between a large draft horse and a typical saddle horse, like an Arabian or Thoroughbred. He was bred for jumping competition. One of the horse owners we spoke to said he used to live in Kentucky, and Kristin went out there a few years ago with this horse and did a few steeplechase races."

"Interesting, Doc, but what's that have to do with our murder cases?" Charlie said.

"Really nothing, but I found it fascinating. If you look inside the stall, you'll see several lengths of teal and gray braided rope hanging there. They're called lead ropes. They're attached to a horse's halter when someone walks the horse out of the stall into the pasture or arena. Kristin has several of them in both of her stalls. Do they look familiar to you?"

Charlie's face tightened, then her eyebrows raised, and her mouth opened. "They are exactly like the rope Eric was tied up with."

"That's what we thought," Doc said. "We looked around and found no other stalls with lead ropes that color."

"When I was out with Sherm talking to people from the original investigation into Sarah's murder, one of Sarah's classmates back then wasn't home," Frank said. "Irish and I stopped by her house this morning and caught the woman before she went to work. She remembered seeing Sarah when she left the school that afternoon and started walking through the woods to the rec center. Guess who she saw leave the school right after her?"

"Kristin?" Charlie said.

"Stretch and I went to the Atlantic Dunes bar for a drink last night," Feebee said. "Spoke to one of the regulars there. He said Anthony comes to the bar a few times a week and has dinner with Kristin there every week or two, but he only saw Kristin there by herself one time. A few nights before Courtney was murdered, Kristin sat at the bar for an hour and asked people if they knew where Eric lived. She said she wanted to send him flowers as a thank-you for taking them to the airport. The man we spoke to didn't know if Kristin actually learned Eric's address or not, but I have his name and phone number if you need to take a statement from him."

They turned when they heard a large horse clomping into the barn. It was being led by a woman in a riding helmet, knee-high black boots, tan riding breeches, and a powder blue long-sleeved shirt.

71

"Hey, Charlie." Kristin removed her riding helmet and shook out her hair. "I'm not surprised to see you, but I figured it would take you a few more days."

"Hey, Kristin," Charlie said. "I had a lot of help to show me I arrested the wrong person."

"I do feel bad about letting Anthony sit in jail. I was going to come clean, but I needed a few more days with my horses."

"I'll have one of my associates find the stable master to take care of your horse, so we can go to my office and talk."

"I've had Athena for eight years, and I've always been the one to groom her after a ride. If you drag me away from here now, I assure you I will do that remain-silent stuff."

Charlie didn't let murder suspects set the rules about when and where she would conduct interviews, but she was willing to make an exception to clear the cases. "We can talk while you groom your horse, but first I need to search you for weapons and narcotics."

Kristin looped her horse's lead rope around a slat on her stall door and stepped back. Charlie patted her down and removed a bottle of pills from her pants pocket.

"I guess I don't get to keep these," Kristin said.

Charlie shook her head. She read Kristin her rights, which she waived. Charlie turned to Feebee, Doc, Beagle, and Frank. "Can you guys give us a little room? Sean and I can handle this."

The four of them walked to the other end of the barn, as Charlie turned on her phone's recorder and started with the date, time, and location, then asked Kristin if she'd been read her rights and agreed to talk without an attorney present. She confirmed both.

Kristin walked Athena into her stall and removed the saddle. Charlie and Sean stood outside the stall, leaning over the railing. "Kristin, this is Sean Tanner," Charlie said. "He's part of the sheriff's cold case team that had re-opened the investigation into Sarah's murder."

"You know, Charlie, if Sarah had never gotten pregnant, none of this would've happened."

"How's that?" Charlie asked.

"Anthony and I grew up together. We kissed for the first time in second grade. All our friends knew we would eventually be married. Then Sarah came around in high school. Cute, bubbly, perky Sarah. Anthony fell for her, but I knew it wouldn't last. Anthony would eventually recognize she was not like us. Anthony and I were going to a good college, and Sarah was headed to community college. Anthony would've figured out she came from a working-class family and that's all she would ever be."

"Then she got pregnant," Charlie said.

Kristin soaked a big sponge in a bucket of water and began wiping down her horse. "How dumb can a girl be to not take precautions? She wanted to get pregnant to trap him. Of course, Anthony agreed to do the honorable thing. What infuriated me was when Anthony's mother gave Sarah her ruby pendant. Ann had told me the story of the pendant a hundred times. It should've been mine."

"Is that why you followed Sarah into the woods that day, to take the pendant?" Charlie asked.

"I intended to confront her. Tell her what a slut she was and how ashamed she should be getting knocked up just to trap a nice boy like Anthony. Then she said Anthony loved her and never really loved me."

"That must've angered you."

"I lost it. The next thing I remember is straddling her with my hands on her throat, and she's no longer moving."

"You then took the pendant from around her neck?" Charlie said.

Kristin wiped down her horse with several old towels, starting at the head and progressing down the body, as she told them how she hid the pendant for all those years. When alone, she'd often take it out of her hiding place, fasten it around her neck, and stand in front of the mirror. In recent years, she kept it in a small box in the back of her underwear drawer. When their house was burglarized, she found the pendant and other items of jewelry missing. It wasn't until the following day that Anthony told her the thief also cleaned out their safe.

"Anthony was clueless," Kristin said. "But I knew Eric had to have been the one who stole everything. I didn't care about anything else, but I needed to get the pendant back."

"Because of the sentimental value or because if someone saw it, Sarah's murder could come back on you?" Charlie said.

"Maybe a little of both," Kristin said. "So I found out where Eric lived and visited him." She told them about parking her Range Rover outside the apartment complex because it was a distinctive vehicle that people would remember. She knocked at his door and immediately pointed a gun at his head. She brought a rope to tie him up, but soon realized she should've brought several to do the job right, so she used duct tape she found in the kitchen. She smacked him on the shins to get him to say what he did with the pendant, but he was stubborn. She then used the hammer on his hand. He finally blurted out that he fenced most of the items, but gave the pendant to his girlfriend, Courtney.

"You couldn't just leave him like that," Charlie said. "He would've told the sheriff's office what you did to him."

Kristin nodded. "I hit him on the head with the hammer. It knocked him out, but he was still breathing, I think, so I put the bag over his head."

"How'd you find Courtney?" Charlie asked.

"She came to me. When I was done with Eric, I left his apartment and began walking back to my car, and Courtney walked right by me, going to Eric's apartment. I guess they had a fuck appointment after she got off work. She knocked at the door for a few minutes, but then gave up and walked back to her car. I grabbed her there."

Kristin tossed the dirty towels outside the stall, apparently leaving them for the stable workers. She retrieved a brush from a locker in the stall and began brushing her horse as she told them about knocking Courtney to the ground and struggling with her. She eventually strangled her with her hands and was enraged when she found Courtney wasn't wearing the pendant necklace. Her plan was to drag the body into the ocean and let the tide take it away. She got the body into Courtney's car, drove to the beach access, and started dragging her across the dunes. Kristin said she was in good physical condition from working her horses, but her back still gave her problems. Halfway to the beach, her back began spasming, and she couldn't go any farther.

Charlie nodded and turned to Sean.

"Why didn't you just leave Courtney's car there by the beach?" Sean said.

"My back was killing me, and I didn't think I could walk back to my car."

"Why'd you leave the gun, bloody paper towels, and hammer in your car?" Sean asked.

"I knew my fingerprints and Eric's blood would be on them, so I put them in the compartment where the spare tire was. I meant to get rid of them but never got around to it."

"How could you allow us to arrest Anthony for this," Charlie asked. "He broke the law to bring you drugs and supported you so you could spend your days with your horses. After we arrested him and mentioned finding the hammer and gun in the Land Rover, which we thought was his car, instead of him telling us it was yours, he refused to talk further without a lawyer. To protect you."

"I'm sorry. He deserved better than me. I kept hoping things would change, but I knew Anthony would always love Sarah. He kept the photo of them from his junior prom in his desk drawer. He was so handsome in his tux, and she had on this skin-tight red dress with a slit up the side and a low-cut top. Sometimes I'd walk in on him at home, and he'd hurriedly stick something in his drawer and shut it. I imagine that he was thinking of her whenever he and I made love."

"Just for the record," Sean said. "We found the bottle of oxycodone pills in your pocket. Are you under the influence now?"

She huffed. "I've been taking these for so long, I'm more normal when I take a pill every four or five hours than if I've taken nothing. Sure, I might take more than one and have a drink or two when I'm home to get a buzz on, but if I'm going to drive or ride, I'd never take more than what my doctor had prescribed."

Charlie looked at the marked patrol vehicle that was sitting at the entrance to the barn. "We've got to go now. We'll make sure the stable master takes good care of your horses."

Kristin kissed Athena's neck and stepped from the stall. Charlie cuffed her and led her to the patrol vehicle.

72

THURSDAY

The sun was just starting to set when people began taking their seats at the big, round table on Beagle's back porch. Annie and Diva jumped into the pool for the fifteenth time, swam to the steps at the shallow end, chased each other around the deck, and jumped in again. The temperature had only reached the low eighties today, and Sean was comfortable dressed in shorts and an untucked polo shirt. And he felt mostly content, still basking in the satisfaction of a murder case that came together. He was a bit anxious over Carson coming home and his refusal to return his calls, and he didn't like the chasm that had separated him and Charlie, but tonight, he'd focus on a job well done with his brother and sister senior-citizen crime fighters.

Sean had been excited to see the text Beagle sent out last night offering to host a celebration at his house. Back in Oakland, the most they'd do after solving a case was share a beer or two at the local cop bar, then go home and get the first decent night's sleep he and his partner had had in many days. It was only fitting Beagle invited Lieutenant Billy Green and Sergeant Charlie Nash in addition to all the Mudflats Murder Club members.

Stretch set a huge platter of grilled New York strip steaks in the middle of the table, while Beagle placed another equally large platter beside it. "This is redfish on the half shell," Beagle said. "It started as an eight-pound red fish, also known as red drum, which was just caught this morning. It was cleaned and halved, then grilled skin side down. You can slide the fillets right off the skin."

People began passing around bowls of salad and rice pilaf and grabbing steaks and pieces of fish when Billy stood. "I just want to raise my glass to the Mudflats Murder Club. Not only did you solve the cold case of Sarah Fitzpatrick, but you were instrumental in helping Charlie bring the real killer of Eric Robinson and Courtney Evanson to justice. What impressed me most was how y'all pitched in and helped without even being asked and took the initiative to look in a different direction."

"In other words, we stuck our noses into her investigations without her permission, but it turned out okay," Stretch said.

"Yeah, that too." Charlie leaned over and kissed the cheek of Irish, who was sitting beside her. "A special thanks to the most experienced undercover operative to ever buy drugs on Spartina Island."

"You mean the oldest," Irish said.

"That too," Charlie said. "Sometimes you guys piss me off when you go off on your own like you did with my investigations—"

"You mean all the time," Feebee interrupted.

"Okay, I admit it pisses me off all the time, but I appreciate everything you did. It was a real team effort."

"Let's not forget all the work Sean has been doing on our missing person's case," Frank said. "You want to tell the group how that's coming along, Sean?"

Sean glared at Frank and wondered how many beers he'd had to bring this up with Charlie present. As with many of his Oakland investigations, the more he dug into a case, instead of narrowing the list of suspects, he ended up with more possible suspects. Now, he had Boyd Moretti, Roger Medcalf, Richard Nash, Andie Mitro, and possibly even Clinton Cannon II. Sean anticipated the list might grow longer before it narrowed.

"The team has done a load of work," Sean said, "We still have people to interview and evidence to evaluate."

Sean glanced at Charlie, knowing she'd realize he was being vague and noncommittal. She smiled. Maybe she wasn't still angry at him, he thought.

As people ate, stories of Irish's undercover work and Frank's deadly cane began growing. Sean figured years from now they'd become legends, as police escapades had a tendency to do with age. The liquor flowed, and multiple conversations began occurring simultaneously and at a higher volume. Sean loved being around cop celebrations, but he preferred them in smaller doses. Music had been playing through the speakers on the porch, and when the old song by King Harvest, "Dancing in the Moonlight," came on, Sean looked out at the full moon over the river. He left the table and walked to the edge of the pool where Annie and Diva were lying on the travertine deck, exhausted from their play in the water.

He remembered driving Lauren back to her dorm on their second date when this song came on the FM radio station in his car. She yelled at him to pull over and stop the car. She pointed at the moon in the sky above them, pulled him out of the car, and began dancing. Sean smiled at the memory. He continued smiling when he realized his mood didn't quickly dissolve into grief over Lauren's death. He sat on a chaise lounge chair and looked out at the river, tuning out the din of the conversations back on the porch. Annie rested her wet head on his leg and looked into his eyes.

"I hope I'm not disturbing you two." Charlie glided toward him carrying two drinks. She wore a sleeveless, jade green, floral sun dress. With her long blonde hair worn down and light pink lip gloss as her only noticeable makeup, she looked nothing like the tough, no-nonsense detective he was used to seeing. He grabbed a matching chaise and pulled it alongside his chair.

She sat down and swung her long, lean legs onto the chaise, either not caring her dress rode up to expose most of her thighs or doing it intentionally to drive him crazy. She handed him a reddish drink in a highball glass. "It's called a sea breeze," she said. "Vodka, cranberry juice, and grapefruit juice. Doc made a big pitcher, saying this was the summer drink at his old country club in Ohio."

Sean pulled the straw out of the ice-filled glass and took a sip. "Not bad."

"How's your shoulder?"

"Much better. I see my physical therapist again tomorrow. I think she'll let me resume normal activities as long as I keep doing the exercises she's assigned me. She did mention that I'm no longer in my twenties, so in the future, I should spend a few minutes stretching my back and shoulders before I pick up people and body slam them."

She took a long pull of her drink through the straw. "My mother and I had a long talk today."

"How'd that go?"

"I don't care that I was conceived before my parents were married. It actually showed my mother was more human. It's just about them lying to me my whole life. I didn't forgive her, but I understand."

"Sometimes that's enough."

"I'm sorry for being such a bitch toward you. I recognize that's my default personality, especially with people close to me. I'm working on it, but Charlotte the bitch will still likely rear her ugly head at times."

"So it might be a while before you become a perfect little Southern belle?"

She grinned. "You were right to let my mother be the one to tell me, and I know that you can't brief me about everything you're doing on my father's investigation. Sometimes I still can't help wanting to know everything, but I'll work on trusting you to do your job and share things with me when you're ready."

To Sean, hearing someone say they were working on changing was the best apology possible. He'd have to remember that if he were lucky enough to have a conversation with his son. "Thank you. I know how hard it must've been for you to say this. What will you do about your new birthday?"

"Changing it would be a real hassle, so I'll just leave it as July twenty-eighth. Only a few people know the truth."

"Maybe one of those people will do something special for you on the other birthday."

"That would be nice," Charlie said. "I've also decided I'm no longer afraid of family secrets, so dig as deep as you need to in your investigation. Whatever you unearth, I can handle."

They sat there in silence for a while, sipping their drinks and looking toward the river illuminated in the moonlight. Sean wanted to ask her something else, but he had not asked a woman on a date in over thirty years. He felt his palms getting sweaty. What if she said no? Finally, he said, "Your mother told me I should ask you out on a date."

Charlie looked over at him with raised eyebrows. "She did, did she?"

"Yeah, three times. I figured I sort of did when I asked you to lunch at your country club."

"Sean, that doesn't count. That was a business luncheon, and, on dates, people don't talk about murders."

Since Sean hadn't really asked her, she didn't have to say no and reject him. He nodded. "You might be right."

She continued to look at him. "I'm confused. Did you ask me something?"

"I guess I sorta did."

Charlie tossed her hair over her shoulder. "Sean, I'll make this easy. This Saturday, you can pick me up at 3:30. You'll drive us to the Cusseta Marina. I'll make sure the Hinkley is fueled up, and we'll sail to Savannah for dinner. I'll pick a restaurant where we can dock the boat."

"I guess that means yes," Sean said.

Without even looking toward the porch to see if anyone was looking, Charlie leaned over and kissed him, letting her lips linger on his long enough to show promise for the future. "Yes, Sean, it's definitely a yes."

A Death in the Deluge
Mudflats Murder Club Mysteries Book 3

The water is rising. Time is running out. And somewhere, a killer waits.

A .22 bullet to the head. The murderer's calling card, left behind with Kimberly Sheehan's body on Spartina Island. Her fifteen-year-old daughter Emily? Vanished without a trace.

Retired detective Sean Tanner and Sergeant Charlotte "Charlie" Nash are racing against a merciless countdown. This isn't the killer's first victim—fourteen years ago, teenager Ashlee Briggs was abducted and executed with the same weapon. Sean's cold case team, the Mudflats Murder Club, had long believed a serial predator was hunting on their turf. Now they're certain.

A third body drops—same .22 signature—and the pattern is undeniable. As a Category 3 hurricane barrels toward the coast and evacuation orders scatter the population, the island empties fast. But is Emily still on it? With official efforts paralyzed by the storm, Sean and Charlie launch a desperate, off-the-books search—cut off from backup, out of time, and heading straight into a deadly trap where the flood hides every trace, the wind drowns every sound, and survival isn't guaranteed...

Brian Thiem, a former detective and cold case investigator, returns with a mystery that's intricately built, character-rich, and full of quiet menace. *A Death in the Deluge* is a must-read for fans of *The Thursday Murder Club* and *Only Murders in the Building*.

ACKNOWLEDGMENTS

Thank you to the entire team at Severn River Publishing: Andrew Watts, Amber Hudock, Julia Hastings, Mo Melten, Megan Copenhaver, Keris Sirek, and especially my amazing editor, Amie Swope. Your support and encouragement have made writing these stories about Sean and Charlie enjoyable.

My most heartfelt appreciation to Paula Munier, Gina Panettieri, and the rest of the team at Talcott Notch Literary Agency for believing in me, guiding me, and never giving up on me.

Loads of thanks to the men and women of the Beaufort County Sheriff's Office, especially Major (Ret.) Robert Bromage for inviting me to join the Sheriff's Cold Case Team and teaching me about Southern law enforcement. I couldn't have come up with the premise for this series without you.

Thanks to Melanie Beckler (Retired Sergeant, Southampton PD), a fellow member of the Beaufort County Sheriff Office's Cold Case Team, for patiently teaching me about investigative genetic genealogy over a long lunch and emails.

A million thanks to my beta readers: Rachael Van Sloten (Retired Lieutenant, Oakland PD), Julie McKenna, and Al Roach. Your insightful comments and thoughtful suggestions made this story immeasurably better.

Thank you, Annie and Lexi, our real Labrador Retriever and Tonkinese cat, for allowing me to turn you into characters in this series. And thank you for your company during the long hours I spend in my office playing with my make-believe characters.

And of course, my deepest appreciation to my most trusted reader, my lovely wife, Cathy, who listens patiently when I talk about the characters in my books and what they're doing as if they were real people.

ABOUT THE AUTHOR

Brian Thiem is the author of The Mudflats Murder Club, the first book in the Mudflats Murder Club series, as well as Red Line, Thrill Kill, and Shallow Grave. In his previous life, he spent 25 years with the Oakland Police Department, much of it working Homicide, and retired as a lieutenant. He's also an Iraq War veteran, retiring from the Army as a lieutenant colonel after 28 years of active and reserve service. He holds an MFA in creative writing and is a member of the Mystery Writers of America, Sisters in Crime, International Thriller Writers, and the Island Writers Network. He lives with his wife, yellow Lab, and Tonkinese cat in Hilton Head Island, South Carolina, where he's also a member of the sheriff department's Cold Case Team, consisting of retired law enforcement professionals from around the nation who examine unsolved murders.

Sign up for the reader list at
severnriverbooks.com